Leah
Making the Scene

Other San Francisco Bay Press books
By Frank Cervarich

Foxhawk It Begins

LEAH
Making the Scene

*Part of the
'Remember Time Never Was'
Anthology*

*The Second Volume in
The Foxhawk Files*

By
Frank Cervarich

San Francisco Bay Press
900 Timber Creek Place
Virginia Beach, VA 23464

Editor: Margaret Cervarich
Photography: Frank Cervarich
Cover Design: Kayleigh Montgomery Morris

www.thefoxhawkfiles.com

Visit the publisher's website at www.sanfranciscobaypress.com

978-1-7346024-7-0 (paperback)

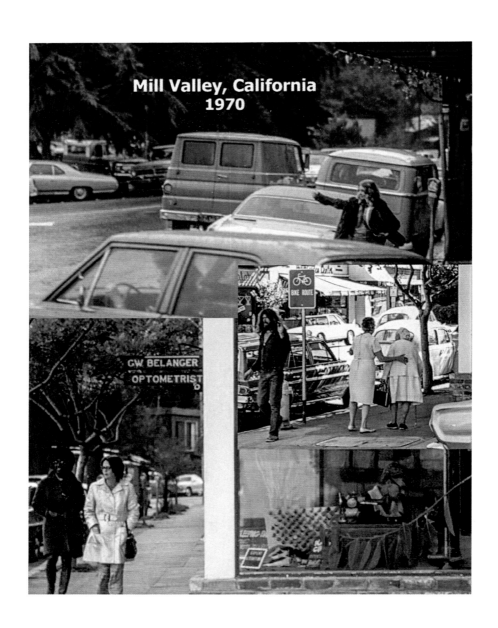

Mill Valley, California
1970

BOOK ONE:
MAYA

My name is Leah Travail

Chutzpah is one thing but setting yourself up for a fall is another. That's what I was told when I, almost 27, revealed my plan to check out the scene in Mill Valley, California before the ink was dry on a divorce decree filed in my hometown, Memphis, Tennessee.

My mother wailed and glared. My father shrugged his narrow shoulders and coughed, a sure sign he was upset. My ex-husband, everyone in our synagogue, and all my childhood friends ganged up on me.

So what? Must mean I'm onto something. My cat, Bianca, agreed. She was coming with me.

The night before I left, I had a dream. I wrote it down on a notepad I keep on my nightstand.

'I am floating rapidly over water toward a distant shore lined with graceful, undulating mountains rising out of the briny sea. Something is going to happen when I reach land, a transforming experience.

Out of nowhere, a man dressed in blue appears, his left hand palm forward, held up in greeting. We joyously rush hand-in-hand together over the sparkling water. Ahead, in the shimmering heat waves, I see something I cannot quite make out that freezes my brain with horror'.

I wake up in a cold sweat.

I somehow know the shimmering land is Marin County, California.

Who is the blue man? What unseen danger awaits me? Am I just anxious – eager to have at it? Is the happening scene in Marin, in the whole of the Bay Area, beckoning me to approach? In the midst of the hippie madness, will I find a way to realize my dreams? Or will I descend into hazy uncertainty?

Hey, I'm up for anything.

To cool out my folks, I arrange to stay with my brother, David, a Jungian psychiatrist by trade, and his family. They live in Mill Valley.

My parents idolize David and I have to admit I think he's pretty wonderful too, even though big brothers can at times be a little too protective, a pain.

While I unpack in the guest room at David's house, his two boys play peek-a-boo with me. Then we sit down together and read a story, Goodnight Moon. We all have a good time, including Bianca. Those two kids are a joy.

Sherry, David's wife, is another story.

Over a disappointingly conventional dinner, Sherry and I jockey for moral high ground while David does his best to stay neutral. Despite the two sweet kids, I know my stay in this house must be short.

First thing, I call my old friend, Big Phil. He obligingly takes me to Miki and Peter's pad, action central for the "family," a loose-knit group of mostly Jewish hipsters with a decided point of view. Miki and I hit it off immediately.

Now there's a girl you can learn a thing or two from while having one heck of good a time.

One thing leads to another. Three very late nights are enough for David and Sherry, so in less than a month, I have a one-bedroom apartment in what was once a sun porch at the back of a single-family home on Lovell Avenue, one block from downtown Mill Valley and down the street from Miki and Peter.

Right away I set about realizing my dream of becoming an artist. I dabbled with calligraphy back home and imagine this would be a good place to start. So, each morning I sit on a cushion before a low table and exercise my hand, Bianca watching. I practice bold strokes, delicate strokes, the art of the fluid wrist.

And, after that, I take a long bath, read some Carl Jung in honor of my brother, and wait for it to be late enough in the day to take to the streets, looking to mix it up with my peers, to see what can be seen.

Oh, I am a lively sight – five feet tall, with black eyes, curly black hair down to my shoulders, and a pale complexion – dancing in my canvas tennis shoes up and down Mill Valley streets.

Miki, my newfound girlfriend, chides me, calling me "the questing heartbreaker." She claims I leave a path of destruction in my wake. She says that trouble is my middle name. Then her dark eyes light up and she laughs her ass off. She laughs because, I admit it, I get a little huffy. She knows damn well I have no intention of becoming *involved. It's too soon after my divorce and contrary to my quest of becoming an artist.*

He is coming, soon - the blue man, left hand raised, palm forward.

And when he comes, I will immediately squint my eyes, trying to discern in those shimmering heat waves the lurking evil that contained so much horror in my dream.

He appears on an ordinary day.

Isn't that the way of the world? And shouldn't we all be continually awake, armed and ready for approaching danger? Potential new directions whiz by each and every day. When is it time to connect with one? When will you, unexpectedly, run headlong into one?

Bang!

I run into this one head-on.

We, the members of my new "family" and I, are sitting like pashas on pillows around a large foot-high circular table that dominates the front room of Miki and Peter's pad listening to Stevie Wonder sing "Keep on Running From My Love."

"Family" members are cool. They play, and I am fast learning how to play, a self-delusional game that some might say is self-indulgent, even self-destructive.

Hey, forget them.

The idea is that we are gangsters, Jewish (mostly) outlaws. We wear the black hats but, in our game, we who wear the black hats are the hip ones, the anti-heroes. We choose our roles as an act of self-expression and an exercise in freedom. As outlaws, we can smoke dope, wear outrageous clothes, say far-out things, think extraordinary thoughts, do things in our own inspired way. And, the payoff is, the straight world turns the other way as we approach or, better yet, we're invisible to them. We're living in Edge City, a place that is seemingly within the confines of the mainstream but is actually nowhere to be seen in this space-time continuum - if you can dig it.

Can you?

Right on. I figured you'd follow me if you're still reading my rant.

On that fateful day, just like every other day, we're passing a cigar-size joint around the table. It goes from Miki to me, the newest member of the "family;" from me to Herman; then to Big Phil, my childhood friend from Memphis; then to Harry, Ida, Gab, and back to

Peter. Gab, of course, declines to take a toke. He's only interested in coke.

Miki Wiseman, my new best friend, is older than I am. She must be in her mid-thirties. She's cozy and tough at the same time. She's got smooth olive skin and dark hair, slouched shoulders and a warm, open face. Her eyes are knowing, penetrating and kind. And her laugh is an explosion of joy. She's also a nudge.

"So. Tell me again why it is that a nice Jewish girl like you would leave your family, friends and husband behind to move out here to wild and wacky Marin?"

"Well, I didn't exactly leave my family behind, you know. Besides, I gained a new 'family' in the process, didn't I?"

"You're not fooling anybody with that story, girlie."

"You got me. To be honest, I'm just trying to do my own thing, participate in the great Human Be-In of life. You know, 'turn on, tune in, drop out.' Can you dig it?"

"Right on," Big Phil agrees with a chuckle.

Miki's eyes twinkle. She smiles.

I giggle, knowing the now-defunct hippie dream is an easy target. "Family" members aren't deceived by idealistic tripe. At least, that's the line. Of course, part of what attracted me to Marin was the whole hippie thing. I mean, in the media it's like a symbol of rebellion.

Albert King interrupts my train of thought with a blues song about a guy whose old lady left him. This guy can't understand why. All he did was go on a bender, two-time her, and beat her up when she complained.

That's Albert King's blues wail, not mine. That's for certain. I'm pulling for my sisters in arms.

According to Big Phil, a Delta blues fanatic, there's a blues song inside all of us just aching to come out (because the blues are just like life). I'm not so sure I dig his logic but I'm trying to get behind it, because it's a part of the scene and came out of the mouth of Big Phil.

I wink at him. I don't have to wink at Miki.

Why? Because we're sisters.

What difference does it make if you attended a synagogue in Memphis or the Bronx? We girls have to stick together, particularly the smart ones, the quick-on-the-uptake ones. We not only know the score; we set the tone and forge a path where none existed before. Or at least that is my thinking on the matter. I mean, guys can be pretty slow and stubborn, resistant to change, if you get my drift.

"Think you're pretty damned cute, don't you?"

Miki pats me on the cheek. I smile with delight.

"I am, aren't I?"

"Nobody loves me but my mother and she could be jiving too," B.B. King abruptly comments.

It's almost one o'clock on this early June afternoon in 1971 and my future has still not walked through the door. But I'm up for it, always ready to stay on top of developments.

Peter, Miki's old man, is drinking his morning orange juice. Self-respecting Marin County hipsters, who thrive by living on the fringe and finding a niche in this outsider world, are readying themselves to make the scene.

The front door bangs open. Maryanne Bergstrom, another "family" member, enters the room and myopically scans it through thick glasses, a warm smile on her lips. Sky, her toddler, rides on her hip. She wears hippie garb: a long, colorful skirt and a blouse that she embroidered with psychedelic doodads.

Sky, shirtless and shoeless, wears tan shorts. His tousled blond hair and brown-as-a-berry body contrast dramatically with his mother's black hair and pale skin. He's a genuine product of free love.

Maryanne puts him down and he immediately heads toward the icebox. He's right at home in Peter and Miki's pad and the happening scene in general.

"You got a minute?" Maryanne asks Miki after nodding to one and all.

"Sure. No problem."

Miki retreats into the bedroom to do business. It's a well-known fact that if you want the finest coke or weed in southern Marin, you better make a beeline for Miki and Peter's pad on Lovell Avenue in Mill Valley, action central for the "family" faithful and numerous hangers-on.

Ida follows the two women into the bedroom. She's probably hoping to hear juicy gossip, news of the scene, and maybe smoke some ganja while she listens.

I turn to Herman and ask, *"Want to finish that game of bones?"* just as Big Phil and Harry split. They've got better things to do than hang out at Peter and Miki's pad all day, even though it's a cool thing to do.

Herman slides over toward the pile of domino bones and observes, *"I once read a story about three ships that were caught in a* horrible storm. One sunk; another one was on its way down. As the one that weathered the storm, packed to overflowing with survivors, limped away, those left on the sinking ship stood on their battered deck and cheered the people who sailed safely away."

"Huh," Gab snorts, wondering when the coke will come out.

"I don't know if I could be that brave and generous."

Did I say that?

Well, yes. I did. I am still a little wet behind the ears.

Herman plays a tile. He's my wise uncle, just like my Uncle Maury back home. But they're wise in different ways. Herman holds forth on macrobiotic diets, Zen, painting, MG engines, how to make it by on the fringe. Uncle Maury is an expert on Jewish dietary laws, retail, pinochle, how to properly observe high holidays, and bar mitzvahs.

Peter, quite often oblivious but always a sweet, lovely, kind-hearted guy and, more important, Miki's old man, picks up the Independent Journal, the local daily. He likes to read the morning paper while he drinks his orange juice.

I've already seen the 48-point headline – DROUGHT WORSENS. Below the headline is a large picture of the Nicasio Reservoir – parched, cracked mud where water should be.

Outside the sun is bright. The sky is clear. No rain is in sight. Low-flow showerheads and bricks to displace water in toilets are the order of the day. Conscientious homeowners note how much water every sink, every shower, every toilet uses. Proposals have been put forward to make watering lawns and washing cars criminal offenses.

It's hot, damn hot, with no end in sight. The drought has been in progress for over a year.

Bang.

The front door swings open

As Bobby Blue Bland is wailing the song "Going Down Slow"

And I look up.

I wouldn't say exactly that it was love at first sight for me but I did get this queasy feeling, one that's hard to explain. It gurgled up from the pit of my stomach, and not because I ate spicy food last night. Oh yeah, for you woman haters out there, it also wasn't because it's my time of the month either.

No.

It was the materialization of my dream, the blue man vision come to life, in what at first appears to be a most unlikely but appealing young man. He's tall and skinny with brown hair. He still has remnants of freckles. He is, of course, wearing a blue shirt and he is already reaching out to take my hand.

Miki comes back into the front room looking for a roach clip and sees Tony, that's his name, standing with his palm upraised in the doorway. He's acknowledging us all. And he's stopped dead in his tracks.

"Tony, have you met Leah?" Miki asks.

"Ah, no…" Tony answers after clearing his throat.

Miki, always tuned into the vibe, chuckles.

Watch out. Avoid matchmakers. I've got other plans. I'm booked solid.

"You want to join us for breakfast?" Miki asks Tony.

Thanks a lot, I mutter mentally, as the knot in my stomach tightens.

"I don't want to put you out."

"Ever the Southern gentleman," Miki quips.

Her New York attitude is the perfect counterpoint to Tony's courtly manner.

"Of course it won't put me out or I wouldn't have asked."

I can't stop myself.

"Are you from the South?" I ask, without batting my eyes or tossing my head so my curly hair bounces up and down.

Early on, I was told by my mother that you have to be very careful about the signals you send to men. That was right after she cautioned me to sit still and keep my knees together.

Bang!

The blue man, unable to control a spreading blush, speaks directly to me.

"It is the Creative that begets things, but they are brought to birth by the Receptive."

"What?" I ask automatically.

But inside my head I'm stunned, bowled over, blown away.

Earlier in the day I spent over an hour struggling to master the yarrow stick method of divination using the I Ching. I got interested in the book after Miki mentioned that Carl Jung wrote an introduction to the Richard Wilhelm translation. My brother is really into the Jungian method of therapy, you know. The reading I got this morning was "The Receptive." Tony just quoted the very words that struck me in the hexagram.

"Far out," I mutter. "Whatever brought that to mind?"

Tony shrugs his narrow shoulders and gives me a lovely smile.

Out of the corner of my eye, I see Herman nudge Peter.

I know. This is no gangster. But he is living on the fringe or he wouldn't be here.

Am I right?

So what's the harm in making pleasant conversation, just as I was taught to do back home?

We discover that we're both artists (well, wannabe artists anyway) and water babies. His name is Tony Vitolinich. He's not Jewish but he does have a non-Anglo last name. In no time we're rushing over glistening water, hand in hand. We are headed into the heart of fabulous Marin where its secrets will be revealed.

What is it that is hidden in shimmering heat waves ahead?

I'm not worried. I'm a young daughter of Moses with plenty of moxie and chutzpah.

My name is Charlie Foxhawk Carter...

Hot and sweaty, I stumble upon a community happening in closed-to-traffic downtown Mill Valley. I've been on a run. The flyer for the event I saw in the Mill Valley Market bulletin board totally slipped my mind. Catching my breath, I survey the gathered crowd as a rock band performs on a riser. It's a bright, sunny day in downtown Mill Valley and everyone seems to be enjoying hanging out, making the scene. I join them, mingling with the crowd. I feel a buzz coming on. Marijuana smoke clouds drift from all directions. The laid-back energy of the scene is infectious. I amble in time to the beat of the music, the ever-shifting dynamics of the assembled crowd.

John Cipollina, a hometown boy formerly with the Quicksilver Messenger Service, is in attendance along with the former manager of the group. Notable drug dealers and hangers-on in colorful attire meander about. It's just after two o'clock in the afternoon, a perfect time of day for sightings of all types.

Attendees have had time for breakfast or at least a cup of coffee. They've possibly smoked a joint (or two) or done up a few lines of coke (or more). They've completed their morning ritual and have decided to take a little stroll down the hill or around the corner.

They talk with friends in small groups that form and re-form. It's a great place to see and be seen. A small-town happening, an event, is taking place in this once hep-cat, now hipster haven just across the Golden Gate Bridge from San Francisco. This is living, Marin County style, at its finest. And I'm a part of that scene and, increasingly, feel that coming-on-to-acid feeling that tingles throughout your body and lightens your brain.

All this activity takes place amid tall redwood trees situated on a tiny island encircled by roadway and in a parking lot where tracks once terminated at a train station. The Depot, as the former train station is now called, has been converted into a coffee shop and bookstore. It's doing brisk business. The parking lot is filled with cars. More people are arriving; others are drifting to various watering holes, notably the Sweetwater, a bar just up the street from the event.

A Bank of America branch, the Mill Valley Market, various boutiques, a thrift store, a hardware store, a few professional offices (mostly on the second stories of the squat two-story buildings), bars and restaurants all done in a style that is reminiscent of a German village, make up the downtown area. Steep hillsides punctuated by streets that, higher up, twist and turn without apparent reason are crowded with homes, a goodly number of them former summer cottages for city dwellers who lived in early twentieth century San Francisco.

My head is spinning. I flop down on a bench and lower my head down between my legs. I take long, slow breaths. I feel like I'm about to pass out and be transported to a familiar out-of-body place I have visited often before. The music, the crowd evaporates.

"You all right, buddy?" someone asks near my ear after an eternity has passed.

I mumble something, trying to nod, from far away.

Another day in Paradise....

Leah
(Several Months Later, Still Summer 1970)

Tony manages to show up wherever I am every day. He's attentive, intuitive, gentle. He takes me very seriously, a compliment to be sure. But wouldn't it be nice to play, to have fun? My recent past was filled with talk about obligations, talk about the sanctity of marriage, talk about what it means to be a Jew, talk about family and home, talk about my obligations as a woman. Well, to be honest, I have to admit that serious conversations have always attracted my attention. So I'm willing to play along with Tony's earnest conversations about philosophy, religion, psychology, all very high-minded and zealous. Small talk consists of sharing notes on the scene, life as we live it. Some courtship palaver, huh? What can I say?

We zoom over the reflective waters, getting closer to the glowing land in the distance. A shiver runs down my spine. That hazy, indeterminate, dark blob in those shimmering heat waves, what is it?

Late one night, Tony touches my face, hands trembling. We kiss delicately, just brushing lips in the darkened room which is illuminated only by a dim bedside lamp, over which I have draped one of my colorful shawls. Electrifying flashes of high-powered energy snap. We kiss again, with more passion and vigor, pressing closer together.

"We're moving fast," I murmur, looking into Tony's blue eyes.

We are high: high on coke, high on weed, high on ourselves. We've spent the evening up at Peter and Miki's, a routine we've settled into, sharing numerous lines of coke, excellent weed, a late dinner, visits by "family" members, a few games of bones, and plenty of music.

Tony urgently eases me toward the pallet I use as a bed. My knees unaccountably give way and we collapse in a heap. We are playing for keeps.

I lie in shadows. The moon reflects off a nearby wall. A fleck of light glitters in Tony's penetrating blue eyes.

His heart races next to mine.

He fumbles to unbutton the top button of my jeans. When I pull my bulky sweater over my head, my braless breasts bounce into view.

Tree branches sway in the moonlight. The room is cold, damp. Goosebumps rise on our skin. We retreat under the covers and press

29

together for warmth. I rub my feet rapidly back and forth on his legs, giggling like a schoolgirl involved in a delightful prank.

"You are so lovely," Tony mutters as the bedding begins to warm.

In the blue eyes of the blue man, I see myself reflected. The reflection captured in his irises is more lovely than I, more generous than I, much more a goddess than I.

Tony – so gentle, so supportive and sensitive...

I pull him toward me. We press into each other, are enfolded in each other's arms, are joined together by an embrace that melds our bodies into one unit, one creature, one organism seeking orgasm.

"Oh, Tony," I gasp.

We move faster and faster, rushing toward oblivion. Our lovemaking is crazed, heated, frenzied. We sail higher and higher.

We are outside ourselves, above the clouds, looking down at Mill Valley. The full moon's silver glow gives definition to the trees, houses, streets and cars. We stretch out our arms and swoop across the sky on wings of passionate delight. Mt. Tam, the goddess fallen to earth, leads us to her essence, the path to the center of this planet. At that center is a black void that is heavier than the heaviest star. We crash through it and arrive at galaxies beyond.

Is the blob in the shimmering haze overcome...or emerging into view?

Tony grunts as I exclaim "Ah" and moan. Stars gush from our hair, our eyeballs, our fingers, our chests, our sexual organs, our toes and fingers. We whirl round and round like a pinwheel, faster and faster. We go off like Chinese fireworks, the grandest Fourth of July demonstration ever staged.

Meaning becomes motion becomes orgasm becomes pleasure becomes male and female becomes yin and yang becomes blending of fluids becomes making of two One becomes making meaningless the material and realizing God-Self-Atman-Brahman.

We lie quiet, spent, in each other's arms. I cup the blue man's cheek in the palm of my hand.

Bianca, my cat, jumps up onto the bed. Tony has usurped her favorite place, snuggled up next to me. She begins to talk in a whining, bossy voice.

"What's her name?" Tony asks, reaching out to pet the cat.

"Bianca," I reply, as she first avoids, then succumbs to Tony's attentions.

The hussy... She arches her back, shamelessly encouraging his caresses.

Guttural, wailing lyrics belted out by Tina Turner rumble through my mind. Tony gently pushes my legs apart, his rapier-like cock leading the way. I am wet with expectation.

We sleep, then awake as lovers, lovers living in Marin, the home of lotus-eaters and pleasure seekers, with the merciless sun riding through a cloudless sky. It shines in through the sun porch windows, eliminating all hope of much-needed rain. My dream moves closer to the "real world." And I ignore my anxiety.

Charlie

I like to solve puzzles, puzzles of all kinds, not just those that come in a box with a picture of the completed puzzle on it. There are puzzles of the mind and heart, puzzles created by the predicaments of friends and others, and so on.

I got fired from Life Beneficial Insurance as a claims investigator two years ago, severed relations with my father (and, as a result, with my family and childhood friends), and took up permanent residence in the San Francisco Bay Area. In the aftermath of all that, I spent many hours solving jigsaw puzzles that come in a box. Unfortunately, I have not had an opportunity to solve any puzzles brought to me by clients of my newly formed detective agency, Foxhawk Investigations. I'm inept at getting the word out about the newly formed agency and I'm short on the cash needed to drum up business.

Puzzles, though, half-finished ones on a card table, await me when I get back to my home of the moment. Hard times have forced me to move around more than I would like. In these, for me, unsettled times, puzzles settle me down. I focus on the task at hand, freeing me up to let my mind wonder and wander. Where it goes I can't really say. But it's a quiet place, a meditative place, a place of needful solitude in the Beyond.

I first became interested in solving jigsaw puzzles when my father took me with him to visit an elderly couple in their apartment. I was maybe five years old. Mr. Vitolinich, the elderly man, was working on a puzzle that day, the one and only time I met him. I was hypnotized and entranced. It seemed like Mr. Vitolinich, wise and thoughtful, was performing a sacred ritual with otherworldly meaning. I was stupefied to learn from my father afterward, "That man is your grandfather."

My father never spoke to me again about this and has steadfastly refused to confirm or acknowledge that relationship. Why? I don't know. For years afterward, this shared secret seemed very important to me.

It achieved even greater significance for me when I met Tony, Mr. Vitolinich's grandson, under rather unusual circumstances at Virginia Beach when I was twelve. A fierce storm was rapidly moving up the coast and the sea was choppy, the undertow dangerous. Getting swept out to sea was a very real possibility if you weren't careful. Tony's mother, standing on the shore, brought Tony to my attention. He was very near that awkward place just before waves start to break for the shore and the undertow hungrily urges floating objects toward the open sea. Being impulsive and full of the confidence of someone my age – wasn't I immortal? – I plunged into the water and, thankfully, helped guide Tony back to the shore.

I'm older than Tony by three years, so afterwards when we became friendly it felt to me more like I was an older brother. But, for unknown reasons, I have never told Tony about our supposed secret kinship. And, what with my father's refusal to acknowledge this secret and my severed relationship with him, I lost interest in the idea that Tony might be my secret cousin. We're just friends, brothers, ex-Virginians living in wild and crazy Marin.

Right now I'm throwing the *I Ching*. I have a notebook in which I enter the results I get. I have pages and pages of results in that notebook. I throw multiple times each day. I require divination for the smallest to the most universal of questions for which I seek answers and/or guidance. I spend most mornings with this Confucian oracle. If I were living in ancient Roman or Greek times, I would probably set great store by the Oracle at Delphi.

Anyway, I'm presently asking the *I Ching* whether this is the right time to make cold calls and, if so, what should I be saying.

Suddenly, it hits me. It's unemployment day. Shit. I'll be late if I don't hurry. In a flash I'm headed up to San Rafael with no time to spare. Forget about oracles for now. I wait in line at the unemployment office, queueing up for my bi-weekly chat with a bored and exasperated government employee.

I've been out of work for almost two years now and my benefits would have run out long ago if I hadn't managed to get temporary freelance work at a very low level for very modest pay in the film business in the Bay Area. Most of these freelance gigs are thanks to contacts that Tony – yes, that Tony – has turned me onto. Oh yes, the Bay Area has a small community of reprobates managing to squeak by in the freelance film business. Anyway, you don't collect unemployment during weeks you work. But, when the gig ends, you get back in line in the San Rafael unemployment office, congratulating yourself that you have successfully extended the benefit period of your unemployment one more week.

"Hello. Long time no see," I pretend to say to my designated government employee while I wait in line.

Then I imagine saying to my fellow unemployed folk, "I'll avoid your eyes if you'll do the same. We'll talk some other time and thank you very much for failing to mention we saw each other at the unemployment office in downtown San Rafael."

"Next in line..."

I jerk to attention. The woman behind the counter is looking at me. I'm standing behind a line painted on the floor, a safe zone of fifteen feet from the counter. Stepping forward, I hand her the paperwork that I had filled out in advance.

I know the drill. "Have you been seeking work during the past two weeks?" "Who have you called about a job, interviewed with, made an appointment to see?" "Were you available for work during the last two weeks?" Drone, drone, on and on, fill in the form in the appropriate spaces, bureaucratic paperwork is the same the world over. Nobody really reads the answers – not me, not the disgruntled employee taking the information, not anyone. Just hand me the check, okay, and I'll go quietly.

I'm a deadbeat, you understand, a good-for-nothing, a hippie, a beatnik, a loser, a Commie liberal pinko fag, taking advantage of the system, living on the dole – does that about cover all the bases? Not by a long shot. I've gone over to the dark side, become the black sheep of the family. I'm living on welfare. I'm lazy, a scourge, not willing to find a fulltime job and keep it even if I hate it, the way everybody else does. I live on the fringe, on the edge, playing with danger and doing nothing to better myself or get out of the mess I've put myself in. No wonder I'm suspect. As the *I Ching* told me this morning, "Youthful Folly... Danger and standstill: this is folly."

Phew...it's over with. See you again in two weeks. I still have four weeks left on my benefit amount. We'll see what comes up in the interim. I head back toward my current temporary quarters, my girlfriend Joyce's place, her Mill Valley pad. Necessary worldly possessions fit in the trunk and backseat of my car with sleeping room to spare, just in case. All of the rest of my stuff is in a storage unit I rented. That stuff consists mostly of things I had shipped to me back when I moved to San Francisco on Life Beneficial's dime.

I make my way onto Highway 101, the main north-south highway in Marin County, just across the Golden Gate Bridge from San Francisco. I'm heading south wearing my square-toed cowboy boots, jeans, work shirt, and blue sport coat. The sport coat is a remnant of my former persona and a concession to the folks at the unemployment office.

I'm medium build and average height; weighing about a hundred and fifty and topping out at five foot eight. My long hair and mustache shake a bit as I look to my right and see Mt. Tam in the distance. In the foreground is a scruffy, low-rent area filled with small repair shops and fly-by-night businesses. There's also a great cheap Mexican restaurant in that area. Their refried beans and rice are plain, stomach-filling, delicious. Could my olive complexion and dark eyes be a sign of Mexican blood rather than the Indian blood that I was told I inherited through my mother's side of the family? Don't think there were too many Mexicans in my neck of the woods, Virginia, back in the late seventeenth century, but I could be wrong. I've been wrong many times but I like to believe I always bounce back.

———————

Leah
(Fall 1970 approaching)

The blue man and I are racing hand-in-hand over glittering waters toward rapidly advancing land. It is filled with tall, graceful mountains rising from the shoreline. The black blob, hidden in shimmering heat waves, is nowhere in sight. With eyelids partially closed to protect us from the intense light and wind, we are suddenly gliding over the shore. Grit works its way into the corners of our eyes. Turbulent winds jostle us, threatening to send us into a tailspin. With horror, I realize the blue man's feet are not winged and pure but pliable, like putty. And they are dark and sinister, just like the black blob.

What is the true character of the blue man?

Without warning we are rushing toward one of the graceful mountainsides. I raise my arms in horror, trying to protect my face. We crash into tangled low-lying undergrowth.

Tony is tapping on my window. Dazed, I sit up in bed and look at him.

Is he real or part of my dream, this gentle man who is so unlike any other man I have ever been attracted to?

He insists I take a ride with him and is very coy about our destination. He puts his finger to his lips and smiles.

Shhhh...

He parks the car in a turnout and takes me by my hand, leading me across Molino Drive, a twisty, narrow road that leads from downtown Mill Valley to Panoramic Drive and, farther along, Mt. Tam; and then the ocean just over the hill. We head toward a path that begins next to a black metal mailbox.

"Tony," I whisper.

A feeling of foreboding floods my entire being. Maybe it's just the residue of my dream. I tug at Tony's hand, pulling away from the path and the future it brings. Tony, an innocent who should be old enough to recognize when to stop, pulls me forward.

What the hell's wrong with me? Am I going to let a frightening moment in a dream hang me up? Don't I trust Tony?

If he's the blue man, maybe I shouldn't.

Our hands lock as we traverse the short path bordered on both sides by massive live oak trees that arch over the pathway. Ivy, planted long ago, covers the ground on both sides of the path, winds up the tree trunks and along the branches clasping them with suffocating force.

Am I about to crash into an ivy-tangled hillside? Is this what the dream was foretelling?

The path, too narrow for us to walk abreast, is only about twenty yards long. Its gently curves only at the last moment, bringing into view a house, a small Japanese-style cottage, sitting near the back of a graveled front yard.

"Whose house is this?" I ask with apprehension as we reach a wooden gate that leads into the yard.

"Let's look inside," Tony suggests, pulling me through the gate. "I think this house is magic."

"Don't be ridiculous," I giggle nervously in response.

35

A wooded hillside, covered with green undergrowth, rises up behind and to one side of the cottage. No adjoining houses can be seen. Nestled in a grassy meadow on the rise of a hill behind the house is a wooden water-storage tank bound together with heavy metal hoops. Wildflowers are blooming in the meadow. This, to all outward appearances, is a remote, idyllic Marin location, a fantasy brought to life that is convenient to downtown Mill Valley.

Tony peeks in a window. With both hands, he forms a cup to shade his eyes.

"Oh look, Leah. It has a free-standing fireplace."

Am I being ridiculous to feel nervous about the tangled undergrowth that surrounds me, the Japanese feel to the place?

I look in the window.

I see a completely empty L-shaped room. The long side of the L is a living room with huge windows running down one side. All of the windows look out onto the rising, tree-filled hillside covered with luxurious green ivy undergrowth. Placed at the L is a freestanding black metal hibachi fireplace. The front door is next to the fireplace on the short side of the L. A piano, built right into the wall, stands next to the door. What use might be made of the small side of the L is mysterious.

"I think it's a Japanese-style dining room," Tony states, seeing the direction of my gaze.

"Japanese? Why do you say that?"

"Because this is our enchanted cottage, our magical place," Tony immediately responds. "Here, let me show you."

We circle around the front of the cottage. A sports car, unseen by us because of the greenery, guns it around the curves of Molino and passes by, going uphill. We approach a steep blacktopped driveway that leads to a carport, inserted into a leveled portion of the precipitous hillside. A small passageway between the carport and the house leads to a back door.

"Let's go inside," Tony says, grabbing the door handle.

"No, Tony. No. Let's not…"

I pull away with vigor. Alarm bells ring. Deep fear and dark premonitions flood my consciousness.

"Look. See? It's unlocked. For us…"

We are separated, disconnected, no longer touching.

Tony walks into an empty master bedroom after passing through a small entryway that doubles as a laundry room.

"Come on," Tony eagerly commands.

One entire wall of the bedroom is windowed. It looks out at the backyard hillside covered with ivy.

"Come on in," Tony commands again. "You'll love this room."

"Tony. Who lives here? Why are we here?"

"Did you know there is another bedroom upstairs, a turret room from which you can walk out onto the roof through a window? And there's a cool galley kitchen. Come on. The place won't bite. Honest. I promise. It's magic...Enchanted. For us... Remember?"

Tony holds out his hand to me. His feet are obscured from view. Time stands still. His clear blue eyes, gentle and insistent, tug on my heartstrings.

What is there to fear?

I float toward him.

Before I realize it, I am taking Tony's hand. We glide through the bedroom into the L-shaped front room and, from there, into the snug but efficient galley kitchen. I am without will or emotion, a windup toy. Tony exudes happiness and excitement.

The cottage is compact, small, remote... ideal for lovers. At one end of the kitchen is a steep set of stairs leading up into the ceiling.

"Come on," Tony urges once again.

He leads me single file up the steep steps. We stand in an empty room that could be used for a bedroom, a study, a hideaway, whatever. Tony pushes open the hinged window.

"It opens onto the roof," he comments, stooping to step out onto the tarpaper and gravel roof.

Momentarily left alone, I get a flash.

Gosh, what an ideal place for a studio.

It dawns on me. This house has possibilities.

Tony's infectious joy, his love and understanding, gushes through my consciousness.

This cottage is enchanted and, yes, does have magical properties.

My feeling of foreboding, my dream warning, is overpowered and seems to disperse.

I step out onto the graveled roof with resurfacing self-assurance and put my arm around Tony's waist. He loops his arm around me in response. Our hips touch as we look off into the distance toward an obscured downtown Mill Valley. What we see are treetops and cloudless sky above. This is truly a storybook land.

"Why did you bring me here, Tony?"

"To show you the dream house I found for us to share together."

I have been putting off Tony's fervent proposals that we move in together. It's pleasant to have a bed companion and Tony has a wonderful heart. He's head-over-heels in love and wants to do everything in his power to make me happy. We feed off each other's energy, tossing around ideas and dabbling with occult matters. I like all of that. I like it a lot.

Then there's Miki. She thinks we make a cute couple and has been egging me on. Her well-meaning, not-so-subtle pressure bears the "family" seal of approval.

But...I made a pact with myself when I got divorced: no heavy-duty romantic involvement until I've had time to come to terms with myself and find a new direction. Take time out and have some much-needed fun.

I'm beginning to find work as an artist, beginning to establish contacts, beginning to realize a new and potent inner self. That new self, and the path of discovery toward that self, is fragile.

"Oh, Tony... No. Not now. Please. Let's let things stay like they are."

Tony Vitolinich takes me, Leah Travail, into his arms. He kisses me gently, lightly, on the mouth. Our lips stick then pop apart, sending tingling reminders of our shared passion up and down my spine.

"I know it's sudden. But this place, everything, is so right," Tony murmurs with passionate conviction.

He kisses me again.

The floodgates break. An overwhelming rush of wild emotion overtakes me. I no longer resist the urgent logic of Tony's erotic fantasy. I embrace the dream of an enchanted cottage, a magical world, our world, and bring it to life for both of us to share.

We will be a couple, a new unit in the "family." We are two souls brought together on the road of life, who will settle in this house and make of it a home. We will give expression to the inner dimensions of our fairy book love in this storybook land.

We will make this cottage an integral part of the crazed party which has been in progress for half a decade in this village-like township just across the Golden Gate and which has ignited the hearts and souls of a generation around the world.

This generation, our generation, is taking control of the streets, of the media, of the country's thinking. We want the world and we want it now. There are no significant obstacles in our way, only a tired and confused group of elders. We will, liberated by the mind-altering vapors in the air and a firm belief in the righteousness of our newfound will, prevail and march into a glorious future that will overturn worn-out wonders of the past while creating fresh new miracles. Karma, yes Destiny, calls.

A dry wind blows, hollow and brisk, up the treacherous hillside. A vulture circles on updrafts high overhead. A merciless and cruel thirst is building in hedonistic Marin.

Where is the blue man with feet of moldering black clay taking me – toward liberation or destruction?

My cat, Bianca, all my worldly goods, and I enter the blue man's inflated dream the very next day.

Charlie

What would Joyce want me to buy, I'm thinking as I shop at the Mill Valley Market for groceries. I don't want her to think I'm a freeloader. I moved in with her a few weeks ago after I wore out my welcome where I had been staying.

Money's tight and Joyce has refused to let me help pay her rent. She has a fulltime job as a librarian. We were dating before I moved in, but were we both really ready to get serious? Is that what this move is all about?

I pick up and put down vegetables and fruits at random. My shopping cart is filling up but it's a slow, painstaking slog. I thought coming in that I'd rustle up the ingredients for some lunches and dinners for us. Now I'm thinking maybe it would be better to focus on snacks and work up to meals from there.

My fall from grace started in late 1968 at the tail end of the Summer of Love when I was transferred to San Francisco by Life Beneficial Insurance. Their corporate headquarters are in Richmond, Virginia, my hometown. I was hired soon after I stopped working for The Office, a top-secret government agency, doing my duty for God, Country and my father in lieu of military service – at least, that's what I told myself and those who asked.

My father, my childhood hero, what would have become of me without your support and guidance? His connections got me both jobs as well as a long laundry list of other things I won't bore you with now.

The Mill Valley Market is right across the street from the Bank of America branch where I cash my unemployment check. I have a checking account with them. The Market, like the Sweetwater, a bar up the street, caters to rowdy young adults looking for action. But I never go to the Sweetwater myself, in spite of the fact that I like their live music. I guess I'm destined to be a stranger in a strange land no matter where I live, an outsider, a misfit, even among fellow weirdos and kooks.

I run into Harry while I'm in the market shopping. I met him when I first moved to San Francisco. He lives just up the hill on Lovell Street. He puts me in mind of Tony. They worked on a lightshow together. I should visit Tony. We haven't hung out together lately. Harry and I salute each other without speaking as I head to the checkout line. I make a mental note to drop by his pad sometime soon.

Shit. At the pace I'm going I'll run out of money before my next unemployment check. The Mill Valley Market is great but it's expensive.

Outside, the weather is magic. It's great just being alive. But my mind continues to rerun movies that have been in my head for the last two years.

My first assignment for Life Beneficial in San Francisco as a life insurance claims investigator was tied to a murder. Tony became the primary suspect. Dirty tricks and undercover operations unleashed by The Office (you know, the one I used to work for) got tangled up in both the insurance and the murder investigation. Their underhanded operations and nefarious infiltration schemes targeted flower children, campus activists, and basically anyone at odds with the establishment, meaning the military industrial complex, the federal government of the good old U S of A. Hello, J. Edgar Hoover.

The Office and its representatives wrapped themselves in the American flag and declared themselves exemplars of "Truth, Justice and the American Way" while, oh yeah, they stunk up both the insurance claim and the murder investigation. But, to me, that wasn't the worst of what came to light.

Core values inculcated in me by my father on camping trips together, playing golf and tennis together at the Club, going to movies together (almost exclusively Westerns), attending church with the family, going on family vacations and participating in family occasions, were deeply lodged. Dad exemplified how the world, society, family life, should be lived. I tried to be a good son, one who lived by the sound principles we shared. I did my duty, obeyed the Scout Law: "On my honor I will do my best to do my duty to God and my country..."

So who should show up after I was imprisoned by The Office during that fateful investigation? My father...and he advocated that I do as The Office demanded, that I rat on my friends to save The Office from unwanted revelations that would smear their name and reputation. How could he do such a thing? Why would he advise me to do something that went contrary to principles I believed we shared, that he had instilled in me, for Christ's sake? In a word, I went ballistic.

I don't mean I lost control. No. That is not the style of either my father or me. I pointed out problems I saw in his argument. My father stuck to his talking points. I did not bend to his will. As he left, the clang of the closing cell door rang in my ears. I waited...and waited...for my father to relent, to no avail. I was released. No charges were pressed. The tangled mess that had ensnared me and my friends was no longer a subject of conversation. It was as if none of what happened had ever happened. And that breaking of a bond and moral code between my father and me, that divergence of views, was bitter and hard for me to bear.

I have not spoken to my father since. Letters from my mother keep me informed about family matters.

My mother gave me a gift two years ago when I was released from custody. On a stretched and tanned hide (a family heirloom; there's Indian blood in her ancestry) a hawk soars on the top left. Below on the same side is a fox partially concealed by a bush. On the right side is a wind god blowing billowing clouds toward the hawk and the fox. There's an inscription below the framed hide. "Hawk flies. Fox cries. Mighty wind." My mother's gift is a constant reminder to always be on the side of the woebegone and forgotten. Bring me your tired, your poor, and your hungry. I plan to hang it in my office when I can afford to get one.

That experience, now two years in the rearview mirror, has me asking constantly – what does it all mean? How do I make myself whole again, living by worthy principles?

To put it simply, I've been having a major breakdown, an identity crisis which puts me in mind of puzzles and the *I Ching*. I used to pride myself on finding solutions to puzzles. Now I spend endless time repetitively throwing the *I Ching*. I'm lost in a maze. Will I ever find my way out? Maybe finding a way out is irrelevant. Live life; stop brooding.

Can't, I'm stuck in a Mobius loop.

Joyce is not home yet. She's at work. She's a librarian at the Marin County Civic Center Library. No problem, I have a key. I put away the groceries. There is a note on the kitchen table.

"We need to talk. How about dinner at La Ginestra tonight," it reads.

Leah
(Fall 1970)

After we wake, a slight whisper of breeze mixes with the rope incense we burn. In loose-fitting clothes we meditate, bringing forth from deep within us the solemn 'Ohm.' When I look into Tony's clear blue eyes, I see myself reflected. That self, my Self, is laboring toward liberation.

Without warning, I remember that my grandmother on my mother's side had the gift of second sight, of prophetic revelation.

As though on cue, Tony picks up the I Ching. I bring out the yarrow sticks. We throw, once for Tony and once for myself. Reading our respective hexagrams in silence, I realize that interpretation is the key.

Will Grandmother be my guide to the mystery lying behind Tony's clear blue eyes and questionable feet?

A rumbling, a slow but momentous breaking up of sedimented gunk, shakes my inner being. Outside, the ivy-covered hillside, overshadowed by live oak trees, remains calm. We smoke some Nepalese hash and play a Ravi Shankar morning raga. There is a knock at the front door.

"I hope I'm not interrupting."

We stare at him, blank, wide-eyed.

"I'm Gandolph. Richard told me about you. I've come to visit."

Richard, a nascent dietary guru who made his fortune running a small chain of local supermarkets, has hired me to create a poster that depicts his new ordering of the food chain. This ordering lays out his dietary philosophy and, with understanding of this arrangement, makes clear his vision of life. That's how Richard explained it to me, at any rate. Gandolph, I recall, is one of Richard's teachers.

"We welcome you into our home," Tony begins.

"You were consulting..." Gandolph interrupts Tony to say, looking directly at me.

"The I Ching,*"* I answer.

Gandolph nods, then picks up the I Ching. The book falls open. He points.

"Hexagram 14 – Possession in Great Measure. A good hexagram for you," he states, still staring straight at me.

"Would you like some tea?" I ask, more impressed with his style than with his execution.

"Green tea, freshly brewed, if you please," he states.

He motions round the room.

"Possession in Great Measure..."

"It's our enchanted cottage," Tony puts in.

Gandolph takes him in for the first time, seems to think of something to say but restrains himself. He smiles.

Will he share his cosmic joke?

No.

I turn to go into the kitchen.

"May I look at some of your drawings while you are preparing the tea?" he asks, seating himself before my sketchbook and opening it up.

The point of his visit is clear. Richard has sent him to put his stamp of approval on me. So be it. The oracle spoke of this visit today (Hexagram 44, Coming To Meet, changing to Hexagram 50, The Cauldron.)

Will the ripe fruit of my work fall and become the seed of Richard and Gandolph's vision? Will all that is visible grow beyond itself and extend into the realm of the invisible?

"Help yourself," I respond from the kitchen.

Gandolph studies my preliminary sketches of Richard's vision of the dietary chain. Tony watches him. Neither speaks.

"Your drawings have weight. Richard has chosen wisely," Gandolph comments after I serve the tea. *"May I?"*

He takes my hand in his to read it. His forefinger follows a line across my palm.

"Your lifeline is deep and wide. Your path will be full of many and varied revelations that offer opportunities for growth. But you must make the most of them. Your time here could be short."

"Does that mean I could, during this lifetime, free myself from the wheel of karma?"

"No palm reader can foresee liberation. That is left to the owner of the palm. That said, your life will be filled with dramatic changes. All of them revelatory… if you are so inclined. Most of them clean breaks with your past. You are an instrument, a lightning rod that collects and then disperses. It's up to you to determine whether that condition is understood as positive or negative."

"My lifeline looks different than Leah's," Tony states, holding out his hand toward Gandolph.

Gandolph releases my hand but not before he gives me another penetrating look. This assures me that we will speak more in private later. He takes Tony's hand in his own, palm upward.

"You will live a long life," he states immediately, with tepid inspiration and little or no thought.

"And I will see many changes as well?" Tony asks.

"You," Gandolph, looks closer at Tony's palm.

What does he see with his inner eye?

I gather he will not interpret what he sees.

Why?

"You too will experience change, dissolution. A long and arduous effort will be required for reconnecting."

He closes Tony's palm, making it a fist, and releases it with a pat.

"You are fortunate to have found each other. Enjoy and strengthen yourselves for the coming storms. You may then prevail," Gandolph tells us at our front door before he leaves.

───────────────

We spread the word to the immediate "family." We let it drop during casual conversations at the grocery store and the coffee shop in downtown Mill Valley. We throw caution to the winds and shout it from the rooftops.

Joy. We're having a party, a housewarming party. Everyone is invited. Enjoy.

At first I cannot help but feel embarrassed about issuing these invitations to our party. I receive all these "I get it" looks, particularly from the women. I flush crimson when Tony proudly blurts out an invitation to Peter and Miki. After that I feel compelled to invite my brother, David, and his family.

Oy…

I won't talk about the looks, the muted questions, the raised eyebrows, the deadly silence that followed that invitation. And the payoff is David never gives me a definitive yes or no to my invite.

But my pals, my buddies, Miki and Ida, jump in and offer to help. That's when the party idea really takes off and picks up steam. And that's also when I allow Tony's enthusiasm to rub off on me.

He is a dear, after all – a great catch.

And, do you know, in no time I'm beginning to feel that magic, our magic.

We make appearances during which we are appropriately awkward about our intentions, tender toward each other, oblivious to others, snared in Cupid's arms.

What to serve as a main course to all our guests is still the big issue. Out of the blue an answer comes. Edge, a dope dealer on the make who just moved to the Bay Area, hears about the party and offers, through Miki, to furnish us a haunch of roadkill deer. I'm ready to refuse.

Hey, I've never met the guy.

But then I rethink his offer.

Sometimes it's best to accept what fate delivers and not question the ins and outs of it too much.

Now we have enough meat to serve an army.

But how do you prepare something like that?

Good old Ida. She knows. Nobody else has a clue. She mixes up a concoction of wine and various herbs in which we marinate the deer meat to make it tender and tasty. We let it sit for four days.

Miki and I put our heads together and come up with appropriate side dishes and noshes.

Tony digs a pit in the yard to cook the deer haunch because it's too large to fit in the oven. Miki sets aside some primo marijuana and excellent blow for the bash, which she'll sell at her cost or below.

We're all excited now. This party is going to be a blast.

Of course, the house is too small to hold everybody.

Well then, the front yard, mostly gravel-covered, will have to be the focal point of the gathering, we reason.

We rake the gravel and pull the weeds.

Seating is a problem. We have almost no furniture.

Well then, the guests will simply have to stand, a minor inconvenience if the proper arrangements (plenty of dope and food, already covered) have been made.

We decide against adding decorations but heavy-duty paper plates, plastic cups, and utensils are a must.

Tony, in a fury of domesticity, cleans the house from top to bottom, washes the windows, waxes the floors. I put out fresh linens in the bedroom and bathroom.

The day of our party, the celebration of the joining together of Tony and me in our enchanted cottage, dawns. The weather is perfect. Not a cloud in the royal-blue sky above.

Birds sing in the trees all morning as we scurry about doing a multitude of last-minute errands. We're nervous, excited, pleased with ourselves. This is going to be so cool, so hip.

Who knows where it will lead?

We won't think about that. Not yet.

I dress in the bathroom. I don't want Tony to see what I'm wearing until the guests begin to arrive.

It turns out that we both chose white.

Is that a magical hoot or what?

Oh well, love is bliss and we are eager to embrace our respective roles.

The first guests arrive.

Great. Two guys I dated once or twice before I met Tony. Edgar, one of them, brings his son, along with his current girlfriend.

Tony gets uptight – which in a way is cute. It's reassuring to see him get his hackles up and amusing to see him make nice because he knows that's the way I want it.

And then it's my turn.

David arrives without Sherry or the kids. I don't know whether I'm offended or relieved. But I know I'm on the defensive. David is my big brother, the one I've looked up to forever, the one I've always wanted to please, the one whose love I need, the one toward which all of my family channeled their hopes and dreams. From the cradle onward, he's captured an unchallenged space in my heart. And our birthdays are less than two weeks apart, of course in different years. Mom did her magic, timing that coincidence.

Immediately I break away to give David a private tour of the house. I can't get a word out of him. He's in one of his moods.

Who knows what the hell he's really thinking?

Of course, I'm thinking all the time that he's judging me and my lifestyle. I try not to seem hostile, even though I feel he's rejecting me. David smiles vaguely and pats me on the shoulder.

Ugh...

Brothers, particularly the oldest son in a Jewish family, what is it with them, a rabbinical gene, an innate ability to make you feel uncomfortable, that you somehow haven't come up to the mark?

Before I can hit him, scream, or cry "No fair," Tony makes his way over to us. I make my escape. No time to obsess about David now. I've got a houseful of guests arriving.

And this is our day, our house, our scene, no matter what old stuffy David thinks about it.

So there...

I see Tony buttonhole David before he can escape into the crowd and chuckle. Tony hasn't got a chance of penetrating David's defenses.

I'm right.

David, ever the gentleman, listens with polite reserve to Tony's awkward overtures.

He smiles.

Is it a smirk or a kindly, knowing look that appears on his noble face?

Tony is diverted by the arrival of a new flood of guests and I am called into the kitchen. David gets to do what he probably came here to do, drift as inconspicuously as possible among the guests. He loves to observe people without being observed himself.

What a joke. He'll stand out like a sore thumb in this crowd. He's tall and pale. And he's wearing suit pants, a white shirt, and a pair of comfortable Oxfords.

Peter and Miki and Ida and Gab arrive at the same time. Ida and Gab's two teenage children begrudgingly tag along.

Miki and Ida give me a big hug. We girls are on a mission to oversee this party and make it a success. With cohorts like these, there's no question what the outcome will be.

Miki fires up a joint and passes it around. Ida insists that Gab come with her to inspect the haunch of venison. Gab is more interested in finding out who's holding the blow. Peter makes his way to the stereo system. He's brought along records and tapes. Music soon fills the air. The party is well and truly begun.

Members of the immediate "family" wait, impatient and awkward, in a queue while others of the immediate "family" exit from the bedroom, clearing their nasal passages and walking with a brighter

47

step. Miki has taken over the bedroom temporarily to conduct business. Joints are fired up inside and outside of the house. Wine flows freely.

Harry shows up. He walked up the stairs from downtown Mill Valley. He doesn't own a car, doesn't even have a driver's license.

No, he's not a foreigner. He's a native New Yorker.

He brings us a housewarming gift, a piece of glass that, upon closer inspection, turns out to be part of a periscope. Tony, puzzled by the gift but pleased Harry thought of us, puts it in a place of honor. Then Tony, beaming with pleasure, gives Harry a tour of the house. They became close pals when they worked together as part of a lightshow group a few years ago. In fact, that's why Tony ended up at David and Miki's pad. Harry turned him on to it.

The house, the front yard, is filling up with guests. The music encourages people to mingle, talk, and dance. Edgar's son climbs out onto a branch of a tree that overhangs the yard. From his perch, he watches the action below.

Tony points out his friend Charlie who has just arrived. That's something else we have in common, people to whom we look up, from whom we want to receive an approving nod, but away from whom we tell ourselves we'd like to grow, now that we are adults.

As Tony leads me toward his friend for an introduction, the crowd separates. We suddenly are promenading through their ranks and are on display. It comes to us naturally that we should greet guests and receive congratulations. Women hug me and men shake Tony's hand.

Someone gives me a bunch of fresh-picked flowers. Tony puts one in my hair. Almost immediately, it slips awkwardly over one eye. Tony leans down to right it. We kiss. Everyone claps, hoots, and yells.

A tipsy celebrant raises his glass and proclaims, "To making love, not war." The righteousness of this sentiment strikes the crowd.

As one, they raise their glasses and repeat, "To making love, not war."

The ceremony ends when we at last reach Charlie.

What do I say? What else?

"I've heard so much about you that I feel like I already know you."

Charlie laughs out loud. Tony squeezes me with adoration.

"Isn't she something?" Tony asks.

Trying to change the subject, I ask him about his work.

"I've never met a detective before. It sounds so romantic."

Charlie laughs again.

"I serve at the pleasure of the woebegone and forgotten, madam," he quips, giving me a polite bow that dovetails nicely with his Southern manners.

"That'd look neat on a business card. You know, like 'Have Gun Will Travel' and all," I respond.

Before I know it I have been commissioned to do Charlie's business card.

What a day!

We've formally opened our enchanted cottage to friends and family. They've graced us with their company. We've shown them our love. They applaud us and pile riches at our front door.

Who knows, maybe this business card thing will lead to other things. Album covers, logos for cool companies, a showing at a high-class art gallery.

Why not?

It looks like we can have our cake and eat it too. The sky's the limit on this day of celebration.

More coke is snorted, more grass consumed. Dancing becomes contagious. Noisy conversations flourish. Command central, the kitchen, is the scene of numerous conferences as food is readied for service.

"See that dude with the goatee and the look of amusement on his face over there?" Miki asks.

I glance across the room, not taking the time to focus. I've got other things on my mind.

"Hmm," I answer.

"That's Edge, the one who donated the venison."

So that's him, I remember thinking, and then promptly put him out of my mind.

"Hi," Edge says, a moment later, by way of announcing his presence.

I'm overseeing Tony as he carves the venison and helping the girls set out the other dishes. I smile, push a stray strand of hair away from my face, and smile again.

"Hi," I respond.

Before our conversation can continue, I am called away. Something dark on the back edge of awareness makes itself known. Edge seems miffed. I guess he was expecting the royal treatment. I mean, he did come up with the venison, the piece de resistance of the event. Anyway, I get a strange vibe from him. It's something, something that requires thought… later, much later. There's too much going on now to get into whatever that weirdness is.

The freshly carved and fragrant venison needs to be carried out. An announcement that lunch is served has to be made. Refilling of emptied bowls must be monitored. The fire in the pit must be put out.

Guests serve themselves buffet style. It's after four and the meat is cooked to perfection. Everyone oohs and aahs over the tenderness, the taste.

Edge gives me a knowing look and even winks.

Cute…

I'm surrounded by a crew of crazed women and all of them want to know what they can do to help. I don't have time for him and his pay-attention-to-me-right-now looks.

What the hell is it with him?

Bottle after bottle of wine is opened. The food table is plundered as the munchies descend on the collected crowd.

Edge pops back up without warning. I'm leaning on Tony's arm.

"To celebrate the moment," Edge states, pulling out a small vial with some white powder in it.

It's lightning in a jar, a psychedelic elixir. I'm sure of it. The dark thing in his snakelike eyes sparkles and beckons.

Hold on. Not now. Not here. This is the enchanted cottage. A celebration is in progress.

"Acid," he explains.

I look at Tony. We agree. The timing isn't right. Many of our friends have never visited us before. Some are total strangers. We want them to have a good time. We want to make a favorable impression. This isn't the time to trip out. Not only would it be self-indulgent, it would be rude. I mean, we're both from the South, where entertaining is taken very seriously.

We shake our heads in unison. Edge's lip curls up ever so slightly. Some sort of animal, some sort of creature, longs to emerge. I can't help watching, fascinated and intrigued.

We were destined to meet. I'm certain of it.

Why?

I'm not given a chance to find out. Edge closes down, bows stiffly and puts the white crystal powder in the small vial back in his pocket.

"Some other time, perhaps," he murmurs.

Shortly afterwards, he splits. No one seems to notice except me.

Some of the guys pull out their guitars and start playing. Gab sings a song of his own composition with Peter backing him up on bass. It has funny lines that make guests laugh. Big Phil performs one of his songs, a rare event. Big Phil is well known for his skill on the guitar but few have heard him play. Fewer still have heard him sing. Don Palgy, former manager of Quicksilver Messenger Service and longtime resident of Mill Valley, jokingly tries to sign them both up.

Night falls. The party begins to break up. Only the immediate "family" remains. We move inside. Fog is beginning to roll in over the coastal range. The temperature is dropping.

Tony lights a fire in the freestanding fireplace. It does little to warm up the L-shaped room, but it does make the place cheery.

Ida, Miki, and I retreat to the kitchen to clean up. A joint passed between us allows us to relive the day with pleasure.

That leaves poor Tony to talk with Peter and Gab. I know that's awkward for him. He likes them but doesn't know how to relate to them. He isn't a musician; well, he can play guitar but he isn't interested in making a living with that skill. He isn't an artisan like Gab. He's not good with his hands. He's a wannabe writer and makeshift philosopher. Nobody in the "family" shows great interest in books or in talking about the meaning of life. These subjects are too weighty, too East Coast.

I'm thankful he hasn't been left alone with Big Phil. He dropped by my place before Tony and I moved in together. Big Phil directed all his conversation in my direction. Didn't seem to think Tony deserved the time of day.

He was sending me a message.

This guy isn't for you. He's not one of us. He's a weakling. He'll let you down.

Well....I love him.

All right...

And he's not a weakling.

He's good and kind and gentle.

The night grows colder. The wind in the trees dies down. Fog envelops the enchanted cottage. Around ten o'clock the immediate "family" leaves and we are left alone. The house is still jangling from all the activity. So are we.

We christen our union by making love on the floor in front of the fireplace. Then we retreat to our bedroom and collapse in a heap on the bed where we drink a bottle of champagne, a rare treat. Tony isn't much on alcohol. The room whirls out of control.

My grandmother calls out to me during the night. I reach out my hand, only to find myself awake and holding Tony's hand. I'm sweating heavily, unable to catch my breath. Tony's sound asleep. The ivy glows – reaching out to strangle me.

What is life but pain and sorrow and the unfolding story of our reaction to this startling fact?

Leah
(Late Fall, Winter 1970)

We live in what seems to be an unending joyful state filled with lovemaking; full-throttle bursts of creative energy; rich, private conversations on serious matters; and rewarding meetings with friends. All of this takes place in one of the most beautiful places on earth, Marin County.

Paradise.

Tony shows an interest in learning about Jewish traditions and does everything in his power to bring me pleasure.

Joy.

Who cares if it doesn't rain and people squawk about it? Who cares if flower children are being displaced by coke-snorting wheeler-dealers? Who cares if we're dead broke and scrambling to make ends meet?

We're in love. We're in love. We're in love.

My poster of the various food groups as envisioned by Richard, the budding dietary guru, doesn't make much money, but creating it was a wonderful challenge.

We planted a garden on the side of the hill near the old water storage tank so I could have specimens to sketch for the food chain poster. I labored to make the fruits and vegetables come to life. It was tough. I've never taken formal drawing lessons.

But that wasn't the most imposing problem. It was the design, the structure for the chart. Richard didn't want his poster to look like the typical chart of food groups. I'm puzzled but he states with *surprising authority, he's not dogmatic or dictatorial, "You'll find the answer."*

Great. I was in a fix, but that just added to the joy of the creative process.

Tony, lamb that he is, had neglected looking for a fulltime job or seeking freelance ones so he can hang out with me. Until we got involved, he had been picking up gigs on film shoots or as a lighting technician at clubs, dance halls, and small theaters. He spends his days playing around with his still camera and a film camera he bought while working for a local TV station and proclaims he's doing just what he wants to do, writing the great American novel. "Working for the man" stifled his creativity, he tells me.

Yeah, right.

The bulk of the time, all either one of us is doing is hanging out together, making love, living our dream. That's our occupation.

And it is a wonderful dream filled with talk about books we have read, mostly on religion, philosophy, psychology, instructive lives. Filled to overflowing, I go up to my studio and work while Tony pretends to do the same. Tony really should be a little bit more organized and disciplined.

Stuffed full on gracious living, we have intriguing visitors and wonderful adventures.

Chock full of happiness and joy, we visit Miki and Peter's pad and there meet up with "family" members.

My moments of clarity and connection with my intuitive ancestor take on greater context and texture. This context modifies my vision, brings insights – some wanted, some unwanted.

Why is it that my liberating partner, the one who trusts me completely and loves me unconditionally, makes me feel trapped, claustrophobic?

Seemingly in every direction I turn, there's Tony with an adoring smile plastered on his face.

One day I come down from my studio. Tony's engrossed in a black-bound notebook. I assume he's writing or making notes, and I approach as quietly as possible, so I won't disturb him. He doesn't hear me. I look over his shoulder. He's drawing a mandala, what Jung calls a centering device, and I interpret to mean a portal to the inner universe.

"What's that for?" I ask into a silence broken only by the scratching of his pen.

Tony finishes a visual thought before he answers. I'm impressed by his concentration, the power and intensity of his design.

"I don't know. Just doodling..."

"That's a mandala."

"Yeah. We used to construct mandala images all the time when I was working with the lightshow. Can't get them out of my mind. So I draw what I see. I wish I had your talent. I guess that's why I write and take photographs. Can't make my hand recreate what my head sees."

Tony doesn't talk much about his lightshow days. I know that's when he met Harry. I also know that's when he met his ex-wife. The lightshow went broke while Tony got tangled up in Charlie's first case as an insurance investigator. Things really got weird and Tony ended up moving back to Richmond, Virginia, his hometown. When his ex-girlfriend showed up at his front door, Tony panicked and married the girl. What would his parents think if they lived together without benefit of clergy?

Big mistake.

They ended up back in San Francisco. She was born and raised in California and hated the East Coast. Tony somehow managed to get a job as a film editor at a local TV station and they rented an apartment in the City. I'm not sure how it happened but he and his wife split up. Tony moved out of the City, quit his job at the TV station, and we met.

I kiss him on the forehead and he pulls me toward him. We embrace.

I wish he'd start serious work on that novel he keeps telling me he has in him. If this mandala is an example of how his creative mind works, the results could be striking.

"Carl Jung drew mandalas," I tell him.

I've already passed Jung's Memories, Dreams, Reflections to Tony, so he's familiar with his thoughts.

"Oh yeah?" Tony responds, interested.

"He even wrote a book about them."

"I'd be interested in studying that book," Tony answers.

When we first met, I mentioned that Jung was into the I Ching. Tony purchased a copy of The Secret of the Golden Flower, for which Jung wrote an introduction.

"Let's buy a copy of Jung's mandala book today if we can find it," I reply, suddenly seeing a potential solution to the structure that holds the food group poster together.

The food chart made its debut in the form of a mandala. It really got the ball rolling for my budding career.

When we weren't holed up in our enchanted cottage, we raced around northern California, sampling the diversity of its landscape: sandy beaches in coves created from rocky cliffs dropping precipitously into the sea, grass-covered mountain hillsides punctuated by clumps of vegetation and dramatically placed rocks, cool valleys filled with redwoods and ferns, open expanses of vineyards laden with grapes soon to be pressed into wine, places with lots of interesting people lurking about. When the conditions were right, we threw off our clothes and soaked in G-d's glorious sunshine. Tony always takes his two cameras with him, one for still photos and the other for 16mm film. He doesn't just capture the surrounding landscape or interesting people. He captures me, exploring, doing my thing.

And it gives me an idea. I buy a large unstretched canvas. I tack it up on a wall. On it I paint a map of Marin County. This map is enclosed in a circle, a mandala, a county globe. Tony prints out his still photos. We cut out the parts of the photographs that interest us and glue the cutouts on the Marin map painting. It becomes an ongoing project, our shared venture.

Miki – strong, capable, knowledgeable – is the big sister I never had. We have wonderful heart-to-hearts. Herman offers advice and drops by our cottage from time to time. Harry visits Tony. And, surprise, David and Sherry come over to dinner. The four of us talk just like we were colleagues, peers, two married couples sharing a meal. No mention is made of our lifestyle choices.

Paradise.

One day a shipment of peyote buttons arrives in the mail at Peter and Miki's pad. With ritualistic fervor we clean the buttons of their hairs so that nothing is left but the dried buttons. The hairs, we are told, are what cause you to get sick. Then we grind the dried buttons up with a mortar and pestle until they are powder. Using liberal amounts of water, we roll the powder up into small balls about the size of marbles.

As darkness falls, we ingest enough of the balls to carry us away. We listen to Indian ragas and chants. We look at meaningful pictures. We talk about many mysterious and wonderful things. We are taken away to the world of visions, the source of all religions and the portal to our origins.

Miki is a holy shaman, an earth mother, a Virgo marvel. Peter is playful, an angelic Libra musician of the spheres. His eyes, his very being, twinkle. And Tony? Tony is kind, gentle, caring, thoughtful, and warm.

I grow closer to my dearly departed grandmother who metamorphoses into an Indian medicine woman chanting Hassidic hymns to a drumbeat created for my ears alone. The meaning and proper interpretation of her chants leads me on a journey beyond space and time.

May this flowering last forever, may this state of grace survive. Paradise has returned to earth.

We daily walk in the Garden of Eden.

Charlie

I slam the car door of my trusty 1965 Volvo S122, four-door, gray-on-gray sedan. I drove it across country when I was transferred to San Francisco. It was the car I was driving when Isobel, my childhood sweetheart, and I were still an item. It's the car I was driving when Heather Chicago, aka Linda Preen, blew into my life here in San Francisco.

I check to make certain I have brought along my old Smith Brothers cough drop tin that fits handily into my jacket pocket. It now contains pre-rolled hash cigarettes.

I wind uphill on Molino, past fledgling redwood trees growing right up to the edge of the paved surface, causing flickering sunlight to strobe my peripheral vision. The last two years flash through my mind.

I took a night school course at the College of Marin that prepared me for my private investigator's license test. I passed with flying colors.

I had lunch with Detective Cooper of the SFPD. I met him while working as a claims investigator for Life Beneficial. Coop promised to keep me in mind if he ran into anyone needing the services of a good PI. I call him every month or so.

I kept my phone answering service so people will have a way of getting in touch with me. Good thing. I no longer have a home phone or a home in which to install it.

I do have a mailbox in San Rafael, the mailing address of my almost nonexistent private investigation agency, Foxhawk

Investigations. If I ever do get a phone, I'll answer it "Foxhawk Investigations, Foxhawk speaking." Foxhawk is my middle name, you see.

Leah made me a business card. I'll have to have a batch printed when I get enough money. On the card is the slogan "Hawk Flies, Fox Cries, Mighty Wind" as well as "Serving the woebegone and forgotten."

I've lost count of all the places I've crashed or hung my hat in the past two years.

And, oh yeah, I still like to think of myself as a seeker after realization, trying to get in touch with my Essence, evolving, stuff most people consider useless garbage since God is dead and it's all about survival of the fittest and going for the gusto (wine, women and song, whatever's pleasurable for me, me, me).

Maybe I've just been brooding, not really meditating or looking to sit at the feet of a guru but, but, but...

And there you have it, for now. More will occur to me. It continually does.

It's another beautiful Fall day in Paradise. My mind is aflame with visions that threaten to overtake reality at any moment. In front of me is the dangerous abyss of the Divine; behind me is a steep, inaccessible cliff. And there I stand in perplexity, the innocent fool, throwing the *I Ching*, putting together puzzles, taking long hikes, exercising, meditating, living in a hashish-laced-with-opium haze sometimes augmented with cocaine "runnin' round my brain." I'm on a steady diet of Cream, Traffic, MJQ, the Jazz Crusaders, B.B. King, Bobby Blue Bland, Vivaldi, Mozart, Bill Evans, Monk, and an endless number of others.

I pull into Tony and Leah's steep driveway and put the hand brake on so my precious car won't end up rolling down the very steep drive, across Molino and on down the hill, only coming to rest when it crashes into a redwood tree.

Leah

"Look inside. Look carefully," Gab Cohen commands, handing a massive, solid-gold ring to Miki.

Gab. Gab. Gab. When will you learn you can't put a fast one over on Miki?

"Far out.... What a trip."

Gab and Miki go way back – back to the time when Miki was the bookkeeper at a coffee house and Gab played guitar and sang folk songs there nightly. Peter played standup bass. Ida was a waitress at the Trident. She fell head-over-heels in love with Gab the moment she saw him. Miki advised caution but there are some things friends can't say to each other and remain friends.

Peter leans close as Miki passes him Gab's latest creation, the ring.

"Look inside."

Peter obeys after taking off his glasses to do so. He squints into the cavity then chortles.

"Cool, very cool…"

Peter often fools people. He looks like a pushover. He's gentle, quiet, reserved. But that hides a sharp, analytical mind. Libras, the scale balancers, have that within them.

Peter starts to pass the ring to me but Gab intercepts it and holds it up for me to inspect.

"See?"

"That's too much, Gab."

What we all see when we look inside is a lump of oddly shaped gold in a cavity of the gold ring. With just a little imagination it occurs to you that this lump could possibly be a fetus in a womb.

"How did you do it?" I ask politely.

I suspect it was an accident.

"Trade secret…"

"Some of Kubrick's people have seen it. He's interested," Dustin adds.

"Well," mumbles Gab, not denying this most likely unfounded piece of gossip.

"Gab's holding out for five figures," Dustin concludes.

Gab shuffles from foot to foot in mock modesty.

Gab is really full of it. And his pal from LA is buying it. There's a sucker born every minute, as the saying goes.

Well, I shouldn't be so hard on Gab. After all, he commissioned me to make a sign for his shop. Peter and Miki insisted on making the delivery of the sign an event. That insistence has the advantage of giving Miki an excuse to visit with Ida. She and Gab are going through a rough patch and, of course, the kids are being dragged right along.

Peter's excuse is it gives him an opportunity to get his precious Mercury Cougar out on the open road. He loves his muscle car with the slant-six engine.

In what seems like no time at all, we pull into the dusty parking lot of Gab's Glen Ellen shop in Sonoma County. Miki, ever the Virgo, looks at her watch.

"What time is it?" I ask.

"Five o'clock."

The drive has lasted a little more than an hour.

We stretch our legs like we've been on a long trip. None of us gets out of southern Marin often except to go into the City.

Tony puts his hands up to shade his lovely blue eyes as he pulls his sunglasses from his pocket. We're night creatures, trapped by the brilliant glare of the sun.

Miki scans the tall trees that partially obscure the hillside on the opposite side of the road.

"Their teepee must be over there somewhere," she mumbles, mostly to herself.

Gab has regaled us at great length about the wonders of teepee living. While he did so, Ida held her tongue. We all know what that means. The Cohens are flat broke and, in desperation, are living in a tent. G-d help them.

Gab's jewelry shop, his latest means of making a living, is in a newly opened, near-deserted, open-air arcade where the shops are connected by walkways. Walkway and shops are built out of unpainted boards that look like they were taken off an old weathered barn.

Gab carefully places his tour de force – the massive gold ring – back on a pedestal illuminated from above by a spotlight, after everyone has appreciated it properly.

"I brought this stuff up from LA."

Dustin stands behind a glass showcase filled with knock-off Native American jewelry. It's all the rage in hip circles now. Miki wears the stuff and I guess I wouldn't mind having some too. Never have been too much on jewelry. My head's into other things.

Before we can admire the silver and turquoise doodads, Gab spots my sign, wrapped in a protective cloth, sitting on top of the showcase.

"Well, what have we here?"

His high, raspy voice makes him sound like a Jewish, pardon the expression, Gabby Hayes.

I can't help it. I blush and lower my eyes.

"Can I see?" Gab asks.

"Of course, I made it for your shop."

I spent over a month creating the sign to hang in front of Gab's shop. He commissioned me to do the work after seeing the mandalic poster I created for Richard, the food guru.

Why shouldn't he?

He got my services for a bargain basement price. I'm doing it for free.

Hey, he's "family."

Anyway, it took a lot of planning. I consulted Herman first. He's the only artist I know in the Bay Area. Making a sign was a new adventure for me. Herman offered vague suggestions, none of which helped. He's hasn't worked as an artist in a long time, poor dear.

What the hell? I went to work.

I selected a slab from a tree trunk as my signboard. After making some tests, I figured out a way to keep the paint from being sucked into the wood, at least for a while.

Then I began thinking about the design. My paper drawing was delicate, intricate. "Go Native," the name of the shop, was encircled by suggestive flourishes and vibrant colors.

Tony assured me I had a winner. Miki liked it too. Thought it would be just the thing for Gab's shop. Peter agreed.

I went right to work transferring my rendering to the slab. It was slow, frustrating work. The uncured wood was obstinate and unforgiving. That didn't stop me. Determination and perseverance are virtues in my book.

The big question still remains, will the paint disappear from the uncured wood before the shop closes its doors or vice versa? I won't hazard an opinion. May they both live long and prosper.

Gab puts his hand to his chin in contemplation.

"You've gone and done it, by cracky," he states at last. "That there is a genuine work of commercial art."

I beam despite myself. Retail is in my blood. Make the customer happy. Gab puts his arm around my shoulders and squeezes me hard, laughing with gusto.

"Come on. Let's see how this thing'll look out front."

Gab picks up the sign and we scurry out the shop door. There we are met with fresh disappointments. The sign is way too small to be read at a distance and the lettering is too delicate to be deciphered. That doesn't stop us. We rush back inside.

"How did you plan to hang this thing?" Gab asks innocently.

Oh no. Something else I didn't think through.

"I…I guess I got so caught up in painting the sign that…well, gosh."

"Hellfire, we'll figure that out later."

Gab puts my sign back on the counter. Everyone crowds around to ooh and ahh.

Gab slips outside to close up shop.

"Look what the cat dragged in," Gab announces, almost immediately reentering the shop.

It's Edge, compact, goateed, pale, and dangerous.

Miki is just firing up a joint so his arrival doesn't cut much mustard, but it makes me uneasy.

Why? Am I feeling guilty about being a somewhat less than gracious hostess at our party?

Well, yes, that's true. But. There's more. He has snakelike, hypnotic eyes that lure me toward him.

I shiver.

"To celebrate the shop and the sign," Miki announces.

She passes the joint to Gab, pot smoke drifting out of her mouth. Everyone laughs. There was a time when Gab smoked weed. No longer. He laughs and shakes his head. Cocaine is his recreational drug of choice. Weed just slows him down.

Where's he going? And who is he going to drag down with him when he crashes and burns?

You got it. Ida and the kids.

Miki passes the joint to me. As I put it to my lips, Edge slips in next to me. No one seems to notice but me. Now he's next in line for the joint.

What else does that put him in a position to receive? Recognition, acclaim, my soul? Why do I feel those snakelike eyes of his want to hypnotize me? Why do my hands feel cold and numb?

Grandmother… speak to me now.

"Cool sign. Is it yours?" Edge asks, turning to me.

I nod, trying to smile pleasantly. I must never let Edge see my emotions, my real feelings, never. I don't know why this is so. I just know it. I feel like a mongoose held enthralled by the swaying body of a cobra.

"I like it," Edge observes.

He relieves me of the joint and appreciatively takes a toke.

All eyes focus on him. That, I perceive, was his plan all along, to draw attention to himself. I'm just a sidebar.

Get your act together, girl. This man couldn't care less about you. Besides, you already have a wonderful old man.

Edge gives the thumbs-up sign to Dustin, the next one in line, as smoke oozes from the edges of his mouth. His snake eyes gleam with amusement. A glass vial filled with crystallized white powder appears in his hand from nowhere. It must have come from his jacket pocket.

"In celebration," he beams, looking around for a chopping block to break up the white powder.

Gab, with alacrity, pulls a marble block out of a drawer. Now he's a happy camper.

Edge chops up the powder and breaks it into tiny lines as the now almost-forgotten joint continues to pass around the room. Edge has succeeded in his plan. He has everyone's undivided attention.

He offers the first hit to me.

What is the meaning of this gesture? Just to acknowledge the sign, or is there something else, something more?

This man makes no careless moves. Everything is planned in advance.

I bend down, making certain my hair doesn't touch the marble block, and suck up one line per nostril. Those snake eyes drill into the back of my head.

Is the sensation soothing, stimulating, frightening?

Edge then passes the block to Miki. While Miki sucks up her two lines, Gab insinuates himself so that he's next in line. The rest of the herd follows.

Tony, the last in line, holds out the block to Edge. There are only two thin, broken lines left. Edge smiles and shakes his head. Tony does them up. Edge then runs his finger over the marble block and rubs the residue on his gums. The block is clean as a whistle.

Wow, I can see everyone thinking. That Edge is quite a guy. He didn't get pissed when there wasn't enough for him. How gracious can you be?

Miki pulls out her coke stash and pours some of it on the marble block. It's only fitting that Edge should be first in line.

A self-satisfied air possesses him as he swaggers to the front of the line. A shit-eating grin comes over him.

What the hell is with this guy? What the hell is with me that I am paralyzed by his eyes?

Now I'm angry, mad.

He can't do this to me. I won't let him.

I'm next in line. Then Gab. The rest of the herd follows.

The room begins to tingle and sparkle. Nerve endings snap and jangle.

"Well. It's been an unexpected pleasure. But I've got some things to do at my ranch," Edge comments with dry mischievousness.

He makes significant eye contact, first with me, then with Miki, and finally with Gab. To the rest, he gives a general nod.

This guy is dangerous. Watch out. Don't turn your back on him. I must never allow him to get close to me, never stop being alert while he's around.

His enigmatic smile returns and, this time, it's noticed.

I can almost hear him thinking - get used to me. I'm taking over.

How? Why? When? Should I care?

I feel very flushed and disoriented.

Touching the top of his forehead, Edge, Mr. Snake Eyes, a trickster, a gangster, a wickedly wily coyote, disappears into the fast-approaching night.

The room vibrates. My stomach churns. The air molecules pop and buzz, smacking together with animated, electrified precision. A fracture, a rupture, breaks the room apart, exposing raw elements.

Maybe it's just me, I think. Probably not a good idea to mention with alarm the disturbing hallucinations I feel welling up from within me. Might make me appear paranoid, a party pooper.

"I think we better get over to the teepee. Ida will be starting to wonder."

Gab's usual upbeat nature has deserted him. A worrisome panic has replaced it. I've seen that look before. He needs to get to a safe place – fast. He wants to hole up. An unknown evil is drawing near with frightening speed.

The six of us leave the shop. Our footsteps echo off the empty wooden walkways and dissipate into the growing night. Stars are beginning to appear in the milky-gray sky overhead. Traffic has built up on the secondary highway that runs in front of the arcade. Another workday over, people are heading for home.

With grim determination, we six pilgrims cleave to reality. The sound of the passing cars is deafening. Depth perception is lost. Death draws near.

Is it the time of day, the uncertain light? What is this fearful, stomach-convulsing thing that is overtaking us? Why am I sweating? Is it because the heat of the day is dissipating and night's chill is beginning to take control?

After what seems an eternity, Gab waves and we all follow him across the road and up a path that leads through a stand of trees to the edge of a cornfield. Only stubble remains, bent and battered in evenly spaced rows. A shiver runs through our collective bones. The moment of autumnal death is upon the land. Doom presses close. Visions of parallel worlds flash into and out of focus. The temporal vortex rips asunder, sucking us into a void.

We stumble along a trail that skirts the edge of the woods-encircled field. Our orderly single-file line breaks apart.

The teepee looms ahead, a white phosphorescent triangle flattened against the blackened trees and the fast-darkening sky.

The wind whispers. A hawk flutters by. A fox cries. A metallic buzz from millions of dead insects roars in our ears.

Without a word, Gab enters the teepee. We follow. Gab picks up a roll of toilet paper, then heads for the woods. We take seats on spread-out blankets that encircle the rock-lined fire pit. A hearty fire burns. The smoke hole above allows us to see stars in the dark heavens.

It's not just me having these feelings. What's going on?

Ida saw the nightmarish glint in Gab's eyes. She's bracing herself for disaster.

"I'm dying, dying," Dustin wails.

His wife cowers in the corner, comforting their big-eyed eight-year old son.

Somehow, Dustin seeks me out for comfort. He puts his head in my lap.

I stare into the fire as sparks jump and float, interlaced in the smoke, toward the opening in the top of the teepee. No time for trivial thoughts now. Prayer is the thing.

Grandmother, draw near. I would commune with you in this moment of uncertainty and infinite possibility.

The meal, which Ida spent hours preparing, is forgotten. Night makes its inevitable conquest of the last hint of day.

Tony leaves the teepee to wander aimlessly among the stubby cornstalks, searching for Gab. The orange moon races across the sky, blocked by clouds one minute, illuminating cloud edges the next, then bursting free with blinding light.

"Gab. Gab," we hear Tony calling outside.

His voice disperses into a soundless, motionless void. Invisible hands drag me into a blinding tunnel of light.

Dustin's moans escape from the teepee through the smoke hole at the top. Designs painted on the teepee transform into mysterious and unknowable symbols. The teepee vaporizes in a white flash. The sky seen through the smoke hole is red one minute and blazing orange the next.

Off in the night, a coyote howls. Wily trickster is on the prowl. Chaos comes closer, closes in, collapses the very air we are gasping to breathe.

Is liberation or destruction approaching?

Tony, smiling beatifically, enters the teepee and sets about encouraging the children to eat.

Peter, Miki's wondrous partner and lover, sits in a full lotus. Thumb and forefinger touch, making a circle. His hands rest palm upward on his knees. His fancy, alligator-skin cowboy boots, Miki's loving gift to him, stand beside him as he surfs insanity, hangs ten on the curl with the Almighty.

I minister to Dustin. My soul is linked with the blood of my Jewish ancestors, nomadic herdsmen of vision and might. I vow to explore all worlds for their meaning in order to free myself from the wheel. Tony squats down beside me and gives my arm a comforting squeeze.

I don't need your tenderness now. I need your power, your strength.

"How're you holding up?" he asks.

He kisses my forehead gently.

Are we together or are we apart? Does his quest mesh with mine? Will we pursue our liberation in harmonious parallel? And another disturbing thought, how would he be holding up without someone else to care for?

He tenderly pushes my hair from my face. We both look down at Dustin.

"Dustin? How're you doing? You okay?" Tony asks.

After what seems a long while, Dustin lifts his head from my lap and turns toward Tony. Apocalyptic visions must be engulfing him. He's learning his first psychedelic lesson, the one that will take him the rest of his life to sort out.

"I'm cold, so cold."

His teeth chatter, even though I have already wrapped an afghan around his shoulders.

Debbie, Dustin's wife, deserts her son on the far side of the tent to join us. Their son looks with unveiled anxiety at the grown-ups. It must be plenty scary for him, particularly in this ill-lit teepee in the dark of night.

"Would some soup help him? We made a whole pot."

Debbie stoops down. The irises in Dustin's unfocused eyes have been swallowed up. He looks lovingly at his wife.

"Debbie? I love you."

"I'm right here, Dustin."

Debbie tenderly takes his hand in hers. Her fingers tremble.

"I'm frightened. Dead and gone…"

"Oh, Dusty…"

Debbie takes her husband in her arms.

The three of them drove up from the San Fernando Valley where, Miki tells me, they live in a comfortable ranch house on a pleasant suburban cul de sac.

I bet Debbie wishes with all her heart she had never agreed to deliver the consignment jewelry and jewelry case to Gab and Ida. She likes to play it safe, despite the fact she hangs out with us crazies.

"See if he'll eat it. It'll warm him up," Miki suggests.

Debbie helps her husband sit up, then feeds him a spoonful of soup. Most of it dribbles down his chin.

"God, it's good," Dustin blubbers with a radiant smile.

Whatever we snorted is beginning to wear off. This too shall pass.

Ida's form flickers in the firelight as she feeds sticks into the fire. Her once firm and attractive body has sagged. Her breasts have fed two children. Her belly has twice been a womb. Weight, always a problem, has begun to win out over vanity. Ida has been on an extended trip ever since she stepped under the wedding canopy with Gab.

It's been a rocky, an eventful, marriage where security is moment-to-moment, hand-to-mouth. This couple, lost souls, proud souls, march to the beat of "doing their own thing" as the bottom falls out of their relationship. And their children are entangled in their descent.

Is that my fate with Tony? Is he strong enough to carry us in safety through the maze toward revelation while living on the fringe, visionary gangsters? And just why am I asking these questions as I emerge from this unsolicited trip?

A dark shadow passes over my soul. I quake.

"Ida? I hate to leave you holding the bag, but…" Miki states.

Miki's tripping too, but what else is new? She's navigated through much more troubled waters than this. In fact, I get the feeling that she's amused, challenged, by this unexpected and unique trip.

What did we snort?

I bet Miki finds out. She'll jolly it out of Edge.

Miki laughs out loud at Ida's rueful look. Ida scowls, then laughs, too.

Dustin looks vacantly up toward the unfamiliar sound.

Is it possible that there is happiness, merriment, in hell? Is that sound a glimmer of hope, a signal of rebirth and renewal?

Just hang in there, Dustin. You'll be okay.

"Yeah, yeah, don't worry. Go already."

Ida shrugs nonchalantly. She knows how to roll with a punch. She's punch-drunk from them.

"Gab'll come down out of the woods eventually. Debbie and I can take care of Dustin and the kids."

Ida hugs Miki and me. Miki puts her arm around my waist and leans close to whisper.

"You hold onto that man of yours. He's a keeper."

Yeah, Tony was there for us tonight, unlike Gab. But…

"I intend to," I whisper back.

And I do, I do intend to hold onto Tony. He's a keeper. He's a good man. But…

While Miki and Peter sit in stony silence in the front seat of the car on the way back home, Tony clutches me tight in the back seat.

Is this an expression of love, of caring, or of fearful weakness? And why am I asking these questions, if we are living out a dream in a storybook land?

The Sonoma countryside whips past. The wind, the wheels, the air itself chants a mournful mantra over and over again.

Dying yet? Dying yet? Dying yet?

The next day I do something I have never done for any other man except my father. I clean Tony's comb with a toothbrush, lovingly removing the crud that has collected there.

Tony is my man, my lover, my friend. He is a fellow traveler. Our visionary gangster path will merge as we seek release from the wheel of life.

I bow down to you, Grandmother. I acknowledge the blue man and scoff at the unworthy image of feet of darkened clay. I choose not to be influenced by snake eyes and dark shadows. We will sail above it all.

Long live Paradise and Harmony... the ruler of this endless series of blue-sky days in lovely Marin County, just across the Golden Gate Bridge from San Francisco, a major spiritual center of the youth revolt whose clarion call has circled the globe and ensnared us all.

Charlie

"Hey, Tony, you're becoming quite the shutterbug."

"And I'm shooting 16mm film too, as much as I can afford," Tony acknowledges, his blue eyes sparkling with excitement.

We're looking at a slide sorter and viewer that holds up to eighty 35mm slides on which he has laid out some of his latest photos. He's been firing off shots of landscapes, sunsets, people, details, all taken in southern Marin.

"Very impressive," I declare, admiring his output.

"Wish I had a 16mm projector. I shoot stuff and then I only get to look at it over a light table or on a Moviscop at Diner's Lab where I get my film processed."

Tony's teaching himself how to make films. He's learning fast but he hit a roadblock when he quit his job at KGO-TV: no more free use of editing equipment, film processing, and field gear. He's been reduced to depending on the kindness of friends. Those friends have also been providing him with freelance work.

That's a minor consideration for Tony, one of the few people living on the West Coast that I knew on the East Coast. He's head-over-heels in love, the lucky stiff. I'm still licking my wounds. Isobel, my childhood sweetheart, married someone else back in Richmond after I threw a monkey wrench into our relationship. The name of that monkey wrench was Heather Chicago; well, as already mentioned, her name really is Linda Preen. She's long gone from the Bay Area scene now.

Tony offers me the last hit of the joint we are sharing. Defensively, I raise my hands in defeat and shake my head.

"I've got to keep my head clear just in case a business opportunity should drop down out of the blue," I tell him, only half in jest.

Tony chuckles, looks blank for a moment and then snaps his fingers, his blue eyes sparkling.

"Hey, that reminds me. There's going to be a *Sunset Magazine* shoot next week in the City. They might need a few extra hands."

"You working on the gig?" I ask.

"I'm synching up the dailies."

Holding the joint with a pair of tweezers because it is so small, Tony lights it and takes a toke. After he exhales, he comments.

"You should give Bill Bishop a call right away if you're interested. I've got his number around here somewhere."

He looks vaguely off in one direction and then the other. Ultimately, his head sways back in my direction.

Has he forgotten what he just said?

Man, are we high.

"Thanks, Tony. I'll call him right now if you can find the number."

Tony struggles to his feet and heads to the kitchen counter. We are sitting in the Japanese-style dining room of Tony and Leah's enchanted cottage. It's cozy to sit on pillows looking out of the many windows in the L-shaped room toward the ivy-covered hillside behind the house. Tony finds Bill Bishop's number on a scrap of paper and hands it to me.

Five minutes later, I've got a three-day gig doing grunt work for the *Sunset* shoot. That might give me enough to pay my share of the utilities and kick in on the upkeep of Joyce's house, if I don't eat anything in the interim and that conversation she wants to have with me still includes me in her movie. Work is hard to come by and detective jobs are just a thought. What I need is someone out there to do some sales. I'm less than useless at it myself. Or that's what I tell myself. Could be the dope talking.

I give Tony a light punch on the arm as I pass him by on the way back from using the kitchen phone.

"Thanks," I say with a smile.

"We all 'get by with a little help from our friends,'" Tony replies, pulling his guitar into position and giving it a strum. He breaks into a blues riff –

"Nobody loves me but..."

I sit down at the piano, built right into the wall of the house, and tickle the ivories. I took lessons as a kid; I prefer the guitar but I hocked that long ago. Leah has the radio on upstairs. We hear her humming. Tranquility rules this house, their union; chaos and disaster threaten from every conceivable direction in the outside world. We are living on the edge, truly strangers in a strange land, as has been proclaimed by numerous contemporary writers and singers.

I segue into a Bill Evans riff and Tony struggles to keep pace. I was the one who inspired him to take up the guitar when we were growing up back in Richmond. I guess it was fated that we run into each other here in the San Francisco Bay Area. Of course, the circumstances could have been a little less tumultuous.

Tony dropped out of college in Oregon and moved down to California, joining countless other hippies in a Tribal Stomp. He was playing the part of a serious lightshow artist, whatever the hell that means, and fell for Jane Preen, a real California dream girl. You're right. Jane Preen is Linda Preen's sister. Then he got himself tangled up in the murder investigation that cost me my job at Life Beneficial and that entanglement ended up costing Tony his equilibrium.

Act Two, the lightshow folds and he ends up on the street with two suitcases holding all his worldly possessions. Then Tony shows up on his parents' doorstep and soon gets a job. After landing a fulltime gig, he moves into the second floor of a farmhouse; tobacco was grown there in former days. It's near his place of employment, a TV station in Petersburg, Virginia, WXEX-TV.

What happens next?

Jane Preen turns up on Tony's doorstep.

So what does Tony do?

He marries the girl, of course (What will my parents say if they find out we're living in sin?) and moves back to California because Jane hates the East Coast.

Surprise, their relationship runs into trouble when they both try to settle down and make a go of it. They really don't have enough in common to see them through the humdrum of married life and entry-level fulltime jobs – the daily grind.

Final Act - they go their separate ways, due to irreconcilable differences. Neither one of them has yet bothered to take the trouble to make their separation official with a divorce decree. Tony moves to Marin from the City after he quits his job at KGO-TV. There he meets Leah and blasts off to the moon, head over heels in love. Again. This time, he tells me, it's the real thing. The two of them sure act like it.

Leah comes bounding down the steep stairs from her studio, her tennis shoes flying. She's a ball of fire sporting black ringlets and flashing, dark eyes. Bianca trails behind her, moving slower, majestic, dignified. She settles down next to Tony and me and begins cleaning herself.

"Charlie. You are staying for dinner, aren't you?" she asks with a smile, sticking her head around the cabinets and countertop that separate the galley kitchen from the dining area where Tony sits playing his guitar. I look up from the piano.

"I don't want to impose," I answer, breaking off my jazz riff to make eye contact.

"Southern gentlemen and their manners," Leah chuckles, putting her hands on her hips and giving me a sisterly smile.

"Okay. You got me," I start, as a worrisome thought makes itself known. "Oh, I'm going to have to pass. Joyce and I have plans. But thank you so much for the offer. Maybe next time."

Meantime, my mind is carrying on a lively conversation with myself.

"Why don't you just break down like everybody else and get a job, any job?"

I mentally answer myself, providing inanities as certainty for justification.

"Well, you've got a point. And maybe, just maybe it has something to do with the fact that this is Marin County, California and this is 1971. Or, then again, you could consider the state of my poor drug-addled brain."

This happens more often than I would like to admit, getting stoned and having conversations with myself.

"How's that working out for you, not having a job, that is?" I ask myself.

I reply, "By imitating water."

"What?" I reply.

I answer. "I overcome obstacles by filling up depressions, by flowing around, through and over obstructions, wearing down granite and washing away earth. Best of all, water succeeds while being dismissed as an insignificant force. That boils down to one word... perseverance. You've got to hang in there, be willing to suffer a little."

"Get out there and start knocking on doors, jackass," I prompt myself.

"Stop trying to be my mother," I whine. "That's not how you go about it when you're in my line of work. To be a champion of the woebegone and forgotten, you've got to have a certain style, an approach, be connected to the higher network that pulses through synaptic links between neurons. In a word, vibes, vibes brought to life in the heavenly sphere that will influence others without their being aware where the influence comes from."

"Give me a break. You're a lazy, no-good crumb bum," I say in exasperation.

"An idealist, maybe; a fool, probably," I answer solemnly.

"Are you familiar with the Chinese curse which states, may you live in interesting times?" I ask myself.

"Funny you should bring that up, considering," I snap back before continuing.

"I mean since Timothy Leary's MIA in Europe and Alan Watts is an alcoholic living on a houseboat at Gate 5 in Sausalito, having consuming thoughts about what Westerners will do with all the garbage they are leaving in their wake, what else is there to do but live in interesting times?

"Oh, forgot to mention, I run the trails and meditate on Mt. Tamalpais, seeking a holy man I once met on the mountain. I wonder while I run, does Mother still hold sway over the dominions of Earth?"

"I know. I know - real space cadet stuff."

"But I'm trying to imitate water. Can't you dig it?"

Leah lights a joint. She has Tony's attention.

Lovebirds... Living in Shangri-La...

"Charlie, would you and Tony please pick some fresh veggies from the garden?" Leah asks.

The kitchen garden is on the hillside above the house next to a modest meadow that gets plenty of sunshine. We could be miles away from the Bay Area, up in the coastal mountains of northern California, as we look out from this spot. Nothing is visible but treetops, hillsides, and sky, that is if you turn off the sound of distant and not-so-distant traffic and the multitude of sounds associated with lots of people living close together.

"The owner of our house is putting it on the market," Tony confides to me while we harvest veggies. "He's given us a month to come up with an offer before he lets the realtor put it on multiple listing."

I want to say, oh Tony, I am so sorry. But I don't. I don't want to hurt his feelings, burst the bubble of this dream world. This is, after all, their enchanted cottage. Tony told me so in the presence of Leah, who did not deny it.

"I called Dad," Tony rushes on to tell me. "Leah called her dad. We asked them for money for a down payment. Explained to them what a good investment Marin property is."

A picture of Tony's father pops into my mind; a picture of Leah's tries to do so as well. I know Tony's dad but I don't know Leah's. Again, I don't know what to say. I don't see either one of them offering to help.

"We figure we can handle the monthly nut and make payments on the loan from our folks. All we need is the down," Tony concludes.

"How long have you got?" I ask.

"Until the end of the month, like I said," Tony replies. "It's going to work, Charlie. I know it will. Our folks just have to get it into their heads what a good investment real estate is in Marin County. This enchanted cottage will have to do its stuff on them."

Ipso facto... QED... End of argument...

Who can resist the logic?

Richmond, Virginia, and the comfortable upper-middle-class circumstances in which both Tony and I were raised are three thousand miles and more than a world away from Mill Valley, California, circa 1970.

"What's up?" I ask.

"Us..." answers Joyce.

"We make fantastic love together."

"True, but..."

Joyce pauses, sticks a fork into her spaghetti marinara, and rolls it up on her fork. She looks at me. I can't think of anything appropriate to say at the moment so I remain silent.

La Ginestra is the local Italian joint. It's loud, dark, and cozy. The decorations on the wall are corny but evocative. We both like the place. It's our place. The owner speaks to us when we come in. He's a friendly guy.

"I think maybe we're moving too fast," Joyce concludes.

"What brought that thought on? Aren't we having a good time?"

"Sure. I like you too. Maybe we're in love, a couple. Only time can tell. But..."

"Great. I couldn't agree with you more. Let's go back to your place and toss it around after we hit the hay."

"I got a call from Big Phil yesterday."

Big Phil was Joyce's boyfriend up until they had a parting of the ways. Joyce hasn't told me what happened and I don't want to know, not even now.

"How's tricks with him?"

"Oh, you know. Big Phil is Big Phil, always the same, always open to trading, making up lyrics, playing Delta blues licks on his guitar."

"Okay, I bite. So what did..."

"He said he'd like to drop by sometime, nothing specific, just that."

"And..."

"It got me to thinking, you know, that maybe we're moving too fast. So I thought we should talk about it at our favorite place to eat out. Don't you think that was a good idea?"

I think I know where this is headed. Maybe she's right. Maybe we are going too fast and maybe I shouldn't have moved in with Joyce. Maybe I needed a place to crash and sort of influenced it to happen without really wanting to think about the implied commitment such a move might indicate.

I don't want to be a heel; I don't want to lose Joyce as a friend, as a lover.

As she said, maybe we're about to discover we're in love.

But, well, yes, I've had to scramble for a place to crash plenty of times in the past two years and I don't want to wear out my welcome and lose out on the off chance this is the real thing, that she's the one. Anyway...

I don't say that to Joyce. I think we both know what the score is. I have to admit free love doesn't mean the same thing to me that it seems to mean to most of my contemporaries. I'm a one-woman-at-a-time kind of guy and, yes, I'm just too serious about life. I need to smile more, to make pleasant conversation, laugh at jokes, particularly when the joke's on me.

For tonight and for this encounter it boils down to the fact that I respond as a gentleman should, just like my mother taught me. I pack up my suitcase and borrow a paper bag to put a few odds and ends into. I leave by the front door with a very friendly goodnight kiss. "Come back real soon, you hear," as folks back home would say. No hard feelings.

Good night yourself, I reply, sitting in my trusty Volvo S122, my handy couch for the evening ahead.

Next morning I'm in more of a daze than normal. And I'm disoriented: for some reason, waking up in my car before sunrise at the end of a deserted cul de sac does that to me. I scratch the beginnings of a beard, smooth down my tousled hair, look around for a creek where I can brush my teeth and wash my face. This is Marin County, California, not Virginia. Creeks are scarce as hen's teeth in these parts. I try to go back to sleep. No such luck. A car pulls out of a driveway heading to work – must be a stockbroker, someone who lives on East Coast time. Got to put some space between me and this parking spot – it looked remote in the dark but it's right in the middle of a neighborhood come daylight.

Fuck it. Right next to my car, I do some elementary yoga stretching exercises I picked up in a book and add a salutation to the sun just for good measure, even though the sun is still a desire in this heavily treed neighborhood in a deep, dark valley surrounded by steep hillsides. Then I hop back into my car, in the shotgun seat, and throw the *I Ching*, the coins landing in the well in front of the seat. I'm hunched down with the top of my head wedged up against the glove compartment. The result is Difficulty at the Beginning, Hexagram 3, hell of an image.

This is the image described in the hexagram: Rain is pouring down from the heavens above. A blade of grass struggles to poke its tip out of the ground. Rocks, mud, all sorts of obstructions weigh the blade of grass down, make it difficult for the grass blade to thrust itself forth and free itself from the nurturing but constrictive soil. Lightning and thunder flash and boom in the sky as heavy rains continue to fall. Caution and circumspection are called for. Hell of an image.

I contemplate that. Do some breathing exercises sitting upright in the seat, back just touching the seat, thumb and first finger making a circle balanced just above my knees. Play a game of solitaire without cards. I love holding numbers in my head, seeing where those numbers lead me. I fall asleep and wake with a start. Someone is knocking on my window.

"You lost, buddy?" a guy asks.

He is holding his morning newspaper in his hand. He's not threatening, more like inquiring. I wave and give him small grin.

"Just admiring the view," I chuckle.

"It's a beautiful morning," the guy agrees.

I start my car and drive away. My car's clock tells me it's 7:00 a.m. Pat & Joe's Restaurant is open. They serve breakfast and whatnot from 2:30 a.m. to 8:30 a.m. So what if it's not quite as clean and shipshape as the town council would like. It's a misfit's kind of place and that includes me. The restaurant is almost empty at this time of day. Peak hours are from 2:30 to around 4:30 a.m., a real late-night hangout. Coffee's good, so are the sunny side up eggs with toast, hash browns and sausage. I'm set up for the day.

The Mill Valley Market is open. I buy things I can eat with little or no preparation, refrigeration, or anything that requires modern-day appliances to keep it okay to eat. Jerked beef, as Louis L'Amour counsels, it's high on my list. You can take it from there.

Back in my car, I pull out my AAA map of Mill Valley and study it before starting up my car. I locate a street to check out for what I have in mind and fix it in my mind. Then I leave the map opened up on the shotgun seat so I can consult it and head up Summit Avenue. It winds around, going steadily upward. I cut off at Fern Canyon Drive. I thought Summit was winding; this street is one big curve and very narrow, just barely room for one car with pull-out places that allow for meeting a car coming in the opposite direction. I know from the map that it dead ends.

There is a steep drop-off on one side of the street. Houses on that side of the street are perched on stilts. They hang out over the slope and have street-level garages or a very small turnout to park their cars. On the other side of the street the hillside goes up, with houses reached by stairs. I'm looking for a place to park my car that is unobtrusive, hidden, one that will not attract attention for extended, particularly overnight, periods of time. I am in luck. There is such a space. In fact, it is large enough for several cars to park. There's a simple explanation. The parking area is located at a trailhead. A redwood post identifies the trail as Temelpa.

I get out my backpack and fill it with the provisions I bought at the Mill Valley Market along with my crunched-up mummy bag. The backpack already has base items, including a heavy-duty flashlight, toilet paper, a knife/fork/spoon kit, a mess kit, all the things Boy Scouts take along with them on a hike, plus some items that I added after taking basic training when I was hired on at The Office. The path leading away from the parking area follows Cascade Creek upward toward the East Peak of Mt. Tam. I'm hoping not too many people take this path. And I'm betting there's going to be a spot or two not far from this trail that will be suitable for a guy in my position to meditate, to hang out, and to establish a low-key, low-impact, temporary campsite. It's back to basics for me, high time that I get my head straight.

I hit my stride and even whistle a little tune as I hike the trail. Sure enough, I come upon several likely spots for camping. I don't settle on one, not yet. I want to explore first. My head feels lighter, clearer, sharper. Taking a breather, I sit on a convenient rock and look around me. I am encircled by young redwood trees. Not much farther up the path I can see golden hillsides leading upward toward the East Peak. I lean back against an equally convenient redwood tree and cup my hands behind my head. I take a deep breath. I feel alive, awake. As a guru might say, I'm living in the Now.

I look for a place to meditate. It appears, as if by magic, on a golden, grassy slope. I tuck my legs up under me and close my eyes, trying to concentrate on the image of a very quiet pond, a large body of water. The surface of the water is like glass, still, unmoving, silent. I focus on my breathing. I relax one body part at a time. I start to feel a tingling sensation, separation from everyday thoughts and distractions. I hear someone squealing, a young woman being playful, with someone else. They are having fun. Sex! My mind alerts the appropriate body parts. My eyelids flicker, letting in light. I try to block out the intrusion. A bug of some sort lands on my arm. Is it a mosquito? I try to resist the urge to swat it. I remember there are few if any mosquitoes in California. Why is that, I wonder? I find myself thinking about all the things that are novel, different, foreign yet wonderful about California. Heather, I mean Linda, appears before me wearing her Indian costume: a leather miniskirt and top with a feather held neatly in place by a bandanna tied tight around her head. Her long, straight blond hair falls to her shoulders. Her pleasing, womanly shape allures. I am aroused. I shake my head and bring my mind back to the quiet, silent, glassy surface of my imaginary body of water and my breathing. The wind picks up. Something floating in the air smacks me in the face. I give up. I'm allowing in too many distractions. Maybe later I'll try again.

I climb up Mt. Tam, reaching the parking place where I usually leave my car. The parking area is packed with cars, as are both sides of the road leading up to the top and an observatory that is closed to visitors. A motorcycle driven by a Hell's Angel type with a fetching girl who has her arms wrapped around his liberal waist turns off the highway and follows a dirt trail beside the road to a prominence. The bike pauses as if it might stop but then rolls down the hill and back out onto the road. It joins a stream of cars moving in both directions. A boy and a girl are sitting on a rock at the top of a knoll. The girl is leaning her head on the boy's shoulder. I don't notice that she is wearing a purple miniskirt and has taken off her shoes until she stands up. She steps onto an adjacent rock just a little higher than the one they had been on. The boy watches her. The girl's legs are long and slim. The boy ogles her and the girl poses for him. On a dusty, grassless trail as wide as a single-lane road, people on horseback, on mountain bikes, and on foot are on parade. Who knows what happens to the people in the cars that reach the top of the mountain? Do the occupants turn the car around and drive back down after a quick look at the panoramic view?

I take my customary path. It leads along the side of a steep, golden-grassed hillside, going neither up nor down. While I hike, I gaze out at the ocean far below and the clear blue sky above. The path leads me onward. The trail seems to go on forever until it disappears around a distant hillside. A guitar-led hootenanny, a sing-along, is taking place fifty feet below the path. One girl, standing, raises her arms over her head and sways in time to the music.

Are they singing the Youngbloods' "Get Together," a popular anthem during the innocent times of "peace and love, brother" back in 1967? Unlikely. That time, that sentiment, is long gone in the Bay Area. More likely "I Wanna Take You Higher" by Ike and Tina Turner. The "me" generation with all its hedonistic aspects on display has arrived. This lifestyle is all about what I want, what I feel, what I deserve, my rights. Yeah, I know I sound bitter, maybe excluded, not high-minded and principled, a bring-down artist, not interested in joining the party. I tell myself that's because I'm an outsider, not a joiner. Cold comfort.

A cloudless sky bodes a not very colorful sunset but it will still be a spectacular sight well worth the wait. There's plenty of room for everyone to pick a spot, spread out and enjoy this fabulous day.

I'm headed toward the collection of cabins I came upon three years ago. One of the cabins was occupied then. A mountain woman was cutting wood in front of the cabin. Smoke rose from the chimney. A man came out onto the porch and watched as I approached. He welcomed me and invited me in for tea. It was an invitation I normally would have refused but there was something about this man. Was he a holy man? I thought so. We sat in a living area on pillows. And the tea took me to a place I'd never been before. The man spoke to me in what seemed like holy riddles. He gave me a pouch which contained totems and a strange blue powder. I have never seen the mountain woman or the holy man again. Revisiting this site might help me settle down and allow me to make real progress on my spiritual journey, if I really am on one.

Is this haphazardly sought goal of spiritual realization, unification of all within the Almighty, my fool's errand? Am I willing to take the necessary steps to reach this goal?

A hawk flies overhead and calls out, a sign to me that magic is in the air. I'm on the lookout for game. Birds sing. I enter a patch of woods and the trail dips gently downward. I round a bend in the trail and the cabins come into view. All is as I remember with one important difference. The cabin in front of which the mountain woman was cutting wood and from which the holy man emerged is unoccupied, as are the other cabins. And they seem to have been that way for some time. Maybe the owners of the cabins have sold out to the government agency that runs this park or their lease has expired. Maybe this just isn't the right time of year for the owners to be in residence. But how can that be? This is the best time of year, at least for weather. Any well-informed local knows that.

The sun is getting lower in the sky. The wind-stunted evergreen trees encircling the cabins hasten darkness. It comes to me that I should camp here for the night. Why not? I have food, bedding, everything I need. I'll pick a secluded spot back up in the trees. What I want is solitude, a meditative space, virtual silence. This place has that in spades. It also has the added advantage of history, a history concerning a mystical and otherworldly event three years in my rearview mirror. Perfect. I could even build a small fire. I would be careful. I could make tea, maybe even heat up some soup. I brought a can or two.

I carefully choose a site for my small fire in a place with good separation from trees and remove all flammable material from the area. I make a circular ring of stones around my fire pit. I collect firewood from deadfall lying about. In the center of my firepit I put very small bits of wood, twigs, tinder, surrounded by a teepee-shaped arrangement of larger sticks with plenty of room between the two so that the flames can breathe. I pull out my mummy bag, spread it out, and sit on it waiting for total darkness. Even though it's noticeably colder, I feel warm, comfortable, relaxed, at home and at one with myself. I think about... nothing, nothing whatsoever. Bliss...

After what seems like an appropriate length of time, I strike a wooden match taken from an Army-issue green screw-top plastic container. The tinder catches with one match. The teepee-shaped sticks catch soon after. I feed in larger pieces of wood. I have a fire. I stare into it with pleasure, something Louis L'Amour, my favorite Western novelist, recommends against. "If danger comes, you'll need to see clearly in the dark right away," he cautioned. I'm not expecting trouble, so no need to bother about that.

I open the can of soup and bend back the still-attached lid so I can use it as a handle. I peel off the label, put it in my backpack, and place the can at the edge of the fire.

Keeping a clean campsite is part of the Boy Scout way. As a Boy Scout, I made Star Scout with fourteen merit badges, was a member of the Order of the Arrow, and went to a National Jamboree in Gettysburg, Pennsylvania where Vice President Richard Nixon spoke. I was dressed, as were my fellow Scouts from the Robert E. Lee Council, as a Revolutionary War soldier. I carried a wooden musket.

I have a cup, a tea bag, and a canteen. I rustle up some hot tea. I eat some jerked beef while the tea is brewing and the soup is heating up. This is living.

I hear an owl hoot. Far away, a dog barks. Is there a ranch nearby or is the dog roaming free? The wind rustles through the trees, an inviting sound. Gosh, it's great that California has so few bugs.

I burn my fingers pulling the soup away from the fire's edge and use my shirt to finish moving it. I break out my knife/fork/spoon kit. I stir my tea. I eat my soup. It's hot. It tastes wonderful. Campbell's chicken noodle, just like we had at home. It's my favorite. I set aside the empty can and the cup to clean up in the morning. I have a Famous Amos chocolate chip cookie, one of my indulgences, for dessert. I break out a hash cigarette and smoke it down to the nub. I contemplate throwing the *I Ching* with quarters but discard the idea. I prefer to idle my time away.

I build up the fire and arrange my mummy bag next to the fire. I look up at the stars. Even in this remote area, the lights of civilization make the night sky not as black as it could be, but still, more stars are visible here than down in Mill Valley. I sing.

"Home, home on the range..."

I wish I had my guitar. Maybe I'll learn how to play the harmonica. That would be fun. I take off my shoes and pants and slide into my mummy bag. I'm staring at the fire one moment and I'm asleep the next.

I am a body of water, a rushing mountain stream, tumbling down a precipitous hillside. Darkness closes in all around me. Tendril-like, skeletal branches reach out overhead, bending to form a circular shape, a target, the center of which is a small island in the middle of the stream. In the center of the island on a small mound is an object. I can't make it out even though I, water, made up of seemingly infinite water droplets, rush closer and closer.

I evolve, become a dark-shadowed form with branch-like arms that reach out in front of me as I approach the mound and the object on it. I see that the object is a leather-bound book. In the scantly illuminated murk of night, three dull silver light-reflecting knives are attached to the book on the top and two sides by strings on which are threaded seashells.

I reach down and pick up the book.

A ten-foot-high ring of fire encircles me and threatens to consume everything including myself. I am not alone in the center of this encircling inferno threatening death. Three other people, I can't make them out, are with me. One of the people reaches out to take the book from me. I think the person is a woman.

At that moment a gush of water breaks through the ring of fire and a woman riding on this wave slides toward me. It's as if she's riding on a surfboard made of water. She speaks. I cannot hear or understand what she says. I strain to make it out. My grip on the book loosens. The woman takes possession of the book and disappears into the inky dark that surrounds us as the fierce flames that had encircled us vanish. I am alone in darkness. I wake up.

The sky above is still dark, studded with stars, but I somehow know that sunrise will soon be upon us. It is that transitional time between night and morning when light is barely discernible. Quietly, a sliver of redness emerges in the heavens. The sun is insisting that it come forth. Red changes to orange changes to yellow changes to a bright ball of light which, when it rises above tree cover, will be visible on the eastern horizon.

I put a few twigs on the coals from last night's fire, bend down, and blow gently on the tinder. Smoke rises. A twig bursts into flames. I add larger sticks. I have a fire. I break out my mess kit and make up a frying pan. Into it I put some jerked beef, frying it like bacon. I pour water into my cup and heat it up. I reuse my tea bag from last night. I eat the heated-up jerked beef. Now would be a good time to throw the I Ching. No, now would be a better time to meditate.

Where would be an appropriate place to do so?

Inside the cabin once occupied by the holy man, of course. I climb the two steps to the covered porch and try the front door. It is unlocked. I enter. It's as if the holy man and the mountain woman have just stepped away. Maybe they are in the woods picking sacred herbs and plants. Maybe they will soon return. I would like to talk with the holy man again.

I sit cross-legged on the same pillow I sat on before. Here, I shared tea and conversation with this holy man. I look out the window which reaches from floor to ceiling in front of the sitting area. As if on cue, the sun lights up the sky. Birds call. The scratching sounds of animals nearby alert me to their presence. The wind has yet to come alive. Still morning light fills the room and glows in my heart, the location many gurus say is a well-known place to meditate on God. I am quiet, still. Without preamble, the glow in my heart explodes, becoming a blinding white light. The radiance consumes me. Floating in this dazzling display is the holy man in a full lotus, a mystic eye in the center of his forehead, his long brown hair hanging down onto his shoulders. His intense gaze penetrates, flashes out laser beams into my soul, even as I am trapped in Maya, between birth and death.

"Not now," I hear him say even though his lips do not move and no voice speaks.

I am grief-stricken, heartbroken.

"Why?" I answer without speaking the words.

I see between the holy man and myself a wall of rope-like vines, obstructers to liberation. I reach out to tear them away. I am pulled toward them. They become the bodies of all the women I have lusted after and the lucre I have desired, the veils of Maya. I wrap myself around an attractive female form. I am filled with desire. I yearn for money, possessions to make life easy, comfortable, emotionally rewarding.

"'You must learn," the holy man says.

"My being feels complete satisfying these desires. How can they be obstructions?" I reply.

"You are a young soul. It takes time to become a true seeker, even longer to journey on the path toward knowledge. Sacrifice and, yes, suffering on the wheel of life are Fate's way of instructing."

"But..." I begin.

"You are not prepared or ready. Deal with the immediate entanglements of life. Remember: the heart is a well-known place to meditate on God."

I am back in the sitting area of the log cabin, in the woods on Mt. Tam, in a wooded glade surrounded by wind-bent trees. The sun is shining higher in the sky. I hear someone on the path that leads to the cabins. I stumble to get up from my cross-legged position on the pillow. My hand bumps against something. I look in that direction. A leather pouch, just like the one the holy man gave me two years ago, is next to my hand. I pick it up and stuff it into my pocket. In a flash, I am out the door and heading up to my campsite in the woods. Two hikers, a man and a woman, appear near the cabin just as I enter the protective trees. The man is using a walking stick. The woman shades her eyes as she gazes at the cabins nestled in the wooded glade. They are not aware of me. I carefully put out my fire and cover it with loose dirt. The man and woman draw water from the hand pump next to the cabin. The woman fills up her canteen; the man bathes his head in the water. They move on. I wash my dishes, pack them up, and put them away. I head back in the direction from which the man and woman came – back toward the road which leads up to the top of Mt. Tam and down toward civilization.

A similar collection of people greets me as I near the road. Still dazzled by the light of my vision, I find their playfulness enjoyable, companionable. They remind me of something I'm already forgetting. What did the holy man say to me? And that dream, what was that all about? Mini-skirted girls with bearded boys who ogle them are delightful to observe, their innocent purity appealing. Maya, Maya, your veil obscures but is so enchanting. People on a dusty path, whether on horseback, on a bicycle or on foot, are all seekers, sweaty and heated and all too human. Hell's Angels on motorcycles with their partners clinging to them from behind are Kerouac figures on the mythical road of life. Their song is not about Dharma bums but about Darwinian predators in sunny California. They don't know the real truth of their existence. But they will learn, as will I. Therein lies the joyousness, the playfulness of Maya. High above, the blinding sun creates brilliant halos around Buddha and Christ images that float in the vibrant blue sky. Fleecy clouds parade by and through these holy men. The Almighty is indifferent to, yet inclusive of, the light-hearted play and inevitable suffering of the collected mortals on this mountaintop. I am included in their ranks. Will I one day commit myself to The Almighty, be entirely devoted to The Almighty, to worshiping The Almighty, and become eternally resigned to The Almighty? Do I have the courage, the determination, the fortitude, the true desire?

At sunset I sit beside a lone tree on top of a hillside, looking down at a group of people celebrating the end of another day. The sun reverses its changes from the morning, going from white light, to yellow light, to orange, to red, to purple, to a diminishing and then dissolved oblong of wavering glow. Mighty clouds assembled in ranks from one side of the sky to the other change color as the sun races toward the horizon. Sky meets ocean. I sit cross-legged and gangly in the moment. As others head toward their cars, I make my way toward the Temelpa Trail, pulling out my flashlight to help me find the way.

Reaching the trees in the last glimmers of light I find a likely campsite and store my gear there. No campfire tonight. After making a cold camp, I nibble on some jerked beef and open a can of peaches. Another Famous Amos chocolate chip cookie is in order. I drink some of the water I hand-pumped at the magic cabin. It is still fresh, cold, delicious. I walk back out into the grassy open area when the moon rises. It's a full-moon night, dotted with stars.

To my right the golden, grassy slopes interrupted by outcroppings of rock and small clumps of wind-bent trees lead to the summit of Mt. Tam. To the left, down the trail fifty feet or so, the trees are less wind-battered than those above. The coastal fog is spread from side to side, low down, well inland. Mill Valley and its environs are cloaked over for the night and most likely will be so well into tomorrow morning. The panorama is spectacular, a sight that sends shivers down my spine. The crisp night air supercharges heavenly thought.

"Om," I chant. "Om," I repeat.

What did the holy man say – that I was a young soul, that it was not my time, that I must make my way through the veil of Maya... and then what? Why? Why is there suffering and pain? Isn't preparing for the shock of inevitable approaching Death enough? How can emotions and thoughts be wrong when they feel on a very deep level to be so right? Why is seeking out and holding onto a partner deceptive and obscuring? Listen. Learn. Stop. Breathe. Come. Go. In. Out.

I hear a fox crying in the night. There must be a den nearby. Is the cry from a mother calling to its young? Is she trying to divert attention from her litter to protect them from harm? Is she on the prowl for food to feed them? The wind picks up. The trees rustle against one another. Gentle tree sounds filter through my bones. I hunch my shoulders and think about the sweater in my backpack. It's time to call it a night. No more visions, no more messages from the holy man or the invisible world.

I un-cup my fingertips and drop my hands to my sides. I take a deep breath and let it out. I gaze at the full moon, the all-enveloping fog below, the dark woods, the steep slopes leading to a Mt. Tam peak. My mind, my inner being, is a void, emptied out. I have received all that I was ready to receive. I head down to my camp nestled in the protective windbreak of the trees. I get in my mummy bag and light up a hash cigarette. I smoke it down to the nub. I stare into the inky darkness. There is nothing to see.

Strange shapes, otherworldly creatures appear as spectral images, swaying tendrils of fog or filamentous beings, in the darkness. In the distance I hear a horn honk, the moaning sound of a siren. Is that an ambulance rushing victims to the emergency room, a fire truck, a police car? A jet plane flies overhead. Its sound is like its trail, long-lasting, far away, slowly diminishing into silence. The wind stirs the tightly clustered trees that engulf my surroundings.

My mind wanders off into whirling thoughts. An image of my father replaces the wavering, spectral shape-shifting forms. He is at one and the same time my guide, the one I seek approval from, and my enemy, the one who encourages pragmatism and dubious ethical and moral positions. I sit with him in that three-years-ago interrogation room. The events leading up to that moment and those that follow it are replayed in my mind. Tangled in the Veil of Maya, captured by Life, sleep closes my eyelids. I am no more – dreamless, drained, an empty shell in a mummy bag, pre-wrapped for coming burial.

I wake and try to meditate. It's impossible. Restlessness has taken hold, propelling me toward what lies ahead in the world below. I'm a fool on a hill, a fool headed back to his car by noon.

Wonder what kind of sandwiches and soup are on offer at Sonapa Farms, what's cooking in downtown Mill Valley? Maybe Joyce has had a change of heart. Tony and Leah should be up by now. What are they up to? I saw Harry at the market. Maybe I should drop by his pad. I remember the upcoming freelance gig.

I head downhill toward the trailhead, my car, and civilization. I can always head back up the trail later in the day or tomorrow.

Yes, tomorrow would be better, much better. Nature has refreshed me; I am ready to meet new challenges, encounter new horizons.

I stuff my backpack into the trunk of my car. The leather pouch from the holy man is in the outside pocket of my backpack, ready for use when the time is right.

The next month is a blur... Nights spent just off the Fern Canyon trail.... Others on couches... Always on the lookout for a shower.... No time for puzzles or solitaire.... Throw the *I Ching* whenever and wherever the opportunity allows... The three-day gig for Sunset offers little relief... My unemployment insurance benefits run out... No gigs on the horizon... I smoke more hash than is my custom. I don't know which end is up... I'm that rolling stone Bob Dylan wrote a tune about.

I get a huge break. The Jefferson Starship is going on tour. The bass player needs someone to house-sit. His girlfriend is joining him on tour. They need someone to take care of a litter of newborn kittens in their Mill Valley pad while they're out of town. Harry convinces them I'm the responsible type and the ideal solution to their problem. The bass player and I hit it off. The tour begins. I move in. I have a place, rent-free, for the coming weeks.

"Neither of our parents came through with the down on the enchanted cottage. It was, it is, such a good deal. The owner isn't willing to work with us. We don't know which way to turn."

Tony looks at me imploringly.

"So what are you going to do?" I ask.

"We've been looking around," he answers half-heartedly.

"Any luck?"

"There's this place we can afford. That's a miracle in itself. It's a little off the beaten path but..."

Tony's thought dries up.

"Where is it?"

"San Quentin."

"San Quentin?"

"Yeah."

"The prison?"

"Well, there's a little village on the road that leads up to the prison gate. It's quaint in an odd sort of way, like something out of an old-time movie or something. There's a beach, open fields on a hilltop, panoramic views."

"And a prison down at the end of the street."

"Crazy, huh?"

Yeah. Crazy.

But who am I to talk? They, at least, have found a place to land.

BOOK TWO:
ENTER WILY COYOTE

Leah
(February 1971)

On the radio a Steve Miller tune – "Gangster of Love." The weighty and palpable presence of violence hangs in the air. For two days I have not been able to find the energy to bathe, dress, or eat, have not called Miki, David, or the police.

Break-in, rape, a dream shattered and turned to shit.

I'm living in a tomb filled with nightmares, terror attacks, and fury.

There's a knock at the door.

"I just had a feeling that I should drop by. I hope you don't mind."

Those snake eyes again, drilling into my head, connected to a powerful, dominating, take-control gangster with a wily coyote smile. Edge.

Why has he come?

My stomach tightens.

Dark curiosity and suspicion emerge within my anger-filled, suicidal dead zone.

"We were just going to have some tea. Would you like some?"

Why do I say that?

"Thank you, yes."

Edge's snake eyes sparkle with malicious and mysterious glee.

The trickster is pleased, just as Ken Kesey and his Merry Pranksters must have been while overseeing their "acid tests." They dosed unsuspecting partygoers with LSD-laced punch while the Grateful Dead played what sounded like a jam session on stage. Some fun, huh, for Kenny and for the Prankster band, but maybe not so much for the unsuspecting partygoers.

Edge dosed us with what I have been told was angel dust on that day we visited Gab and Phyllis.

Did he intend to give us an "angel dust test?" Or was he just trying to amuse himself, to flaunt his power, to demonstrate his control over us?

"Leah? Don't you think..." Tony begins.

I don't want to know what Tony thinks. I push him aside, using Edge as a wedge.

Tony. Don't hover over me, worried, uncertain, weak. I need decisive, protective, strong. Not a visit from the blue man with feet of black clay.

Our dream is over, shattered. All has been revealed.

What remains?

Determining when and how I can extricate myself from this murderous rage, this never-ending, cloying, claustrophobic entanglement.

"Grandmother, hear me. Give me the strength to see and act with resolve and insight."

Silence resounds from the vacuum. Infinite separation and panic attacks, snake eyes, the tumbling of karmic dice.

Edge is leering at me, smacking his lips.

Or am I imagining that, fantasizing about it?

No. He's watching my ass as I cross the room.

Am I wanton to think of encouraging him to take me, this strong and dangerous man, this gangster of love?

Tony says nothing, does nothing.

Weakling. Coward.

I want to be protected! I want to feel safe.

Tony stands rooted to the spot, a blank expression on his face.

Calm yourself.

The intruder held a knife to his throat.

Fucker.

Tony didn't have to beg and plead. He didn't have to forget about everything but his own skin.

Stop. Stop. Stop this right now. It's not healthy, it only leads to the same painful reflections and conclusions.

Neither Edge nor I acknowledge Tony's existence.

Does this mean that Edge knows something? Or does it mean I am the only reason he is visiting?

What should I do? How should I act? How long have we been alone in the kitchen? Have I put the water on for tea? What has been said?

Tony puts on a record, the Mozart sonata for flute and oboe. Then he picks up a book, Dune by Frank Herbert.

Who's he trying to kid?

I realize I'm laughing just as the teakettle begins to sing.

Is Edge being witty and charming? Am I being coy and flirtatious?

Tony looks up from his book. Edge pours hot water into the teapot. I put Melba toast on a plate. We parade into the front room. It has dramatic views from windows that cover an entire wall looking out toward the upper end of San Francisco Bay. Ivy growing up the side of the house has insinuated itself into the room by pushing apart the window casements and pressing through those openings. The sun outside is bright; the sky is blue. No rain in sight.

I am hollow within, a jumpy, raging, haunted being that I do not know.

Edge motions for Tony to join us.

Am I Edge's hostess? Am I under a spell, his spell?

Ridiculous.

Which is more ridiculous, being his mistress or wallowing in self-destructive thoughts?

No. No more cowardly acts. There's been enough of that.

"Help. Please help me, Grandmother. Send me a sign."

Silence resounds.

"Come on, Tony, while the tea's still hot," I call out.

After taking a ceremonial sip of the soothing chamomile tea, Edge pulls out his stash.

"A friendship offering," he states, his snake eyes darting from Tony to me and back again, his teeth flashing.

"It's Maui Wowie," I hear myself bleat with pleased surprise.

Edge carefully breaks a bud of the weed apart and rolls the crumpled, fragrant flower into a joint. My palms are sweaty. I'm dizzy, nauseous. Get a hold of yourself. You've got to be the strong one in this household.

Forgive me, Grandmother.

"For a deserving old lady," Edge states, passing the unlit joint to me.

Is that the way I want it? Is it?

Being his old lady would be one avenue of escape, a way to make a clean break. And what else?

The weed is potent. I take a hit and pointedly pass the joint to Tony, not Edge, afterward. Edge makes no comment.

Is this whole complicated scene just my head trip?

Help. Help me, Grandmother.

Silence resounds.

"I'd like to see some of your work," Edge says, his attention concentrated on me.

"I still have a lot to learn," I answer.

I sound like a schoolgirl.

What's wrong with me?

If you want to be this man's old lady, you've got to be powerful and strong.

"Why don't you let me be the judge of that?" Edge replies.

"I don't think..." Tony begins as he passes the joint to me.

"Is this your work?" Edge interrupts.

I nod.

I had been doodling at something that became a mandala drawing at the dining room table when Edge showed up at the door. The result, in my mind, is meditative therapy, not art.

"This is fantastic."

He takes a hit and passes the joint back to me.

"Thank you. It's nothing – really."

I take another hit of the joint.

"No. No. You're onto something here."

Edge puts down the drawing as his snake eyes take in my portfolio. He ceremoniously opens it up on the black coffee table that came with the house and begins to look through it. We pass the joint back and forth until it is consumed.

The weed takes effect.

Edge turns in what seems to be slow motion toward Tony. Disconnected and distant growls and roars come out of his beast-like mouth.

Tony frowns, uncomprehending.

Edge laughs.

Contagion strikes the dulled edges of our consciousness. Tony and I laugh too.

Wily coyote has taken control of the henhouse. I am laid open.

What does Edge see? What does he want?

My soul, my work, my heart, my art – they are dead and gone.

I sit shiva over them.

Help me. I've been violated. I can't do this alone.

Grandmother, come to my rescue. Spare the walking dead from this sacrifice, from becoming the bride of Lucifer.

"Can I see some of your work, too? I've heard you're a writer," Edge requests of Tony, making that request sound like an insult somehow.

"Well," Tony manages to say.

"Listen to this poem," I respond, trying to cover up what we all see so plainly, Edge's hostile act, his charade.

"On a peak looking down to the ocean
"Walking through a cloud
"They heard, as one together
 "A mental rattle of communication
"Devoted to Self-comprehension.
"Was not all a dream
"Round the fleecy bowl of sky?"

"That's really heavy shit," Edge states solemnly after a brief silence.

I go on.

Am I rubbing it in, destroying all traces of feeling, humanity, innocence? Is that what must be done? Is that the way back from or further into this Underworld that I now inhabit?

"Monopoly, Scrabble, dominoes, checkers.
"Peyote - the cleansing agent for the mind.
"Sparkles up those neuron endings.
"Synaptic crackles, clean and tight.
"Motor units in the brain unclog and clear.
"The long spinal column snaps, pops, and straightens.
"Your back's as good as new.
"Peyote - body cleanser, healer.
"Peyote good medicine, you bet."

"Right on," Edge agrees.

Tony ducks his head and blushes. He's starved for recognition.

"Hey, I've got to split," Edge says abruptly.

The ceremonial tea has grown cold, is forgotten. Primo weed and wily coyote have seen to that. Tony and I rouse ourselves from our stupor. Our guest is standing up to leave.

"Oh. I almost forgot. I want you guys to have this."

He reaches in his pocket and pulls out a vial.

Why does that vial frighten and excite me at one and the same time?

Suspicion, paranoia, fear, anger, hate – I'm a bundle of emotions going in sixty-four different directions.

Face it. Get over it. Deal with it.

I can't. Too soon… I'm sorry.

"It's crystal LSD."

Edge hands the vial to me. I hold it up to the light to inspect it.

"Take very small amounts. This stuff is pure. Two granules will keep you high for a week."

There is enough in the vial for more than a dozen trips if what Edge says is true.

"Too much," I hear myself say.

"Cool," Tony blurts.

I can see that he does not think this gift is cool.

Why? Fear? Jealousy? Paranoia?

All of the above.

Suck it up. Get used to it. Get over it.

It's over – the dream is dead. So is my soul.

So what?

I'm sorry. I can't help it. It happened. I can't change that. I can't go back and close that door. I can't undo it. I can't change what Tony did or what happened. I can't not think whatever it is that I'm thinking and feeling. Change. Move on.

Tony, you fucker, you let that man hurt me.

I can't forgive you. I can't forget.

It's over.

Fear, anger, sorrow, pain.

I'm living in a putrid Underworld, being readied as the bride of Lucifer, the gangster of love.

Is that the answer for a soulless individual - seeking out a stronger will?

The very next day I take a double dose of Edge's acid. Tony, explaining that he will be my guide, takes a smaller dose.

Who the hell is he kidding?

I can see the fear in his eyes.

Take me. Take me – into a psychedelic dreamscape lined with hot coals. I have been expelled from the home of my ancestors, just as Jews have been expelled throughout the centuries.

What else is new?

So be it.

I know now life is hard and cruel, not kind and gentle.

Deal with it.

Get over it.

I can't.

Not yet.

I'm sorry.

Help me.

Grandmother, where are you?

After angry, tortured, tear-torn reflection ---

Dear Tony,

I felt this morning that it was time for me to go.
I started to cry (again) but my heart
Said
Love is Eternal.
Change is
Illusory experience
In this Hall of Mirrors.
Thank you for the Love you have
Blessed me with.
Thank you for the Love you blessed me
Receiving.
I pray our light will always
Shine. For one another.
Now & always.

Leah

Charlie

Tony pushes his Polaroid sunglasses away from his watery blue eyes and slumps down into a cloth-backed deck chair, throwing his feet onto an adjacent chair as he does so. His trademark tennis shoes held together with gray duct tape jump prominently into view as he does so.

"You want some coffee?" I ask.

Tony, looking way, way down in the dumps, shakes his head. He's a skinny, six-foot tall, woeful question mark.

We're both sporting long hair but I've got high cheekbones. That makes some people think I'm Native American, which in a way I am. On my mother's side of the family there's Native American blood. People really get confused when they hear my Tidewater twang. Had one guy ask me if I was an Aboriginal. Tony favors the English roots on his mother's side of the family. He's got brown hair and blue eyes and sunburns easily. Don't get me started on where my influences come from when you get to the mental side of things.

With a mighty sigh, Tony launches forth.

"I've lost her. And it's my own damn fault."

Oh no. Watch out.

He picks up steam rapidly.

"I'm a coward. That's what I am. I didn't come up when she needed me. I'm a disgrace to the 'family,' to everyone, to myself. I don't deserve to be alive."

Tony, Tony. What have you gotten yourself into?

I pull out some primo weed, pre-rolled, from the pack of Sherman's in my shirt pocket and light a joint.

Getting high definitely makes time stretch out and warp. Some say it clouds the mind; others say it clears it of clutter. I say right now it helps blow away the gloom threatening to drown childhood friends. Well, at least we're sharing our pain.

We drift together into the marijuana haze still engulfing much of the Bay Area, a hangover from the free-and-easy hippie days that are now rapidly dissipating in northern California.

Nothing can stop Tony from spilling his guts now. Stop. Listen.

"Leah's gone, man."

"What do you mean, gone?"

"Split. Flown the coop. Vamoosed."

"What happened?"

"I screwed up bad, Charlie. Real bad."

Tony begins to cry. "Tomorrow Never Knows," a cut from the Beatles' Revolver album, starts to play on the record player. The Jefferson Starship bass player and his wife are still out on tour. The mother cat and litter I'm babysitting are doing just fine, all but the runt of the litter. Even his mom pushes him away. Tony tells his sad tale, with long, anguished spaces in between snippets of his story.

"A man broke into our house…"

"Tomorrow Never Knows" plays in the silence.

"It was hot. We had the doors open…"

Continued psychedelic music playing in the silence.

"We'd smoked some hash and passed out on the bed…"

Crazed fragments of orchestral moments ring through wild lyrics and audio altered instruments echo into the deep silence.

"I woke up with a knife at my throat…"

Deliberately distorted instrumentation and William Blake lyrics wrapped in Eastern mysticism warp deep, dead silence.

"I lost it. Completely. I begged him to spare my life – without a thought of Leah."

Dramatic wailing and crying, echo effect with drone dragging curdles deep, death silence.

"I'm a coward."

Tony pulls a pack of cigarettes from his pocket - Players. He doesn't hear "Tomorrow Never Knows," doesn't see the dry, sunny day or the deck where we sit. He only sees the nightmare that runs in a continuous loop inside his head. The song ends. He taps out a cigarette from his Players pack, lights it, takes a drag, starts up again, this time with fewer painful gaps in this tale.

"The man put a pillowcase over my head so I wouldn't be able to identify him. I had visions of suffocation. I felt the chill of death creep up my legs. I whined and pleaded. He dragged me into the bathroom and hog-tied me to the sink drainpipe.

"Leah and humiliating fear occupied my mind. I prayed she had run from the house.

"All I could hear were pre-dawn sounds - birds beginning to waken and call, cars far off in the distance, nothing else.

"My heart was pounding. I was very conscious that I was lying on the bathroom floor.

"After a very long time, Leah came in and untied me.

"She saw me like that, Charlie.

"She heard me beg for my life.

"I didn't think of her, didn't save her. I didn't...didn't..."

Tears of despair, tears of anguish, tears of disgrace pour down Tony's face. He's awash in overwhelming emotions of self-pity and emasculation.

His innocence has been revealed as weakness by an unknown evil. The blinding tentacles of the burning sun eat soothing shade away from the deck. Bleary-eyed Tony puts one hand up to protect himself as a shocking bolt of sunlight illuminates his tear-stained face. A windblown tree branch sways. He awkwardly drags his chair, retreating into the shade. The silence hums with parched and despairing bitterness, a void Tony tries to fill unsuccessfully with words.

"Leah told me she had been raped.

"She didn't want to call the police.

"She didn't want strangers in the house.

"We hugged but it didn't help. Our arms were blocks of ice.

"Even though we were sitting on the couch right next to each other, we were far apart.

"I wanted to plead my case but couldn't.

"It wouldn't have made any difference. It was too late for that.

"I failed the test. And I lost Leah."

Is there such a thing as Fate, predestination, Karma? Is anyone whole, complete, perfect that is not a saint or divine, I wonder.

"When she left, did she take all her things with her?" I ask.

Tony looks at me with pleading eyes. He yearns for absolution that I cannot give.

"Did she take all of her things? No. She left lots of things, including her cat. Do you think that means she might come back?"

"What have you done to find her?"

"I was frantic. I contacted all our friends, the rest of the 'family.' No one knows where she is. Or that's what they told me. They know. I could see it in their eyes. I...I..."

"Do you think she just wants some space, some time?"

"I don't know...I wish...I just need to know that she's all right. Is that wrong?"

Oh, my woebegone and forgotten friend. I pat him gently on the shoulder but Tony's too far gone in his private nightmare to notice. How can I help?

"I'll find out where she is for you if that's what you need."

Tony nods, then looks down at his hands. A giant tear falls on them.

During the rest of the afternoon and well into the night, I listen to the mental wanderings of my scorned and tearful friend on the deck of the bass player's Mill Valley house. Clear-cut slices of his great love affair with Leah emerge from Tony's endless stream-of-consciousness monologue.

Why? Why does life attack the innocent – is that not all of us – with these testing moments of horror and pain? Why? So that we can fail? So that we are forced to confront our flaws and vow to improve on them? So that we can emerge as heroes filled with courage? So that we can receive instructions that direct us along the path?

"Guide us," I shout silently, mad with the weight of eons-old human consciousness shrouded in the Veil of Maya.

––––––––––

According to Tony, Miki and Peter's tucked-away cottage is action central and the community bulletin board for "family" members. Tony and Leah used to drop by their pad on Lovell at all times of the day and night to hang out, get high, buy drugs, play games, listen to music, play music, pass the time, and pass on information. Their visits would consume a large part of many days and nights. Time zoomed by.

I assume my best low-key but inquisitive manner as I head toward the stone steps that lead to Peter and Miki's. The place was built long before the Golden Gate Bridge was finished, a rough-and-ready retreat that a San Franciscan constructed for weekends and summers. It seems unchanged. It sits on a small plot of land that is reached by going up a set of stone stairs. There is no direct street access. These stairs take you behind a wood-shingled duplex where

Harry, Tony's friend from their lightshow days, lives, and through a gate into the yard of the cabin.

When you enter by the gate, you look uphill into a yard that lacks vegetation. It's mostly hard-packed dirt. The tree-covered lot gets almost no direct sun. A Malamute eyes me as I come up the walk but does not bark. Standing on the front porch is like stepping into a time machine. No other houses are visible. Seemingly distant street sounds echo off the hillside. Birds talking in the trees overpower the outside world.

Inside, Aretha Franklin cries out for a little respect.

Is Tina Turner cued up next? Will Gladys Knight and her Pips follow?

The Malamute – black and white with blue eyes – settles down into a pile of odds and ends on the porch, no longer bothering to watch me. I knock on the door.

It gets quiet inside. Knocking on doors must be for squares or the cops. After a longish pause, I open the door myself. All eyes are directed at me.

"I'm Charlie, Tony's friend," I announce, thrusting a business card Leah mocked up for me into the hand of the person nearest the door.

Half a dozen or so people sit cross-legged on pillows around a low circular table. The dude I hand the card to passes it on without looking at it. A tall man facing the door takes the time to look at it when it reaches him. He has a mustache and long black hair tied back in a ponytail. He wears heavy, black-rimmed glasses. If his pale skin is any indication, he doesn't get out in the sun often. He has a reassuring face and an easy smile.

"Oh yeah... I remember Leah talking about this card," the man states, his face lighting up into a smile.

He leans toward a balding older man with tufts of gray hair and a well-tended goatee to show him the card.

"See - woebegone and forgotten. Remember?"

The older guy chuckles, then looks up to me with a smile on his face revealing gaps in his teeth. He needs to see a dentist.

That card really is an icebreaker. I'll have to have more printed up when I can afford it. I take it back from the gray-headed guy.

"I've only got a few," I explain.

Not a cool move. But what am I supposed to do?

"So you're Tony's friend," the pale, tall, dark-haired man politely states. "Make yourself at home. My name's Peter and this is my place. Miki, my old lady, is on the phone. You ever meet Herman?"

Herman is the older guy with the goatee, it turns out.

"I've seen him around."

How could you miss Herman riding his rattletrap bicycle around Sausalito or hanging out down at the Depot in downtown Mill Valley? He's a fixture, a part of the scene.

Herman smiles again. He has highly intelligent eyes that twinkle mischievously and he looks just like what he turns out to be - a transplanted New York artist who migrated to the Bay area when Beatniks roamed free.

I'll find out later that he lives rent-free at Gate Three in Sausalito in what was once a machine room for a Naval shipyard. "Gate Three" refers to an entrance gate into the shipyard where ships were built during World War II. Herman scavenges food from the dumpster outside of the Big G Supermarket near his house but spends most of his time hanging out in pads that welcome him.

He has a wealth of esoteric knowledge; he's not really a guru, not really an artist, not really a deadbeat. He's a hip moocher with bad teeth.

"You want to smoke some weed, do some blow?" asks Peter, ever the gracious host.

Being a Southerner, I appreciate his style.

A small pile of white powder is sitting on a marble block next to a razor blade. A bowl filled with potent-looking marijuana is nearby.

"Don't mind if I do," I chuckle.

Peter waves his hand toward the marble block, indicating I can do the honors. Picking up the razor blade, I chop up the coke. I try to look cool as I divide the small pile of coke into lines. Then I take out a dollar bill from my pocket, fumble as I roll it into a tubular shape and, eventually, manage to snort up two lines, one for each nostril. I haven't really done much coke. Not that I'm against it, you understand.

"Good stuff. Thanks," I comment, pushing the marble block toward Peter as an electrical charge surges within me and I feel an urgent need to blow my nose.

Hello.

My brain lights up. I see immediately why coke is popular these days.

B.B. King plays hot blues licks to a tune called "Nobody Loves Me" on the record player. Lucille was in good form the day B.B. recorded this song. So was B.B.

As Peter finishes honking up two lines, Miki bustles in from the bedroom.

"Tony's friend, Charlie, just dropped in. You know, the one he's always talking about?" Peter immediately comments as Herman snorts up the last two lines of coke.

Miki hesitates only momentarily, then she too turns into the gracious hostess. These folks have got the entertainment thing down cold. After all, that's what they've been doing every day for who knows how long.

"Oh, right. Hi."

"I've heard so much about you," I mutter, feeling the heat of her inquisitive eyes.

She's definitely the one in charge. I like the feel of her – capable, solid.

"You seen much of Tony lately?" she asks.

"That's what I came here to talk with you about."

She picks up on my implied suggestion right away and switches gears with no visible effort. She's fast as well as sharp.

"I know these two guys would like to finish their game of bones. Why don't you join me in the kitchen? I've got something on the stove I need to stir."

"Nice pad. Cozy," I comment, looking for something to say after we reach the kitchen.

"You and Tony have a wonderful accent. Has anyone every told you that you sound like you're from Australia?"

"I get that and New England, also Canada. It's the English influence in words like out, house and about. Virginians are very proud of their heritage. The first permanent English settlement in 1607 and all." Miki looks blank, maybe even a little distant. "I learned that in school," I add.

Hey, I don't feel very connected to that heritage and all it implies either. I mean, look at me. Do I look like a Southern aristocrat?

I switch gears. I'm on a mission, a mission of mercy for my woebegone friend, Tony.

"I spoke with Tony yesterday. He's pretty shaken up."

A big pot filled with a reddish mixture bubbles on the stove. Miki turns the gas up on an empty burner. It sparks and ignites. She pulls her black hair away from the side of her face and lights a joint directly from the flame. After taking a toke and passing it to me, she begins vigorously chopping up scallions. She's making spaghetti sauce.

"What happened to those two was a tragedy," Miki sympathetically allows.

I nod in agreement.

After taking a toke, I hold the joint so that Miki can take a toke without interrupting her work. We both exhale. Two clouds of marijuana smoke fill the room.

The kitchen has two small windows, one opening up onto the porch and the other, above the sink, looking out over the side yard. The whole yard is filled with young, skinny but tall redwood trees. The kitchen is painted a dirty tan. I bet the lights stay on in this room day and night.

"You seen Leah lately?" I slur out of the side of my mouth.

The combination of coke and weed has hit me hard.

Miki sticks her head into the refrigerator and looks into the vegetable bin. She pulls out mushrooms and olives.

I take another toke and hand the joint back to Miki when she returns to the butcher block and her chopping knife. Miki eyes me pointedly as she takes another toke. Then she puts the joint in an ashtray for future use. Her look has spoken volumes.

"You and Leah are pretty tight, aren't you?" I ask, forcing myself to concentrate.

Miki begins washing the mushrooms. The faucet makes a loud hissing sound that, in my altered state, seems to imitate a rushing mountain stream. A ray of sunshine suddenly penetrates into the dark room through the window above the sink and shines on Miki's long black hair, which seems to explode and glow as if it were on fire.

Miki and Peter have mighty fine drugs. I feel like I'm coming onto acid.

"She's like a sister," Miki admits, talking loud enough to be heard above the hissing faucet.

"You seen her lately?"

"She doesn't want to be found, Charlie, particularly by Tony."

It's my turn to withhold comment. Miki anticipates what she believes I'm thinking.

"Tony is a good man, a gentle man. Peter and I both love him. But if he really wants to be a mensch, he won't go looking for Leah."

"He still loves her, very much. He just wants to know she's all right."

Miki turns off the water. The washed mushrooms are on the counter beside the chopping block. She picks up the knife but does not use it, not yet. A "family" member, one of her best friends, is being talked about. No misunderstanding should occur.

"She's trying to start a new life. She wants to forget about the past which, unfortunately, includes Tony. It's hard for all of us."

"In order for Tony to find a new life, he needs closure."

Is that what Tony needs? What does that mean? I hope the thought is headed in the right direction, for all concerned.

"Leah was the one who was raped."

"And Tony was threatened with a knife and tied up to a drainpipe with a pillowcase over his head."

Miki looks at me with exasperation. I hold up my hands.

"You're right, of course. It's just that... he's my friend... and I told him I'd help out. I'll see he doesn't make a nuisance of himself."

Harry, who introduced Tony to the scene at Peter and Miki's, clumps onto the front porch. He looks in the kitchen window, taps it with a knuckle, and waves to Miki and me.

He has long, curly reddish-blond hair. He's burly and hairy and wears wire-framed glasses. He has a ready, devilish smile that indicates powerful intelligence mixed with loads of street smarts.

He's another transplanted New York Jew, a graduate of Bronx Science, a dropout from Bard College, a draft dodger who tried to buck induction by taking acid and riding in the front subway car all night before showing up for his draft physical. He was classified 1-A, then he dropped out of sight. He's been on the lam ever since.

We hear Harry greet Herman and Peter when he enters the front room. Miki sighs.

"She's moved in with Edge," she confides. "They live on a ranch up in Sonoma. It's his hideout." She seems to be finished but adds, "I haven't seen either of them lately."

Do I detect a hint of concern in her voice?

I don't have time to question her about it before Harry enters the kitchen.

"What's happenin'?" he asks, with a laid-back chuckle that belies the feverish activity of his brain and his life.

Harry is an electronics genius. He has his ham radio license and he loves to tinker with tubes, wires, and other electronic paraphernalia.

Besides acting as road manager for Hot Tuna, he builds studios for well-heeled musicians. In his previous incarnation as a lightshow artist, he did some electrical work for them too.

"Where've you been hiding yourself, stranger?" Miki asks, beaming her high-voltage smile at Harry.

"Oh. I've been spending a lot of time out in Bolinas helping Banana build a studio."

Banana is a member of the Youngbloods. Harry turns his attention to me. He's not interested in talking about the studio at the moment.

"You seen Tony lately?"

"Just saw him yesterday. He's still pretty shook up."

"Tell him to drop by. Maybe he'd like to see the studio I'm building."

"Anything to distract his mind is a good thing."

Harry shakes his head in sympathy, then turns his attention to Miki. He's here on business.

"Can you make up a little care package for me? I'm a little low on staples."

"I think I can scare something up," Miki answers, smoothly making the transition from cooking to dealing dope.

"Excuse us a minute," she mumbles as she and Harry head toward the bedroom.

I soon find out that the bedroom is for transacting business and parleying on other high-level, secretive matters. A balance beam scale sits on the floor next to a small desk. It's used to weigh up and break down coke and weed.

The spaghetti sauce simmers on the stove. The washed and sliced mushrooms and olives await introduction to the sauce. Miki is constantly being jerked from one role to another.

Herman and Peter are playing bones in the front room. The marble block, now empty, sits near the center of the table. The bowl of marijuana has disappeared under the table. Before I get a chance to say anything, the door opens. It turns out to be Big Phil.

"Ta-da," he exclaims throwing his arms wide and beaming broadly. "I have arrived."

He's heavyset. He looks like a butterball but closer inspection reveals that what might be thought of as fat is mostly muscle. He's as strong as an ox. He has short, reddish-brown hair and a mustache, both of which he keeps meticulously trimmed. He wears serviceable, well-tended, sturdy clothes – jeans, a plaid shirt, well-polished cowboy boots. He carries a trading pouch over his shoulder and holds his guitar in his hand. In his pockets and his pouch he carries one-of-a-kind items which, according to whim, he offers for sale or use. He's a man of great energy and charm, always ready for the unexpected. Nothing catches him off guard. He's also a wealth of information if he decides to take you into his confidence. And he was Joyce's boyfriend for a time, maybe still is.

The room comes to life. Big Phil rolls a joint from a sinsemilla flower top that's purplish and has glittering crystal tips that he carefully crushes and strips. He tells us the history of this weed as he performs this operation. The weed is, of course, the finest. Big Phil explains why at great and fascinating length.

Peter, continuing his role as gracious host, pulls out some coke and begins chopping it up. Miki and Harry come back into the front room. Greetings are exchanged all around.

The joint and the coke are passed around the room, then Big Phil plays one of his original compositions, a line of which strikes me as appropriate to Big Phil's humor and mindset.

"Strictly running in the black... My brand new sixteen track just came in today."

Everyone hoots in appreciation when he finishes. Harry takes his leave of the group. He's not into hanging out at Peter and Miki's even though he lives just down the hill. I'm left sitting dazed and befuddled next to Big Phil.

A day at Miki and Peter's is more than a time warp. It's a voyage into a parallel dimension.

"Cool guitar work. What's that phrasing you use?" I ask.

"Just some blues riffs I stole from some Bayou pickers," Big Phil answers.

"Are you from Louisiana?"

"Memphis," Big Phil answers, suspiciously.

"Isn't that where Leah is from?"

"Small world," Big Phil replies with a twinkle in his eyes.

"I'm Tony's friend, Charlie," I rush to add, showing him my card.

Hey, it worked once. Let's see whether it goes over big again.

Big Phil takes it, studies it.

"Leah's work... I'd recognize it anywhere. Mind if I keep it? Who knows? Maybe I'll run into some woebegone and forgotten soul that needs some help."

Before I can think of a snappy comeback, Big Phil starts to turn away. I blurt out what's on my mind to stop him.

"You ever been to Edge's place up in Sonoma?"

"Could be," he answers then adds. "You interested in trading at all?"

"I might be."

There's something in the way Big Phil answers me that makes me think he's well aware of my short fling with Joyce. Peter puts a Bobby Blue Bland record on the turntable. More visitors come in the door. Miki is swept away into the kitchen and then into the bedroom. Herman leaves. I guess he doesn't like to hang out when the scene gets crowded. I negotiate a trade with Big Phil for a buck knife. During the course of conversation, I get my business card back and directions to Edge's ranch. Big Phil laughs when I explain why I want the card.

The tree-covered mountainside filled with rocky outcroppings, the winding road, the ramshackle houses bring to mind the Blue Ridge Mountains back in Virginia where my parents have a cabin.

Tight-mouthed, suspicious locals watched our family drive past from their porches and sat in stony silence at the local store when we came in to shop while we were on summer vacation. Luke, the monosyllabic son of the man who maintained our cabin, showed me where to catch mountain trout. I never found out why he bothered. I don't think I was exactly loveable or even likeable for that matter.

Each fall, Dad took me on an outing to a VMI football game. He graduated from this venerable military school just in time to serve as an intelligence officer for The Office during World War II, the same organization I worked for after graduating college. He was also actively involved in Office business during the Korean conflict.

We had some real father-son chats during our weekends at our cabin in the Blue Ridge. Things were different back in Richmond. It wasn't that we never talked or interacted. We did. But there was this silence about my father that no one seemed to penetrate. All that changed when we were alone in our mountain cabin. Maybe that's why I have a predilection for silence myself.

Will I ever re-connect with him and receive his blessing? Despite what has happened, I still yearn to receive it. Will I allow it to happen? Will he?

Us Carters are a bunch of pigheaded damn fools, most of us; well, me at any rate. And don't get me talking about Vitolinich character traits, if I'm actually related to them, that is.

I think about Dad as I hoof it two miles up a bunch of switchbacks. It's hot, sweaty work. But no way in hell I'm going to drive my battered, gray Volvo S122 sedan up the ill-kept road that leads to Edge's hideaway.

At the top of the rise, there's a level, open area that was bulldozed long ago so that a ranch house and outbuildings, now weathered and worn, could be built. Natural succession has begun reconverting the compact hillside fields, tidy apple orchard, and fenced-off areas for farm animals back into forestland. Chokeberry, ragweed and thistle abound.

The outdoor hand pump squeaks, but cool, refreshing water almost immediately pours forth when I work its handle. I let the water splash over the back of my neck, then wipe my forehead with a handkerchief before putting my hat back on.

Nothing stirs in the late afternoon heat. The dust I kick up with my boots hangs in the air. The sun is hot, unavoidable.

Off in the distance a shot is fired. A gasoline-powered engine fires up. A lone hawk cries high above this wild and lonely place.

Why the hell would Leah agree to move up to this remote ranch, Edge's eagle aerie?

From what I know about her, Spartan conditions contradict her style. She's more suited to paved city streets, sidewalk cafes, and quaint restaurants cluttered with city-bred intellectuals. She's a Southern lady, an Easterner, a Jewish-American princess camouflaged in worn-out dungarees, sloppy shirts, and cute-as-a-button tennis shoes.

Does she really believe she's cut out for a back-to-nature experience?

I step onto the bowed front porch and knock on the doorjamb. The door is ajar.

"Hello. Anyone home?"

No one answers, not even the wind.

A chair is overturned in the front room and the kitchen table is rammed into the wall. The table smashed a window when it collided with the wall. Broken glass is on the floor.

What the hell does that mean? I ask myself.

I step inside and leave a business card on the kitchen counter. Never hurts to announce yourself, even when it appears no one's around. It'll give Leah a kick to see it.

There are no dishes in the sink or drain rack, no pots or pans on the stove, no glasses or cups on the counter, no brooms or mops standing in the corner. A light layer of dust has already collected on surfaces. That would happen in short order around this place, particularly with the door and windows open.

The refrigerator – almost useless without power (a gasoline generator must be hidden somewhere) – contains a moldy, half-eaten loaf of bread, a pitcher of water, some potatoes, a dried- up bunch of celery, a package of carrots, several of which have started sprouting roots, a shrunken lime, and two bottles of flat seltzer water.

In the pantry are a few cans of soup, canned vegetables and fruits, a big bag of brown rice filled with mouse droppings, a box of powdered milk, a big, almost-empty box of cornflakes, and some jerky in a large jar that is wedded to the pantry shelf by glistening spider webs. That jar of jerky has been there a good while.

The bedroom closet and several dresser drawers are filled with clothing that must be Leah's. The curtains in the bedroom and a rug on the bathroom floor look like Leah additions. A spare bedroom has become her workroom. Assorted tchotchkes from the Mill Valley enchanted cottage and the San Quentin residence add colorful touches to this otherwise drab, almost foreboding interior.

Edge has made little impression on the ranch house. The furnishings look like they came with the place. Nothing of his hangs in the closet. Some underwear and socks are in one drawer of the dresser. Some work shirts and dungarees are in another. They could be anybody's.

Is there some very simple explanation for the overturned furniture and smashed window, the absence of visible habitation?

I head back outside and stand on the rickety front porch where I light a hash cigarette and take a toke or two, only to stub it out for later use. It keeps company with other half-consumed joints and hash cigarettes in my metal Smith Brothers lozenge container.

The kitchen garden has gone to seed. Two gigantic, fruitless zucchini plants overrun a row of radishes, a row of carrots, and a row of lettuce. Chinese peapods have wilted and died back from the wire mesh fence to which they once clung. One lone watermelon grows at the end of a long vine, seemingly deriving its vital juices from the demise of the other vegetables.

I absentmindedly crouch to thump the watermelon. The sun is racing toward the horizon. The night air will turn this place into a cold, dark, sinister place in no time flat.

A battered, unpainted wooden outbuilding with a brand-new door, standing near the perimeter of the leveled portion of the hillside, attracts my attention. A steep and treacherous slope composed of loose gravel and dirt drops off precipitously behind the outbuilding. You wouldn't want to fall down that hill. You could easily break a leg or, worse yet, your neck.

As I turn the doorknob to open the outbuilding door, a bee buzzes lazily by my head. I raise my hand to shoo it away. A shot rings out. I fall against the door pushing it open. I am lost to the world...

I groggily put my hand to my head and pull it away. It's sticky with dried blood. Night has almost recaptured the landscape.

I'm lying on the floor of a primitive drug lab. Shattered lab bottles on a nearby countertop glow dimly in the uncertain and failing light. The bullet that grazed my head must have smashed into them before lodging in the wall. My body wedged the door open.

I sit up slowly and shake my head to clear it. I pull myself to my feet. Boot prints glowing in the mixture of moonlight and the last glimmer of sunlight lead me to a ridge that overlooks the leveled plain. Someone wearing those boots stood near some shrubs just under a deformed apple tree, an orchard remnant. The shooter smoked a Pall Mall cigarette here. A .22 rifle shell casing lies on the ground. Tire marks clearly indicate where a truck parked and drove away.

Is Leah in danger? Who is this Edge creep and what is he up to other than drug dealing? Did he take this potshot at me?

––––––––––––

My hair clots the blood and stanches its flow. I have a whopper of a headache. A swing by Miki's pad reveals that Leah and Edge have not dropped by. Strike one. Down the hill, they haven't made an appearance at Harry's apartment. Strike two. David Travail, Leah's older brother and a practicing psychiatrist, is listed in the Mill Valley phone book.

I hop back in my trusty gray Volvo. My head rings with the throbbing of the car engine as I wind along narrow and ill-kept back roads. Heat hangs heavy in the air.

When the hell is a rain-filled front going to break the back of this drought?

"Yes?"

A hard-to-make-out man stands in the hallway shadows of a house that is nestled beneath looming redwood trees near the neck of Blithedale Canyon.

"Dr. Travail?"

"Yes? I'm David Travail."

"I'm Charlie Carter. We met at a housewarming party given by your sister and Tony Vitolinich. Tony is a friend of mine."

I hand him one of the last business cards that Leah dummied up for me. His hand emerges from the shadows to take it. A long, ponderous silence follows.

"Leah made a card for you?" he asks in a softer voice.

"That's right."

It doesn't seem like he's going to say anything else so I jump in.

"I hate to intrude on you and your family without notice, but I'm concerned about Leah. And Tony. Have you seen either of them in the past few days?"

Travail steps out of the shadows. He's a tall man, lean and gaunt. His eyes have a brooding tenderness about them. He is, after all, a man who, by profession, listens to the troubles of others. He has a knowing, a shopworn way about him.

He sighs, a long, deep sigh. Then he raises one long-fingered, expressive hand upward and lets it drop to his side.

"Leah has been staying here with us for the last few days."

"Can I speak to her, please?"

Travail makes no move to oblige.

"Like my card says, I'm a private investigator – for the woebegone and forgotten."

"Are you on a case?"

"Tony asked me to find Leah and talk to her for him."

"I see."

"He's upset. His life is in turmoil. He needs to know that Leah's all right."

Travail shakes his head.

"Maybe it's best they don't see each other right now."

"Normally I would tend to agree with you. But..."

"He's your friend."

"Yes. And I have reason to believe both of them might be in danger."

Travail sadly, sagely nods without committing himself.

"She's not here right now, Mr. Carter. What makes you think they might be in danger?"

"I assume you know that Leah has taken up with a man named Edge who lives up in Sonoma?"

Travail puts one of his expressive hands to his chin.

"And that concerns you?"

"I went up to Edge's place in Sonoma. Have you been there?'

Travail shakes his head, this time with traces of concern.

"It's a lonely, desolate, unused place, not a fitting place for Leah to live, if I may say so. I discovered a crude laboratory in one of the outbuildings. It looks like it's being used to make designer drugs of some type."

"Yes? Go on."

"Someone took a warning shot at me. It creased my skull. Whoever it was didn't want me hanging around."

"That explains your head. You really should have that looked at."

"First things first. Do you know anything about this Edge character?"

"Not as much as I'd like."

"Do you think he's capable of taking a shot at someone trespassing on his property?"

Travail raises his eyebrows in a qualified assent.

"Is he selling drugs?" I ask.

"I don't know. What I do know is that Leah and Edge are staying in our guest house out back."

"Do you think your sister might be in trouble?"

"Edge is smart, paranoid, deceptive. He has a huge chip on his shoulder. I believe he's had a troubled upbringing."

"Why do you say that? Did he confide in you?"

"Leah confides in me, up to a point."

I wait two beats. This time it works. Travail opens up just a smidgen.

"We were very close when we were young. We still have a strong bond."

He sighs again. Whatever he's thinking must be none of my business, at least in his mind. He tosses the ball back in my court.

"Do you think my sister is in immediate danger, Mr. Carter?"

"I don't like the feel of this setup. But I have no specific reason to think Leah is in immediate danger unless you count this crease on my head."

Travail gravely rubs his chin with his hand. Realizing he is doing so, he looks at it as though it were an alien thing, pulls it away, and drops it to his side.

"Thank you, Mr. Carter. Thank you for sharing your thoughts with me. I will most certainly have a heart-to-heart with Leah when I see her. Unfortunately, I must spend most of my time at the Institute in the City. And my wife and Leah don't... well..."

Travail begins closing the door as he steps back into the shadows. He seems to be retreating into his professional persona, an acquired habit to protect his psyche from constant attack. He knows the dark secrets of too many people. They must haunt him.

The door closes silently, then clicks as the bolt is thrown from the inside. I step away.

I light up a Sherman's into which I have stuffed bits of Nepalese hash and turn on the radio. It's tuned to KMPX, the hottest underground FM station in the Bay area. They are, as usual, playing cuts from LPs, long ones with no interruptions. Jimi Hendrix whispers amid the clickety-clack of drumsticks. His lyrics speak of death. He's defiant, posturing.

A growling bass guitar and Hendrix's wailing licks overtake the song as a small red Nash Rambler putters round the corner and parks in front of David Travail's house. It's Leah's car and she's alone. Edge must have found something more important to do. My stakeout has borne fruit.

I put the hash-laced cigarette in the car ashtray before getting out of the car. Wouldn't want to start a fire in this dry weather. The dry-as-toast trees clatter against each other, applauding my thoughtfulness as I walk, hands in my pockets, toward the Travail house. The front porch light goes on.

"Leah. It's me. Charlie, Charlie Carter."

Leah's face looks drawn. Her being has aged. Yet her spirit continues to burn with fierce energy and determination.

"Yes?"

"Tony asked me to see if you were okay."

Leah's face is transformed. Her spine straightens into regal lines. She is a Sphinx, a fierce yet silent Buddha. I feel I must justify my presence.

"I went up to Edge's ranch. I got this for my trouble."

I point to my head. Leah looks at the angry bump and clotted blood with concern.

"Who did this to you?"

"I was hoping you might be able to help me with that. Do you think Edge has it in him?"

"Well no... I mean, I don't know... I..."

"Maybe you should hang out at your brother's house for a few days and kind of think things over while I..."

"No. Don't interfere. I'm perfectly... I'm all right. Really... It was probably accidental, what happened to you. Unintentional... You won't press charges, will you?"

"Leah. It's me, Tony."

Tony steps out of the shadows.

Where the hell did he come from?

I start to say something but Leah interrupts.

"Tony, you shouldn't be doing this. Edge is on the way."

"I only want a chance, Leah. A chance..."

Leah does not answer. A cat, not Bianca, ambles out of the door and twists through her legs, then clings to her feet.

"Please. I love you. Give me a chance."

"Tony. Now is not the time..." I start.

Leah shakes her head with solemn determination. In retrospect, I believe she realized at this moment that even if the rape had never occurred their love would not have stood the test of time.

"It's too late, Tony. Leave. If you really love me, you'll respect my request."

"Don't make me do that, Leah. I'm begging you. Please."

"Tony."

Leah speaks in soothing, gentle tones but offers no mercy.

The air is still. The earth is parched and dry.

She retreats into the shadows just as her brother did.

What protective persona is she fading into?

"Leah? Please, Leah," Tony pleads.

Neither of us can see her face. Only the vague impression of her being remains.

The door closes silently. The bolt again clicks home on the other side of the door. The dry branches in the trees rub together.

Will they ignite before rain comes to soothe Marin's overheated landscape?

"Come on, Tony."

I take him by the arm and gently lead him away from the house. Tony doesn't bother to answer, just gets into my faithful chariot. As we pull away, Edge's truck rounds a corner and passes us. We make the rest of the ride in silence.

When we reach Tony's place, I follow him up the steep path toward the back door of his San Quentin house. It's dark and menacing. In the middle distance off to the west, the prison, well-lit with guard stations along the wall, dominates. In front of the house, the upper reaches of San Francisco Bay are framed by the Richmond-San Rafael Bridge, the East Bay, and the back side of the Belvedere/Tiburon peninsula.

Tony's shoulders are slumped. He's beaten down, low and mean. I wish I could help him find a way out of his situation. But that's impossible. He's got to do his own suffering, poor woebegone and forgotten one. I'll just hang in there in case he wants to sing the blues to a sympathetic friend.

I bunk on his sofa. Tony does not bother to comment, just goes into his room and closes the door.

I look around at the strange surroundings as I smoke the rest of my hash cigarette while lying on the sofa in the dark. All is shadowy, indefinite, ill-defined. The place is in a sad state of disrepair. It needs a whole heap of tender loving care.

Evil lurks in the corners. That menace is not just about the proximity of the prison, a fellow traveler to this house since it was built. It's also about the circumstances, the events that have transpired in the short time since Leah and Tony moved in.

The wind picks up during the night and the house makes pained rattling sounds that bring to mind suffering, loneliness, displacement, and isolation.

The arms of Lethe welcome me with a cold embrace. I sleep a dreamless sleep.

"That's one hell of a goose egg," Tony comments, walking in on me washing my head in the kitchen sink.

Tony apparently didn't notice it last night. I'm encouraged that he does so now.

"You want me to drive you over to the emergency room?" Tony asks.

"I'll be all right."

I look at Tony without lifting my head from under the faucet. The cold water feels good. I see a stricken face. Tony has retreated into his shell. My goose egg must have reminded him of other recent injuries, physical, mental, spiritual, cataclysmic. Another reminder, the appearance of Leah's cat Bianca, doesn't help. She settles down under the kitchen table next to the stool that was once Leah's seat.

"What about you? You all right?" I ask, pulling away from the faucet and picking up a dish towel to dry my head.

Tony snaps out of his funk, sort of.

"Yeah. Sure. Where did you get that goose egg anyway?" he asks, trying to appear engaged.

I know better.

I decide to take a gamble on Tony's mental health. I need another perspective on my recent encounter. I pull the .22 casing from my pocket and place it head up on the kitchen counter.

"Target practice?"

"Yeah... On me..."

I dry my head with care, then turn on a burner on the gas stove. A half-full pot of coffee sits on the counter nearby. I put the pot on the burner.

"Where did this happen?" Tony asks.

"At Edge's hideaway," I answer.

Tony sags into one of the two chairs at the kitchen table. I use the burner to re-light a hash-laced cigarette.

I exhale a cloud of smoke from the corners of my mouth. Tony shakes his head when I offer him the cigarette.

"Was... was Leah there?"

"I didn't see anyone," not answering his implied question.

Tony eyes me. He's hurt, tortured. I can't hold his gaze. It hurts me too much.

We're a pair. Two losers inhabiting a beat-up shack of a place in San Quentin Village, right down the street from the prison and just around the corner from one of the most self-indulgent places on Earth, Marin County, California.

Where does that leave us?

I take another long tug on my cigarette while pulling two cups from a cabinet. The coffee is heating up fast.

"Who shot at you?"

"Didn't see."

"And Leah is living there with Edge?"

"You saw her. She's at her brother's house."

A tear forms at the edge of Tony's eye. I look away.

"That's right. I saw her. At her brother's house."

Tony's voice is dark and hollow. I look in the refrigerator. Eggs... Bacon... Toast... I set about fixing us some breakfast. Another beautiful day has dawned in sunny Marin. The drought remains unbroken despite last night's threats of rain.

How long? How long?

"You still need a place to crash?" Tony asks, after wolfing down his eggs.

This is no time for pride. Besides, if you can't let it all hang out in front of friends, secret cousins (family, one of my family?), who can you do it with?

"The Jefferson Starship get back from their tour tomorrow so I'll be back on the street," I answer.

"You can crash here for as long as you want."

"I'll chip in on the rent, as much as I can."

I still have some cash left and, fingers crossed, a paying gig might fall in my lap. Stranger things have happened.

"That would be a help."

I finish off my eggs, soak up the bright-yellow egg yolk with the toast and polish off my bacon, then begin to clean up the dishes. Tony remains seated at the kitchen table, staring off into space.

Is there a trail around here where I can run? I need exercise. Got to clear away some of the cobwebs. I've got to shake off the vibes that are getting me down, from the inside out. An *I Ching* reading seems like a good idea. And, of course, I wouldn't say no to sharing a number or two.

My name is Miki Weinberg
The Visit
(Very Early Spring 1971)

Peter, my beloved Peter, is practicing, floating away on the strings of his sitar. I listen, thrilled, ecstatic in a quiet, low-key way, just doing nothing really, looking off into space, out the window.

The air is dry and still. Birds call in the distance. A car guns it down Lovell. A snap of a rug being shaken, a fragment of a conversation, echoes off our walls. It comes from somebody's back porch. We are safe and sound in our Mill Valley cabin on no fixed day, in no particular time or place.

Suddenly it approaches, a humming from out of the ether. I am possessed, taken up. I don't scream and shout or foam at the mouth. Yet I know. Or, more precisely, I get a vibe. A shadow is lurking, poised to place an icy hand on my left shoulder. Night in the midst of day approaches.

I shiver.

The front door flies open.

"Well, look what the wind blew in."

My face lights up but my heart pounds with apprehension. Leah, my precious little sister, rushes in. All about her is the smell, the almost tactile impression of this approaching night.

"Hello, Miki."

She smiles. In her voice I hear her pleading for sympathetic female conversation, the ear of a friend, in the safe arms of "family." Something has gone very, very wrong. And whatever it is is poised to pounce on all of us with destructive force.

"Don't just stand in the doorway. You're blocking progress."

Edge pushes Leah inside with forced goodwill.

Peter puts down his sitar and uncoils himself from his half lotus position. I pull my bathrobe closed as I stand up. I just got out of the

136

shower and I've been toweling off my hair. I embrace Leah with joy, with concern, with the paralyzing knowledge that we are on the edge of the abyss.

Sisterly affection radiates between us. I know we must talk. Now, today.

Peter reaches in and gives Leah a bear hug. Leah's body visibly relaxes into our embraces. She is home, back in the arms of the "family."

"You want a smoke?"

Peter pulls out the ever-ready bowl of weed sitting under the front room table. Leah smiles in Peter's direction, then in mine. She's a happy girl. That conversation can wait while we share a joint. Edge usurps center stage.

"Let's try this instead."

He pulls out a 35mm film canister from a leather pouch he carries on his shoulder.

"What's that? Acid?" Peter replies with a chuckle.

The night Edge tricked us into snorting angel dust, particularly Gab's reaction, has become a "family" legend.

Edge unscrews the film canister top with a smile and holds it up to Peter. Peter backs away, his nose wrinkling.

"Smells like a chemical factory."

"DMT..."

"Where did you get that?" I ask, looking at the tar-like substance.

"It fell into my lap."

I look at Leah. She smiles back. Give it a go, she seems to say.

"Just give me a minute to change."

I scurry off into the bedroom.

Why did I allow myself to be diverted from an immediate conversation with my little sister? Why did I bypass an intuitive flash, that certain feeling?

I don't know.

Edge's magic?

I don't think so.

The scattered nature of my life?

I don't want to think that's so.

Leah's return and her wonderful smile?

Maybe...

But that's no excuse.

"Leah, there's some coffee in the kitchen. Why don't you pour us all a cup," I shout from the bedroom.

It's nearly noon. The lone window in the bedroom glows. It's going to be another long, hot, beautiful day in Paradise. I begin to whistle. Leah's here. Thank goodness.

Peter puts an Ike and Tina Turner album on. "Proud Mary" plays. Edge fills a small brass pipe with a dark, gummy substance that promises an exotic high, a scrape with death.

"Oops."

Leah dips and twists, avoiding a collision with me as I rush toward the front room. We meet at the intersection of the bedroom door and the kitchen door at one corner of the front room.

We both laugh.

It's been too long, we say with our eyes.

We'll sort everything out when we talk, we silently agree, joining the men at the table.

Edge impatiently glares at us. That boy does love to be the center of attention.

"One hit is all it takes."

He fires up the bowl, holds in the noxious smoke, then passes the pipe to me. He's coughing out smoke as I pass the pipe to Peter. Peter takes a hit and passes the pipe to Leah. She relights the sputtering chemical tar and takes a hit.

The beautiful day explodes with colors and blinding light. The real world metamorphoses once, twice, three times, a dozen, a thousand, a million times. All life freezes, shatters, clattering to the floor. Emptiness, the Void, takes us.

We rush into outer space. For an indeterminate period of time we are without form or body.

Then suddenly we are back in this space-time continuum, sitting in our front room on pillows around the ceremonial "family" table. Tina Turner is still wailing. Hot coffee, still steaming, sits in front of us.

And I, in reaction, shake my head in appreciation.

"That stuff has one hell of a kick. You willing to part with any of it?"

Edge smiles his enigmatic smile, his eyes twinkling. I get an ugly flash.

Edge thinks he's got me right where he wants me.

What could a creep like him want but power and attention?

He doesn't deserve my apprehension.

138

He better not hurt Leah in any way. Or else.

Creeping dread, a shiver from a shadow over the left shoulder, returns.

"Am I willing to part with any of this? We'll have to talk about that," Edge answers. "First, let me offer you another hit."

I have to be nice to this guy. He's Leah's old man. I hold up my hands and wave them back and forth in mock defeat. Guys love it when you seem to surrender.

"Hey, I just want a cup of coffee right now," I plead with a chuckle. "I just got up. I need time to adjust to the situation."

"This is for you," Edge comments, holding out the small vial of DMT. "There's not enough of it being made to sell."

The wind blows through my hair. I'm watering the plants on a deck reached by climbing up and down a set of stairs installed in our bedroom window. One of our carpenter friends installed it in exchange for some blow. The trade was well worth it.

I turn off the hose and look at Edge. He wants to talk. This was the purpose of his visit. I'm a patient woman. I motion for him to sit down on a bench after taking the vial without comment.

"Thought you might be interested in this as well."

Edge pulls a large baggie from his pouch. In it are smaller baggies filled with weed.

"It's chemically treated homegrown. I'll let you have this pound, already broken down to ounces, for $150. My cost... You should be able to get some free smoke out of it. It's real heavy-duty shit."

"I really appreciate the offer, Edge, but..."

To be polite I open one of the ounce baggies and smell the grass inside. Then I gently press a bud between my fingers. I can smell the chemicals. But there's plenty of resin in the flowers.

"But I've got the weed angle covered," I say.

"Let's call it a token of appreciation for things down the road."

"I don't follow."

"I've hooked up with a major supplier. Acid, hash, grass, speed, coke, smack, the whole gamut. In large or small quantities," Edge answers with a sly smile.

"That's nice. I hope it works out for you."

"We could enter into an arrangement that would be mutually rewarding, if you get my drift."

"That's certainly something to think about."

"I can beat anybody's price. We could really make out."

"I'll think about it. Come back in a week. We can talk then."

Inside, Leah plays dominoes with Peter. I want to talk with her before I answer Edge. For now I just shine him on.

Day is turning to night and fog is rolling in over the coastal range. The parched soil eagerly breathes in the ocean-moistened air. The golden hillsides are covered with dead grass.

Where is the rain? When will relief come? Who hears the suffering of the land until its howl halts human progress?

I do – Mother Earth, a Virgo. I hear.

But do I respond? Do I get a move on, even when an icy hand reaches out to touch my left shoulder?

The front door opens. Al blows in. His smudged coke-bottle glasses defy penetration. His pale bald head glows beet red. He has a shy smile and a jolly face when he grins. Everyone agrees Al is a real pal. He's a great and constant friend.

The room comes to attention.

Al is also "the man," my coke connection. More to the point, he's one of the biggest cocaine wholesalers in northern California. Peter and I rise to greet our friend.

"Al," all shout brightly in unison.

Taj Mahal is playing one of his eclectic songs on the record player. Peter is gearing himself up for his studio session with Taj later.

Peter and Al hug and exchange greetings. They go way back, back to a time when Al was not dealing but making his living as a still photographer and Peter was working as a standup bass player in a folk group. Coffee houses and meaningful conversations were the order of the day. Windy City Al was just a user, albeit one with heavy-duty Chicago connections.

Those connections set Al up in business. They wanted a piece of the action on the West Coast but their style made laid-back Californians skittish. Al was the perfect middleman; bland and unassuming, low-key yet fast on his feet. He became a real pal to the locals. In fact, everybody calls him Al the Pal.

Supplying me with coke gives Al an excuse to visit. He hasn't forgotten his friends. Problem is, he's too busy, too stoned out, to make the trip often and too nervous to stay long when he does come.

"Still playing those things?" Al asks pointing to a corner in which a stand-up bass, an electric guitar and a sitar sit.

"Sure. Want to hear a tune?" Peter asks, deliberately reaching for the sitar instead of the stand-up bass.

He knows Al meant the bass. The sitar is one of their standing jokes. Al has a thing about swamis, meditation, and such things. Peter spent six months in an ashram before he was lured back into the "real" world by female persuasion and his love of music.

Al shakes his head and holds up his hands. Both men chuckle good-naturedly.

I pick up Edge's brass pipe which is lying on the table and teasingly offer it to Al.

"Try some of this, Al. It'll knock your socks off."

Al takes the pipe and smells it. His nose crinkles. He makes a face. Everyone laughs. It's a well-known fact that Al snorts coke. Exclusively.

"Too heavy-duty for me," he chuckles pleasantly, handing the pipe back to me.

"Sit down. Join the party," Peter offers.

"Like to. Like to. But..." Al murmurs almost inaudibly.

He tilts his head to one side nervously and grimaces a smile. He samples way too much of his own product. Peter slaps him on the back. Al chuckles and pulls a folded piece of paper from his pocket and hands it to Peter.

"Spread this around while I talk with your old lady for a minute," he whispers, partially obscuring his words as he wipes his hand across his mouth.

Coke has destroyed his nasal passages, put a rasp in his voice, added a wicked cough, done things to his cortex that medical science hasn't a clue how to diagnose, let alone treat.

"You bet," Peter answers, taking the coke from Al.

I don't focus on it then but Edge stood up when Al entered. He moved over next to Peter, expecting an introduction that never came.

Hey, Peter's not perfect. He forgot to introduce Edge.

Most people would shrug it off. Not Edge. He grabs Leah firmly by the elbow and whispers something menacing in her ear.

Asshole.

Al turns and looks at me with a nervous smile. I worry about his health. He doesn't look good at all. I keep telling him he needs to get away for a while but he won't listen. All he has eyes or ears for is blow – the feel of it exploding into his sinuses and lighting up his tired brain.

He plops down on our bed and wheezes. Time to blow his nose again. Time to bring his swirling mind into focus.

Al, where have you gone? I miss you. I don't want a pal. I want my friend back.

Is this where we all are headed, what we'll all end up becoming?

I shiver.

Is he the root of my premonition?

Is he the initiator of this left-shouldered ill wind?

"Miki."

I turn my head in surprise. It's Leah.

What the hell is she doing in here now?

She knows not to interrupt when I'm doing business, particularly with Al.

"I just wanted to tell you that I have to go."

Then she's in my arms before I have a chance to say a word.

A rush of panic filled with fears, questions, overpowering anxiety assails me with her embrace.

She needs reassurance, guidance, a friendly "family" ear, help.

She – her union with Edge – is the source of this ill wind. I know that for certain now.

"We haven't had a chance to talk," I whisper in her ear.

"Edge… Edge wants to go," she answers.

Then she rushes from the room. I follow, ignoring Al. He doesn't seem to mind.

Before I reach the front room, Leah is being dragged down the hill, spirited away.

My friend, my precious little sister, needed attention, a good listener, and maybe even someone to take some action. She's in trouble and I didn't make time for her.

What kind of woman have I become? What have I allowed to happen?

Leah
Dead Soul
(Late Spring and Summer 1971)

Is the desire to be protected the reason I've separated myself from the "family," Bianca, Tony for my new role in life, the bride of Lucifer living in the Underworld? I'm not up to being analytical right now. I'm too scattered. Fact is, and I don't know why, I'm playing the gangster moll to the hilt. Edge digs it. We make love in every conceivable position. He turns me on to a battery of his designer drugs. My mind fragments and spins off in six thousand different directions.

We go down to LA on business. We visit the Whiskey A Go Go, where Edge is treated like royalty. We hang out with band members of Led Zeppelin and a new group called the Eagles. They're holed up in a rented house in the Hollywood Hills. Next day Edge has a meeting with some Colombians at his shack up in Topanga Canyon. He tries to charm them but they're not having any of it. It's obvious there's history between them that goes way back. He orders me into the bedroom when discussions get heated. Afterward, I hear him talking on the phone to someone about business dealings in a twisted, multi-layered, sinister way that makes me wonder who's on the other end of the line.

My mind creates all sorts of possible answers, none of them pleasant.

I realize with startling clarity that I'm in over my head.

Who is Edge really? What is he up to? How exactly do I fit into his world?

When he gets off the phone, Edge pulls out some smack and his works. He shoots us both up. Before I know it he's beating me up, calling me a whore, glaring at me without recognition.

Later, much later, in the car on the way to the airport, he tries to make it up to me.

I'm no moll. I'm just a girl in trouble. I need someone to talk to, someone sympathetic and wise like Miki, my best friend, den mother for the "family" and a descendant of Mother Earth herself.

I'm frightened. Every heartbeat repeats the mantra - Over my head. Over my head. Over my head.

Surprise...

Edge stops by Miki and Peter's pad on our way back to the ranch. How does this fit into his agenda? I vow to sneak in my longed-for heart-to-heart with Miki during the visit. Then the bottom drops out. Edge is insulted, overlooked, when Al the Pal pays Peter and Miki a call. Edge drags me down the hill to his pickup.

"Jewish outsider hip gangster cowboys living on the fringe... What a joke," he declares as we drive toward the ranch on a moonless night.

No more fun and games with Edge. I finally realize that I was a means to an end: a connection to the "family" and Miki that would establish an instant network to distribute Edge's drugs and expand his drug empire to northern California. That possibility removed, I'm a punching bag, expendable.

Mean, caustic, angry, unpredictable, vicious – the new Edge uncovered.

Who does Edge work for? What do his employers want out of this venture besides money? Power. Control. Inside information. How will that added value be used? How soon will I be disposed of and in what manner?

One thing is certain. An ill wind is set to descend on my "family" and friends.

"Stay here until I get back."

Edge scowls at me, then hops into his pickup and drives away. I watch him leave from the front porch.

I'm stuck. My car's in Mill Valley. From Edge's ranch it's more than two miles over very rugged terrain to the nearest house and over a dozen miles to the nearest town. Living in the nearest ranch house are friends of Edge's. I'd have to walk right by their house to get to town, unless I try to cut through the woods.

I'm not the outdoorsy type. I'd get lost.

I stay put – for now. Something else has to turn up.

After three days, I run out of cigarettes. Then the generator that powers the electricity refuses to start. Food is running low.

Should I make a break for it?

I'm powerless, immobile. For the first time in my life, I have lost my self-assurance.

I try to tell myself I can handle this, but I know I'm lying to myself. I try to work. I've lost my voice, my nerve. Maybe it would be best if I did starve to death.

What good am I to anyone in this state of mind?

Edge returns. Red, who calls himself a business associate but really is just an errand boy, pulls in behind him on his chopped Harley. Edge, ignoring me, heads to the outbuilding he uses as a lab. Red stomps into the house, pours himself a cup of coffee, pulls out a pill, pops it, then gulps down the coffee.

"Where's Edge keep that journal of his?" he asks.

"Pardon?"

"You know what I'm talking about. The journal with his transactions, formulas, everything. I'd like to take a look at that. I'd keep it between us."

Red winks and gives me a goofy, lopsided grin. Is this guy kidding? What is he, some kind of idiot? Does he assume I'll join him in idiot corner?

"You'll have to ask Edge about that."

"You don't get it, do you? It'll be between us. You dig? I'll read it right here and leave it here too. No harm, no foul."

He taps the tabletop. I put my hands on my hips and give him my "no fucking way Jose" disgusted glare. Without warning, he grabs me by the arm and pulls me toward him. I resist but he forces a kiss. I pull away and laugh. He tightens his grip on me and reaches for the top button on my jeans. What a jerk! Chutzpah like his deserves what it gets.

"You're a real hot potato, baby. Need a real man to tame you."

"And you're that guy?"

"Darn tooting, sweetheart."

My knee comes up, hard, right into his manly parts. He releases his grip on me and grabs himself. He's not even worth laughing at. The guy is an imbecile. He needs a minder. A muzzle and a chastity belt wouldn't hurt either.

"Bitch," he hollers in pain.

He reaches out to grab me. I pick up a kitchen knife from the counter. He advances, still crouching in pain, hands out. He's tall and outweighs me by maybe a hundred and fifty pounds. No matter. I'm going down fighting. I lunge at his approach. He stumbles back awkwardly.

"Get lost, creep. Out on the porch…"

"You're going to regret this, bitch," Red replies, backing up until he's out the front door and standing on the porch.

I slam the door in his face.

Life with Edge is brutal. Memories of the rape and Red's assault mingle and merge with Edge's constantly abusive treatment.

My paintbrushes collect dust. They have been laid aside. The oppressive silence of this mountain retreat enfolds me. I smoke one cigarette after another, drink one cup of coffee after another, see all around me nothing but death. Here on this ranch the Underworld has found a place above ground in which to exist. Edge, the Lord of this Underworld, separates me from my eternal soul.

"Fix me something to eat, woman."

I turn to the stove, pick up a spoon and begin to dish out a bowl of stew. Without warning, the spoon slams down onto the counter.

Has a Dybbuk entered my empty shell and taken control of my body?

Don't be foolish.

I wipe away a tear for my conquered pride mixed with despair and force myself to turn around and face this Devil Incarnate.

"I'm leaving," I announce.

Edge doesn't bother to look my way.

Has he heard? Does he care? What will he do?

He chuckles with malice.

"You're not going anywhere."

"And why not?"

"Because I say so."

Our eyes lock.

How can it be that Edge's eyes glitter? He's sitting in a dark corner.

He breaks the silent impasse.

"What do you think brought that intruder to your San Quentin pad? Fate? Was that how your rape and the humiliation of your pitiful old man came about? Are you that stupid, that much of a fool?"

"What? What!"

I can't find more words. I look left; then right.

Panic, petrified horror overwhelms me.

Is Edge that evil, that insane?

"And Red..."

Edge nods, a malicious smirk on his face.

"Red is a little slow on the uptake and could use some work on follow-through. But what sort of fate, what sort of karma, will follow you if you leave me, I wonder?" Edge asks, harsh and quiet.

Did Edge really plan these foul events? Did he instruct Red to molest me only to have Red screw it up? Did he delegate someone to break into the San Quentin house? What will he do if I step out of line again?

I am frozen with hostility, hate, fear, and uncertainty.

I cook breakfast and clean in the morning. Then I work in the kitchen garden while Edge chops wood for the stove and fireplace.

Stripped to the waist, whaling away with rhythmic, demonic intensity, making chips fly hour after hour, his eyes glittering with unholy fire, he swings his two-edged axe.

I try not to watch. I bend diligently over the tender young vegetables. But I hear. Hear his breathing, grunts, roars, the everlasting sound (crack, whack, thwack) of the axe he wields, connecting, cutting, splitting, shattering.

We break for lunch. Afterwards he takes a notion, fucks me and force-feeds me drugs.

I wander into dark, dank places. Torment pursues me. I am in a place where there is no hope, no future, no sunny sky above. Into the descending night my reeling mind leads me.

Red reappears after sundown. He and Edge talk heatedly near the outbuilding that houses the lab. I can't make out what they say. My mind's in a fog. When Red splits, Edge bangs the door to his lab shut and locks it behind him. I hear the clink of glass against glass. He's working. I peek in the window. He's making notations in his journal.

Edge's homemade lab offers no protections, no controls. Edge inevitably gets high while he's experimenting. These highs are unpredictable. The dosage, the exact mixture of each batch, is never the same.

After he finishes in the lab he talks to invisible strangers, has close encounters of the mysterious kind. One moment he's crying; the next he's in a rage.

"You're a spoiled cunt, a goddamned Jewish princess. And you make bad choices. First you chose a weakling for a lover; then you chose someone who has nothing but contempt for you. You're less than nothing."

He spits in my face. I lash out angrily, all fingernails and kicks. Edge grabs my wrists, twists my arm until it feels like it might break, slaps me hard in the face.

"Don't imagine anyone from your precious 'family' is going to show up to protect you. They're just a bunch of deluded Jewish losers, not tough, hip gangsters. Get used to it."

Crumpled on the floor, I start to crawl away. Edge kicks me hard in the butt, then turns away in disgust as tears stream down his face. Nobody wants to understand why you are crying, Edge, not even you.

"Don't let anyone onto the property," Edge states, after force-feeding me another one of his concoctions. "Particularly Red."

He's not eating. Something's bothering him.

Good.

I slip into a dream state that resembles narcolepsy. Unable to move, my eyes fixated and open, I relive the horror, the evil, which has become my life.

Dry tears flow for lost innocence. My sorrow builds toward anger.

Edge returns. A 30.06 hangs in the rifle rack of his truck and a .357 Magnum is shoved into the belt that holds up his jeans. On the seat beside him is enough ammunition to start a war.

"What are you planning to do?" I ask.

"Shut the fuck up, woman, or I'll stomp your face in."

Edge slams the door shut on the battered truck after taking the rifle and ammunition out of it.

That night he sleeps in the lab.

Next morning he appears carrying his rifle, the Magnum still shoved into his belt. He sets up a row of bottles and cans for target practice.

The targets fly away or apart with surprising regularity. Each shattered bottle or riddled can symbolizes Edge's cruel anger, the malevolent struggle of a trapped, wily coyote.

Does he see my face on one bottle? All of them?

I slip away into the house and lock myself in the bedroom. Edge beats on the door and kicks it.

"Open this fucking door, bitch."

I curl up in a ball between the bed and the wall. A shot rings out. Another. The door flies open.

"Don't you ever lock me out of my own goddamn bedroom again," he mutters.

I play dead. After an eternity, I hear retreating footsteps. He has left me alone, this time.

Edge is in his lab. I am weeding the garden. The door of the lab bangs open. Edge emerges carrying his rifle, the Magnum stuck into his belt. He has not changed his clothes or shaved. His eyes seem to point in different directions.

He walks briskly toward me. I stand as he approaches. When he is near, I smell his foul breath. A strange chemical stench permeates his body.

"I'm going to give you what you deserve for saddling me with that bastard brat of yours."

Edge raises his rifle to his shoulder.

"Edge... I'm Leah. You're having a bad trip."

A bullet whizzes past my ear before I can throw myself out of the way. Behind me, a deer falls in its tracks.

Edge rushes by me and begins methodically gutting the deer with a hunting knife. Blood and guts spew everywhere, on his hands, his clothes, the ground.

I hear someone screaming. I realize it's me. I can't stop.

Edge leaps up, knife in hand, gun still pushed into his belt, and slaps me as hard as he can with his free hand.

I spin to the ground. A blood-splotched handprint appears on my face.

Something snaps. Edge's evil spell, his web of chemical nightmares, breaks apart and loses its power over me.

I will escape. And I will make certain Edge never again has the opportunity of creating a nightmare like this for me, or anyone else.

"You should eat this soup."

I push a bowl and a spoon across the table. Edge comes out of his angry trance and mechanically picks up the spoon. My heart pounds.

"Whatever it is that's bothering you is only being magnified by the drugs you're taking," I tell him in a monotone.

"Meth makes me think better."

"It's obviously not helping you solve your problem. Let me help."

"What do you know about my business?"

"I kept books for my father. He taught me about the rag trade. What difference does it make what the product is?"

"Did his competitors and potential business partners have enforcers willing to kill on command? Did he partner with the Devil? With almighty sovereign powers? Did he?"

"Is that what's... I mean... who's threatening you? Should we be leaving this place?"

"Figure it out for yourself. You think you're so damn smart."

Edge pulls out his journal and slams it on the table.

I open the leather-bound volume. Edge's handwriting is crabbed and small, hard-to-read speed-freak strokes. Detailed and extensive lists of transactions, formulas, observations fill page after page. Rapidograph drawings line the margins, eat up quarter pages. I look up at Edge.

The food is slowing him down. He's been up two days without eating. His eyes snap shut, then pop back open just as fast.

"The rag trade," he snorts. "My old man bought and sold people like your father. What do I need with the daughter of one of them? You're less than useless."

He sluggishly finishes his downer-laced soup. His eyelids shut. I watch closely. Conversation stops. He sways in his chair. Nothing moves or stirs. Then, with a small sigh, Edge pitches forward. His head lands in the soup bowl.

Now is my chance to escape, maybe my only chance.

I'm afraid to tug at the truck key attached to his waist. No matter.

Just before I leave, I snatch up Edge's journal and hide it below a loose floorboard in an unused closet. Cobwebs abound. I make certain not to disturb the thick layer of dust. I hope Edge never finds it. I feel as though I have concealed the heart of his dark matter. Will that end Edge's evil influence, curtail it, or have no effect? I can't worry about that. Escape.

Outside, the stars burn bright in the heavens above. Freedom!

The obvious way, the steep, deeply rutted and treacherous dirt road Edge uses in his truck, will be the first place he looks when he wakes up. I take to the woods, racing downhill, with a shoulder bag stuffed with hastily grabbed items.

The woods are blacker than black, darker than the darkest ink. They are a black hole that leads to the void where there is no up or down, left or right. Above me, I see tentacles of barren branches that seem to whirl round and round in dizzying fashion. I step outward from a rocky platform into thin air and fall forward, tumbling downward. My head strikes a stone when I come crashing to earth. I'm out like a light.

I'm awake. Standing over me is a man holding a rifle. Bright sunlight turns him into an inky silhouette. I bring my hand up to shade my eyes, trying to focus. The man laughs a chilling, cold-blooded, heartless laugh.

It's Edge. He's the one possessed by a Dybbuk, not me. I'm certain of it.

At first, I cannot understand his words.

Is he speaking in Underworld tongues, words that connected are omens and curses, words that will bring down cataclysmic pestilence?

"Get up and hurry up about it," I at last understand him to say.

He motions with his rifle. I collect my bag without bothering to brush myself off. We retrace our steps. I am surprised to discover how close we are to the house. What had seemed like a long, perilous journey into the ever-engulfing night is only a few faltering steps away.

Without paying further attention to me, he locks me, shoulder bag and all, in the closet where I hid his journal and leaves the house. Good. At least he doesn't know his journal has gone missing. If it's my time, at least there's that. I hear his pickup pull out of the yard.

I am alone. I bang on the door. It's solid. There's little hope that I will be able to get out until and unless Edge returns.

What will he do to me when he lets me out? Will I still be alive when he opens the door?

I curl up in a fetal ball on the floor of the cramped closet and concentrate on entering a state of hibernation, just as though it were Samadhi, the ultimate state of realization. Hate, anger, revenge keep me alive, not oneness with the Eternal.

I must... I must... I must...

What? Kill? Will thoughts and actions like that help me achieve release from the karmic wheel of life? Are those trapped like an animal in a zoo worthy of the free will to make choices?

"Grandmother! Help! Please!"

Miki

"I need your help. I'm worried about Leah," I confide to Charlie, after we've settled into my bedroom office.

I've told no one, not even Peter, about that icy hand reaching out of the shadows for my left shoulder. But I haven't forgotten it. Not for one minute.

"Are you trying to hire me?"

"Well, yeah. I'll pay you... in trade. What do you say?"

"You're serious?"

"I'm serious. Will you take me on as a client? Do you have the time?"

"Well..."

"Come on. Be a pal."

I take Charlie's arm and squeeze it. He's a mensch. He relents.

"All right... I'll do some checking around. But I can't accept payment."

"Don't be silly. Here's something on account."

I hand him a baggie filled with weed and a little vial of coke.

"I knew you'd do it."

"Why's that?" he asks.

"It's right on that business card you had Leah dummy up - private investigator for the woebegone and forgotten - and I'm very woebegone and forgotten at the moment."

"That'll be the day."

Charlie chuckles and shuffles uneasily from foot to foot. On his first try, the baggie won't fit into his jacket pocket. I kiss him on the cheek before sending him on his way.

We're all depending on you, Charlie. We, the "family," friends of Leah, wish you well.

I hope I haven't waited too long.

Charlie
Case Closed?

I approach the porch of Edge's ranch house, gun in hand.

"Hello. Anyone home?"

No one answers.

The front door is wide open. My business card is still on the kitchen countertop. The place seems deserted but then again, it seemed deserted last time I was here. I pause in the doorway.

"Hello. Anyone home?"

No one answers.

A pot of soup is sitting on top of the wood stove. A long wooden spoon lies on a nearby counter. Dishes sit in the drain rack. Dregs of days-old coffee remain in a Pyrex pot on a burner.

"Hello? Is anyone here?"

Still no answer...

I edge down the hallway, my gun raised in front of me. I throw open the door of Leah's studio and find dried-out paintbrushes, forlorn doodles, and an ashtray with long-dead cigarette butts and joint ends.

I throw open a second door. The bathroom. No one, nothing, not even a tube of toothpaste.

I throw open another door. The linen closet. A towel tumbles from a shelf. Dust motes float in the air. Opening and closing doors has disturbed their rest.

I sigh, raise my gun, advance. The last door along the hallway flies open. I yank it hard.

Leah, still wearing her shoulder bag, flops out onto the hallway floor. She must have been leaning against the door. I check her out, gently. She has no broken bones, deep cuts or bullet wounds. She's breathing. Must be weak from lack of food and water.

I pick her up and carry her to the bedroom, then rush to the stove and ladle out some soup. It's unheated but looks nourishing.

"Are you all right?" I ask, putting the full soup bowl down on the night table.

Leah's eyes are open but she is unable to speak.

"I'm going to feed you some soup," I tell her.

I cup my hand under her head and hold her up as I dish up a spoonful of soup. The first spoonful dribbles down her chin and onto her chest.

I wait to see her reaction. Nothing... I try again. This time Leah coughs, spitting out the soup.

"Water," she croaks.

I rush back to the kitchen. There's a hand pump next to the sink. I take a glass from the drain and fill it.

"Let me help you," I command on my return.

Water, the source of life, revives her. An enormous tear rolls down her cheek.

Looks like I'm a momentary hero. I've rescued Leah Travail, just as Tony would want, just as Miki asked, just as Leah, evidently, needed. That about wraps this sad muddle up for Leah and Tony, I think, as I help her gather her things and support her as she walks toward my trusty car.

BOOK THREE:
CASE NOT CLOSED

Tony Vitolinich
Bloody Knife

Tony Vitolinich lies sprawled out on the front room floor of the San Quentin house, his still camera and 16mm film camera still awkwardly strapped around his neck. Next to him, in a pool of blood, Edge lies, very, very dead of a knife wound to the chest that punctured his heart. In Tony's outstretched hand is the murder weapon, an ordinary but very sharp kitchen knife. Tony has been out cold, starts to come around.

"Nothing. Void. Blank."

He stirs, touches the back of his head gingerly. His fingers come away covered with blood. He is groggy.

"Delirious. Spaced. Scattered."

He slowly shakes his head from side to side.

He feels, thinks, "Can't focus."

Unsteady, nauseating fingers of Death crawl up his icy body.

He recalls Edge's crazed laughter. Leah under attack. Attempt to save her. Noise from behind...

"Stroboscopic flashes. Whirling. Tumbling. Blurred. Topsy-turvy. Out like a light."

His brain repeats these unhinged nightmarish images. He gags, coughs, can't quite hold back the noxious bile that dribbles out of the side of his mouth.

"Edge in a pool of blood. Me, holding a bloody knife," he concludes to himself.

Tony drops the knife in horror. It clatters as it hits the floor. Tingling pieces of brain matter rattle around in his disordered, discordant cranium. He tries once, twice, then succeeds in struggling to his stumbling feet. He thinks he might be sick again, thinks he needs to lie down, imagines he is dying. He realizes, no chance of that, just as he ceases to exist.

"Nothing. Blank. Void."

He stumbles, weaves out the back door of the house. Goes up the hillside and through a gate in a fence that encloses a large, grassy hillside. Battered perception is causing him to lose his sense of being, his hold on reality. His mind shouts,

"Leah? Leah!"

He asks himself,

"Did I plunge that knife deep into Edge's body? Did I force it through his blood vessels, into his vile heart, and press against it – hard – to make it stop – for all eternity? Did I? Did I murder Edge?"

Lights snap off. Goodbye, Tony. Can't be put back together again...

"Blank. Nothing. Void."

The stench of murder, rape, cowardice, needful redemption hangs heavy in the poisonous, prison-drenched air, warping innocence out of Tony's existence, mocking all that is good and true. He whimpers,

"Nothing for all time without end?

"Black. Nothing. Blank. Void."

Charlie

(The next morning)

The front door swings open and closes. Footsteps approach, interrupting a dream in which Charlie and his father are on a camping trip somewhere in Nepal, high up in the mountains. They are chanting. Charlie tries to hold onto the words they chant. They are gone. He rolls over in bed. It's nine o'clock.

"What respectable Marinite would be up at this time of day?" he wonders.

A police officer, pointing a gun at him, stands in the center of the sunlit doorway. Charlie got back late last night and came in the back door, as is his custom. He brushed his teeth, took a pee, and crashed out, all without even turning on the lights. He was bushed, wiped out.

"I want to know why the hell you are here and who you are. Right now. You hear me, boy?" the back-lighted officer stridently demands.

"What?"

Charlie wants to rub his eyes, stretch, shake off the dregs of sleep, to convince himself that he's awake and has not descended into a ludicrous new dream in which a big fat-bellied cop like the one in Smokey and the Bandit is striking a pose one would assume at a gun range preparatory to firing a large pistol.

"Are you real? I mean, serious?" Charlie mumbles.

"Marin County Sheriff 'Tex' Whelan, son... And you are sleeping in my crime scene."

"Crime scene?"

Charlie feels sure that there was no crime scene tape, or any other sign of things being out of the ordinary, when he came in last night.

"What's going on?"

He makes a move to get out of bed and Whelan shakes the gun in Charlie's direction.

"That's a no-no, son," leisurely comments Whelan.

"I'm Charlie Carter. And I share this place with Tony Vitolinich. His name is on the lease. Now can I get up? I need to take a pee."

Whelan lowers and holsters his weapon as Charlie crawls out of bed. He thinks, "Thank god I slept in my shorts and T-shirt." Most nights, he sleeps naked.

He heads for the bathroom. It's in the back of the house, just past the kitchen and right next to the back door. Charlie checks the back entrance again. There is no crime scene tape. Was that an oversight?

He pees, throws water in his face, shake his head vigorously, then pulls a bathrobe off a hook on the back of the bathroom door and slips it on. Whelan is waiting for him in the kitchen. Charlie is still half asleep.

"You said something about a crime scene?" Charlie asks, remembering his Office training – keep calm and collected, assess the situation. You'll have the high ground.

Sheriff Whelan, hands resting on his gun belt, legs wide apart, stands in the doorway that leads from the kitchen into the room Charlie has been using as his bedroom. That room must have been designed to serve as a parlor of some sort. It's large, open, and airy. Leah used it as her studio. The unstretched canvas on which Leah painted a topographic map of Marin within an Earth-like globe, covered with still photos taken by Tony, still hangs in the room complete with photos attached.

Whelan chomps on a cigar, spewing forth fumes as he spits out, "You've got some explaining to do, boy. Give."

"Coffee, sheriff? I was just going to make some for myself."

"I asked you for an accounting, boy."

Charlie purposefully turns his back on Whelan, reaches into the refrigerator, and takes out a bag of ground coffee. He needs time to think, time to pull himself together. The coffee maker is already on the stove. He fills the bottom with water and pours the grounds into the top section. Whelan sits down in the seat Tony usually uses at the kitchen table.

"Maybe I will take some of your java after all," Whelan informs Charlie. "If you don't plan to water it down. It'll give me something to do while you explain yourself."

Charlie turns on the gas burner and then answers.

"I'm totally in the dark here, Sheriff. You've got to help me out. Give me a hint, a clue."

Whelan's more interested in his stogie than giving an answer at the moment. Charlie takes two cups from the cabinet and pulls both milk and brown sugar from the refrigerator. In a surprisingly short time, the kettle sings. That's what he likes about gas cooking.

"What's going on, Sheriff? Really, I don't have a clue," Charlie repeats, still standing by the stove.

"When's that java going to be ready?"

Whelan shifts from one buttock to the other uncomfortably on the wobbly chair. The boiling water begins to perk through the grounds. Charlie lights a cigarette. The stimulating aroma of coffee fills the air, driving away the smell of whatever was causing Whelan discomfort.

"Good grief," Charlie can't help but think. "What has this man been eating in the last few days to cause such a smell?"

The two remain silent while they wait for the coffee to perk. They both need a jolt.

"None of that sissy stuff for me," Whelan comments, as he takes a healthy slurp of black coffee. Charlie adds milk and brown sugar to his morning cup.

Whelan smacks his lips and emits a satisfied sigh.

"So... what's on your mind other than coffee, Sheriff?"

"John Wentworth Rutherford. You know him?"

"Never heard of him."

"Called himself Edge, I hear tell."

"Is that past tense?" Charlie replies.

"Deader than a doornail," Whelan allows.

"In this house?"

"My crime scene. Tape's on the front door."

"Not on the back one. Where I entered last night."

"Front room," Whelan enlightens Charlie.

Charlie sips his coffee and takes another drag on his Sherman's cigarette, all systems on high alert.

He tells himself, "Play it by the book, The Office approach, cool, calm, and collected.

"Let's see if I can blow a smoke ring around that tan cowboy hat of Whelan's that's perched on his fat head," he fantasizes.

Whelan, oblivious, asks, "Anthony Vitolinich of this address… How does he tie into this character, Rutherford?"

"John Rutherford and Anthony Vitolinich have a tie-in? You've got me there, Sheriff," Charlie replies.

"You want to take a ride in my patrol car?"

"No, sir," says Charlie. But he allows himself to think, "Asshole."

"That's more like it," Whelan continues. "Now, you said you were living here with Vitolinich?"

"Just bunking here until I can find a place of my own. Any law against that?"

Whelan holds up his finger and shakes it. He has a wacky smile on his face. More unpleasant odors come from his direction. Charlie's face muscles begin to tingle right about where he imagines Whelan would like to land his fist.

"Great, just great," Charlie ruminates. "The threat of violence and a smell to match the situation. This really stinks."

"I'll ask the questions, Sonny Buck," Whelan chuckles unpleasantly.

He takes another big slurp of his coffee, then slides the cup across the kitchen table.

"Got any more of this? It's making a new man of me."

"You could have fooled me," Charlie opines to himself.

He refills Whelan's cup.

"So, what else is on your mind, Sheriff?"

Whelan glares at Charlie like he's going to say something. Or, worse yet, he may be hatching a plan of action that will rearrange Charlie's anatomy.

"And he won't need a license to practice as a chiropractor to do it," Charlie reflects.

Whelan gets down to business – thank goodness.

"We found Rutherford's body on the front room floor of this house yesterday. He was stabbed with a kitchen knife which was lying beside his body," Whelan allows as he reviews the basics of the crime scene. "A half-filled piece of paper in a typewriter on the coffee table in the front room had some pretty nasty things to say about Rutherford. You type them?"

"No."

"Seems like that makes this Vitolinich character the one who typed it... which makes him number one on my hit parade of suspects... And it makes you an accessory after the fact."

"How do you figure that, Sheriff?"

Whelan shakes his finger at Charlie again. His cheeks are rosier. His disposition has improved a thousand percent. But he's still a dedicated son of a bitch.

"Where were you the night before last?"

"At my girlfriend's house."

That's almost true. Charlie was at Joyce's. She's no longer his girlfriend, though when they parted last month, they were on good terms and last night they got very friendly.

"I'll need her name and address. Be interested in talking to someone dumb enough to do the dirty with you."

Whelan chuckles and sucks down more coffee.

"Touché, asshole... Score one for you," Charlie mutters to himself.

Charlie refills his cup. Whelan smacks his lips with pleasure before continuing.

"Where is Vitolinich right now?"

"No idea. And I've got news for you. The guy's a peacenik, a flower child. Butter wouldn't melt in his mouth."

"Yeah, right, Baby Face Nelson looked like a real pushover too, and look what he done. I give it to you, however, even a pissant should get extra points when he stands up for a friend."

"That's right. He is a friend. Of long standing."

That coffee is starting to kick in for Charlie as well. It is good; it does perk you up.

"We were childhood friends growing up in Richmond, Virginia."

Charlie doesn't think Whelan needs to know about the mercy errand he went on that involved Leah, or the rivalry, if you can call it that, between Tony and Edge. He'll spill those beans to Whelan when and if he thinks the time is right; which would be about at the point where he's taken his last breath, based on the impression he has of Whelan at this point.

"Childhood friends, Richmond, Virginia... Is that so? Well, I do declare."

Whelan's eyes twinkle maliciously. Then he changes the subject.

"This Rutherford - Edge – is he just another loony tune? How would you place him in the scheme of things?"

"Just another creeper on the vine, Sheriff..."

"You trying to make fun of me, Boy? The backseat of my patrol car is eager to accommodate you."

Whelan shoves away from his chair and ponderously rises. He's fat but strong. His hairy fists look like they have convinced many a reluctant felon to confess.

"As far as I know, Edge was just another unemployed no-good hanging out on the scene with no visible means of support. And, if you're planning to catch the real killer, you'd do well to get a move on before the trail goes cold."

"Huh? What's that you say?"

Whelan wiggles his leg. Another pungent odor floats in Charlie's direction.

He really should watch his diet, Charlie thinks.

"What did you say your name was again?" Whelan demands, glaring at Charlie.

"Charlie Foxhawk Carter."

Whelan hollers over his shoulder to his deputy in the front room.

"Hey, Jackson, slip on down to the patrol car and run a check on one Charlie Foxhawk Carter, wants and arrests," before muttering under his breath, "What sort of name is that anyway?"

Charlie's detention while trying to close out the insurance investigation pops up. Before you can say lickety-split he's cuffed and in the backseat of the patrol car being taken in for further questioning.

Welcome to sun-parched Marin. Welcome to a whole new ballgame. Welcome to a fucking mess. Welcome to what looks like another chapter of incarceration for Charlie's childhood friend Tony Vitolinich, and possibly Charlie as well.

How the hell did two lovebirds keeping house together lead to a violent murder? Did Tony lose it and kill Edge in a fit of jealous rage? Is that really what happened? Did he really do that?

After three long hours of questioning that goes nowhere, Charlie is taken to a cell.

"Got to hand it to Whelan, the food they serve here is better than I got at that undisclosed location used by the Feds three years ago," Charlie reflects.

But the cot in the Marin County jail is just as hard, just as uncomfortable. He spends a long night looking up at the few stars he can see overhead. He's out of cigarettes but, thank goodness, no one is put in the holding cell with him.

Without breakfast or a word of explanation, he's released the next morning. He's already been warned not to leave the jurisdiction without notice, to get a good lawyer, to stay out of the Marin Sheriff's Department's hair until this case is closed. Charlie catches a cab back to Tony's San Quentin place so he can pick up his car. Whelan made it abundantly clear during their long chat that he didn't want Charlie within a country mile of his crime scene. Charlie will just have to make do with the clothes on his back and the fast-diminishing greenbacks he has in his wallet.

At the nearest phone booth, he calls his answering service, hoping to hear good news – a high-paying gig, a reassuring call from Tony, a surprise call from Heather saying she wants to see him, someone other than Tony or Leah confessing to Edge's murder. None of the above messages have been left but he does have one.

Fred's Place in Sausalito is the ultimate greasy spoon and one of the local breakfast hangouts for lowlifes like Charlie. Florid-faced Fred stands over the stove smoking a cigarette. The kitchen help bustles around him, keeping him supplied with materials. Fred passes plates to the waitresses who scurry about the room, delivering and taking orders and perpetually pouring coffee.

Seating is on a first-come, first-served basis. Tables are communal. Charlie sits in his regular spot, regular in the sense of coming in here once a month or so. The table is empty but it's littered with discarded San Francisco *Chronicles*, folded to meet the needs of breakfasters long gone. Just as well this table's cleared of people. Charlie's not in the mood for Marin gossip today. He places an order, looks off into space, and pretends to read the newspaper. He remembers he hasn't done his morning routine: bathroom, shave, shower, *I Ching*, stumbling attempt at meditation, feeble attempts to get a job search going. Despite the coffee in front of him, he could use another forty winks. Sleep would be a pleasant release from his current state. A shadow passes across the edge of the table. Footsteps stop by his side. He looks up.

"Mr. Carter?"

David Travail, his sister at his side, sticks out his hand. They shake. Charlie rises and waves them to a chair.

The message was from David. He wanted to talk, but not on the phone. Charlie was hungry so he suggested Fred's. He loves Fred's Swedish omelet (beef patty, fried eggs, cheese, caramelized onions). David has other things on his mind than food, urgent things that cause him, uncharacteristically, to initiate a conversation rather than wait for someone else to open up.

"I've contacted a lawyer to represent Leah. He recommended we hire a detective to run down leads for her possible defense."

Charlie picks up his coffee cup and puts it down untasted. David cuts him off before he can ask why.

"Leah was questioned by Sheriff Whelan about Edge's murder yesterday. Her state of mind made her less than credible."

"David overreacting," Leah mumbles, now seated at the table.

She has a lopsided look in her eyes that seems to be more than distracted, closer to lost in space. And what's with her speech pattern? Charlie is well-raised, polite, a true-blue Southern boy. He does not bring the subject up.

Instead, he catches the waitress's eye. She splashes coffee into brown mugs for David and Leah, then rushes away. A crowd at the back of the room is clamoring for her. Charlie stashes the newspaper he was reading on a nearby chair where a pile of discarded Chronicles has already collected.

"Your brother may have a point, Leah. I just spent the night as the guest of Sheriff Whelan and the Marin County Sheriff's Office because of Edge's murder. I don't think you want to get on their shit list."

"It will pass," Leah mechanically replies.

Leah's manner is giving Charlie a queasy feeling. Charlie can't help thinking, What's with her? Is anybody home? And that halting speech pattern, what brought that on?

"Are the police aware you've got a pretty good motive for killing Edge?" Charlie asks.

165

"Do you really believe Leah could do such a thing?" David Travail shoots back.

"For the moment, Tony is Whelan's prime suspect," Charlie explains. "That's what Whelan made abundantly clear to me during our extended conversation yesterday. That must have been before he grilled Leah."

He has the floor and he makes his point.

"Be honest. Both Tony and Leah look good for Edge's murder. By the way, any idea where Tony might be? His car is parked in the turnout up at San Quentin but he's not around."

David Travail drums his fingers on the table and shakes his head. He's uptight, worried, but solution-oriented. Leah shakes her head as well. Charlie isn't sure if her head shake is a distant signal from the Void or a response to his query. He catches himself remembering Leah flopping out of that dust-laden closet on Edge's remote mountaintop hideout in Sonoma County. They had a long, quiet ride back to southern Marin that day.

Mental torment and abuse, along with liberal doses of substances known and unknown, can turn creative, carefree, self-absorbed and intelligent individuals into a multitude of things: rage-filled murderers, candidates for the funny farm, or new cemetery residents.

A passing waitress slaps a plate on the table. It's Charlie's Swedish omelet. He digs right in but still manages to hold up his end of the conversation. Leah and David slowly down their coffee.

"Where did you talk to Whelan?" Charlie asks. "What did he ask you?"

There is a longish pause before Leah answers with no change of expression or nod of recognition to her surroundings, only a breath that sounds something like "humph" that gets her started.

"David's house," she answers and drifts away somewhere no one else will ever see or contemplate.

"What did he ask you?" Charlie repeats gently, looking intently at her.

She clicks into gear, haltingly.

"Edge... who, what, where... "

"What did you say?"

From far away, she responds.

"Edge gone... No idea... "

"You still pretty upset about what happened to you up at Edge's hideout?"

That wakes her up.

"You saw..."

David looks down at his hands. Leah holds her head high but her breathing is rough and irregular. Her eyes are glassy and out of focus.

"Did the police ask you where you were on the night of the murder?" Charlie asks, softening his tone further.

"Yes."

Her lower lip begins to tremble.

Charlie reflects. Is that from trauma or anger or something else? Do I want to find out? What would I do with the information if I did find out – clear her of murder or make her a candidate for a new pair of bracelets she doesn't want to wear?

Leah looks down once more, looks up, shakes her head. Her forehead is damp. Ringlets of hair droop over her forehead.

"David did the right thing when he insisted you get a lawyer," Charlie confides.

No reaction. Leah has just checked out. She needs a complete rest cure. That's not on the menu for her in the foreseeable future.

"They grill you on Tony's whereabouts?" Charlie follows up.

"No." There is a long pause before Leah asks, "Why?"

"The police did tell you they found Edge's body at the San Quentin place, didn't they?"

This time she's clear, firm.

"Tony not kill Edge."

"What do you suppose Edge was doing there?" David asks quizzically.

"Good question worthy of a good answer," Charlie snaps back. "I've got a few more. Who called the police to report the murder and how did they get Leah's name? Any ideas?"

Both David and Leah shake their heads with honest conviction.

"Everything so wonderful... then nightmare," Leah manages with equal parts hints of anger and despair. "Guess need help..."

Charlie asks himself, what sort of help would that be? Are they hoping I can find an out to a murder rap? Or a recommendation for a good place for a rest cure?

Despite that thinking, Charlie knows he must ask.

"Did you murder Edge, Leah?"

Leah locks eyes with Charlie. She struggles to focus. Quiet tremors run up and down her body. She clears her throat. With a tremendous effort she answers in what Charlie imagines she must believe is a calm but challenging voice.

"Think me capable?"

"You didn't answer my question."

"Don't know," she answers after a very long pause.

Charlie hasn't got a clue what her answer means. In her present condition, it seems unlikely that he will be able to get to the bottom of things with her any time soon.

Another disturbing thought – Will anyone, including herself, ever be able to get to the bottom of things with her? Leah Travail is in a very bad place from which there may be no return. May it not be so.

"Do you have any idea who might have done it?" Charlie asks, not really expecting an answer.

Leah looks like she's standing on a narrow ledge five hundred stories up. It's a long way down but a short trip to Infinity.

The look in her eyes, what her whole being projects, is the nightmares in her immediate past: a rape, abusive treatment, high-powered drugs, murder.

Charlie is thrown back on himself, thinking, Christ, I don't know if I'm cut out for this investigating stuff. Particularly when both of the prime suspects are dear friends, almost like family. Is it enough to just do my best for them? Will I only make things worse?

Suddenly, a fragmented, choppy answer, call it a madwoman soliloquy, is torn out of Leah's shattered consciousness.

"Edge rub people wrong way... wanted respect from 'family' ... Marin drug kingpin... Ha... Own worst enemy... "

She unconsciously puts her hand up to her cheek as though she'd just been smacked, hard.

What is she remembering, he thinks but doesn't say.

Tears bloom on the edges of her eyes. She angrily wipes them away.

Charlie inwardly sighs. If Leah murdered Edge, he deserved it, he thinks. And if she sounded like this yesterday when she talked to the police...Oh boy...

"Take your time. Charlie is going to help," her brother soothingly states, using his best bedside manner.

There's a tender sweetness in his concern for his sister. This man is a mensch.

Charlie doesn't want to think it but he does: Could David, in a moment of anger, take the life of someone who hurt his beloved baby sister? Could David Travail look good for this murder? Agreeing to help put the pieces of this puzzle together is going to suck, any way you cut it, even if I end up succeeding, he concludes.

Charlie probes again, hoping against hope that Leah will help herself and Tony with her answers.

"What was Edge up to? Do you know?"

"I...." Leah begins as an angry tear rolls down her cheek and recent horrors are reflected in her eyes. "I..."

She cannot contain a deep sob, a cross between a wail and a moan that creates more violent trembling. David takes her by the elbow. She struggles but collects herself.

"Take your time," Charlie offers.

Leah nods, then continues.

"Red...."

"Who's Red?"

"Edge runner... big... biker... pops pills... asshole... "

Charlie has never heard Leah use a curse word before. Red is a man worth finding out more about.

"Go on."

"Had heated argument with... Some big deal... "

Charlie keeps his mouth shut. He waits and listens with heartfelt sympathy.

"Edge super paranoid... Bought handgun and rifle... "

Her halting, choppy commentary goes into pause.

Charlie tries not to show it even though he thinks it: Is she checking out for the duration?

He gets an answer to his thought at last.

She lets out a moaning sigh, then gets it together to continue.

"Tried run away... Locked in closet... You showed up... " She goes into pause again, then marshals herself. "Dealing drugs... power and control... All he cared about..."

"He's not going to hurt you any more, Leah," David protectively comments, putting his arm over her shoulder. She sniffles, allows David to comfort her, then shrugs gently away from his arm.

They're close and have high regard for each other.

All three sit in silence. Charlie lights up a Sherman's. Traffic zooms up and down Bridgeway outside. There are only a few customers left in Fred's. It's a time of day in a joint like this that seems disjointed, isolated from all other times. Charlie breaks the silence.

"Have you seen Tony since that night in front of your brother's house?"

Leah has run out of gas, lost the will or need for speech. David jumps in.

"Will you work with Leah's lawyer on leads? I'll gladly pay your rate plus expenses."

"This is an open case, Doc. I get caught nosing around and I could get my license revoked."

"But if you told the authorities and turned over whatever you uncovered to them and it just happened to clear away any suspicions about Leah's involvement..."

"I charge $200 a day plus expenses, that's if the authorities clear me to do some poking around. And all that might get you is dead ends that leave Leah on the hook."

"That means you would be willing to look into things?" David insists.

"What about you, Doc, where were you on the night of the murder?"

"You don't think that I had anything to do with, with, with this?"

"You never know what you may turn up when you start trying to solve a puzzle that involves murder."

"That means you'll take on the case?"

"What's your alibi, Leah?" Charlie asks.

"Don't know."

Leah, one of the walking wounded, is deep down in the muck again, Charlie reminds himself. I don't have any idea how to help her out of the place she's in. I'm not a psychiatrist or a doctor. But, since she asked me...

"You've hired yourself a detective," Charlie agrees.

David Travail writes Charlie a retainer check for six hundred dollars, three days of Charlie's going rate. Charlie calls the lawyer, Ernie Feldman, from a phone booth outside of the 7-Eleven convenience store right next to Fred's Place. Feldman welcomes Charlie aboard and, in almost the same breath, informs him that this is his first criminal case. He mostly works on divorce cases and private property litigation. Charlie asks Feldman if he has any leads he wants him to check out.

"I thought that's why David wanted to hire you, to find leads," Feldman replies.

"I'll be in touch," Charlie answers.

Charlie's on his own. He cashes David's check and gets a room at the Fireside Inn, on the highway between Sausalito and Mill Valley. The room has a phone. Local calls are free.

"Detective Cooper," Coop barks into the phone when he answers.

"Coop. Charlie. Charlie Carter."

Charlie met Coop while working on that insurance claim investigation tied to a murder. He was straight with Charlie, even gave him some latitude when he needed it most. And Coop has always taken his calls since Charlie got his PI license.

"Charlie. Wish I could say someone just asked if I could suggest a good PI but I can't. Anything new with you?"

"Just wanted to let you know that I have a client, my first, Leah Travail. She and her brother want me to do some nosing around into the affairs of a drug dealer who was murdered. This dealer lived in Sonoma County but dealt in Marin. His name is John Wentworth Rutherford, a.k.a. Edge."

"That's out of my territory. Your courtesy call should be to Sheriff Whelan."

"You're absolutely right, but… "

"What?"

"Funny thing… Rutherford was murdered day before yesterday in a house rented to one Tony Vitolinich. You know, the guy who was accused of murdering Bob White. That's Tony, my childhood friend."

"Where was this house?"

"San Quentin Village."

"San Quentin?"

"That's right. And I'd been crashing at Tony's pad for the last week or so until I find something more permanent I can afford."

"Cozy."

"And that's where Marin County Sheriff Whelan woke me up at gunpoint yesterday. I was sleeping in his crime scene." Charlie hurriedly goes on to add before Coop can ask an obvious question, "I went into the house by the back door in the middle of the night and there was no crime scene tape on that door.

"Whelan took me in for questioning and I ended up spending the night in county," Charlie concludes.

"You've just ticked off a long list of red flags there, Charlie," Coop answers. "I know you've waited a long time to get your first client but why stick your nose in where it's likely to get bitten off?"

"I got shot at up at Rutherford's place in Sonoma. The bullet creased my skull. My client, Leah Travail, a former live-in girlfriend of Tony's, moved in with Edge. She got beat up pretty badly by him before she left him."

"Let Whelan do his job."

"There's that. There's also the fact that Tony is Sheriff Whelan's prime suspect for Edge's murder. Sound familiar? Leah Travail is running a close second."

Coop cups his hand over the phone and says something to someone in his office. Then he's back on the line.

"What did Whelan tell you when he questioned you?"

"He told me to stay the hell away from his case and his crime scene. But he turned me loose this morning without a word of explanation, or breakfast either. Probably figures I'll lead him right to the break he needs in this case. That'll give him something to crow about while he's arresting me and all the rest of my degenerate friends."

"Tread carefully, Charlie, very carefully."

"Could I call you in an hour or so to see what you can turn up on Whelan's case and anything you can get on John Wentworth Rutherford, a.k.a. Edge?"

"Sorry, no can do concerning what Whelan has. Professional no-no. But you should clue Whelan in even if he busts your chops for it. You worked hard to get that PI license, and this is your first case. What I can do is look into Edge. Call me later."

"Okay. Okay. I get the message."

Charlie is surprised by Whelan's response when he informs him that he has been hired to do field work for Leah's lawyer as a private investigator. Whelan reminds Charlie not to leave the jurisdiction without letting him know and repeats that this is an open case, an open case in which he, Charlie, might be implicated, not just Leah Travail. He also tells Charlie to keep him up to date on anything he uncovers and reminds Charlie not to disturb the crime scene until he, Whelan, says that he can. He, mercifully, is not able to transmit over the phone the unpleasant odors he emitted while Charlie was in his company. Charlie sincerely hopes Whelan finds a remedy for that malady, for the sake of all in his employ or vicinity.

Then he takes a break to shower, shave, and brush his teeth. He bought the essentials after he cashed David's check. Unfortunately, he can't change clothes. What he's wearing is all that he has at the moment.

I need to do something about that, he thinks.

He looks at his watch. Almost an hour has gone by since he talked to Coop. He gets back to him.

"Turns out you're not the only one who would like to know a whole lot more about John Wentworth Rutherford, a.k.a. Edge," Coop begins. "The Los Angeles DA's office, the LA mayor's office, the LA police department, even the dealers Edge was in competition with, would like to know a whole lot more. But none of them have been able to get a fix on him. The rumor is that he has friends in high places. Which side of the law those friends are on is hotly contested."

And he gives Charlie the name of a confidential informant – a CI – down in LA who might be able to get him more on Edge. Charlie thanks Coop and dials the CI's number.

"Sal, Charlie Carter. I'm a PI up in Marin. Detective Cooper of the SFPD told me to give you a call."

"He did, huh? Did he tell you I don't just talk to anyone and, when I do talk, I come at a price?"

"That can be arranged."

According to Coop, Sal attended Brown University on a scholarship until he caught Timothy Leary's act and decided to turn on, tune in, and drop out. How Leary's message was converted into a move to LA that leads to his being a CI for the cops is a mystery Charlie prefers to leave unexplored.

"In that case, what can I do for you?" Sal responds.

"Looking for a line on two guys. One of them was just croaked up here in Marin."

"In the capital of laid-back northern California? Tell me it ain't true."

"Well, the guy moved up here from LA. Must have brought some of those nasty LA vibes up here with him."

"This is Surf City, haven't you heard? Clean living and wholesome character is what we sell. What was his name?"

"Called himself Edge. Real name was John Wentworth Rutherford. Made designer drugs. Had a runner named Red."

"What does this Red look like?"

"Biker type, big, burly."

"And this Edge character?"

"Small, wiry guy sporting a goatee... Shifty eyes and plenty of tics... He was heavy into crystal meth."

"There's a guy lived up in Topanga Canyon that might be the dealer. Red's too much like a lot of characters down here to place right off. Why?"

"A close friend of mine has the misfortune of being the prime suspect in this character Edge's murder."

"When do you need to hear back?"

"I'll call you tomorrow. Give you time to touch the easy bases. If you don't have any luck, we'll talk about it."

Charlie hangs up and keeps on dialing. He may not know how to get an investigation off the ground but he does know how to work the phones.

"Must be old home week," says Molly Kovauc. "Tony dropped by and stayed to dinner a few nights ago."

When Charlie first met Molly she was playing den mother for a lightshow group. Her husband, David, and Tony were members of the group. That was over three years ago. Now, David sells DayGlo posters and assorted hippy-trippy stuff to head shops to make ends meet, foregoing his calling as a music composer. But he wouldn't say no if someone offered him a composing job. Molly tends to their two toddlers.

"Tony had dinner with you? He must have craved some of your home cooking."

The Lovin' Spoonful's "What a Day for a Daydream" is mixed with the sound of children playing in the background on Molly's end of the line.

"What's wrong, Charlie?"

Molly's no fool. She's a graduate of Barnard and she has a nose for nuance.

"The guy Leah moved in with up in Sonoma..."

"Edge?"

"He was murdered the night before last."

"Murdered?"

"Murdered at Tony's San Quentin house. Tony tops the list of suspects, with Leah coming in a close second."

"Oh no. That's horrible." Molly turns her head away from the receiver. Charlie hears her placating one of her children, then she's back. "Tony's been pretty choked up about Leah for a while, as you know, and he wasn't happy when he found out she had moved in with Edge. But Tony as the primary suspect? That's crazy, insane. And Leah?"

"Your typical crime of passion to the cops, if they find out about Edge stealing Leah from Tony and Tony's current love life or lack thereof, combined with his state of mind, in the dumps and looking for redemption. As for Leah, she and her brother just hired me to help sort things out."

"Is she all right?"

"Leah's in a state of shock bordering on total collapse. Only time will tell if she's able to weather this storm, particularly after all that's happened to her lately."

"Anything I can do to help?"

"What that woman needs is a total rest cure, pronto. Not likely to happen just yet."

"You talk to Tony yet?"

"No. I really need to get in touch with him but he's AWOL so far, as they say in the military."

"He stays in touch with Harry, of course."

"He's on my list."

"Then there are his two cronies at Pier 42, you know them too, right? Augie Cinquegrana and Glenn Carroll. They've thrown lots of PA and assistant editing stuff his way since he quit KGO."

"Also on my list..."

"Oh, and a long shot, an old college chum of mine, Sonya Bergstrom."

"Sonya?"

"She might have talked to him or seen him." Charlie doesn't respond so Molly elaborates. "Tony was so hangdog I suggested he call her. He needed some strokes. I knew Sonya liked him. Her number's 542-3811. Tell her I told you to call. She's a little paranoid by nature."

"You're a jewel. Oh, and by the way, if Tony should get in touch with you, tell him to stay out of sight and get in touch with me right away."

175

"Got it. And you stop by when you get a chance. It's tough talking to toddlers all day long. We can solve the problems of the world and maybe get you fixed up with a date."

"Thanks, Sis."

Sonya is out. Charlie leaves a message on her answering machine. Who knows when or if she'll call back? She's just a long shot anyway.

"Charlie. Wish I could say I have some work I can throw your way," Glenn Carroll, an independent film producer and a real mover and shaker, states with bonhomie.

"So do I, Glenn. But the real reason for my call is I'm looking for Tony. You seen him around lately?"

"He dropped by. I didn't have time to talk with him. Let me buzz Augie for you. I think they had lunch together."

Glenn and Augie work at Pier 42, a loosely connected group of independents working in the film industry. Augie confirms Glenn's recollection but has little to add.

"Yeah. We had a quick lunch together but all we talked about was the project that Tony synched up dailies for. You were on the shoot, weren't you?"

"Last film gig I had."

"That right? Want me to keep you in mind?"

"You bet. By the way, you happen to know where I can reach Tony today?"

"When we got back from that shoot, Ed Dudkowski's secretary had left a message for Tony to call her. Tony worked on a doc with Dudkowski a while back and it turns out Ed wanted to meet with him to talk about finishing the project. It was put on hold, lack of finishing money. The funding that dried up must have come back."

Mimi, Ed's secretary, confirms that Tony has an appointment with Ed on Friday at two o'clock. That's in three days. Besides his home phone, Mimi knows no way of getting in touch with Tony. She hasn't heard from him but will definitely tell him to get in touch with Charlie right away if he should call in.

Charlie needs forty winks. He leaves a wakeup call at the front desk.

It had been another glorious day in Paradise. The morning fog burned off. Afterward there was not a cloud in the sky. Birds sang

176

plaintively in the trees. And it was dry as desert sand. Thermometer must have reached eighty, a scorcher by Marin standards. Villainous humidity leaked into San Rafael near sunset as fog began pouring through the Golden Gate, cooling things down.

"This is ridiculous," Charlie tells himself when he is awakened from a restless sleep. "I need a change of clothes, this-and-that, maybe even some staples from the kitchen."

There's a small refrigerator in his room and a hot plate.

"I'll tell Whelan later," he tells himself to calm his apprehension.

When he gets to the San Quentin house, it looks as if Tony just stepped out for a moment. His bedroom is neat and orderly. His mom would be proud of him. There's no evidence of flight. His toothpaste tube, neatly capped and rolled up from the bottom, sits next to a clean razor with a new blade at the edge of the sink in the bathroom. Fresh towels hang on the towel rack.

"I didn't put them there. He must have," Charlie observes.

Orderly rows of clothes hang from hangers in Tony's closet. *Ishi*, *Black Elk Speaks*, *Dune*, and the *I Ching* are on his bedside table. There are throwing coins on top of the *I Ching*.

Tony hasn't dusted for a while.

His mom would mark him down for that oversight.

Several strains of black, curly hair, definitely not Tony's brown locks, cling to a splinter in the doorjamb leading into the front room.

Most likely they're Leah's. When did she deposit them there – on the day Edge was murdered? Could be any time.

In the front room, a typewriter sits slightly askew on the coffee table. Manuscript pages are scattered all over the top of the table and on the floor, a real mess. The police search probably helped create the mess. Tony would never have left this manuscript in such a state. A quick survey of a few of the pages reveals that Tony is writing a disjointed, semi-autobiographical, stream-of-consciousness novel.

His childhood in Richmond does not figure in this chronicle but Leah does, heavily. She's angelic, a goddess come to earth. Edge takes a real beating. He's the devil incarnate and worse. And Tony takes a beating too.

He always was a bit of a masochist, would have made a great penitent, Charlie thinks. He'd be the one wearing the hair shirt, flagellating himself and repeatedly banging his head against stone walls.

No need for anyone to read too much of this sad story. Motive for murder jumps off the page: Tony made the mistake of using Leah's and Edge's names in his "made-up" story. That accounts for Whelan's interest in Tony. It also informs Charlie how Whelan was put onto Leah.

On the floor next to the table is a sizable pool of blood. A floor lamp is knocked over. Maybe Edge banged against it after he was stabbed or grabbed it as he fell.

There are no signs that anybody has dusted for prints or collected forensic evidence. Guess Whelan never took that course when he was cramming to get the sheriff's job. Must have missed out on the crime scene tape seminar as well, Charlie muses.

Charlie does some collecting himself, finding three long strands of hair - two red and one auburn – next to the pool of blood.

Tony or somebody wrote down a phone number on a pad next to the phone. The impression of that number is left. 332-4496.

Charlie's answering service number. Great, more reasons for Whelan to tie me into the murder, he thinks. And a good reason to cut me loose. If they follow me, who knows where that might lead?

What the hell was Johnny "Edge" Rutherford doing at Tony's place anyway? Who else could the murderer be, other than Tony or Leah?

If one of these red hairs is Red's, that most likely puts him at the scene of the crime. Leah saw Red having a heated conversation with Edge.

But why would Red, if he is the killer, murder Edge in Tony's house? Did Red just take advantage of a golden opportunity?

And, assuming neither Tony nor Leah murdered Edge, were they present when the murder occurred?

What else? What else? There's something more. He knows he's missing something – something important. What is it?"

Then he sees it, or rather light sparkles off of its surface, catching his eye. It's an object partially hidden beneath the abundant ivy cascading into the room, an old-fashioned brooch. A delicate gold chain slipped out of the eyelet and disappeared into the fold of the long sofa that came with the house. He stoops down to retrieve both the brooch and the gold chain.

He hears footsteps coming up the rickety front doorway steps. They are ponderous and slow.

Whelan?

He heads for the back door but does not make a break for it. Instead, he does his best to see if anyone is watching. It's almost impossible to know. A tangle of overgrown vegetation obscures the view in every direction except directly out of the glass-windowed back door. And it's dark, very dark.

The front door lock clicks and the door slams into the wall. A gust of wind must have blown it open.

Charlie takes advantage of the noise to slip out of the back door. Before moving away from the cover provided by the much-too-tall shrubs, he looks around.

Nothing.

He hears voices and footsteps moving around in the front of the house. He heads uphill and ducks behind the cover of an overgrown patch of blackberry bushes. He's careful not to get too close to them. After a very long time, two suits exit the house. They get into an unmarked car.

They don't look like anyone who would be working with Whelan. But where else could they have come from? And, if they are from some other agency, is it county, state, or federal?

The possibilities are endless – and disturbing.

Edge's murder has just moved into a new realm of conjecture. Charlie finds himself thinking about The Office.

The Office muddied the waters but good in that murder he investigated as an employee of Life Beneficial.

He's mad, frightened, exasperated at the prospect of their, or a similar agency, being involved in this case. He storms down the hill and heads back into the house. He packs some clothes, collects some toiletries, staples from the kitchen, even adds a supply of weed and, of course, his precious *I Ching*, before exiting the house.

As he scurries down the hill to his car in the turnout, he wonders once again just why Whelan let him go without further grilling.

Is a game being played out in which he is the only one not aware of the rules and all the other players in the game?

The muddied waters of that damned insurance claim tied to a murder he investigated seem to tug him deeper into the murk.

He tells himself, "Forget idle thoughts and speculation, along with metaphysical conundrums, idiot. Activity, solutions to problems, fitting pieces into the puzzle, is what is now required, no, demanded. Cool, analytical thought, traits my father admires and traits I admired when I was little because I admired my father, that's what's called for. Put up or shut up. Piss or get off the pot."

He puts the samples he took from the crime scene along with a brief note into an envelope, planning to mail it to Coop's attention at the main office of the San Francisco Police Department tomorrow morning first thing.

Leah is at Miki and Peter's pad. That's where David, her brother, said he thought she was headed, despite the fact he pleaded with her not to go.

"Wait at least a few days until things settle down a little, I said to her. She just shook her head and that was it," David told Charlie. "She always was willful. Mom and Dad could be having cat conniption fits. Leah wouldn't listen."

"Anybody want a bagel? There's some lox and cream cheese in the fridge," Miki announces, coming out of the kitchen.

Miki and Peter's place is action central and the "community bulletin board" for "family" members and friends. The toilet flushes and Peter comes out of the bathroom.

"Hey, gang. What's going on?" Peter asks.

His hair is still wet from the shower. So is his pale skin. He has his bath towel wrapped around the lower half of his body and he's barefoot. He looks as innocent as a newborn babe with his black-rimmed glasses off.

"Bagel?" Leah asks from within her internal abyss.

"Sounds good...and lots of hot coffee, too," Peter replies, wiping his glasses and putting them on. "I've got another heavy session with Taj tonight."

It's after one o'clock in the afternoon and Peter is ready to settle down with the *IJ* while he waits for breakfast. The headlines scream – FIRES BURN OUT OF CONTROL NEAR SHASTA. This drought is getting out of hand.

Charlie follows Leah and Miki into the kitchen then pulls out and lights a pre-rolled joint filled with Panama Red and Nepalese hash, his special mix. He takes a hit and passes the joint to Leah, who takes a hit and passes it to Miki. The two women nod approvingly.

Before Charlie takes his second hit, he asks Leah, "Yesterday, you said you were a little fuzzy about the day Edge was murdered... Still feeling that way?"

He then takes a toke and hands the joint to Leah. While Charlie exhales, she answers.

"Can't. All mixed up. Sorry."

Leah takes a toke and passes the joint to Miki. Miki looks my way and then in Leah's direction with a meaning look. Give the girl a break, she seems to be saying. Her brain is fried, hopefully not for keeps. We all love her.

"Nothing, not even tiny fragments?" Charlie asks anyway.

Leah exhales and passes the joint to Miki before she answers. Would she prefer that those hours in her life never get clear in her head? If so, Charlie has a message for her: You better hope those memories come back. They could get you and Tony out of very hot water.

"Blank. Can't..." mumbles Leah.

Miki takes a toke and hands the joint to Charlie. She sends a silent signal as she does so.

Charlie interprets it to mean, Cool it, okay?

Leah shrugs and sighs. A long shiver runs up and down her body. Her forehead is moist. Her eyes are working, working hard. On what, with what, what's left of her poor mind?

Charlie takes another toke.

"Try, but... " Leah concedes, "all messed up."

Charlie exhales. Leah shakes her head when he offers her the joint again. Charlie puts it in the ashtray. The remains of several other joints lie there. Marijuana and conversations of this nature don't mix, even for hardcore marijuana smokers like these three. The focus of conversations can get lost, which is great when you are looking to make far-out connections but not so great for deductions and recollections.

"Where were you before you blanked out and where were you when you started remembering again? Maybe that will help," Miki interjects, showing some sympathy for the task Charlie has undertaken.

Miki and everyone in the "family" want to find a way to get Leah and Tony off the hook. Getting rid of those bad vibes Edge brought in the door with him would be welcome as well.

"Driving. In car," Leah answers right away.

"Where were you?" Charlie asks.

181

"101."

"Heading north or south?"

"Not sure."

"Was that before or after you blanked out? Or both?" Charlie pursues. But Leah has left us again. Where does she go? What does she see?

Charlie nods, hoping to encourage her, to bring her back. Miki looks thoughtful. Charlie reminds himself, Be like water, try to go with the flow. Overcome obstacles by filling them up with water until the obstacle gets overflowed by water.

There's a long silence, not unusual after you smoke really good weed. But this is different, another ball of wax. Miki puts the bagels, cream cheese, onions and lox on a plate.

"Did Edge make a business proposition to you, Miki?" Charlie asks, giving up on Leah taking part in the conversation for the moment.

"Me? What does... " Miki looks cool as a cucumber. "What does that have to do with anything?"

"I don't know. Just speculating," Charlie stammers. Then he picks up speed. "Might be a motive for murder. Maybe your dealings with Edge went sour. Maybe... I don't know. I'm just looking for a way forward, answers, putting puzzle pieces together in their proper places so everything will make sense," he admits.

Miki gives him a look that makes him feel less than comfortable.

"What a woman," he thinks. "She'd be worth riding the river with."

Miki's game though. She's willing to play twenty questions. Maybe it's because she hired Charlie to find Leah and get her to safety and Charlie did just that. Maybe it's because he's "family." That would be a new experience for Charlie. No longer just an outsider, but also part of a group of outsiders.

"Well," she confides. "Edge wanted to become my supplier. He claimed he had a bigtime connection. Told me we'd make a killing. I told him I'd think about it. I'm not really into chemically treated weed."

Leah puts cups and a pot of coffee on a serving tray without looking in Miki's direction. But she's listening.

"He laid some designer drugs and exotic weed on me. But why would I go for his scheme? I already have the best connections in Marin."

Miki and Leah exchange a woman-to-woman look. Then Miki barrels on.

"Is it a crime to humor a guy because he's living with one of your best friends, one of the 'family?' I figured Edge wanted to be friends and this was the only way he knew to go about it, by showing me what a big man he was. I played nice. It seemed to get him off."

"Why did you hire me to check up on Leah, if that was the case?" Charlie follows up.

"Edge was acting weird, wired, borderline crazy. Leah wanted to talk about something when the two of them last visited here. We didn't have a chance. He dragged her away, down the hill. I was worried about her."

"Did Edge ever mention or introduce you to a guy named Red?"

"Red?" Leah asks in a low, inward-facing tone.

"Red," Charlie answers, hoping he might stimulate her to cautiously reclaim a small piece of what is now blocked out in her mind.

"The muscle," Leah allows. "Edge the brains. Only… "

"What?" he asks, not really expecting an answer.

"Can't… Can't… Sorry."

Silence. Quiet. This is not a quiet you'd want to spend an eternity in.

"Try a little tenderness… " Otis Redding suddenly wails.

Peter has turned on the record player in the front room.

Damn. Double damn, Charlie exhorts himself. I hate fumbling around, not knowing what to do next, figuring out things on the fly with people I care about looking to me for answers and me not having answers or even a clue – other than answers none of them want to hear. Tony's lost in the ozone somewhere and so is Leah, presumably for different reasons. Hope is fading fast. Where is the cavalry when you need them?

"Did Edge mention any of his business associates to you?" Charlie asks Miki.

"Trust wasn't high on Edge's list of character traits."

Miki snorts. Leah nods in agreement, looking like a ghost ready to fade from view. Charlie grimaces mentally. Leah's had a rough time. And yes, I'm going to give her plenty of latitude because of that. But…

"You said you thought this murder was drug-related, right, Leah?" he asks, giving this conversation one last try.

"Yes," Leah replies.

Miki comes to the rescue.

"Somebody in the 'family' might know something. You could ask around. Kind of thing that probably should be done in person, not over the phone, though. Could take a while."

"Big Phil. Edge talked to," Leah suddenly interjects, putting together an inverted complete sentence.

"That's right. He did," Miki responds with a chuckle.

There is a slight pause before Miki continues.

"Edge thought he had a free pass to hit on Big Phil for intros to all the heavy-hitter drug dealers because he was Leah's old man," Miki concludes, putting her hands on her hips and shaking her head in disdain.

"Hey, are you guys going to hog the bagels or what?" Peter hollers from the front room.

"Nothing's going to tear this 'family' apart," Miki comments as she takes the plate loaded with bagels, cream cheese, onions and lox to the front room.

Before Leah follows with the coffee and cups, she adds, "You hungry?" to no one in particular.

Sitting on comfortable pillows, Charlie and Leah share breakfast with Peter and Miki around the over-sized short-legged circular table, the sun streaming in through the big window in the front room. When Miki begins clearing the table and Leah gets up to help, Charlie touches her on the arm.

"I'd really appreciate it if you'd sort of show me around, help me find and follow up on leads, Leah. Would you be up for that?"

The front door bangs open. In walk Gab and Ida and the kids.

"I'm told this is where you come to get a whiff of the finest coke in Marin County," Gab announces to the room in general with a huge, shit-eating grin on his face.

"You've found the place," Peter replies with a chuckle.

Miki rushes out of the kitchen. Ida and Miki hug. Gab and Peter shake hands. Their grumpy kids are crowded into an awkward corner of the room. Leah and Charlie slip out and head to Harry's pad, just down the hill. He's not home. The day can disappear quickly if you're not careful at Peter and Miki's pad, particularly if you're one of the "family."

Leah

In the enclosed bubble of Charlie's car, the outside world whirls and swirls in kaleidoscopic flashes of Marin countryside flying by.

There's nothing wrong with Leah's eyes and ears, at least as far as the here and now goes. Not that she would advise herself to take a tough final exam or prepare a legal document. The real problem is the connection between her mind and her words. She can't seem to put two words together most of the time. What's more, there are some huge holes in her ability to summon up memories.

The upside is that her brain is still clicking along, collecting images, thoughts, impressions, etc. What she's shaky on is putting them in the proper order without losing track of who and where she is. She's also a little confused about where, when, and how her brain sends out these images, thoughts, impressions, etc. All brain activity seems to register as fragments, disconnected and mutilated, particularly where memory is involved.

"Grandmother, help...please help," she reflexively mutters.

Charlie doesn't seem to notice.

She asks herself, Did I say that inside my head or just not loud enough for anyone to hear?

They park in front of the Record Plant, a recording studio located in Sausalito's Gate 3 just down from Tiki Junction. They enter Studio One where a session is in progress.

"Anybody interested in listening to the playback?" the engineer asks, using the talkback mic to communicate with the rock musicians in the studio.

At first none of the musicians answer or move. Then, the bass and lead guitar players pull their guitar straps over their heads, prop their instruments against speakers, and amble out of the room. The drummer thumps his drum with a nervous foot pedal, then dumps his sticks on the snare head and splits. The singer sniffs once, looks vaguely off into space, and heads for the soundproofed door. The back-up vocalists follow.

As Leah watches them, her mind reruns what it has been playing over and over about the day of Edge's murder.

Edge...Hit me...Struggle...Darkness...

Jumble...Flashes...Shouts...Anger...Fight...Void...

Black…Blank…

All messed up, she comments to herself. Was I fighting with Edge? Did I murder him? Don't know. Trauma. Fried my brain.

The engineer industriously sets levels and adjusts EQ settings on a massive thirty-two-track mixing board covered with knobs and buttons that stretch out toward a window opening onto the studio.

With an explosion of air, the heavy, soundproof door swings open and the singer enters the control room. He's got a serious sinus problem. He picks up a bottle of tequila and pours himself a shot.

"Watch out for the worm," Big Phil comments.

What the hell am I doing, asking around among "family" members about drug deals, the underworld, murder? Leah worries. Am I digging a deep hole for "family" and friends to get stuck in and, at the same time, horning in on Big Phil's chance to get a tune he wrote recorded in a studio by friends who are in a well-known rock group?

Find leads… what leads… charlatan… me… a charlatan… ha ha… funny… Big Phil hired The Charlatans to play in the Red Dog, his saloon up in Virginia City, Nevada, back in the day.

"Whadda you think?" the singer asks, ignoring Charlie and Leah.

"You don't like it, you've got plenty of empty tracks," Big Phil states with a shrug as he plays short, explosive riffs on his guitar, his fingers wandering up and down the bridge and neck of the instrument.

"Play the thing," the singer orders the engineer.

The engineer pushes the play button and the band's latest cut blasts out of the control room speakers.

Leah's internal muttering never stops.

Confess. Killed Edge. Hatred… Anger… No regrets. Cell door clanging shut… Did I really do that? Did I?

The singer shakes his head, reaches over to the mix panel and rams a fader to full volume. His voice is ear-splitting; it dominates the room. He laughs with boyish insolence.

"Give 'em what they want," he shouts with glee.

Cute, but he needs to develop better manners, Leah mentally shoots right back.

The singer slurps down the rest of his shot and sloshes another into a dirty glass. Big Phil chuckles at his antics.

Gosh, Big Phil, do you have to encourage this jerk's knee-jerk? You've got more class in your little finger than he does in his whole body.

"Just a minute," the engineer says, pushing the rewind button on the machine.

He makes adjustments with focused, frenetic skill. The tape reels jerk to a stop. The play head separates from the tapes and the massive deck sends the reels silently whirring in reverse. A stop tab halts the machine at the head leader. The engineer pushes the play button. The song begins playing again. The singer's voice is mixed hotter. An EQ adjustment adds a raspy edge to his voice.

The drummer enters. He's got a serious sinus problem too. He grabs the tequila bottle, slops out a shot into a paper cup, and tosses it down.

"I can't hear the snare," he states with indignation. "Bring it up."

He slumps down into a chair next to Leah, ignoring everyone and everything, including whether the engineer turned up his snare.

"Nobody has a bloody clue," he mumbles darkly to himself. "Nobody... "

Great... This guy is beyond autopilot. He's lost in some serious brain fog, Leah thinks. She can't and won't stop the running commentary in her head.

Another longhaired, wiry fellow scurries into the room. He's not one of the musicians.

Who the hell could he be?

He's obviously not the studio engineer. Peter, the only studio engineer Leah knows, never comes on like this guy does. This guy is too self-absorbed.

He isn't a roadie. He doesn't have Harry's matter-of-fact, down-to-the-nitty-gritty techie attitude.

He isn't a poster artist or a light show artist. He hasn't got Tony's ethereal spaciness.

He isn't a dealer. He hasn't got Edge's narcissistic arrogance.

Leah stifles the urge to scream. Her palms are sweaty. Edge's infection is suddenly trying to take control within her again.

Want to go home...

You have no home...

Want to lie down...

You have no bed...

Want to disappear...

It's not time for you to die...

You are barred from the invisible world.

"Take it from the top, Ed," the longhaired fellow directs the engineer. "And set the levels the way we discussed. I want Jim to hear it that way."

Ed again re-cues the tape. This time, before he pushes the play button, he pre-sets levels to marks he has made on pieces of tape next to the faders. The EQ panel comes heavily into play, as do the echo and reverb. The nervous, longhaired dude stares fixedly at the speakers mounted above the window opening onto the studio in which the instruments remain, creating a musical still life.

The tune, a ballad with a wicked, insinuating beat that builds throughout the song until it reaches a crescendo, begins. The lead singer wails, mixing blues intonation with liberal doses of torch singer.

Everyone is silent, worshipful, praying for magic, inspiration, a mega-hit. Big Phil told Leah the group's been in the studio for almost six months now and they're scheduled to start touring in two weeks. The tour was set up to herald the completion of this album. The boys are still not satisfied with any of the tracks. Three songs have yet to be laid down. Big Phil's tune is one of them. With no final mixes but a firm delivery date, the front-office bean counters are nervous.

These rockers are the living embodiment of the bad rap Bay Area band members and the San Francisco sound in general has received in the industry. The bad rap goes -all they do, even at work, is spend all of their time getting high. They show up late, if at all. They have hangovers or some form of withdrawal when they do, causing them to be anti-social to their bandmates and unable to function. They're all sex-crazed in one way or another. Groupies are constantly running in and out of the studio; so are drug dealers and a host of other hangers-on, bringing the session to a crashing halt. The music sounds more like a loud, messy, long jam session than an arrangement. They refuse to cut a three-minute commercial version of their hottest tune. The engineers struggle to please out-of-control band members, wired producers, and a panicked front office. If the engineer fails to meet all these contradictory and ludicrous demands, he's fired.

In this particular case, the group had a fluke hit single that rose to number ten on the pop charts two years ago and they haven't done a thing since. To make matters worse, the band members have already spent their advance money on this album, courtesy of a contract signed shortly after the release of their first album. And they're crying for more cash.

The song rolls to its inevitable conclusion. The longhaired dude with all the nervous energy looks at the lead singer; the lead singer belches loudly and forces himself to fart, signaling, Leah supposes, that he's unimpressed. She hopes he messed his pants.

"Where's the goddamn lyrical edge," the singer comments, glaring at the man.

"That's your job, sport," the nervous dude answers testily.

"He's the producer," Big Phil whispers in Leah's ear. "They're getting ready to dump him."

The producer glares at the lead singer pointedly. The lead singer deliberately and meaningfully scratches his crotch. The producer erupts.

"If you'd stop putting coke up your nose and drinking that rotgut you'd see what's going down, Jim. For Almighty Christ's sake, we're supposed to be getting ready to go on tour."

"Ain't gonna be no fucking road trip if we don't finish this goddamn album and finish it right."

"Don't you get it? If you don't finish this goddamn album and get out on the fucking road, the label's going to dump you. They'll cancel any future albums. That'll be the end of the big time for the band."

The door pops open and the lead and bass guitar players come in. They have their ladies on their arms. They also have serious sinus problems and an urgent need for tequila. That bottle is emptying fast.

"Is it a wrap?" the lead guitar player asks, barely suppressing a giggle.

"Who's the narc?" asks the bass player, nodding at Charlie.

"Let's get some air," Big Phil comments, getting up. "These boys need to conference."

Leah and Charlie follow Big Phil out into the hall. It's past ten o'clock and the session is just gearing up. No way it'll break up before dawn, the way these guys are going at it. Plenty ups, downs, and sideways are yet to come this evening.

"I hope they don't decide to cut my track from the album. I helped write the lyrics. Pretty cool, huh?"

"I hope they pay well, and in front," Charlie replies.

Leah knows from the way Big Phil talks about this band he's proud of his work. It's a sure bet that Charlie's comment hurts.

"So, you solved Edge's murder yet? Joyce tells me you're aces but I'm not sure in what department," Big Phil tosses back with a testy *yet jovial chuckle laced with plenty of edge, one of his trademark characteristics.*

Uh-oh. There's heavy innuendo in the mention of Joyce. Are they both balling the same old lady?

Charlie smiles right back.

They're quite a pair. Big Phil is rounded, squat, powerful, and pale with plenty of go; Charlie's a shrimp with an olive complexion and a mellow manner that obscures a determined core.

Oh boy.

"I'm working on it," Charlie responds, not specifying exactly what he's working on. "Say hello to Joyce for me, will ya?"

"If the subject comes up," Big Phil replies.

They both, as if by mutual agreement, decide to drop Joyce from the conversation... for the time being.

Leah helps by changing the subject.

"Miki thought... "family" help... Find Edge murderer... Drug related... Maybe...."

"Leah," Big Phil starts, then stops.

A look of concern appears on his face. He uncharacteristically stammers.

"What...What's wrong, Leah? Are you okay?"

Another awkward silence during which Leah can offer nothing coherent.

Charlie, tactfully ignoring the comment on Leah's speech pattern, jumps in to clarify her jumbled delivery.

"Leah and Tony are looking good to be charged with Edge's murder. And the Marin Sheriff's Department would like nothing better than to put Leah and Tony away, along with as many of their known associates as they can sweep up. We're thinking the murder might be drug-related and Miki suggested maybe a 'family' member might have heard something that would support that theory."

"That," Leah adds, pointing to Charlie and nodding, abashed by her current lack of verbal skills.

Big Phil and Leah go way back, back to their hometown, Memphis. After synagogue one time she told her mother Big Phil pushed her into the mud in the playground. That's when – well, after this actually – they became friends. Big Phil told her in no uncertain terms she had to learn not to squeal. He was a year older. She took his advice to heart.

"Let me see," Big Phil answers mildly, rubbing his chin and raising his eyes skyward in reflection.

Leah wants to give him a great big hug for not dwelling on her speech problem.

"Edge... At Peter and Miki's... " Leah prompts Big Phil. "Gave him runaround..."

Big Phil gets it. He comes right back.

"Yeah... Yeah. Okay. Right... What a laugh. That weasel wanted me to introduce him to the rest of my pals. Creep – that guy was an affront looking to get silenced – no offense to the dead."

Charlie replies.

"What did he say exactly?"

Big Phil, feeling things out, thinking, figuring how he can help Leah, elaborates.

"Oh, he bragged about what a big man he was. Wanted me to introduce him to my friends. Tried to buy me with his fucking designer drugs. I blew him off. That rat needed to disappear down the hole from which he emerged."

"You spread this story?" Charlie asks.

"Next best thing. I improvised some verses that spoofed Edge's act while some of us were jamming over at Palgy's place. Gab was there; he can tell you. Gab claimed he'd dropped by to get a group Don was managing interested in this song he wrote. All he was interested in was getting his nose packed for free. I got carried away. Gab ate up the routine. It was a way to pass the time."

"Who else was there besides Palgy and Gab and the guys you were jamming with?" Charlie wonders.

"Luigi..."

"What did you say in this spoof?"

"Oh, I created this character based on Edge. Made him into a kingpin dealer working the angles. But he's a fuckup. You dig? This guy screws up the count on the weight and loses money on a deal. He struts into the room and stumbles over a chair. He pulls out a piece and uses it as a cigarette lighter. He's a narc gone rogue who thinks he's a dealer. I don't know. I was just winging it. Variations on a theme. Gab was digging it. So was Palgy. I built it up."

The band members file out of the control room, heading back to the studio. The bass player's girlfriend tugs him toward her and presses her body suggestively into his. Then they grope each other's privates.

Very romantic, very hip, very productive, Leah thinks.

The heyday of this group has passed them by. Do they realize that? Maybe... They're not fools. Maybe they're afraid to release a new album. Maybe they think the new album will expose them as frauds. Maybe, maybe, maybe they should write a song about their indecision, the precarious nature of fateful karma, something.

And maybe I shouldn't be so judgmental, she thinks. Look at me.

Leah becomes aware that Charlie is responding to Big Phil.

"And the essence of what you were telling Gab and the others was that Edge was trying to set up shop in Marin and use Miki to catapult him to the top. Use her connections to set up his ring."

"I'll have to get back to you on that," Big Phil replies, not wanting to say more.

"Who's this Luigi?"

"Just this guy... He works on feature films and commercials as a second unit director. He and Al go way back... to Chicago. They both hail from there originally."

"Al?"

"Al the Pal... You know, Miki's main man."

"And does Luigi have anything to do with Al's business?"

"I wouldn't be surprised if Luigi hadn't fronted Al bread on occasion back in the day when Al was just getting started. They're tight. But no, Luigi does his own thing."

Charlie asks Big Phil to put out the word for information about Edge's drug-dealing activity. Big Phil nods.

Leah feels like crying. She's feeling pretty rocky.

How many more of these visits will be necessary? How many can I take? She wonders.

———

Leah and Charlie head back to Mill Valley. Harry still isn't at home, so they go up Molino Drive.

Charlie knocks on the front door of a low-lying mid-century modern house, all redwood, stone, and plenty of windows large and small, nestled on a hillside above downtown Mill Valley. A beat-up Ford truck is parked next to a black E-type Jag in the carport.

"What you selling, man?" Don Palgy, a man in his forties with long dark hair and hooded, worn eyes, asks with cautious laziness after he finally opens the door.

Bebop from the Beat Era plays in the background. From out by the hot tub on the deck, floating on stilts on the steep hillside, a warm woman's voice harmonizes with the music, lacing a lazy scat riff into the beat. Incense and pot smoke billow past Palgy and assault Leah and Charlie's noses.

Leah feels that she and Charlie are playing a bad joke on Don. I'm a pipsqueak, a spaced-out hippie chick with black corkscrew ringlets, pale skin, and wrong eyes, she tells herself. A Betty Boop cartoon in torn dungarees and a tie-dye shirt. And Charlie is an unlikely hippie version of Peter Gunn and Philip Marlowe, disguised in a swarthy face that close inspection might lead one to conclude is American Indian. In my book he's the ace detective in a dime-store novel, smoking a cigarette with attitude. Who needs a fedora when you're defending the woebegone and forgotten?

"Hate to crash in on your scene at this time of night, man, but I need to ask you some questions," Charlie begins.

Palgy starts to close the door. Charlie slips his foot forward, blocking it open. Palgy shrugs, snorts.

"Well, you obviously ain't the fuzz… so what gives?"

"It's about that guy Edge who was murdered. Leah here and a friend of mine have gotten tangled up in his murder investigation. Big Phil and Miki thought you might be able to help us out."

"Okay, make it quick. I've got some unfinished business out in the hot tub, if you get my drift."

"Right on. Big Phil dropped by your place last week and did a rap about Edge, the dealer that was offed. From what I hear it had you, Gab, and Luigi rolling in the aisles."

"Big Phil's got real talent, genius. Too bad he's throwing it away. So what else is new?"

The scat singing stops but the music continues. A woman shouts into the night air, "Donnie. It's awful lonely out here. Are you going to take all night? I might get mad if you do." Her voice mixes with small waves splashing against the wooden side of the hot tub.

"Cool it, Sally. I'm coming."

Palgy gives them a meaningful look. Charlie clears his throat.

"Heard any noise about Edge planning to move in on the drug-dealing action in Marin?"

"How's that again, stranger?"

"I'm trying to take the heat off of Leah here and my pal Tony Vitolinich, that's all. Looking for an alternate target for the heat to home in on."

"What kind of guy do you take me for?"

Charlie holds up his hands, palms forward, and slightly lowers his head, begging pardon. Palgy settles down.

"No offense intended." Charlie continues, "Heard any buzz about Edge on the scene? Squirrelly comments about him or his act?"

"I hear lots of things, most of them mindless."

"Okay. I can dig that. You know anything about a biker type named Red? Edge used him as a runner."

"Can't say I do."

"Cool, I'm out of here. But do Leah and my friend a favor, will you?"

Palgy doesn't answer but he doesn't slam the door in their faces either. Charlie ploughs on.

"We're thinking somebody on the scene didn't take kindly to Edge. Maybe it was somebody who got bent out of shape because of something he did or said. Maybe it was because he was trying to push into territory that others already had staked out. Whatever… Our theory is, somebody murdered Edge or had Edge murdered because of his drug-dealing ambitions. If you hear anything, I'd appreciate it if you'd let me know. Here's my number. It's an answering service so you can get a message to me, night or day."

Palgy takes Charlie's card, looks down at it, back up to Charlie.

"Woebegone and forgotten… Are you for real?" he asks with a chuckle.

"Ask my card designer," Charlie answers with a straight face, pointing to Leah. "Maybe she has a catchy slogan in her hip pocket for you."

"Maybe she does. Maybe she does," Palgy answers, slapping the card across his knuckles with a speculative look in his eyes that have drifted Leah's way.

Leah is amused and pissed at the same time.

Palgy closes his front door.

"Hop in," Charlie says as he opens the car door for Leah.

Leah whispers to herself, "Where're we going? Toward what? Leads? Life in prison?"

She rides with her arms crossed, sitting bolt upright in the shotgun seat of Charlie's Volvo. They're winding their way back down the hill toward downtown Mill Valley.

Charlie pulls out a joint, lights it, and takes a toke. Then he hands it to Leah as he comments quietly, politely, "I don't want to seem like an insensitive asshole. And I don't want you to feel like I'm trying to pressure you. But, well, when your brother hired me I told you that you and Tony were my primary suspects for this murder until you proved otherwise."

Leah takes a toke and offers it to Charlie. Charlie, concentrating on the road, doesn't notice. Instead, he finishes what he feels like he needs to say.

"I know, I know, you can't remember or can't get it straight enough in your head, to spit out anything that might get you guys off the hook. And I sympathize and I understand that your head's a mess because of far too many unwholesome drugs and the horrible things that have trashed your life, not to mention your head. But I guess what I trying to say is, I hope you feel better, sooner rather than later."

Leah sits silent. She thinks, I can't. Can't get a clear picture, or even a slightly off-kilter one. Mouth still not synched up to my brain. And my brain...oh brother...oh brother. Trying to show I want to be helpful. But... Miki's idea... why not? Good as any.

Then she says.

"Thanks... Sorry... Messed up mind..."

She sighs, takes another toke of the joint before putting it out in the ashtray. It looks lonely and precarious balanced on the edge of the metal compartment. The night is dry and hot. She's feeling low and mean, hard, brittle, and beyond dead. Maybe what she is is an edgy automaton.

Charlie stops at the stop sign at Throckmorton. He looks both ways. Nothing coming or going as far as the eye can see. He pulls out into the intersection before ruminating out loud, "Tony's a childhood friend. Also, he may be a cousin of mine, Leah. I've never told another living soul that fact, including Tony. He may be family. What more can I say? And you, you and the rest of the gang, you're, in a special sense, 'family' too. I want to solve this puzzle in the worst kind of way, wrap it up with a bow and present it to the world, make everything turn out right."

Leah listens to Charlie, looking at his profile. When he stops talking, she looks out the car window. Cozy downtown Mill Valley

195

passes by. The architecture, the substantial redwood trees, the steep streets leading away from downtown, hint at a mountainous European village. The Germanic founders of this town would roll over in their graves if they saw the hipsters who cruise their streets.

Leah had such pleasant dreams when she first arrived in town. If that dream had flowered, by now she might be doing an album cover for Taj Mahal. The fact that Peter is mixing his latest album might have given her an in.

Over. Empty. Mixed up. Walking train wreck. Disaster, her mind tells her.

"Luigi tomorrow?" Leah asks.

"Drop by Harry's first..."

Leah hears a jail door slam shut. She's caged, trapped. There's evil in the world and it can't be allowed free rein. It must be killed off, put down.

Has vengeance been served? Is that it? Is that what went down? The cocky girl who invaded Mill Valley almost a year and a half ago, was she and her high-minded aspirations a joke? Was she a buffoon, and oblivious to the fact? Did she get ground up in the meat grinder of life, turned and twisted until she's dangling, lost, addled?

Is there anything ever that is "justifiable" about homicide?

Charlie

Charlie takes a run at sunrise, up on the trails of Mt. Tam. No one is about. Fog still clings to the hillsides, pressing down heavily on the morning dew. Birds chirp in manzanita bushes, announcing the new day to all and sundry.

His brain comes alive. He's alert – in the moment – aware that the real world is filled with shadows, a dream. The invisible world is everlasting. Ultimate Reality, the Absolute, is the whole of existence.

How to truly realize that and maintain that realization? Is that what I should be focused on? he thinks.

A word breaks through to Charlie's consciousness –

Remember.

What is it "I" should remember?

The leather pouch, still in the outside pocket of his backpack, is ready for use when the time is right.

My real "I" and the Universal are one? How can that be so?

He's sweaty and breathing heavily as he jogs down the path leading to the small park at the end of Blithedale Canyon and the street that David Travail lives on. A shower, a shave, fresh clothes, a cup of coffee, maybe breakfast in downtown Mill Valley will set up his day just right.

After the visit to Palgy, Charlie stopped by the Fireside to pick up some notes to show to David. When she saw the dreary motel, Leah insisted he stay at her brother's house. David echoed Leah's insistence. They gave him the cottage out back and Leah moved to a room in the main house.

As Charlie jogs into the driveway, David is leaving the house. They nod to each other. David looks grim. Another thankless day of listening to people's troubles awaits him.

Inside, Leah is still asleep. Charlie overcomes his tendency "not to intrude" and makes himself some coffee. He cuts up a banana and mixes the slices with some fresh strawberries in milk. It's easier than heading downtown and he can get some work done.

He eats listening to the classical music station. They're playing Bach and Albinoni this morning. He lights a cigarette and picks up the phone.

There are no messages left with his answering service.

Sonya still does not answer her phone. Charlie has already left her a message. No sense leaving another.

Sal down in LA has not turned up anything useful. He tells Charlie to call him back later. He needs a little more time.

"How much was that you were going to pay me and when will I get the cash?" he asks.

Charlie promises to wire him his money and hopes David Travail will agree to the expense.

Now for a hunch call.

"Walt? How're they hanging?"

Walt is Charlie's one and only friend still working at The Office.

"Probably not as good as with you out there among all that free love and those hot hippie chicks."

"Free love has pretty much gone by the board."

"From what I've heard, any California girl would be good enough for me."

"I'm with you, but an agreeable one is just as hard to find here as it is on the East Coast."

"Tell me it ain't so. You've punctured my fantasy."

They both laugh. Charlie takes a deep breath and dives in. Hunches always seem stupid when you bring them up in open conversation. Charlie would never admit it but he blushes as he does so now.

"Walt. I know you're going to say I'm paranoid or worse but I've gotten a whiff of something that's giving me a very sick feeling."

"How come? You eat something that disagreed with you?"

"I saw two plainclothesmen coming out of a house, a crime scene. They did not look like locals to me."

"Well, you know how it is."

"That's exactly why I'm calling. I do know how it is."

"You working on something The Office might have an interest in, Charlie? I warned you last time not to do that and look where it got you."

"This is my first real case as a private investigator. Got my PI license and everything."

Walt laughs. Charlie chuckles himself before continuing.

"But those two guys came out of nowhere, left field. Why would the feds be interested in a local murder with a possible drug-dealing angle?"

"You're right. You are paranoid. You smoked some bad stuff?"

"Murder victim's name is John Wentworth Rutherford, a.k.a. Edge. Would you mind putting some very low-key feelers out to see if his name comes up in connection with any current federal investigations?"

"Gosh, I don't know, Charlie. What's in it for me?"

"Glory, Walt. A job well done. A pat on the back."

"How about a trip to Frisco and a meet and greet with one of those wild West Coast women of easy virtue?"

"You'd actually submit yourself to the wild and woolly West Coast?"

"Try me."

They both laugh... hard.

His next call is to Coop at SFPD. Coop is his usual self, direct and to the point.

"Sheriff Whelan received an anonymous call from a woman that led him to the murder scene. An all-points bulletin has been put out for Tony Vitolinich based on evidence found at the crime scene. Leah Travail's connection to Vitolinich has surfaced. She's running a close second on the suspect list. That means the sheriff's office is most likely paying a visit to all of Travail and Vitolinich's known associates. From what you've told me, none of their friends can stand up to any kind of scrutiny. I suspect Whelan has visions of cleaning out a rat's nest that infests his jurisdiction, using this case as the battering ram. Wouldn't that look fine when election day rolls around again? You are also in his sights. You made quite an impression on him the other day, it seems. In a word, watch out. And warn your friends to do the same."

"Great. Heard anything more on Edge?"

"There's some sort of rumble going on but I haven't got a fix on it yet. That usually means the Feds are mixed up in there somewhere."

"Red, the biker?"

"Nothing."

"The forensic evidence I sent you yesterday taken from Tony's place, would it be possible to get it analyzed?"

"You looking for anything in particular?"

"If I knew that, I wouldn't need them analyzed."

"I can't promise you anything but I'll do my best."

Leah

"Tony seems to have vanished into thin air," Charlie comments, just making conversation after Leah and Charlie have stopped by Harry's. Harry isn't around so they go on their way. He's often at home alone for days playing with his ham radio, drawing, tinkering with electronics or reading, mostly textbooks. Harry's taking classes at the College of Marin in mathematics and computer science.

Maybe he's on the road. He's the road manager for Hot Tuna, Leah's mind tells her.

Charlie pulls out a joint and lights it. They're rushing along toward Stinson Beach. As they slam around sharp curves magnificent vistas open up. Steep canyon drop offs, seen through breaks between

199

tall evergreens, reveal the Pacific Ocean shimmering in bright sunlight in the distance. On the uphill side of the road, breaks in tall evergreens show pockets of grassland and rocky crags that lead to the higher elevations of Mt. Tam.

"So what's Luigi's story?" Charlie asks.

"From Chicago. Worked on 'Bullitt,' second-unit director. Stayed on."

"So what made him move out to Stinson Beach? It's kind of inconvenient for someone doing what he does."

"Tightwad...Got deal on house... Gutted it..."

"The house really needed that much help?"

"Previous owners crazed, peyote-dealing Texans... Used front room to gut deer shot on Mt. Tam... Place so rank stood empty two years... "

Luigi's house is surrounded by live oaks and is set back from the road. It sits on a bench that overlooks Stinson Beach.

"And you are?" Luigi asks when he opens the door.

He does not ask them in. Not yet. Luigi is a cautious man.

"Charlie. Charlie Carter. Work as a private eye. I'm doing some legwork for my friend Leah here and Miki Weinberg."

Charlie hands Luigi his card. Luigi takes it but doesn't look at it.

"You two know Miki?"

"Yes."

"What's on your mind?"

Luigi is swarthy, short, and nondescript. He looks tough and gentle at one and the same time.

"Mind if we come in?" Charlie asks. "It's mighty unfriendly talking on the front porch."

Luigi shrugs and steps aside.

Leah and Charlie step into a dream. The paneling, which was once permeated with the smell of game, has been stripped away and replaced with rich, polished, natural wood. Master craftsmanship and liberal amounts of cocaine have led to a glossy and intricate series of niches, alcoves, and insets. A magnificent view of Stinson Beach and the ocean beyond from windows along two walls of the massive front room reinforce the impression the sparkling interior suggests. What a payoff.

"Nice place," Charlie states with conviction.

He looks for an ashtray as he pulls a cigarette out of the pack. Luigi shakes his head. Charlie pushes the cigarette back in the pack.

"Yes," Leah comments.

Luigi smiles graciously and allows his eyes to stray to the curves of Leah's body.

"You're both very kind and I'd love to show you around sometime. But I've got a meeting in less than an hour in downtown Mill Valley," Luigi prompts.

"Been hired by Leah here and her brother to look into the murder of a character calling himself Edge, real name John Rutherford. You know him?" Charlie begins.

"Name sounds vaguely familiar."

"Big Phil did a rap about him over at Palgy's the other day. You were there."

"He did, huh?"

"He was a dealer, just like your friend Al the Pal."

"So are a lot of people."

"How do you suppose Al would react if he heard Edge was about to move in on his territory? Would he feel threatened?"

"Talk is cheap. Personally, I never pass along gossip. Poor policy... You know what I mean? Now, if you don't mind."

Charlie doesn't give up easily. He makes a run at Luigi.

"Are you Al's connection to the Chicago mob?"

Luigi throws his head back and laughs.

"Despite what Mario Puzo and Francis Coppola have to say on the subject, mobsters and mob bosses only exist in the fertile imagination of writers of fiction and screenplays. The people you refer to as a mob are businessmen, pure and simple."

"But you're not denying that you back Al?"

"I'm in the motion picture business, period. Just because Al is an old friend of mine doesn't mean I get mixed up in his business dealings or, for that matter, sample his products."

"Since, as you say, there are so many dealers in the area, can you think of any one of them who might not take kindly to Edge moving into their territory?"

"Like I said, I'm in the motion picture business and I'm not a user. I really wouldn't know. Does that about cover it?"

"Guy named Red, a biker type: big, burly, red hair. You know him or heard anything about him that would help us locate him?"

"Sorry."

Luigi looks at his watch pointedly, signaling an end to the interview.

"Would you mind letting us know if you hear anything that might help us turn suspicion for Edge's murder away from Leah here and my friend, Tony Vitolinich?"

Luigi is non-committal but he doesn't say no. At the door, he bows graciously again.

"You are welcome back at any time," he comments, looking directly at Leah before closing the front door.

The merciless sun beats down on the car and the parched hillsides as Leah and Charlie negotiate the curves on the back road leading from Muir Beach to Mill Valley.

"You can take a cat nap if you want."

Leah shakes her head, then presses her palms into her eye sockets. When she pulls them away, she looks in the rearview mirror. Leah feels unmasked.

My face looks old, tired, spent, she thinks.

"Can't. Okay," she says aloud.

"Do you think we're wasting precious time?" Charlie asks, a new tone in his voice.

"Could be. Suggestions?"

"Well, I don't think Sheriff Whelan is a patient man. And you and Tony are still in the center of a bullseye."

Charlie pulls out a hash-laced Sherman's from a special cigarette pack in his shirt pocket, lights it, takes a hit, and passes it to Leah. Leah starts to decline, then thinks better of his offer.

Charlie asks once again, "Are things getting any clearer in your mind about what happened the day Edge was murdered?"

Leah exhales. A billow of smoke floats Charlie's way as she passes him the cigarette. As Charlie takes a hit, Leah tries to concentrate before giving an answer.

"Edge angry... Raised hand... Slap... Fight back..."

Leah stops gathering herself, struggling with interior gaps and confusing images.

"Anger... Whirling... Tangle...Shouts... Darkness..."

Her rehearsal is making Leah's breath come in short, shallow gasps. Her forehead wrinkles. She clinches her fists and shakes her head.

"Don't know... Jumble... Can't make out... Mixed up... Not helpful... Trying... Sorry..."

Charlie comforts her.

"That's okay. It'll come when you're ready. I'm sorry I have to put you through repeated questions. But when you do remember, I'm thinking it might clear everything up."

Leah takes another hit. The hash cigarette makes their conversation seem cerebral and removed from reality. Leah doesn't need more of that kind of feeling. She's had more than enough of that already.

Is the drug dealing angle just hot air, pure fantasy, a waste of time? All Leah knows for sure is that Edge was murdered. As for the rest, from her perspective all she's got are a series of flashes and fragmentary images.

She wonders, do I keep coming back to the idea that I'm guilty because somewhere deep down in my distorted and corrupted mind there's a memory of me doing Edge in?

Charlie asks again, "If it's true that Edge's murder was drug-related, what was Edge doing at Tony's house?"

"I don't...can't..."

Charlie's gets a flash.

"Could he have been looking for something?"

"Looking?"

"Was something hidden at the San Quentin house that got Edge murdered?"

"What?"

Leah whispers to herself in the back of her cranium.

Grandmother. Help a dead woman, she mentally screams.

Hash smoke trapped in the confines of the car has settled and clarified the chamber's air. Leah breaks the pregnant silence between them.

"Edge journal – names, formulas, transactions. Maybe... "

"Did you take it and hide it at the San Quentin house?"

"Found me in closet. I... "

Something nags at the corner of Leah's brain.

"What is it? Did you hide Edge's journal at Tony's house?"

"Edge might... maybe... don't know...can't... "

Again she asks herself, did I lure Edge to the San Quentin house and then stab him and kill him? Is that what happened?

"If this journal is not hidden at the San Quentin house, wouldn't it most likely be at Edge's hideout?" Charlie asks, thinking out loud.

"Maybe. Don't know. Maybe."

Help me, Grandmother, she pleads internally. I'm in pain. I'm lost, without a soul. Wake me from this nightmare. Lift me up from amongst the dead. Grandmother! Grandmother!

————————

They creep up the long drive to Edge's ranch in Charlie's Volvo sedan, fruitlessly trying to avoid deep potholes and boulders they meet along the way. At long last, they pull into the sunbaked front yard.

"Oh... my," Leah hears herself mutter.

The stark desolation makes shambles of her already tenuous thinking. She has returned to a place she vowed never to think of again in her life, much less revisit. She opens the car door. The horrific vibes lingering in this fetid and remote spot assault her.

Here I wandered in the submerged land of the dead, she thinks. Here I was violated. Here I cohabited with evil incarnate, of my own volition.

She feels like she might retch but instead forces herself to her feet.

The kitchen garden is overgrown, hardly a memory. The porch needs sweeping and the front door is wide open. Inside, the main room is covered with dust, deserted.

"Front room," Leah mutters.

Charlie asks no questions, doesn't speak. Thank goodness. Leah moves briskly down the hall. "Activity disperses nightmares" – *or so she tells herself.*

"Hid journal..." *she mumbles over her shoulder as she opens a door that leads into the spare room.*

It's the same room in which Charlie opened a closet door and Leah flopped out of it. The room is filled with cobwebs. The windows are caked with the dirt of years. Peeling wallpaper threatens to pull away from the wall. A bed frame with sagging metal springs and a weathered gray and white mattress sits in a corner of the room.

Who knows what went on in this lonely and austere place before Edge bought it? Leah always thought something sad, something tragic happened. She romanticized, speculating that this might be the place where the last gasp of the dream that drew settlers westward died.

She opens the closet door and pulls a light cord. Nothing happens.

"Damn. Generator off..."

Charlie pulls a flashlight from his backpack and switches it on. Now Leah sees the loose floorboards. They pop up with ease. She reaches down into the revealed space. It's empty.

"Was the journal here?"

"Nothing..."

From very far away, Leah hears someone whispering. It's almost audible.

Grandmother...Are you trying to contact me, to warn me? Too late... I'm already burning in hell. Is that my sentence for the foreseeable future? Is it justified?

"There's no other place he might have hidden the journal on the ranch?" Charlie prompts her.

"Lab... Maybe..."

She wonders, does Charlie believe me about the journal, that it's real?

Pain, agony, hatred, vengeance - a cluster of violent emotions overtakes her.

Murder most foul! Is it ever involuntary, accidental, justifiable – homicide?

Can't let this place get to me...

Refuse to relive the nightmare I endured here.

Won't let it torture me again. Won't!

Charlie takes her by the arm and gently leads her back down the hallway and out the front door.

"You wait on the porch. I'll check out the lab."

Charlie heads to the lab while Leah sits in a rocker, the one she put out here to take advantage of the view. She rubs her face with a distracted hand, one that seems unattached to her body. She's weary, weary but her brain continues its running conversation with herself.

Got to snap out of this... Can't give up... Get free and never look back.

Is that possible...in this situation? What is the situation?

Death hangs heavy in the fetid air. It's hot, hot and dusty. Charlie's boot heels kick up small clouds of dried dirt. The drought that has held the Bay Area captive for over a year is everywhere apparent on this g-d forsaken ranch.

A vulture floats lazily in and out of the burning glare of the sun and drifts on the updrafts high above.

Why does it circle? On what or whose death does it wait to feed?

As Charlie opens the lab door, a woman bursts out of the shabby outbuilding, dragging a young child behind her. She rushes over the rim of the ridge and down the hill. Charlie, right on her heels, leaps after her. Leah rushes over and is just in time to see Charlie grab the woman's arm. The child, a girl, stands by her mother's side with her thumb in her mouth.

"What the hell?" the woman growls.

"Need help?" Leah shouts down the hillside.

Charlie shakes his head and smiles. A colorful floppy hat, a rainbow of glorious hippie colors, makes it impossible to see the woman's hair and most of her face. But the open hostility of the woman is readily apparent.

Charlie

Has fate brought us a legitimate lead? Are Tony and Leah about to be delivered from their encounter with evil and misfortune? Charlie wonders.

"Who you?" Leah asks, after Charlie struggles up the hill with the woman and child. "Why here?"

The woman's hostility has magically disappeared. She is now timid, demure. She clutches her child's hand fearfully. Her eyes are opened wide in astonishment.

"Meant no harm, ma'am. Just tryin' to find my Johnny. He done run away from me."

The woman is diminutive, sturdy and attractive. She has green eyes. Underneath the gigantic floppy hat, her clear, smooth skin accentuates wonderful features. Her backwoods, down-home Southern drawl is laughable, though.

"Johnny?" Leah asks. "Dark hair curly... goatee?" Leah holds up her hand to indicate height. "This tall... Eyes gray?"

"That be him. That be him," the woman responds with idiotic joyfulness. "You know where he at?"

"Johnny's dead, ma'am," Charlie interrupts to add.

"Oh no..."

The woman moans and wails in much the same manner that grieving women captured by news cameras in faraway places do. Charlie and Leah watch from the audience.

"How... how do it go down?" the woman at last asks when it is clear that nobody is rushing to comfort her.

"He was murdered, stabbed to death," Charlie answers.

"Lord have mercy," the woman wails, falling to her knees and crossing herself.

The child patiently watches her mother and the proceedings with big-eyed silence. Charlie leads the child over to the porch. The woman, realizing everyone has stopped watching her act, follows. Charlie boosts the child up into the rocking chair. Leah goes to fetch a glass of water.

"Where you from, Richmond?" the woman asks.

Charlie is taken aback.

"How did you know?"

"I done passed through when I was a wee thing," the woman answers, looking off into the distance.

She takes her child into her arms and exposes her breast so the child can nurse. It's clear the child was weaned ages ago. Charlie sits on the edge of the porch with his back against the rickety porch roof support and looks pointedly away from her maternal labors. He lights a cigarette and takes a drag.

"When did you last see Johnny?" Charlie asks.

The child's uncomfortable grunts have diminished. Leah is not back with the glass of water. The woman, as if she is seeing Johnny at some distant time, delivers her answer.

"He done left me and my baby down in his Topanga Canyon house nigh onto six months ago. Said he was a-comin' up here on business. Huh, I thought. What kind of business? Woman business? That's why I've followed, to hunt him down. I did. I done track him down to this house. I knowed it was his by the makings out back."

"You know a biker type named Red?"

The woman's eyes narrow with suspicion. She knows Red all right.

"He be somebody I seen from afar. A fighting man... He be strong but not in the head..."

"You know how I can find him so I can talk to him?"

The woman takes her time as if she's considering where Red might be and then she shakes her head. Leah reappears with the water and starts to hand the glass to the child. The woman intercepts the glass and offers it to the child. The child ignores the offer. The woman gulps the water down.

"How Edge make living?" Leah asks the woman.

"Thank you kindly." The woman hands the empty glass back before answering. "Johnny, he liked to play with powders and poultices and such like. I told him they'd bite back. Is that how come he done got murdered?"

Leah looks at the woman with frank incredulity without answering.

"Were you his woman, too?" the woman asks.

Leah clears her throat, then nods her head.

"Child his?" Leah asks in return.

"She lovely, ain't she," the woman comments, pushing the girl forward for Leah to inspect without answering Leah's question.

Leah chucks the child under the chin. The little girl looks back, grave, mute. Suddenly and without warning, Leah pulls the child compulsively toward her and hugs her to her breast. One great tear appears on the rim of one eye.

Will childish innocence bring Leah back from the near dead and start her on the road to recovery from the traumas she has endured? Charlie wonders.

The woman, taken aback, starts to grab indignantly for her child but catches herself and pats Leah on the shoulder instead. They stand well apart.

Charlie sighs as his mind whirls with speculation. Why would these two women be attracted to Edge? He not only didn't appreciate them, it appears, but he also abused them. And he was not the kind to father a child. He was not careless. So... Why has this woman appeared at Edge's ranch? What does she want? Will she help solve the Johnny Rutherford murder mystery puzzle? And who will benefit from her tale?

Leah looks into the woman's eyes, then kneels down so she can look into the child's eyes at the child's level.

"How get here?" she asks. "Where staying, sweetheart?"

Before the child can speak the woman jumps in.

"We flopped in a deserted houseboat down in Sausalito t'other night, ma'am. We sleep and eat wherever we can. And we hitch ourselves rides."

"Would you like a ride with us back down to the city?" Charlie asks.

"I don't mean to be no trouble," the woman drawls.

"No trouble at all," Charlie starts.

"Stay with us," Leah suggests. "For night..."

Charlie looks quickly at Leah and then back at the woman.

"That's right kind," the woman agrees, taking the child's hand.

Leah reluctantly relinquishes her hold on the child.

"Your name?" Leah asks the woman.

"It's Peggy, ma'am. Peggy Crawford."

"Your name?" she asks the child.

The child does not answer.

On the long and convoluted drive back to Mill Valley, both Peggy Crawford and her child sleep, or seem to. Charlie and Leah have nothing to say. Wild flashes of thought, flashes of inspiration, zap between them.

We're headed for the heart of the matter now, come hell or high water, Charlie thinks, picturing the blue powder in the pouch he has in his backpack.

God bless and keep us. Amen.

The front door flies open and Sherry Travail, David's wife, runs down the path.

"Thank goodness you're here. A woman named Miki Weinberg called about a half-hour ago looking for Charlie. She sounded desperate."

Miki Weinberg sounding desperate, races through Charlie's mind. This is serious.

"Go. Go," Leah says, grabbing the child's hand and pulling her in the front door.

As Charlie roars away, his car raising dust clouds, he reviews the pertinent facts of this case.

First off, Edge was murdered at Tony's house in San Quentin.

Who was there to either witness that murder or commit it?

It seems logical that Tony must have been.

What about Leah? Her tangled attempt to recap the day of Edge's murder seems to indicate she might have been.

What about Peggy Crawford?

It's possible that Red was there and, come to think of it, Peggy as well. Those hair samples I found. They might be a match for those two.

What about those two plainclothesmen I saw exiting the San Quentin house? How do they fit into the picture?

Are they connected somehow with The Office?

Does Edge's drug dealing have any bearing whatsoever on his murder?

"Enough with the questions," Charlie tells himself out loud. "I need some answers."

One thing seems certain to Charlie: Edge knew his murderer. Edge was the paranoid type, particularly when you add his meth use, but the murderer got the drop on him. Edge must not have thought the murderer posed a threat. Or he dropped his guard.

With that in mind, his logic tells him either Tony or Leah is the likely murderer. Edge would not drop his guard in front of Red. And he doesn't think he'd drop his guard in front of Peggy Crawford, or with anyone associated with those two plainclothesmen either. On the other hand, it's hard for him to believe Leah or Tony would stab Edge, even though they both have damn good motives to do so.

So, eliminating the possibility that this was a crime of passion, a possibility that most definitely is not off the table by any means, it's possible that Red or Peggy or those two plainclothesmen or someone higher up could enter the picture. And that could make this a crime about drug dealers or power players in general jockeying for position.

According to Leah, Edge was putting together a big deal but he was having trouble with it. Red, his runner, was maybe playing both ends against the middle while looking for a way to move up the ladder himself.

Okay, he says to himself, but why would Red, if he is the murderer, stab Edge in Tony's house?

Let's assume that Edge was looking for his journal at Tony's house.

How would it have gotten there? Did Edge find it? Did Tony? Where is it now? Would it help solve the case if it were found?

Will Red, when found, become the missing piece that solves the murder mystery puzzle?

When Tony shows up, will he put to rest my concerns? Guilty or innocent, will my childhood friend ever see the light of day again? Or be in prison the rest of his life?

When Leah puts together what she knows about the events of Edge's murder, will it be in the form of a confession or will it implicate someone else – like Tony?

What about Peggy Crawford? What the hell does she have to do with anything?

I'm not even going to bother to formulate a question yet that covers the two plainclothesmen, a mysterious superior, or The Office.

Christ! This whole thing is a mess.

Am I going off on another wild-goose chase while my friend and his former lover, the ones with the best motive for murdering Edge, get closer and closer to being arrested and put away?

The police already have an APB out on Tony. And I've just left Peggy Crawford and her daughter at David's house, two very good leads in the case. Will they still be there when I return?

Oh Lord, please don't let Tony and Leah be the ones.

What am I saying?

Loved ones are not murderers – Ever - particularly Tony and Leah. Tony's a sweetheart, a standup guy, even if he is too idealistic and impractical and not exactly the hero type. And Leah's a free spirit. She's headstrong but not violent. They're family.

The gate leading into Peter and Miki's yard is open. Misha the Malamute is not on the porch. Charlie bangs on the front door as a feeling of foreboding swells within him.

"Peter. Miki. Are you inside? Are you all right?"

No one answers. No movement inside. Silence. Nothing.

Charlie circles around to the deck in the back of the cottage. The window entrance to the bedroom is open. He steps inside.

"Peter, Miki," he calls with more urgency.

The bedroom is torn apart, a chaotic mess. The bed is overturned. All the drawers in the desk have been pulled out and flipped over on the floor. The dresser had the same treatment but afterwards it was shoved away from the wall and toppled over. Clothes, linen, shoes, hats are strewn round the room.

Was this an act of willful destruction or was someone looking for something – like a journal?

In the front room, the round table that served as the centerpiece for "family" gatherings is on its side. Peter's precious stereo system has been smashed. Record albums have been jerked out of their sleeves. Quarter-inch audiotapes have been ripped out of their boxes and unrolled. Peter's stand-up bass has a broken neck. The strings on his electric guitar have been cut and the guitar speaker has been kicked in. The sitar is bent, broken.

"Peter. Miki. Where are you?"

No answer. Silence...

211

"Family" members and the rest of the regulars will have to find somewhere else to hang out, somewhere else to score, somewhere else to sample free dope, somewhere else to get all the latest gossip on the scene. Miki and Peter's pad has been ransacked and pillaged. This "happening scene" is closed for the duration.

Where are Peter and Miki? Are they hurt?

Charlie double-times it down the path to the street and almost runs into Peter, who is turning toward the stone steps leading up to his house from Lovell.

"What's going on?" Charlie exclaims, grabbing Peter's arm to keep from bowling him over with his forward momentum.

"Misha got out of the yard. And two plainclothesmen came knocking on our door."

"They tossed your house?"

"That happened before. That's when we called you."

"You find Misha yet?"

"No."

"Did you let the plainclothesmen enter the house?"

"No. Miki saw to that."

"What did they want?"

"Information about Edge..."

"Nothing about you guys?"

"No."

"What did you give them?"

Peter ticks off a list.

"The fact that we knew him... That he had visited our house... That we had no idea who might want to murder him... That we knew Tony Vitolinich and Leah Travail... That we had not seen either of them recently... That neither Tony nor Leah would ever, under any circumstances, murder John Rutherford, aka Edge... "

Peter has a very orderly mind for someone who seems so gentle and unassuming.

"Any idea who tossed your house? Did they find your stash?" Charlie asks after Peter finishes.

"That's what freaked us out. The stash was untouched. We were hoping you could help us figure things out."

"No problem. I'll add it to my very long laundry list of mysteries that need an explanation. Where's Miki?"

"Driving around trying to get a fix on Misha's whereabouts."

They both look up, then down Lovell, hoping Miki will appear with Misha. Birds chirp cheerfully. Neighbors work in their yards or head out on errands. Cars meander down this low-key street. The sun is warm on their faces. It's another magical day in Paradise, another day without any rain in sight.

"Sorry about your dog."

"It's happened before. He just needed to run. Or he got the scent of a bitch in heat. Malamutes roam. It's in their blood."

"Sorry about your house and the undercover guys too."

Peter gives a weak smile and shrugs. Such is life.

Charlie sighs. There's only one way he can figure two plainclothesmen showing up on Peter and Miki's doorstep looking for information on Edge and not showing any interest in what goes on at their pad. A tail has been put on him, Charlie; a bug in his car, a tap on the San Quentin phone. Something.

Is The Office involved? Or someone with a connection to Whelan's office? Charlie muses. If that's so, who tossed Peter and Miki's pad? Could it have been the murderer? Someone working for the murderer? Just possibly, could it have been the police? Maybe it has something to do with drug dealing in Marin, not about Edge or me.

Out loud he says to Peter, "You haven't been getting any weird vibes lately, haven't noticed anything out of the ordinary?"

"I've been real busy. Taj needs to get this album out. Money pressures."

"No strangers showing up on your doorstep to score? Nothing to indicate the cops were on to you?"

"No."

Charlie decides – better safe than sorry. He tells Peter he's likely the reason that two plainclothesmen showed up on their doorstep.

"The way I figure it, there's a tail on me. That's why two plainclothesmen showed up at your house. Nothing else makes sense."

Peter's sharper than he looks. He's also pragmatic.

"We need to tell the rest of the 'family' – in person. Our phones might be bugged. Who else have you visited?"

"Big Phil at the studio... Don Palgy at his place... And Luigi over at Stinson Beach..."

"I'll see Palgy at the studio tonight. That leaves Big Phil and Luigi."

Peter and Miki's Mercury Cougar pulls onto Lovell Street with Miki behind the wheel. She looks pale and drawn. Misha is sitting on the seat beside her, happy as a lark.

Even before she rolls to a stop in front of the steps leading to the house, Charlie and Peter are beside the car. Peter, leash in hand, grabs Misha. Charlie opens the door for Miki. She nods.

"Thanks for coming."

"I'm probably the reason you got rousted by those plainclothesmen. They most likely put a tail on me," Charlie confesses.

"We've got to get the word out to the 'family,'" Miki immediately concludes.

"It's not safe. You guys have to cool it for a while. Is there somewhere you can go?"

"Ida might..."

"Maybe you could head out of town for a few days, at least until I can get this thing sorted out."

"I've got my sessions," Peter replies. "But Miki could go."

"Miki?" Charlie asks.

"The 'family' needs..."

"You can't help them if you're in jail or battered by the maniac who tossed your house."

Miki hesitates but finally nods grimly. Charlie's still not so sure Miki really agrees.

"Is there somewhere the two of you can stay?" Charlie asks Peter.

"With my parents, I suppose. They live over in the East Bay."

"Give me their number so I can stay in touch."

Charlie pushes them, dog and all, toward the Mercury Cougar. When they're inside the car, Miki rolls down her window and passes a piece of paper to Charlie with Peter's parents' phone number on it.

"Could you run down to the Western Front and warn Al? He can get in touch with Luigi," Miki asks.

"Sure. What about Big Phil?"

"Palgy or Al are sure to see him. They can warn him."

Charlie slaps the side of the car.

"Done... Now you guys get the hell out of Dodge. I'd hate to lose two good friends right after getting to know them, particularly founding members of the 'family.'"

David chuckles quietly; Miki's eyes light up. The Mercury leisurely rolls down the quiet street.

"Anybody home?" Charlie calls in a conversational tone.

A shaggy head pops out of a doorway to a backroom.

"Looking for Al…" Charlie states.

"And you are?" the shaggy head responds.

"Charlie Carter, a friend of Peter and Miki's. They sent me."

"Send him back," a voice from the backroom calls.

It's Al. He's in.

Charlie gets right down to business, outlining the case he's working on, its direction and the latest twists – the tossing of Peter and Miki's pad and the visit by the plainclothes officers. He includes the fact he might be the one that put the plainclothesmen onto Peter and Miki but does not mention the potential Office angle.

"They sent me here to warn you – Luigi and Big Phil too if you run into them. I visited both of them – Luigi at his place out at Stinson."

Al nods.

"Miki and Peter okay?" he inquires.

"Real troupers…"

"Son of a bitch who tossed their place ought to be shot. You're not likely to find two more beautiful, gentle people. We go way back, you know."

Al's Coke-bottle glasses magnify his gentle eyes and make them seem to pop out of his narrow, pallid, clean-shaven face. Charlie pats him on the shoulder.

This guy should take better care of himself, he reflects.

Al is in his forties but he looks like he's in his sixties. He's lost most of his hair and the skin on his face hangs loose around the jawline. He has a deep, all too constant cough. His nasal passages are shot. Al has unwittingly become a poster child for the deleterious effects of cocaine on the anatomy.

"Hey, man, I hate to do this, but I need to know… " Charlie starts.

Al smiles, then chuckles. Charlie cannot help but wonder how the hell he can see out of those glasses. They're thick and they look opaque.

"We all got a gig. Do yours, partner," Al allows.

"Well, Edge kept a journal, a record with all his transactions, all his formulas, maybe even his contacts."

"Hmm. Not cool. Hope that wasn't what got him murdered."

"That's not all. He told a number of people that he was going to take over the dope-dealing scene in Marin. It could tie into a deal he was working on. That threaten you in any way? Make you think you may lose territory?"

"You've seen too many movies. I don't have territory. I have customers, mostly friends."

"He wanted to take those customers, those friends, away from you."

"I've seen a lot of wannabe kingpins come and go in my time. And one thing I've found out. There's plenty of action in this county, plenty of room for all, particularly at the level he was most likely doing business. Why should I bother to have him killed?"

"It's rumored that you're backed by the Chicago mob. Maybe they wouldn't be as generous as you are if they found out about Edge's activities."

"Again with the movies. My Chicago friends are businessmen, plain and simple. They don't rub out my competition. They don't need to. They let market forces do the work."

"Any new action on the scene lately that might tie in with this Edge deal?"

"There's always something. I just let it slide."

"Maybe it's time to focus on 'em. Might help me with my case and avoid a repetition of what happened to Miki and Peter."

"You got something there. I'll do some checking around. You get back to me?"

"I'll make time. Kinda on the run right now..."

"You want a toot?" Al asks, pushing a compact piece of marble on which he has created long, jagged lines of coke toward Charlie.

He smiles as he does so. Al's a real straight shooter, a good pal for anybody to have. Charlie gets a number and a home address from him so he can catch up with him later. He walks out of the Western Front with a more jaunty step and a mind racing six different ways at once.

"Cocaine... Cocaine... Runnin' all round..."

———————

A question presses hard on Charlie's consciousness.

The journal, the journal – is finding it important enough to toss the pad of two unsuspecting people, important enough to murder Edge? he wonders. That journal of Edge's, is it at Tony's place?

217

Charlie steps into the Sweetwater and uses their pay phone.

"Miki and Peter?" Leah asks after Charlie identifies himself and before he can update Leah.

Charlie hears her breathing into the phone. In the background whales are singing their eerie songs.

"Miki and Peter's pad was tossed," Charlie tells her. "Two plainclothesmen came knocking on their door, probably because of me. Miki and Peter have gone into hiding. Top predators are circling, getting ready to move in for the kill. Was Edge's journal valuable enough for someone to kill Edge for it? And if so, is it at the San Quentin house?"

The moaning whales continue their mysterious calls. The oceans of the world allow their voices to carry for miles on currents. A part of Charlie's mind follows these calls. Are they talking about the meaning of life? Are they reaching out to family members, offering a helping hand so those near and dear can avoid unforeseen dangers?

Leah, after a very long pause and several gut-wrenching sighs, answers Charlie's question about the value of Edge's journal.

"Loose board... Behind toilet bowl... San Quentin bathroom... Worth checking..."

When Charlie rescued Leah from Edge's hideout, she left with more than the clothes on her back. She had her purse with the long leather strap with her, too. Did she have the journal in it? Is that why she's suggesting... Charlie asks himself before asking Leah,

"You were at the San Quentin house the day Edge was murdered?"

"Not sure..."

"Did you murder Edge?"

"Can't... Don't... Maybe... You think I did?" Leah answers in a voice lower than a whisper.

"It doesn't matter what I believe."

"Drug dealing angle..."

"More 'family' members might get dragged into this."

"Low profile...This too shall pass..."

"Sheriff Whelan, law enforcement officers in general, are likely to arrest you and Tony as well as any other 'family' members they can get their hands on, file charges of various kinds, and let the chips fall where they may. The way they'll see it is that would be a huge win for the American way and the criminal justice system. So what if the charges get bounced later, much later."

"No. No way. Not right. Not… " Leah voice and her emotions have gone up a notch, maybe two, laced with hostility and frustration.

The line goes dead. Charlie is left standing in the Sweetwater bar looking out at cars passing on Throckmorton.

The bar is empty. It smells of stale beer, extinguished cigarettes, urine, and vomit. The help are washing down the floor. It's early for the Sweetwater and its steady stream of regular customers.

Forehead pressed against the glass folding door of the phone booth in exhaustion and frustration, he realizes that if Edge's journal is in the hiding place Leah mentioned at the San Quentin house, it could make some pieces of the puzzle fall into place. It could also lock Leah in as the prime suspect in Edge's murder.

There's no sign of Tony, no indication that anything has been moved or rearranged by the cops or the two plainclothesmen. The journal is right where Leah said it might be.

Charlie opens it up and flips rapidly through the pages. Edge's handwriting is cramped and hard to read, typical speed-freak hen-scratches. There are detailed descriptions of meetings. When people are mentioned, they are referred to in code. Places and transactions are also coded. Pictographs often replace descriptions of action. Careful study might reveal clues. In the back of the journal are four full pages of what appear to be the formulas for Edge's designer drugs. There's no mystery there. Any chemistry major worth their salt should be able to follow these recipes. This is very valuable information indeed. If Edge's murder is drug-related and if a new syndicate is moving into the area, Charlie is holding dynamite. If those meetings and contacts are in some way connected to covert operations, this journal is radioactive.

I've got to find Tony. Now, Charlie realizes.

There's a phone in the kitchen. Charlie makes use of it. Maybe it's not bugged. Maybe...

"Molly, it's Charlie. You heard from Tony yet?"

"No."

Damn. Where is that boy?

"You making any headway?" she asks.

"I'm being tailed and, as a result, the pad of two friends was tossed. If you call that progress, I'm making plenty."

"What can I do to help?"

"Tell everyone we know to keep it very cool for the next few days. I think the lid is set to blow off. People will get hurt."

"Coop. Looks like Edge's murder could actually be about a big drug deal gone sour or maybe a power shift, I don't know. That means laidback southern Marin is likely to experience some sudden changes."

"What happened?"

"Somebody put a tail on me. And I've uncovered a journal Edge left at Tony's."

"You need to turn that in. It's evidence."

"Okay... "

"Who tailed you, someone in law enforcement? Who?" Coop adds before Charlie can continue.

221

"Good question."

"If this murder is drug-related, how about bigtime dealers or people who could profit by getting their hands on that journal?"

Long, awkward pause...

"Is Vitolinich or his girlfriend really part of this?" Coop asks.

"Probably just pawns. That's what I'm hoping, but who knows. Any news on the forensic evidence?"

"Just arrived on my desk."

"Appreciate it if you can run the samples."

"I'll see what I can do. And you, take care of yourself. Looks like you're in the soup."

"Thanks, Dad."

"You're welcome."

Next, Charlie gets his LA contact on the line.

"Sal?" he asks. "Charlie Carter. What you got?"

"That money you promised?"

"Hey, look. Things have gotten a little crazy up here. But I promise you, it will get to you."

"I don't know why but I believe you."

"Thanks."

Sal chuckles.

"Okay. John Wentworth 'Edge' Rutherford, late of Los Angeles, formerly of Dearborn, Connecticut and reform school, has not resided in the county or city of Los Angeles for at least six months. He owns a shack up in Topanga Canyon that's surrounded by estates. The shack was once a caretaker's shanty.

"Edge hung out with the flashy set at the Whisky A Go Go, most of them wannabes. But there were a few well-known musicians and budding starlets in the group. Edge was their supplier. He peddled designer crap that typically sends you in six different directions, none of them positive, all of them frenetic. His drugs of preference were meth, heroin, angel dust, DMT, AMT – all mixed up in various combinations. He wasn't much of a fan of consciousness-expanding drugs.

"Peggy Crawford and her illegitimate child, Jennifer, live on the property. It's not clear whether Edge had a long-term relationship with her or if he fathered the child. But Crawford is definitely involved in Edge's operation. It appears she brought in most of the customers and kept everything afloat while Edge was spaced out on his own drugs.

They say she was the brains behind the operation and only tolerated him because he knew how to make the drugs and she didn't want to get involved with that end of the business herself. Smart thinking, I'd say, considering what happens to most of the people mixing the chemicals."

"This Peggy Crawford, you got anything else on her?"

"Born in Tennessee. Story has it that her dad was a moonshiner. You know, Thunder Road and all that. She was raised by him, some say with the use of a very heavy hand. One thing for certain, she's a beauty. She was for a very brief time talked about in the same breath as Tuesday Weld and Ann-Margret. She had other plans than becoming a pin-up, however. Money, lots of it, that's her scene, until she had that kid at least. Could be even more so now. No one seems to know who the father of her child is."

"I want to know everything you can find out about her. In a hurry."

"You got it, after I get that money order."

"This Red character. Got a line on him?"

"There was a biker type hanging out on their scene, had red hair. It's all pretty vague. Maybe some of your cop contacts will be able to fill you in with more. He probably has a rap sheet."

"Could Edge be fronting for someone else, maybe even narcs? You hear anything about that?"

"Anything is possible on a scene like Edge had going. It would explain why he never got busted, though. The guy was a real loose cannon. Never failed to make a big splash when a small wave was all that was called for."

Next call.

"What you got, Walt?"

"I got nothing definite, Charlie, not even rumors, which does not reassure me. I'd advise caution, serious caution," is Walt's reply. No small talk today.

Charlie is off the line in a hurry. He doesn't want to know more. The line is probably tapped.

Charlie paces, thinking. He jumps when the phone rings.

"Charlie!"

"Leah? What's wrong?"

"Gone..."

"Crawford and the kid?"

"Gone... Searched my room... "

As Charlie hangs up, he hears the front door open and close. It's too late to make a break for it. He tosses his traveling joints into a tin filled with flour in case it's the cops. Then he slides Edge's journal into the bookshelf above the oven, hiding it in plain sight among the cookbooks. He steps forward to meet whoever is approaching.

"Stop right where you are."

A raised gun is pointed in his direction. One of Sheriff Whelan's minions holds the gun.

"Don't get excited. I'm not planning on making any sudden moves," Charlie answers. He raises his hands and puts them behind his head.

"You've been a busy boy," Whelan hoots.

Charlie is mashed into the back seat of a patrol car parked in the turnout. Whelan, squeezed into the backseat with Charlie, smiles. The caps on his teeth look like they came from a five and dime. They probably glow in the dark, Charlie surmises.

It's a good day for Whelan.

"That's right, Sheriff, I've been a very busy boy. The least you could do is put me on retainer."

"Don't know as we have the budget for that, son. Besides, what do I need to go and do that for when all I have to do is watch you? Look at what falls out of the trees. You and your bunch of low-life druggies. Who knows what might turn up next? No sir. I don't think we need to put the squeeze on our puny budget to pay you."

Sheriff Whelan is pleased as punch. He's smoking a stogie in celebration. Sharing close quarters with him is trying, very trying. The odors are the final touch, a very putrid, stinky one.

"If I'm helping you out so much, why am I sitting in this patrol car with you? Looks like you get more benefit out of me running around loose."

"I thought about that, but busting your chops was just too tempting."

"On what charge?"

"Unlawful entry into a clearly marked crime scene."

They both know that's not going to stick. There's still no crime scene tape on the back door. But how long will it take for Charlie to be released from custody if he's hauled in?

"So? What's on your mind?" Charlie replies.

"County food should be on yours."

"You got a major break in this case?"

"You located Vitolinich yet?"

"I wanted to leave you something to do."

"This whole sick scene you're part of is coming down, Mr. Private Dick."

"Am I under arrest?"

"What were you doing up in that house before we got here? Your pal leave some incriminating evidence behind that needs covering up? What?"

It comes to Charlie in a flash that the two plainclothesmen may be connected to Whelan but maybe not on the county payroll. Has Whelan been working with a federal agency on an undercover operation?

"Why was I in the house? Well, besides packing a change of clothes, I'm concerned about Tony Vitolinich. You remember, he's my childhood friend. And my client, Leah Travail. There's a hard-working county sheriff who's just aching to run them in on all the charges he can think up. I'd like to find Tony so I can clue him in and I'd like to find evidence that removes both of them from suspicion."

With jovial and calculated indifference, Whelan jabs Charlie in the kidneys. The blow is well placed. Charlie doubles up. Whelan has had plenty of practice in his interrogation room back at the station house. Whelan takes a puff on his stogie, further fouling the air in the already close patrol car.

"That's funny. Real funny..." Whelan chuckles.

Then he rolls down the window and spits before shouting to one of his goons waiting nearby. "Got the keys for the cuffs?" Whelan hollers.

The deputy nods and hustles over to the patrol car as he reaches into his pocket for the keys. He hands them to his boss. Whelan shoves Charlie forward to undo the cuffs. He gets Charlie in a position that will tighten the cuffs on his wrists and threaten to pull his arms out of their sockets.

"You're right. You're more valuable to me on the loose," Whelan comments nonchalantly as he wiggles the cuffs up and down a few more times, pretending that he is struggling to undo them.

They pop open. Charlie rubs his wrists. Whelan chuckles.

"Tell your friend when you find him his ass is grass."

"I already told you, you'll be the first to know when I find Tony."

"Right, you did say that. Well, keep this in mind. The fact that you live in this crime scene might motivate me to search the house for contraband if you don't find Vitolinich soon. Who knows what I might come up with? Chew on that."

Peggy Crawford

Peggy Crawford traveled to the Bay Area just like most visitors do, by plane. She rented a car at the airport. She drove to her lodgings, which she had arranged for in advance, and dropped off her suitcase. She also eats out, just like most visitors.

"What say I toss that San Quentin pad again?" Red, her underling in the business, irritable, frustrated, asks. He often is. He has little patience and is not noted for his cleverness.

Crawford quietly takes a bite of her cheese omelet, ignoring him. The coffee shop where they sit, in the lull between breakfast and lunch, is almost empty. Jennifer, Crawford's daughter, looks at Red with big, impassive eyes, not trusting, not fearing. Crawford notices.

Good girl, she reflects. Just like I taught you. Don't trust anyone, particularly men.

"That detective needs to be diverted. He might queer the deal," Red snaps.

"Let's stay focused on Edge's journal. Got it?"

Crawford takes a long, languid sip of her coffee. She loves having a late breakfast. It's soothing. Looking out the window, she pictures herself alone with Jennifer somewhere far away, someplace without men, without any threats or intrusions. Cars and foot traffic pass by beyond the plate glass window. The dive they're eating in is on Fourth Street in San Rafael. Crawford finds that comforting.

It's a nice, quiet little town, she ruminates. Never know you're a hop, skip and a jump from Frisco.

226

The waitress, sitting on a stool at the counter smoking a cigarette and drinking a cup of coffee, reminds Crawford of Ma. Both have had too many one-night stands, too many nights with the bottle, too many brief encounters in cheap hotels. Shanty Hollow, Tennessee, circa 1955 is alive and well in upscale Marin.

Face it, girl, there's no way you're going to escape your past or the pressing needs of the present. Get down to business, she says to herself.

Aloud she says, "We need to find that journal."

"You checked his ranch?" Red replies.

Red drove up from LA on his bike. It's parked near Crawford's lodgings. He's riding with Crawford and Jennifer today. Crawford reflexively starts to admonish Red but changes her mind.

"Lots of hiding places there. I was interrupted. But, yeah, I checked out the most likely places. I also checked the brother's pad, the one that chick Edge shacked up with lives in. Who knows, maybe somebody else got wind of it and took it."

"What about hiring some extra muscle to help out?"

Crawford has a caustic answer for that.

"Never tie up loose ends with more loose ends."

Tony

Nothing... Black... Void...

Tony Vitolinich is passed out in the grassy, open field above the San Quentin house. He has been in and out of consciousness since he managed somehow to get out of the house on the day Edge was murdered.

The straps of his still camera and his 16mm camera still are wrapped around his neck. It's a miracle they have stayed in place.

Nothing... Black... Void...

Tony does not dream. He does not move. He is looking up at the sky but he sees nothing.

Dark of night... Blank... Void... Sunrise...

There are brief intervals when his sightless eyes see and his appendages make awkward attempts at movement.

Get up...

Sway... Tremble... Weave... Stumble... Fall...

But they are feeble efforts with no rewards.

Nothing... Blank... Void...

Nonetheless, his body keeps going through the motions of activity, of life, even as his consciousness remains unattached.

Weave... Stumble... Fall... Get up... Fall...

His attempts are fruitless.

Blank... Stumble... Black... Weave... Void... Fall... Out

He remains under the influence of a powerful, untested, unregulated pharmaceutical. Will he recover from the effects of this drug...ever?

Blank... Darkness... Void...

Miki

Misha is busy trying to stick his nose into every hole and orifice in the teepee. Ida and the kids are forced to stand up in the small space. That makes Misha think they want to play. He gets more rambunctious. It was no picnic, being cooped up with a Malamute in the Mercury Cougar for over an hour.

"Take that dog out and help him to blow off a little steam, will ya, kids," Ida commands.

"Yes, ma'am," her two children grudgingly agree.

Who wants to do your mom's bidding when you've just become a teenager? Rebelling against your parents is just part of the deal, isn't it? With parents like theirs, rebellion might be training to be a Green Beret or walking a dog.

"Where's Gab?" Miki asks Ida.

Miki dropped Peter off at the Larkspur Landing ferry terminal. He must be on his way into the city by now. Got that session with Taj… Before Ida can focus on an answer, Miki rattles on. "Peter and I are supposed to meet up at the studio in the wee hours, or that's the plan at least."

"Where's Gab?" Ida snorts, not at all surprised to hear Miki jump from a question to another subject. They're old friends and their conversations often are constructed this way. "He went slinking out of here the minute he got a chance. I'd say he's on the lookout for more blow."

"That's too bad because Charlie picked up a tail. Could be the authorities are turning up the heat. Or else a drug syndicate moving into Marin. Our place got trashed."

"What! We've got to tell the rest of the 'family.'"

"Precisely…"

"You want to crash with us until this thing blows over?"

Ida's a real pal. She'll share whatever she's got even when she has nothing. Miki answers Ida's question with a statement.

"The plan was to hide out at Peter's parents' house in the East Bay. But getting the word out to the 'family' is more important than hiding out."

"Just give me a minute to pack some things," Ida responds.

Personal safety means nothing to Miki when "family" members might be in danger. Same goes for Ida. They're on the case.

"Okay if I leave Misha here with the kids? We've got some ground to cover."

"Believe it or not, I have someone I can call to take care of the kids, and Misha too."

Charlie

Charlie and Leah are on the deck behind Leah's brother's house. It's another beautiful day in Paradise, as danger threatens all about. Charlie is thinking out loud. He's too worked up to notice that Leah picks up Bianca when she joins them on the deck. Leah presses Bianca to her chest. Bianca purrs with pleasure. Leah has a faraway look in her eyes as she scratches and rubs her. Is she paying any attention to what Charlie is rattling on about?

"Okay, let's look at what we do know.

"We know that Peter and Miki's pad has been tossed.

"We know that Sheriff Whelan smells blood.

"We know that Peggy Crawford and her kid have vanished.

"We know that Tony is lost in the ozone somewhere while an APB is chasing him down.

"We know that two plainclothesmen are so out in front of us that they have us looking in our rear ends to find some answers.

"And we sure would like to know exactly what happened the day Edge was murdered..."

Charlie stops, suddenly aware of Leah. She looks far away, fragile, storm-tossed.

"How are you feeling? Things clearing up in your mind at all?"

The phone rings inside, loud and insistent. Leah doesn't seem to hear it. She is absorbed in petting Bianca. Charlie catches it on the tenth ring. It's Big Phil.

"Come on," he announces to Leah after finishing a brief conversation.

Leah puts Bianca down and gives her one last stroke. Bianca arches her back and slowly saunters toward the sliding glass door that leads into the house. Charlie doesn't stop to consider just then how Bianca got to David's house. Last time he saw her she was at the San Quentin house. They've got to get a move on.

The Trident in Sausalito is filled with ferns and custom woodwork. The same craftsmen that remodeled Luigi's house did their magic here. A well-endowed waitress wearing a leather halter top and skimpy denim cutoffs escorts Charlie and Leah to the bar. Other equally attractive young women hustle back and forth, waiting on tables.

There's a dynamite view of the Bay and the San Francisco skyline out of the floor-to-ceiling windows. The deck outside is almost empty, too windy and exposed for hedonists concerned about their looks. Inside, sunlight pours onto plants artfully placed around the large open space.

Sitting in the spacious built-in wooden booths and wooden-topped cocktail tables are upscale hipsters, movers and shakers of the "me" generation, all dressed to the nines and throwing cash around like it was going out of style.

"You see Big Phil? I don't," Charlie observes after they have been directed to stools on a remote edge of this glamorous scene.

Rock music blares from hidden speakers. The babble of conversation blends into the music.

Without acknowledging Charlie, Leah surprises him with an observation.

"Humpty Dumpty... Can't put together again... "

Distracting sounds suddenly seem far away, muted, in their remote corner. Charlie pats Leah's shoulder. She looks down at a beer bottle stain left on the glossy bar top.

"I wish I could think of something upbeat and positive to say," is his sympathetic reply. "I mean, when a bunch of disastrous things hit you all at the same time and that is complicated by the introduction of a mixture of drugs of unknown potency and effect... Well, I guess you just have to find a way to weather the storm, with a little help from friends and family."

Charlie takes Leah's hand and squeezes it, hoping Leah gets the message that he wants to be part of that help. Leah watches as her Dubonnet on the rocks and Charlie's draft beer are placed in front of them. She doesn't respond, but Charlie is convinced Leah is listening somewhere in her fragmented mind.

They're holed up in a meat market where the folks are decked out like they're going to a masquerade party. All present are ready to boogie on down. They have no interest in discovering the meaning of life. The first wave of seekers on the Summer of Love scene, given the name "hippies" by the media, have been replaced; no, overshadowed by carpetbaggers looking for easy ways to cash in on free love, drugs, and rock-and-roll. This carnival of life, this self-indulgent, overblown,

Fellini-like circus, raves on to the self-fulfilling beat they hear in their own heads.

Leah surveys the scene, drumming her fingers on the wooden bar top.

"Where is Big Phil? I thought he called from here," Charlie reminds himself.

Unexpectedly, Leah speaks. "Nick Reynolds owns... "

"Oh?"

"Kingston Trio... Has Oregon ranch... girl Harry dated there too... She's gorgeous."

Leah is getting more coherent. The effects of the drugs in her system are beginning to diminish, but Charlie hardly notices. He's absorbed in a different way by Leah's comment.

Leah is talking about Heather, he reflects. My Heather. Dressed as an Indian maiden, she initiated me into love hippie style, the northern California variety, with decidedly calamitous results. And Leah's right. Heather is gorgeous...

Too bad Leah arrived on the scene when she did. If she had come pre-Summer of Love, would what's happened to her have happened? Timing... Karma... the twists and turns of Fate... Then again, arriving on the scene pre-Summer of Love didn't keep Tony from taking some pretty wicked blows.

What he says out loud is, "Tony was doing lightshows with Harry and the guys when I was transferred here just after the Summer of Love." He doesn't really expect an answer but he gets one.

"Not meant to be... "

Charlie thinks, That's probably true. But that's not how he replies.

"Tony doesn't react well to adversity, it's true... Anyway, as far as I'm concerned, you're both family."

Leah nods.

"Yes... " she agrees.

She is solemn, stone-faced, as a tear rolls down her cheek. Her verbal skills may have deteriorated but her dignity and honesty show through as she expands the thought.

"Was angry... Made bad choice... Evil... " Pause. Then.

"Murder..." Pause. And.

"Fuck."

A good Jewish daughter is confronted by a grim reality that has played havoc with her life. Charlie listens, watching Leah closely.

Will she reconnect with her indwelling, life-giving spirit? Will she forge a new persona? Will she undergo this change behind bars or as a free woman?

Leah downs a good portion of her Dubonnet on the rocks. Charlie takes a sip of his beer after slipping the bartender a five. The bartender gives him a look of disdain, taps his fingers on the bar top, makes his getaway. Did he expect a ten spot?

"Over there by the window," Big Phil whispers, appearing from nowhere to lean between the two. "You see the smarmy dude wearing the leather pants and lots of jewelry? That's Jorge. He's Colombian."

Charlie and Leah jerk their heads in the direction Big Phil discreetly points.

Jorge has one arm propped over an adjoining chair. In the other he elegantly holds a cigarette. His eyes glitter. Insolent, indolent, slippery as a snake, he rules over conversation at the table. The waitress and the two dudes sitting with him are licking his boots. He is dark, wiry; a vision of South American good looks.

"So?" Charlie whispers back to Big Phil as Big Phil sits down next to Charlie and Leah.

"Al has it from a reliable source that he's the front man for an organization gearing up to move in on the drug scene in Marin."

Out of nowhere a blond bombshell, curvaceous hips undulating, well-formed breasts seemingly ready to jiggle out of her low-cut dress, approaches Jorge's table. The hippie waitresses look like chopped liver beside her. Hollywood has come to Marin and is taking the room by storm. She looks familiar. Leah gets it first.

"Peggy," she whispers.

Indeed it is, but she's totally transformed. She's every male's wet dream. She's erotica to the nth degree. She's Sophia Loren and Marilyn Monroe rolled into one.

Jorge looks at her over the top of sunglasses pulled down to the end of his nose. He thumps the glasses up as he straightens in his chair and says something that Crawford takes her time answering.

Does it matter what they say? Charlie thinks, You bet your ass it matters. He needs to get closer.

"You know her?" Big Phil asks, unable to conceal his astonishment, putting a hold on Charlie's advance.

"She and her kid showed up at Edge's ranch," Charlie answers.

"She has a kid?"

234

It is hard to believe the tough, savvy, hardboiled looker taking a seat next to Jorge could be anybody's mother. She's a take-charge-grab-'em-by-the-balls momma. And Jorge, even with his dark Latin eyes, looks like her pigeon.

It strikes Charlie that Crawford won't have much to say to this guy. She'll want to talk with to the big boss.

Charlie reconsiders getting closer to eavesdrop. I need to follow them, he decides. Getting too close would blow my cover. If we split up, maybe Big Phil will be willing to help out. For a big man, he's extremely light on his feet. And he's smart.

Big Phil catches Charlie's eye and nods in a new direction. Luigi has arrived on the scene. He sits by himself on the deck, looking in through the window toward the table where Jorge and Crawford are seated.

'Is Luigi more involved in Al's business than he's let on?' Charlie wonders.

Three people need to be tailed. This looks like an honest-to-God, Heaven-sent lead that might end up getting Tony and Leah off the hook.

"Peggy Crawford," Leah whispers to Big Phil. "Edge's LA girlfriend... Not sure whose child..."

"No shit," Big Phil whispers back.

It occurs to Charlie, 'Dare I start to believe that Edge's murder has nothing to do with Tony and Leah? That it's really all about a high-powered drug deal gone south or an undercover operation in progress and not a crime of passion?'

"Big Phil. Leah. You up for a little detective work?" he asks.

Big Phil chuckles, a twinkle in his eye, and nods. You bet he's ready. Leah looks solemn, determined. She nods as well.

"Okay. Here's what I want you two to do..."

Charlie asks Leah if she's up to driving his car so she can follow Crawford. Leah holds out her hand for the keys to the Volvo. Big Phil agrees to tail Luigi. When Jorge exits, Charlie follows him on foot, knowing it will be easy to find a taxi if the three Colombians get into a car.

All the bases are covered. In one hour, they will exchange information by calling Charlie's answering service and leaving messages. Failing that, they'll meet at La Ginestra for an early dinner.

With supreme indifference, Jorge and his two companions join the crowd of tourists boarding the Sausalito ferry into the City. Charlie stifles a smile.

'Where's the black limo with the tinted glass? What kind of thugs are these guys anyway?'

Leah

'Damn... Not used to this car.'

As Leah pulls out into oncoming traffic, the car bucks and sputters. A car horn sounds. The car engine starts to die, then catches. A driver gives her the finger. She lurches forward into the flow of downtown Sausalito traffic.

Got to keep Peggy's Mustang in sight...

The fire-engine-red Mustang, two cars ahead of her, pulls onto Highway 101 north. Right away it pulls away from Leah. The snappy new Mustang weaves through traffic guided by the confident hand of an LA driver. Leah's not in high gear and the engine roars as she hits eight thousand RPMs. At sixty she figures how to get Charlie's car not only into fourth gear but also into overdrive and the car thanks her by settling down.

Peggy crests a hill and disappears over the top.

When Leah finally gets to the top of the hill, she sees Peggy way ahead of her in the far right hand lane.

She's going to take the San Rafael exit.

There are two possibilities, Sir Francis Drake Boulevard East going toward San Pedro Point or Second Street heading towards the Miracle Mile. Leah picks the Second Street fork.

Luck is with her. After she exits, she hits a red light. Peggy's Mustang is also waiting for the signal to change. The light turns green. Leah finds herself right behind Peggy's car. She scrunches down in the seat, hoping Peggy won't catch a glimpse of her in her rearview mirror. In convoy, they head west to San Rafael's Miracle Mile. After a mile or two, Peggy abruptly turns left into downtown San Anselmo.

Crawford parks. Leah drives past her. The rear end of Charlie's Volvo sticks out dangerously after Leah's attempt to parallel park fails. No time to straighten that up now. She yanks on the door handle. It *won't open. She gives it two hard pulls before she realizes she needs to unlock the door.*

There is no sign of Peggy.

Damn. She must have gone into a shop, she thinks.

Leah hurries up the street feeling conspicuous, exposed, while telling herself she's being ridiculous. She's just another hippie hanging out on the scene. San Anselmo is a Mecca for them.

A restaurant near Peggy's car seems like a likely destination. Leah starts to scurry across the street in the middle of the block without looking both ways. A car screeches to a halt, almost causing the car behind it to crash into it. Heads turn. People on the crowded street with marijuana-dulled eyes are slow to figure out what's going on.

She jumps back onto the curb. Someone grabs her elbow, hard. Before she can look around she receives a command from a familiar voice.

"Just act like nothing at all unusual has happened. Otherwise I'm going to have to hurt you."

She's pushed, none too gently, toward the crosswalk.

It's Red.

Red thinks he's got me where he wants me, she thinks. But he's got another think coming if I have anything to say about it.

Big Phil

Big Phil takes the direct approach. It's quite often the best. Learned that from my pappy. Cotton trader. Knows how to handle people and situations, just not me. I'm a handful, he tells himself.

"Hey, Luigi... What bought you to the Trident?"

Luigi is not easily taken by surprise. He's cool as a cucumber. A laidback chuckle erupts from his throat but his eyes twitch from side to side.

He flashes Big Phil a toothy grin. He has a mouthful of healthy white teeth.

"Big Phil, as I live and breathe. Wish I could chew the fat but I'm in a hurry."

Luigi is headed down the Trident steps toward Bridgeway. Big Phil joins him. They dodge back and forth through the ever-streaming crowd of dawdling tourists. When they get to the ferry dock, Luigi slows down.

Passengers board the ferry in small groups while the blue and white craft rocks on the calm waters of the Bay. There's not a cloud in the sky. It's another beautiful day. Not a drop of rain in sight.

A group of three men – one of them Jorge, the other two his South American minions – leisurely walk up the gangplank. Charlie is buying a ticket at the small wooden ticket booth near the gangplank.

"I dropped by Al's pad earlier. You talk to him lately?" Big Phil asks as he and Luigi watch Charlie follow Jorge and his companions onto the ferry.

"I've been working on a commercial the last few days. Anything new?"

"Looks like a dealer with some muscle plans to move in on the Marin scene. Those three Colombians getting on the ferry are part of his syndicate."

"That a fact?"

"You're also hot," says Big Phil. "Charlie – the detective who visited your house, you know, the one getting onto the ferry right behind them – he's had a tail on him for the last few days."

"That's very unfortunate."

The ferry's engine revs up as crewmembers remove the bulky ropes that secure the ferry to bollards. Jorge and his companions join other passengers on the open-air top deck to watch the procedure.

Luigi spots them. His Mediterranean face tenses, then relaxes.

"Nice seeing you, Big Phil, but I gotta run. Production meeting in the city in less than an hour."

Luigi turns to leave. But Big Phil isn't having that. He grabs Luigi and the smaller man stops dead in his tracks.

Pappy always said I had a grip of steel, Big Phil thinks.

Aloud he says with a chuckle, "You're coming with me."'

"Now why would I want to do that?" Luigi calmly replies, his jaw tightening.

"Because it's important to straighten some things out."

Luigi puts a mild, blank look on his face, but he can't hide the real Luigi Santucci from Big Phil, who feels like he's seeing him for the first time.

"You wouldn't by any chance be a silent partner in Al's operation, would you?"

"I'm in the movie business."

"Tell that to Al. That's where we're going."

"I said I had a meeting."

"Call 'em when we get to Al's. Tell them something's come up. Push back the meet."

Charlie

Charlie shrugs his backpack off and opens it. The wind whips through his hair. Tourists armed with cameras take pictures of every animate and inanimate object in sight. Seagulls call overhead, begging for easy pickings.

The ferryboat points its nose toward the rocky shores of Alcatraz. Once one of the most famous maximum-security prisons in the country, it now lies abandoned in the middle of San Francisco Bay.

Rummaging around in his backpack, he discovers the plain, unimpressive brown and white cameo brooch he found at Tony's place. He takes it out and opens it up. Inside there is a black-and-white picture of a man with a three- or four-year-old child sitting on his knee. The man is weathered and his suit is rumpled. He has a handlebar mustache. It's hard to tell if the child on his lap is a boy or a girl. Opposite the photo, engraved into the soft metal, are the words "With love, Poppa Bob 1954." The look on both of their faces is stern and drawn, possibly indicating straitened circumstances. The brooch – its weight, the picture, the very ordinariness of it, picking it up on Tony's floor – unsettles Charlie.

Why didn't I look at it sooner? What significance does it have, if any? Whose brooch is it? he wonders.

He looks up. Jorge and his companions have left the top deck.

Damn. Where are they? The ferry will be docking in less than twenty minutes.

He stuffs the brooch in his pants pocket and throws his backpack over his shoulder.

Charlie makes a pit stop. The ferry's restroom is cramped and smelly.

A gun prods into his kidneys as he exits. One of the South American minions holds the gun. He doesn't seem to be in the mood for small talk. He is, however, in the mood to take Charlie's wallet.

The three gangsters hustle Charlie into a taxi for the short ride from the Ferry Building to the Hyatt Regency Embarcadero. They ride up the interior glass elevator in silence. They enter a spacious room overlooking the bay, where Jorge peruses the contents of Charlie's wallet.

And finds his private detective license.

The three confer in Spanish. What they say is lost on Charlie. They don't bother to question him. Charlie realizes that he's just a nuisance.

One of the thugs slips a blackjack out of his pocket.

Here it comes, Charlie thinks. Are they going to terminate me? Or just knock me out?

The blackjack slaps him on the back of the head.

The blow stuns him but he stays conscious. They drag him into a corner of the room. Jorge and his companions babble on in Spanish with great animation. One of Jorge's companions seems to favor putting Charlie out of his misery. The other looks like he'd like to split... in a hurry. There's a whine in his voice.

The bedside phone rings. Jorge picks it up. His two partners in crime go silent.

"This better be good," Jorge states stridently.

Jorge's attitude undergoes an immediate change. A long silence follows while Jorge listens. He nods his head curtly twice. Whoever is on the line has Jorge's total and undivided attention. He listens until it's his turn to speak.

"I told the girl where and when you wanted to meet. I gave her a number to call if she got hung up for any reason. And we waylaid a private detective who was tailing us. You want us to handle that on our own?"

Jorge looks with malevolence at Charlie before nodding again with abrupt, military sharpness.

"Yes, sir," he acknowledges before hanging up.

Jorge says something to the compatriot who likes to hurt people. That thug looks briefly in Charlie's direction and lets loose a torrent of words in Spanish – seemingly he objects to the order he was given. Jorge slaps him across the face, hard. The whiny one clams up and shrinks back toward the door. Jorge hollers at both of them and points to the phone as he does so. That clinches it. He gets no more complaints.

The whiny one glares at Jorge. He's the kind who'd stick a knife in your ribs when you're turned the other way. The violent one kicks Charlie in the kidneys, sending stabbing pain up and down his body, then cracks him over the head with the gun for good measure. Lights out.

Leah

"You shoulda kept your nose out of this," Red informs her.

"Your babysitting job?" Leah answers.

"Jennifer isn't my job."

Jennifer's big blue eyes turn Red's way. She's eating a sundae. Vanilla ice cream and a hint of chocolate syrup run down from the edge of her mouth to the bottom of her chin. Leah's opinion of Jennifer is confirmed. She's an angel.

She wipes Jennifer's mouth, chucks her under the chin and smiles. Jennifer smiles back. Leah is charmed. She has a lovely smile.

"Jennifer. Pretty name. Like to draw?"

Leah pulls three crayons out of her leather pouch. Leah's nephews love to draw with them. Jennifer reaches out, pauses, looks at Red.

"Don't worry about him, honey," Leah confides. "Friends?" she then asks.

Red dismisses Leah and Jennifer with a grimace and a growl and takes a seat in the booth across from them.

That fucker will get his, Leah promises herself.

Jennifer puts a pudgy yet delicate finger to her cheek and cleans away some chocolate. Then she sticks her finger in her mouth. Her cherubic face is grave, solemn. After due consideration, she nods her head. Yes, she would like to be friends.

Has she ever had a friend before? Leah wonders.

"Good. Like that too," she tells Jennifer.

"What we're doing is waiting for Peggy to get out of the can," Red interrupts to inform the table at large. "When she does, we're going to leave here without any trouble. You got that?"

Leah wonders what he thinks he's going to get out of his current arrangement – power, influence, money, Peggy Crawford as his old lady?

Whatever it is, he's in deeper than he can handle, that's for sure, she thinks.

Peggy emerges from the bathroom. She's changed back into her hippie outfit. She's no longer the high-rolling LA swinger, the electrifying blond vamp. She's down-home Peggy from somewhere in the deep South. Her floppy hat makes it difficult to tell exactly what color her hair is but it's for damn certain not blond.

Is all of this changing of clothes necessary to put her in the proper mood for the job at hand? Or are the clothes just part of the sleight-of-hand? Leah mulls.

"Where did you run into her and why has she joined us?" Peggy asks, jerking a finger in Leah's direction as she takes a seat next to Red.

"I saw her tailing us so I nabbed her. What do you want me to do with her?"

"She might come in handy. We'll keep her."

"Where Southern accent?" Leah asks.

Jennifer looks up from the drawing she's creating on her place mat. Her sundae is forgotten, melting in the bowl.

Peggy doesn't bother to answer Leah. She's all business. Her eyes are hard, tough, calculating.

"Get up. We're leaving."

Leah's reaction is a silent 'Fuck you and the horse you rode in on.'

Slowly, deliberately, Leah wipes Jennifer's mouth after moistening her napkin with some ice water.

"Leave my kid alone and get up. We're leaving," Peggy barks.

'Well, a chink in her armor,' chuckles Leah mentally.

"You need any help, Peg?" Red asks.

"You've done enough already. Just pull the car around front."

Her vibes are overwhelmingly powerful. And she hasn't moved a muscle. Red folds.

Leah finds him disgusting and detects the same reaction in Peggy's demeanor.

"Give me your hand, Jennifer."

Peggy extends her hand. The misty inward smile that had taken possession of Jennifer while she was drawing disappears. Her mother is the boss, the top sergeant in little Jennifer's life, the only constant. She holds out her hand.

Leah steels herself. No way I'm going to let these people out of my sight, she decides.

Leah slides out of the booth and follows Peggy and Jennifer out of the restaurant. Jennifer still clutches Leah's three crayons in her pudgy left hand. Crawford gives them a baleful look. Leah takes the opportunity to chide Crawford.

"Won't hurt her. Might enjoy,"

Peggy stiffens, then shrugs.

"They aren't going to change what happens next, sister. Business is business," Crawford strikes back.

Leah opens the door for Crawford and Jennifer.

"What?" Leah asks.

Peggy pauses, pushes a feather mounted on her floppy hat out of her eyes, and looks at Leah with an icy stare. The force behind that look does not stoop to hate or love, but it does convey a willingness to step on you and crush you with the heel of a boot.

"We're going to take a ride together. Got it?"

"Got."

The tires hum hypnotically, taking the car through pleasant Marin suburbs. Scenes of everyday life pass by their window - the community college, Bon Air, Petrini's Plaza. They're headed back toward Highway 101.

Leah is ready to act if an opportunity comes her way.

Thank you, Grandmother, for your strength, she thinks.

Big Phil

"Luigi... I told you not to get involved."

"I got a call from our mutual friends in Chicago, Al."

"We both made our own bed. I'll sleep in mine."

"Bullshit," Luigi shoots back. "I told you it would come down to something like this one day. Stay out of it, I said. I could have gotten you a gig on my shoots as the still photographer. You could have had everything you want without this grief..."

Al's rejoinder is to lift his arm from the kitchen table and then lower it slowly back to the table.

He lives in a rundown split-level near Tam Junction. It looks like it was built to house the Cleaver family. He hasn't bothered to furnish the place, fix it up, or maintain it. Keep away the neighbors and cut down on visibility, that's Al's approach to this house and his business philosophy. Overgrown hedges and peeling paint hide lots of sins.

Al, Luigi, and Big Phil sit at a rickety kitchen table jammed into a cramped breakfast nook. Coffee is always on the stove – one of Al's concessions to domesticity.

Luigi, being his usual fastidious self, wipes the chair before he sits down. From somewhere in a back room, cool jazz blows down a hallway and filters into the room. Outside, birds are hitting a feeder that Al keeps stocked.

Big Phil is not interested in listening to bickering between two old friends at the moment. The clock is ticking here.

"This Jorge guy, you think he may have murdered Edge? Some sort of drug or territory dispute?" Big Phil asks.

"I told Big Phil about Jorge, Luigi," Al clarifies without answering Big Phil's question.

"Jorge, I was told by our mutual friends in Chicago... " Luigi replies without answering Big Phil's question either. "...is fronting for someone called Mr. Big. Our friends have had dealings with this Mr. Big in the past – and they weren't friendly ones."

"So... " Al lets that tired "so" hang.

He blows his nose and looks out the window.

Must have sinus problems above and beyond his coke habit.

When in Heaven's name is it going to rain?

Marin is as dry and hot as the inside of hell.

Luigi looks at his friend. Big Phil heard they worked together at an ad agency in Chicago and shared an apartment. It's hard to imagine it now but they must have been eager, young, making the scene – probably in smoky Beatnik bars where bands played hot jazz and Chicago blues.

"Who's the looker with the LA swagger that showed up for the meet?" Luigi asks, carefully folding the handkerchief he used to wipe down his seat and putting it back in his rear pants pocket.

"Leah told me her name is Peggy Crawford. She lived with Edge down in LA," Big Phil responds.

A lull falls in the conversation. Big Phil asks himself, Why does Al need this grief? I hear he has plenty of cash hidden away in offshore accounts. He's got a clean record. Why doesn't he just fade into the woodwork? Then he mentally answers his own question: Maybe it sounds corny, but maybe it's because Al really is a pal. He's worried about his friends, people like Miki and Peter. He wants to protect them, keep track of them for their own good.

"What else do you know about Peggy Crawford, Phil?" Al asks.

Big Phil obliges.

"She and her kid turned up at Edge's place and laid a line on Charlie and Leah. She pretended to be a dumb-ass country bumpkin. Then she skipped out on them the first chance she got. Shows up at the Trident totally transformed, looking like this cool, tough LA broad with plenty of street savvy, tons of moxie, and the curves of a starlet. Looks to me like she's planning to pick up where Edge left off. She's a player – in a big way."

"Are our Chicago friends planning to make a move on these people?" Al asks Luigi.

"They said they'd wait until I checked it out. But who knows? They're not patient and there's already bad blood."

Al nods, coughs. His head twitches.

"Will you be able to get them to hold off on the muscle?"

"Maybe..." Luigi speculates. "But your operation brings in a lot of dough and Dominic has a short fuse. You know that, Al."

"I'll call him. You guys spread the word to friends and family to keep a low profile. This could turn nasty in a hurry."

Charlie

Charlie slowly returns to consciousness. Total darkness and the smell of disinfectant surround him. He's in a closet, his backpack beside him. He pushes the door open a crack. No one is in the room. He pulls on his backpack and looks around the room. Not that there is much to observe. There are no suitcases. No shaving kits. No clothes in the closet. No one's slept in the bed or used the bathroom. Not even lint on the carpet.

He wants to turn his predicament into a lead. Leah and Tony's freedom might depend on it. What to do?

The doorknob turns. He slips out through a sliding glass door onto the narrow concrete balcony.

Looking down, it's a long way to the ground. Looking up, this room is close to the top floor. Great. Charlie does not like heights.

Calculating his chances, Charlie vaults over the metal railing and lowers himself until he's hanging from the edge of the balcony by his hands.

Someone steps out onto the balcony. No time to waste. Charlie swings out and in, then drops onto the concrete floor of the balcony of the room below. His head bangs into the sliding glass door.

From above, a head appears. It's the goon with the killer instinct. His head snaps back after he makes eye contact with Charlie. Charlie yanks the sliding glass door handle. It's locked.

"Shit."

Making it around the dividing wall to the next balcony requires everything Charlie is in short supply of at the moment - coordination, timing, strength, and concentration. The wind picks up. The entire hotel seems to sway.

No panic attacks now. Not allowed. Just don't look down, whatever you do, he tells himself.

There's just enough clearance to jump onto the adjoining balcony.

Thank god, this sliding glass door is open.

Inside, a couple is making passionate love. Charlie bolts for the hall door. Two heads jerk up, startled.

"What the hell?" the man blurts.

"Ed," the woman shouts pulling the covers up to hide her chest as she struggles to sit up.

"Carry on, Ed," Charlie suggests over his shoulder without pausing.

He's out the door and into the hallway before either of the lovers manage to get out of the bed.

Will they go back to their recreational activity or call security?

With my luck, well, let's not speculate, just run like hell, he thinks.

The stairway door slams open. Jorge and his compatriots, guns in hand, burst into the hallway. Charlie sprints toward a stairway exit at the other end of the hall, his former captors in hot pursuit.

246

No room for trickery here, just a test of stamina and speed. Charlie pours it on. Soon he's three floors ahead of his pursuers but out of breath. An adrenaline jolt will do that for you.

There's still the problem of getting away clean.

The lobby's safe, crowded with conventioneers. They're wearing funny hats and have on badges.

The Lions... The Elks... The Masons... Who knows? Charlie sees safety in numbers. He wiggles in among them. They chat as they move toward an inner room where they sit down for a seminar on how to be successful under-assistant West Coast movers and shakers.

Charlie's pursuers appear. Almost immediately they spot him. They dance at the edge of the group, trying to isolate Charlie from the crush. As Charlie and the conventioneers enter the seminar room, the thugs holster their weapons and lean against a pillar near the door.

Jorge nods for his compatriots to cover the exits.

What's next? Charlie asks himself. Looks like the secret pledge of the organization, followed by an afternoon nap brought on by the drone from a long list of speakers and the rubber chicken, just consumed at lunch, that needs digesting.

"Mr. Cutler will now present the Lions Club International's strategic plan for 1972. Mr. Cutler."

The room breaks out in polite applause as Mr. Cutler steps to the podium. He adjusts the microphone and taps it once, causing ear-splitting feedback. He looks with uncertainty around the room.

"Can you hear me all right?"

A deafening silence greets his question. His armpits are wet. He clears his throat, takes a sip of water and adjusts his pants. His jockeys are probably bunched up. He looks like he could use some air.

"If someone would turn down the house lights..."

Miraculously, the lights go down.

Jorge, trying to blend in with the crowd in the back of the room, looks around. Charlie crouches low and heads toward a rear exit, ignoring the protests of the groggy conventioneers he bumps into.

Now is not the time for niceties. Just get away.

He opens the door a crack. One of Jorge's compatriots is standing nearby. He's momentarily distracted by a waitress who's hustling down the hall with a tray of food held high above her. Her hips move invitingly.

My, oh my...

Charlie slams the door into the distracted goon, knocking him to the floor, then bolts across the hallway to another exit door. He's in a series of corridors and passages designed for the help to use so they can move unobtrusively throughout the building.

He rushes down a set of concrete steps lined with metal railings, looking for a way out of the building. Bare overhead bulbs, some burned out, provide the only illumination. Inky shadows interrupted by patches of light lead Charlie along.

A door slams open above. Distorted sounds bounce and echo off the cinderblock walls as several pairs of shoes scuffle down some stairs.

A collection of trashcans beside a battered green door jumps into view. Through the door is an empty loading dock and freedom.

The outside world.

Hallelujah.

Charlie circles back around to the hotel lobby.

Time to turn the tables on these bozos. I'm calling in the cavalry, he tells himself. He finds a pay phone and dials a familiar number.

"Coop. I'm in a tight fix over at the Hyatt Regency Embarcadero and need wheels right away. Can you have someone meet me at the front entrance ASAP?"

"You got it."

Leah

"I want Edge's journal. I want it fast. I want it now."

Peggy Crawford paces, hatless, her auburn hair flying loose. Jennifer has disappeared into a corner of the room. Red sits impassively in front of the only table in the ramshackle houseboat. If they bothered to look out through sliding glass doors, Peggy, Leah, and Red could see Richardson Bay from the cheap seats at Gate Five, Sausalito. They are distracted by the drama taking place inside. Leah looks innocently at Peggy.

"Journal?"

Peggy hauls off and slaps Leah as hard as she can. Leah stumbles backward, crashes into the wall, and lands hard on her fanny. Her throbbing cheek reminds her of another slap in another situation. Did Peggy get slapped around by Edge too? Leah wonders. What did she get out of the experience, her charming disposition?

It taught Leah you have to stand up to violence, even if it means death.

"I don't have time to waste on this kind of crap," Peggy almost whispers getting in Leah's face. "I'll feed you to Red...You don't want to know what he'll do. Believe me."

"Got nothing," Leah replies.

"Your messed-up way of telling me you never saw Edge writing in a bound notebook, not even once? He was so secretive and all-powerful that he pulled the wool over your sweet, innocent eyes? Is that your story?"

Peggy laughs, shrugs, sighs, carries on, replaying past scenes which took place in Edge's Topanga Canyon pad in her mind.

"Huh. He was bright some ways, not so bright in others, particularly where women are concerned. I know. I lived with him, too. Remember? Now give. Where's Edge's journal?"

Leah decides to try a different tactic.

"What for me?"

Peggy raises her hand and takes a threatening step toward Leah. Leah braces herself but holds her ground. Then Peggy chortles.

"The real Leah emerges. Is that it? What about your life – is that inducement enough?"

Before Leah can answer, the phone rings. Peggy jerks it from its cradle.

"Yes."

In seconds, Peggy's expression transforms itself from anger to cool calculation, from fiery hellion to power-hungry LA goddess on the make. She listens attentively without interrupting.

"I told your messenger that I keep my promises. I'll deliver. Don't let some two-bit detective playing hero change your mind. Just ease him out – one way or the other."

She listens again, this time for a shorter length of time.

"Okay. But I'd like to be there when you do it. Afterward, what say we close this deal?"

She snaps her fingers at Red. She needs pencil and paper to write down an address, make a note or two. Afterward, she hangs up the phone.

"What's up?" Red asks.

Peggy gazes unseeing at Richardson Bay. Sailboats and pleasure craft are enjoying the late-afternoon wind. The back side of Treasure Island seems incredibly close. Water laps against the edges of the houseboat, rocking it gently back and forth. The tide is in. The mudflats are not exposed. It's another sunny day in a fool's paradise.

And it's hot and dry – way too dry.

"Got no time to help you remember right now, sweetie pie... But don't you worry. I won't forget you," Peggy snarls, looking down at Leah.

She turns to Red.

"Watch her until I get back from this meeting. Oh, and she better be in one piece, totally intact, when I do get back. Got it?"

"When will..." Red starts.

Peggy slams the door to the bedroom shut, creating a vacuum of disturbed silence. Minutes later she sashays past them, transformed once again into the blond bombshell, and heads out the sliding glass door.

Jennifer watches her mother leave, her finger in her mouth.

Charlie

A gun pokes Charlie's rib cage.

Charlie is caught again.

This time Jorge and his goons stuff Charlie on the floor in the backseat of a Lincoln Continental. The gun is now casually pressed into his temple. He cools it, gun bouncing off his head with every bump. The streets of San Francisco are full of bumps.

The car has moved away from the hotel and the waterfront. It twists and turns, starts and stops innumerable times as it makes its way through city streets.

The roar of heavy traffic recedes. The sound of cable cars fades away. Wind, the distant thunder of waves crashing against a rocky shoreline, the call of sea lions and gulls, children playing in a school yard, a church bell ringing in the distance – they're passing through outer neighborhoods.

No one in the car speaks. The radio is off. These men are serious about their work.

Hope, fear, despair, joy fly away and sit on the shoulder of God as Charlie reflects.

I'm in the fickle hands of Fate, Karma's twin. The veil of Maya, God's sport, is playing rough today.

Tony

Tony wakes in the open field above the San Quentin house. It's night. Bright moonlight bathes the hillside.

The awakening is unpleasant, even horrifying. He suffers multiple seizures. He throws up on himself. For a long moment he thinks he will drown in his own puke but he manages to roll onto his side.

Clutching his arms across his chest, he shivers and shakes. His mouth is dry, parched.

In the distance, the Richmond-San Rafael Bridge glows. Its wavy reflection can be seen in the waters of upper San Francisco Bay. The back of Tiburon and the refineries in Richmond, in opposite directions across the Bay, are inky shadows in the infinite depths of night.

Tony, unable to control his body, weak and delirious, messes his pants. He has another seizure. He shivers and shakes.

Blank... Void...

In hallucinatory flashes of unsettled consciousness, Tony sees.

Bloody knife... Edge... Pool of blood....

Unconscious... Blank...

Unsteady, he struggles to his feet and stumbles through the gate in the fence that encloses the grassy hillside. He makes his awkward way downhill.

He approaches the house by way of the small back porch and enters through the back door. Passing the bathroom, he staggers, almost falling, as consciousness begins to slip away once again. His hand reaches out and grabs the kitchen table. It steadies him. The moonlight shines into shadows of the kitchen and lights the room in which he slept as well as the room Leah used as a studio.

Nothing... Empty... Void...

He sticks his head under the kitchen faucet and rinses the vomit from his mouth. Then he starts to gulp down life-giving water. He puts his head under the cold water coming from the tap. He changes into clean clothes, throwing the dirty ones in the kitchen trashcan.

Flickering back and forth like the stroboscopic light the lightshow members, including himself, used back in the day, his mind, his being, knows not what and where he is. Yet he continues animate and upright.

He finds his backpack and thrusts into it a change of underwear, a shirt, a pair of pants, and socks. From the kitchen he takes some staples, beef jerky, a can of peaches, snow peas, graham crackers, saltines, sardines in oil. He fills his canteen with water.

His mind still in chaos, belching and feeling nauseated, he stumbles, a ludicrous charade of his normal gait, patches of moon light further destabilizing the room. Hefting his backpack on takes time. His still camera and 16mm camera are still strapped around his neck. They make it even harder to put on the backpack. Before leaving the house, he picks up a bag that contains his most precious possessions, his slide collection and his rolls of exposed 16mm film.

At long last, slow and fumbling, in and out of this world, he stops at the turnout. There, he opens the trunk of his slant-six blue Plymouth Duster and struggles to take off the cameras. The straps are a tangled mess. The backpack fights with him. His mind is lost in the Void.

But he revives and puts the backpack, the two cameras and the bag with his treasure trove in the trunk of the car. He looks with grave, disoriented suspicion up and down the deserted street. The nearest streetlight is dark. A cat scurries across the lonely road. Tony reacts with a shocked jerk of his head. He shivers and shakes but does not have another seizure. He is sweating profusely; the damp cold of the night is unsettling. He did not bring with him a blanket or a jacket. He tenderly wraps his cameras and the bag containing his treasure trove in a tarpaulin he keeps in his trunk. Then he takes a tin of sardines and a can of peaches from his backpack.

The moonlight illuminates the small cove and the sandy beach reached by going down an embankment at the edge of the turnout. A lone tree on a point at the far end of the cove is highlighted by moonshine, an inky presence. San Quentin Prison, brightly illuminated, is visible off the shoulder of the point.

The wind whispers, mysterious and ominous. Tony shakes his head. On, blink, off, blink, here, blink, there, blink. He is still standing.

With his first tentative steps on the path leading down to the beach, he is deceived, seeing creatures known and unknown obstructing his progress. He stumbles and falls, clutching the can of peaches and the tin of sardines. He is winded, weary, frightened. He passes out again. He is alone. When he rouses himself, he is lying on his back at the edge of the sandy, unappealing beach. He seeks shelter in a clump of bushes as the sun begins to rise over the East Bay.

Blackness... Blank... Void...

Miki

Those who have places to go are taking a trip. Those who are left behind go into hiding. The word is out on the streets. The authorities are busting people. The Mafia is moving in, taking over the drug scene. They want to control the action, make a profit from the community's alternative lifestyles.

There's more.

It's said that the authorities are in league with the Mafia. Thugs with shifty eyes and deceptive smiles will turn the beautiful people into creatures that do their bidding. Pods will be attached to the backs of the necks of the whole of Marin. The living dead will rule in Paradise.

So say the doomsday soothsayers.

They go on.

Kangaroo courts will process offenders. Those who resist will be sent to work farms, forced-labor camps where overseers will rule with fists, whips and guns. Marijuana fields planted without the okay of the mob will be sprayed with Paraquat. Cocaine not sanctioned will be impounded by the authorities in league with the mob. Heroin, getting a fix, will become the preoccupation of pleasure seekers. Hipsters will be stooges, junkie snitches, for the syndicate.

This is laidback Marin? Miki wonders. This is a place where the rules that dominate the rest of the world are irrelevant?

First things first, she tells herself.

"Family" members, it's time for you to fade into the woodwork.

Al, take a much-needed vacation.

Leah, get your act together, girl. You're hip deep in danger.

Tony, come out of hiding and face the music. We'll stand by you.

Charlie, may G-d guide you toward some answers. We need them.

Peter, you damn well better take care of yourself. I'll kill anybody who disturbs a hair on your beautiful head.

Miki and Ida are just leaving the no name bar in Sausalito as Al enters.

Miki grabs him by the arm.

"What are you doing here?" Ida asks.

"When was the last time you two dropped into this place?" Al responds, shaking his head and letting loose with his trademark nasal laugh.

He has a coughing fit. Al always does when he laughs too hard.

KJAZ plays on the radio. Regulars, remnants of the Beat generation, sit on wooden benches attached to the wall playing chess, sipping drinks and smoking pipes.

Miki asks Al, "Did Charlie run into you at the Front and give you the news?"

Al nods. He answers, "Looks like the scene is about to go through some heavy changes."

"We're looking for Herman so we can warn him. You seen him?" Ida asks.

Al shakes his head.

Is he answering Ida's question or rocking his head in time to the beat of the jazz tune on the radio? That swinging head movement has become habitual with him. He smothers another cough. Miki has the same thought she's had way too many times: I'm worried about Al's health. He won't listen, just laughs and smiles.

Al asks, "I'm looking for Luigi. He here?"

Miki and Ida shake their heads. Al sighs, shrugs, and pulls a cigarette out of his pocket. He lights it.

"What about Gab, you seen him? Ida asks plaintively.

"You lose your husband again, Ida?"

Ida blushes like a schoolgirl.

"What are you going to do, Al?" Miki asks.

Al shrugs, blows out a cloud of smoke, coughs.

"Normally, I'd just close up shop until the bad vibes blow over. But this isn't your usual storm. This is a killer tsunami."

"What's the story?"

"There's bad blood between my backers and new players on the scene."

"Maybe you could set up a meet, kinda cool it out or something."

256

"Nay. And, by the way, stay clear of Gate Five. A houseboat flying a God's-eye flag is one of their drops. Tell Herman too when you find him."

Miki grabs Al and gives him a hug. He needs mothering just like everybody else. Al hugs back, tight.

"You take care, now."

"You too," he mumbles, his head bobbing up and down, his feet already heading out the door.

Detective Cooper

The police radio crackles on.

"Lt. Cooper? No sign of Carter out front of the Hyatt. What should we do? Over."

"Park and take a look around inside. I'll put out an apprehend and notify dispatch on the scanner for him."

Cooper sighs. What the hell has Carter gotten himself into this time? Thank goodness it's not my case.

Check that.

It might become Lt. Cooper's case if some of the action moves into his territory, assuming the brass are willing to commit to it. Last time Carter got into hot water, there was a whole lot of foot dragging, lots of phone calls behind closed doors, orders from on high to keep him handcuffed, and, to top it all off, the Feds busted into the act and made off with all their meager evidence, the sum total of the SFPD's imposed-from-on-high-less-than-diligent work. Coop didn't like it, not one bit. Mercifully, coverage of the case melted away and so did the case. Cooper has other more personal and immediate thoughts.

"Oh boy. I was planning to take Helen out to dinner tonight. That might have to be put on hold. Should I alert Whelan? If I did, what would I alert him to?"

Lt. Cooper is certain Whelan wouldn't take kindly to the fact that a pain-in-the-ass PI, Charlie Foxhawk Carter, has been calling him and pumping him for information about a certain murder investigation taking place in Whelan's territory.

I'm Luigi

"Al's too easygoing, Luigi, and you know it. We're gonna have to fix things."

Luigi is looking out at the Pacific Ocean while talking on an outdoor pay phone at Muir Beach. His house is hot. Plainclothes cops are parked out in front. The sun is setting and the temperature is right around seventy degrees.

Dominic, his childhood friend on the other end of the line, will be looking out over Lake Michigan where the sun has already set. Luigi imagines there's a cold wind off the lake and snow is most likely in the forecast.

"Marin isn't Chicago, Dom. No muscle. Please."

Luigi zips up his windbreaker to ward off the approaching darkness.

"You've gotten soft, Luigi. Didn't the old neighborhood teach you anything about control and how to keep it? By the way, you should call your mother. She complains about never hearing from you."

"What about you, you old palooka? All you do is sit in a leather chair and smoke cigars."

"Don't smart-mouth me, kid. I got friends in high places."

"Says you..."

They both laugh bitterly at their respective acts. They're too real. Old times. That's about all that can make them smile anymore.

"So when are you coming to your senses and moving back to the Windy City?"

"Why, so I can become a bum like you?"

"Hey."

Dominic is Luigi's best friend from childhood, the one who stuck up for him when the chips were down, and he's far away, in another world.

Looks like that world is about to collide with laid-back Marin.

"Look, Luigi, this thing with Al has been a headache right from the start. We both know that. But – and this is the important thing – it has turned out to be a very profitable venture. We depend on that revenue. And we aim to protect our investment, do whatever it takes to keep it safe and secure. Capisce?"

"Al's gonna holler."

"I'll straighten him out. You cool him out from your end. End of story."

"He doesn't want to hear that from me."

"You tell him we're saving his ass. This syndicate's trying to push in on our action. They ain't choir boys like our mothers wanted us to be."

"Let me tell him about the muscle before you let 'em loose."

"Too late. They're already on their way to Frisco and you're their contact."

"They'll stand out like a sore thumb, particularly on the scene where Al does business."

"Can't be helped. You talk to Al, pronto. Line up a car, two clean pieces, and be ready to prep these guys. Help them get in and out without a hitch. Okay?"

Better me than someone else, I suppose, Luigi thinks bitterly, even as he predicts disaster. Nobody else is listening.

Charlie

Charlie's now sitting up in the back seat of the car, a gun pressed into his ribs, looking out at a breathtakingly disturbing day. Gigantic, billowing clouds, dark and angry, rush across a windy sky. Moses climbed Mt. Sinai to receive the Ten Commandments on a day like this. The end of days prophesied in Revelations will be heralded with skies like this.

Ahead, an oversized, modernistic house beckons. It stands on well over five acres of carefully landscaped grounds overlooking San Francisco from just below the final approach to Twin Peaks

Charlie chuckles to himself. "Looks like it's about to become my house of horrors. The location of my final solution." He's a fan of dark humor, to the very end.

The black Lincoln Continental passes through an impressive wrought-iron gate sporting its own guardhouse and follows the main road within the compound. Numerous outbuildings dot the landscape: a carriage house for the live-in help and security, the guardhouse, several gardening sheds, and a building whose purpose is not clearly defined near a steep drop-off at the lower edge of the property.

He's dragged out of the car. His ankles smash into each granite step leading to the front door. Inside, floor-to-ceiling windows draw guests' attention toward a massive deck that has an award-winning view.

The humble abode of Mr. Big, I presume, he thinks.

The three South American thugs walk in lock step. Two are dragging Charlie. Jorge walks in front. There's no time to appreciate the interior, with its marble walls and columns set in open airy space; the deep, plush Oriental carpets on sparkling parquet floors; the tasteful arrangement of museum-quality pieces ranging from artfully constructed furnishings to Picassos on the wall illuminated by indirect lighting.

"Make mine Ripple with a twist," Charlie mutters as he's unceremoniously dumped in a study just off the gargantuan front room.

One of the goons, the one with the killer look, pulls the sap out of his pocket and wags it in Charlie's direction. That tames him.

Oh, yeah.

The study reminds Charlie of a movie set, a bad movie that gets no box office. There's an impressive cherrywood desk and a large globe on a stand. An ancient manuscript protected by a sealed case is on display. A spotlight mounted on the ceiling illuminates it. The walls are lined with books. Ladders that slide on tracks mounted in the ceiling allow access to the topmost bookshelves, which are nearly hidden by lengthening shadows.

There's a media center, a nod to the modern age, filled with television monitors and various pieces of electronic gear, in a setback near an arched window that looks out over a formal garden. The paneling and its detailing are worthy of closer examination.

"Too bad I haven't got the time," he thinks. "I'll have to come earlier in future when I won't have to rush through the experience."

What Charlie sees most intimately is the thick Oriental carpet. It's old, massive, and smells faintly of camel dung. He struggles unsuccessfully to get into a sitting position. One of the Colombians thoughtfully puts his foot into the small of Charlie's back.

"I've always wondered whether it's really worth the money to visit a chiropractor. If I survive this, maybe I'll find out," he says aloud. He gets no reaction.

An oversized dark-wood door swings open noiselessly. The elegant, tasseled shoes of an elderly man appear at Charlie's eye level. Mr. Big smiles with benevolent ferocity down at him.

"I didn't ask you to bring Mr. Carter here in this manner. Please, help him up."

He turns his back while his underlings, with very little goodwill, toss Charlie into a black leather, high-backed armchair. These goons don't like being scolded by the boss, particularly in front of Charlie. Mr. Big turns around.

"Brandy?" he asks pleasantly. "The Calvados is quite satisfactory. In fact, I think I'll have a glass myself."

He snaps his fingers.

"If you wanted to talk... I'd..."

Mr. Big holds up his hand. Two glasses of brandy magically appear – one for Charlie's hand, the other for Mr. Big, who raises his glass.

"To reliable information," he states, before downing his drink and putting the empty glass on the edge of a nearby desk.

Charlie prefers to sip his drink.

"I'm not much of a brandy drinker. But I gotta hand it to you, this brandy tastes smooth and mild, even to my uneducated palate."

Before Charlie can get any further, Mr. Big again holds up his hand.

"As a courtesy to your father, Mr. Carter, I have had you brought here alive so I can tell you in person that you are sticking your nose in where it does not belong. In this case, that could mean getting yourself hurt. Badly. I would regret this because of my aforementioned regard for your father. Be that as it may, my associates, in case you haven't noticed, have very barbaric methods for handling a nuisance."

Mr. Big looks at Charlie, smiles pleasantly, then smirks.

Charlie is dumbfounded.

"My father? How?"

"Does that upset you, Mr. Carter? Have I been too brash, too crass, for your refined taste?"

Charlie flinches. He wonders, Will he offer me a Havana cigar or a last meal? Will my father walk into the room as a surprise guest on my "This is Your Life" get-ready-to-die program? Or will Mr. Big call him on the gold-plated phone next to his arm?

Mr. Big returns to his monologue, or is it a soliloquy?

"Your well-intended investigation," Mr. Big continues, "will force me to do something repugnant to my nature. By the way, what have you uncovered so far, hmmm?"

Might as well answer what is probably a rhetorical question. Who could it hurt but me, Charlie asks himself before answering Mr. Big.

"It looks like the murder of John Wentworth Rutherford, a.k.a. Edge, had something to do with a big-time drug deal of some sort, a drug deal that is likely to be tied in with federal agencies and international political intrigue. It's hard for me to imagine Edge, ah, Mr. Rutherford, as a serious player in such a deal, so I'm assuming he managed to put himself in harm's way much as I have done, by accident or stupidity.

"Or, possibly, his father too had the pleasure of your acquaintance. Whatever the case, Mr. Rutherford was eliminated for his trouble. My problem is, this messy and unfortunate termination took place in the home of my friend Tony Vitolinich. He and his girlfriend, Leah Travail, are on the hook for this puzzling murder."

"Please. Do continue."

"I liked the murder weapon, a knife. It takes you back to prison movies."

Charlie looks inquiringly at Mr. Big. Is he a big movie fan? Evidently not.

Charlie plunges ahead.

"The cops are looking for Tony, ah, Mr. Vitolinich, and they're asking a whole lot of questions that are embarrassing other friends of mine and, I presume, questions that could upset the sedate quiet of your retreat."

Charlie's hand is in the pocket where he stashed the brooch. Peggy Crawford and Red flash through his mind.

"Should I include them in my recap to Mr. Big? Nay. Let him wonder," Charlie decides.

Mr. Big smirks, then lights a cigar before bothering to reply.

"Full of spirit – very good. You'll go far – in gangster movies filled with pretty boys and unconvincing heavies. On the other hand, this is real life. Yes, real life."

He allows that thought to settle in. Charlie takes another, a longer, sip of the brandy.

It's good, just like Mr. Big said it was.

The old man is winding himself up by strutting back and forth across the room.

"I like your sensitivity and your loyalty, Mr. Carter. Very commendable. But again, this path will lead toward more painful experiences."

He pauses in his stroll and looks Charlie's way.

"Now, I'm going to let you in on a little secret. This unfortunate murder had nothing whatsoever to do with the business dealings to which you allude. I should know."

He points at Charlie for dramatic effect and raises his voice just enough as he says, "No. It was a crime of passion. Your friend lost his composure, something I'm sure you would never do, and took the life of John Rutherford, a.k.a. Edge. Most unfortunate. And I have the sheriff and his department backing me up in my position."

He puts his hand to his chin and seems to reflect on what he has just revealed before concluding, "I advise you to stop what you are doing and remove yourself from the scene. Take a vacation. Visit family and friends back in Virginia, the home of presidents and the first permanent English settlement. Perhaps relocating to your homeland might be in order, hmm? A change of scenery is often beneficial. You could carry my best wishes with you for your father."

"Can't do that, Mr. - what did you say your name was?"

"That is not important."

Mr. Big snaps his fingers once again. From behind and to the side of his chair, arms reach out and take hold of Charlie. His sleeve is pushed up. A needle appears out of nowhere. Its contents are injected into Charlie's arm.

"Sweet dreams, Mr. Carter. I leave you in the very capable hands of these professionals."

The room goes fuzzy and vague. A drug-induced delirium spreads rapidly throughout Charlie's body and draws him down a velvet-lined tunnel toward an unknowable destination.

As Mr. Big's image vaporizes, the smell of perfume assails his nostrils.

Charlie's thoughts become disjointed: Is Peggy Crawford in the room? Is she a gangster's moll? Did that old dog, Mr. Big, back her in a porn flick? Will Peggy ask me to come up and see her sometime? Will I say, haven't we met somewhere under more pleasant circumstances? Care to look at my etchings?

Oh, sweet mystery of life, I've found you.

Leah

He's coming toward me. I'm ready.

"Admit it. You wanted it. But you couldn't let yourself enjoy it then. Relax, I ain't no drug-crazed madman who can't get it up."

Red unzips his pants. His schlong leaps out of his opened fly. With all the force Leah has in her body, she kicks him in his privates.

"Umph," Red groans, grabbing his crotch.

Leah moves in for the kill. Her hand finds a brass lamp. She raises it over her head, then, furiously swinging it, smashes it into Red's head.

"You wanted it? You got it.

"Up yours. "

Charlie

Charlie realizes that his mouth is flapping. He's talking. Good God, he's talking. Can't stop himself.

"What do I know about Edge? Drug dealer. Likes to beat up on women, particularly girlfriends. Can't figure out who killed him. Might be drug-related. Might be mixed up with Office business. Makes sense. Some sort of big deal gone sour in the crazy world of international intrigue. Good theory. Take the pressure off Tony and Leah."

Jorge, Charlie's interrogator, has a smooth Latin voice. His English is excellent. Probably grew up in LA. "This drug deal, who're the players?" he asks.

"Where's Peggy Crawford?" Charlie slurs in reply.

He can still smell her perfume.

Another needle goes into his arm.

Another chemical rush.

He feels cold, sweaty.

His body trembles.

He descends into a nightmare, a hallucination, in which he is kissing the red-haired woman, now covered in shadows.

Don't swallow my eyes. Don't swallow me, he mentally pleads.

She knows who he is. Knows all. Knows the deepest, darkest secrets that he hides, that his family hides, that placid society hides.

Her eyes are green. No, they're black, a maelstrom ready to suck him downward out of existence. She is real – in the room. He knows it.

"Peggy Crawford is a henna-haired Delphic oracle," Charlie speculates to himself. "She's the one.

"Oracles don't do the dirty work of unworthy leaders. That would be the end of all hope, the suspension of all dreams as we know them.

"Warn them. Warn them all."

He wants to shout, and does.

Who is that groaning? Is that me?

"This drug deal. Who are the players?" comes the voice again.

"B...B...Blood...truth."

"You've given him too much, you fool. Ease him back a little."

Peggy Crawford

Mr. Big sits next to a blazing fire wearing a quilted smoking jacket. His pale skin seems to have turned blue. Old age must be playing tricks with his circulation. The room is overheated and stuffy but it looks like he's freezing. That doesn't stop him from making predictable, condescending conversation.

"If you can produce a substantial quantity of each of the drugs specified in this list by the end of the week, we have ourselves a deal. If not, you're out."

"Christ," she asks herself, "How many times must I be forced to curry favor from men like this? At least I don't have to bury my face in his lap. That time is past."

Crawford has already been informed by Mr. Big that she should be proud. Supplying him with plenty of Edge's specialty products is her way of doing good for her country and showing good faith to Mr. Big's organization. Crawford has no idea what he's talking about. And she doesn't care – about her country or Mr. Big.

The formulas for those specialty products are in Edge's journal, the journal she is still seeking. Along with cocaine and heroin supplied by Mr. Big, the designer drugs will complete the inventory of the West Coast arm of Mr. Big's worldwide organization. Crawford will, she has been promised, run the day-to-day operations of this arm if she delivers.

Worth whatever it takes to cement this deal? You bet your ass it is. But that one-week time limit is a killer, she worries.

Perfect. Now he's looking at me. Fine. That's what I'm dressed for – to be looked at, to be gawked at - by pigs. Look at my hips gyrate. Imagine what it would be like to fondle my breast. I'll cut off your balls if you try. Meantime, let's see what we can get out of you.

She stops in front of him and leans forward. Her tits strain at the tight leash of her dress. Mr. Big coughs some phlegm into a handkerchief.

"I can deliver, but I need three weeks," Crawford answers in her honey-toned voice, soothing and in total command. "Edge let our supply dwindle. He was half crazed in the past few months, harder and harder to control. You'll supply the coke as agreed?"

"I'm old-fashioned enough to believe that young women deserve added courtesy," Mr. Big, the old geezer, replies, trying to match Crawford's oily delivery but failing miserably. "Even when it goes against my better business judgment," he adds.

He clears his throat before concluding.

"So – two weeks to deliver the required goods on your end and we have a deal. Our connections for cocaine will, of course, be alerted to your needs."

She takes his palsied hand in hers. Their eyes meet.

"What the hell," she thinks, "might as well get something on account."

Aloud she asks, "That truth serum, mind if I take a few doses with me? I have a problem it just might solve."

"Of course, my dear. Nothing would give me greater pleasure."

His trembling hand starts to grope in her direction. Crawford smiles and pats his cheek.

"A cup of nice warm tea and a biscuit before you go?" he inquires, looking pointedly at her breasts.

Well, in all fairness, how could he avoid them? She's practically poking him in the face with them.

"That's very kind of you but business calls. Shall we schedule it for – two and a half weeks from now?"

"Quite... Quite," the old fart answers.

On her way out, she can barely maintain her placid exterior. "Quite," bite my ass, she thinks. "When will I no longer need to kowtow to venal old men, men who want nothing more than to touch, to fondle, to hurt, to probe, to disrobe, to humiliate and dishonor? Bastards – fuck you. Fuck your painful, penetrating protection.

I can take care of myself, thank you very much. I don't need your help and I don't want it.

Well, after I close this deal, that is, she admits to herself with a chuckle.

Charlie

"What should we do with him, boss?"

"What do you suggest?"

"Head on a post therapy?" Jorge answers with a jovial grin.

"Very creative, Jorge... And may I suggest we observe what happens when we inject our naughty patient repeatedly with that concoction?"

Mr. Big smiles at his henchman. Jorge is a favorite. They're two peas in a pod.

Charlie smiles and nods in agreement.

It is wonderful that life brought them together, isn't it? Charlie chuckles contentedly to himself.

"You got it, boss. Head on a post. Repeatedly..."

Jorge rubs his hands together in a whistle-while-you-work manner. Mr. Big smiles benevolently.

Does Mr. Big even know he's smiling? Charlie from somewhere unknown vaguely speculates. Would I be smiling at Jorge knowing that one day, maybe sooner rather than later, I'd have to dispose of him... or else?

Charlie looks down at his comatose body from somewhere far above. The Void, the space between lives, beckons.

Peggy Crawford

Creating an explosion of wind and noise, a helicopter touches down at the heliport wedged in between mudflats and marsh. Passengers, eager to make a connection at the San Francisco airport, head toward the chopper. The last rays of sunlight are disappearing from the white sides of pleasure craft struggling to combat ever-increasing winds on Richardson Bay. Ominous clouds are rapidly filling the darkening sky. In the wavering half-light, Belvedere and Angel Island beyond are distorted, thrown out of focus.

Magical Marin does not slumber when the sun sets. Hipsters and born-again entrepreneurial flower children finishing their day's work are readying to dash to pleasure troughs. According to their predilections they will scatter – to bars, restaurants, psychedelic havens, to uppers and downers and out-of-body experiences that soothe and stimulate their pleasure-seeking hearts.

In this fool's paradise, a pragmatic outsider, Peggy Crawford, is seeking to profit from these dreams and fantasies, a modern-day carpetbagger on a happening scene.

She slides open the door of her rental houseboat on the outskirts of Sausalito.

"What the hell's going on here?"

Leah is out cold on the sofa. Her panties and her jeans are shoved down to her knees. Red is unbuttoning his pants, schlong at attention, readying to rape her.

"I told you to watch her, not screw her. Where's Jennifer?"

Red does not respond to Crawford.

"I asked you a question," she repeats.

Red shakes his head and his smile broadens. Leah groans, then spits.

"Give the little bitch a double dose of this," she commands Red.

She tosses the serum she got from Mr. Big to Red. He has to let go of his pants to catch the vial. They fall down to just above his knees.

"Do your own dirty work," he says.

Red has only one thing on his mind.

Peggy, ever the pragmatist, replies, "After we're through, you can have her."

Red chuckles and steps out of his pants. He loads the syringe with serum and jabs it into Leah's arm.

He's history when this deal closes, Peggy promises herself.

Leah's not new to chemical torture; Edge saw to that. Her irises grow large as the yellowish liquid squirts into her veins.

"Real spunky... Perfect for pulling a train – after I'm through with her," Red observes with pleasure.

He pats Leah's ass.

Tears of frustration and anger overtake Leah. No matter how hard she tries, she's unable to strike back.

"Down to business," Crawford says. She turns on a gooseneck lamp and adjusts it to shine into Leah's eyes.

"Tell me, where is Edge's journal?" Crawford asks as tonelessly as possible.

Leah moans.

In a surprisingly short period of time, her mouth begins to flap, just like Charlie's did. She tells all.

Jennifer and I are well on our way to being free of others, free to do whatever we want, Crawford announces to herself with pleasure and a sense of achievement.

I'm Jennifer

Red hurt Leah. Now Mommy is hurting Leah.

Why?

When Uncle Edge hurt Mommy, Mommy said he was wrong to do what he did, that he had no right to hit her and he should be punished. Mommy said she would find a way to do that. But Mommy never did tell me just how or when she would get back at Uncle Edge.

Now Red has hurt Leah and Mommy not only didn't help, she's hurting Leah too.

Is Mommy wrong? Should she be punished? Will she punish me for liking Leah?

Run. Run. Run away and hide. Get away.

It's easy for Jennifer to slip out of the houseboat undetected and scamper down the walkway while Red and Crawford focus on their own agenda.

Her tummy hurts. Her heart is pounding. Her mouth aches. She can't swallow. She's cold. Her nightgown is thin.

Jennifer shivers in the growing wind, retreats further into a space only little people would notice.

Dirty...Smelly...Ugh... Shaky dirty wooden walkway...

Uncle Edge locked Mommy and me in a closet. It was dark. I was so afraid. Mommy held me close and I stopped crying. There's no one to hold me now.

Red hurt Leah. Mommy is hurting Leah. Red does what Mommy tells him to do.

Did Mommy tell Red to hurt Leah?

Red scares me. Mommy scares me too when she acts this way.

Don't scream. Mommy will hear and get mad. Red will punish me too – just like he did Leah. I will get hurt, be abandoned, left alone.

Charlie

A fast, belching, roaring train of consciousness sends sparks of terror in all directions as it blasts by, transforming with its dizzying power the nerve endings of awareness. Charlie tries to focus, tune in.

"What movie is playing? What universe am I in? What planet am I on?"

Far away at the top of the ceiling is a spider's web. A very intricate and delicate pattern of filaments spins out from the Master's wheel – origin, the cosmic hole/whole – and laces back and forth, back and forth, until the room is consumed.

The body of the one called Charlie Foxhawk Carter is wrapped, covered, in the spiderweb cocoon. He, a chrysalis, will chew his way out of his wrappings only when his body has metamorphosed. His teeth become fangs. His head flattens and elongates. His hands grow claws. Feet are unknown quantities – unseen in the enveloping darkness.

He awakens into a dream.

Peggy, Isobel, Linda, Leah fused. They are the Multi-headed Goddess of Light with which his new self must mate, to learn the secret, to evolve the soul, to make a whole. By broaching, broaching, broaching a subject just beyond the level of verbal articulation and human comprehension.

A madhouse express of consciousness flashes by at speeds beyond those of thought, before a finger can snap, at the moment when light is brought to a stop.

His hand, even though it is securely fastened, is, somehow, held out to reveal the skeletal system inside.

Awesome.

Bones melt away and collect in a gritty pile. Where this essence goes, all go. Nothing can be found.

How could a search be initiated from the invisible realm by something that is not even a cipher, unknown?

From his far-off vantage point, Charlie hears, "What should we do with him, boss?"

"More head on a post. But let him administer his own dose."

Jorge looks quizzically at his mentor. Mr. Big explains.

"Put a pitcher of water in the room. Allow Mr. Carter to pour himself a drink to slake his thirst."

"Right on," Jorge replies with satisfaction.

Jorge, trained in the art of torture and denial, sees value in pain and suffering.

Will he rule his master's kingdom when he has fully learned the wily arts of inquisition and the wielding of power? Charlie wonders, then decides, I place my money on Mr. Big – but his dream is empty, too.

All hopes and dreams are no more real than this timeless, antiseptic basement room furnished with a metal bed outfitted with fasteners for legs and arms, a chair, a table, and a pitcher of deadly water.

We're Tough Guys from Chicago

We're in the stinking San Francisco airport – two guys in white trench coats and fedoras; surrounded by faggots and beatniks wearing hippie beads and phony-baloney jewelry.

Who gives a shit? thinks Frankie, one of the tough guys from Chicago.

These people smell like overripe sewers, listen to music that fries your brain, and cram drugs down their throats that'd turn any self-respecting person into an animal. End up snapping their fingers, bobbing their heads up and down and spouting words like far out, too much, groovy.

Christ. Frisco...shit.

Who the hell wants to get sent here?

The two tough guys from Chicago, Frankie and Eddie, stride rapidly through the terminal, Frankie in the lead.

Where can you get something decent to eat? Who would you want to shoot the breeze with?

Fuck that.

We're on a job. Not here to soak up the sun and fuck the broads. Not here to eat pasta or have some yucks. Only thing I'm interested in is doing these hits and getting back to reality, the windy streets of Chicago, the place where a man gets the proper respect due to his position in life.

Without pausing, Frankie looks up at directional signs. The terminal is crowded. Several flights have landed at the same time. Frankie sneers.

The yokels in this burg have no concept, no understanding.

What a toilet, a real nowhere place. Bunch of degenerates.

No wonder we had to come in and clean up this mess. No one here could.

Besides, it's our business and we're good at it. The best.

So fuck this crummy town. We'll put up with it for as long as it takes. Then get the hell out.

"Hey, Frankie... What you want to do first?" Eddie asks.

Frankie glares at Eddie and spits out of the side of his mouth.

"Head for the fucking parking lot, Eddie..."

"Okay, Frankie. Sure. But what..."

Frankie cuts him short.

"Luigi said he'd stash our gear and directions in the trunk of a turbo-charged black Pontiac GTO in Lot D of short-term parking. You got the plate number I gave you?"

Eddie reaches in his pocket and pulls out a piece of paper, waving it in front of him as they walk. He nods.

"We check to make sure everything's cool. Then we do the hits. Clean up the stinking mess. Get the fuck out of this rotten weirdo town."

Eddie nods again.

Frankie is not placated. Eddie should know better. He knows I don't like to talk before a hit.

"Yeah. Sure, Frankie," Eddie answers.

"Christ," Frankie mutters. "Have I got to do everything myself?'

Miki

"What the hell are you doing here? Don't you know it's dangerous?"

Gab's brighter-than-bright eyes meet Miki's. White powder lines his nostrils. He's out of his gourd on coke.

Peter and Miki's place is empty and no one except the authorities is likely to drop by. Miki only came because she needed some personal stuff.

"Miki. Try some of this blow. It's pharmaceutical," Gab blabbers.

Before Miki can answer, Ida barges through the door, almost bumping into Miki as she does so.

"I got tired of waiting in the car," she begins.

Then she sees Gab.

"What the hell are you doing here?" she growls.

"Have some," says Gab, offering his coke stash to his wife.

"What are you doing? Don't you know what's happening?" Miki adds as she heads into the bedroom and begins throwing some necessities into her shoulder bag.

Back in the front room, she hears Ida yelling at Gab.

"Tell me right now where you've been and who you've been talking to. Right now."

Gab makes no answer. At least Miki doesn't hear him say anything. Coming into the front room, Miki joins the conversation.

"She's right, Gab. It may be important. We're all in danger."

Gab stumbles to his feet, trying to maintain his hold on his stash. Some of it spills out. He lurches to correct course. The coke stash falls to the floor. Miki scoops up a handful and throws it out of the window.

"Freddy gave that to me," Gab shouts, leaping to save the coke.

"Are you crazy?" Ida moans, pushing him away.

Miki steps between them.

"We've got to get out of here right away. The authorities are watching this place."

Gab's head jerks from side to side like he's the foil in some slapstick comedy.

"Authorities. Keep 'em away from Gate Five. That's where the action is," he blurts out.

"Come on."

Miki pushes Gab in the direction of the front door. Ida, the last one out, slams it shut. They scurry down the path toward the street, three dazed Marinites wondering if the trashing of Miki and Peter's pad is the first tentative wave of the tsunami Al predicted. The air is freshening. The wind is picking up. Miki's intuition is working overtime.

"What's that Gab said about Gate Five?"

That's the second mention of it Miki's heard in less than an hour.

Gab runs his mouth while they cut across a backyard to avoid coming out on the street at the path leading to Peter and Miki's pad. It's the coke talking.

"The houseboat with the God's-eye flag. Gate Five, Sausalito. That's where Freddy got his stuff, from a biker named Red."

"Right," Ida answers, slamming the door of the Cougar.

"This Red is connected to the new action taking over the scene – real tough guys," Gab babbles knowingly.

Miki has an idea: Maybe David Travail or someone at his house knows where they can get in touch with Charlie.

There's no doubt in Miki's mind that Charlie should check out the God's-eye houseboat at Gate Five. That cold hand is tapping her on the shoulder. Danger is near.

The front door of the Travail house is wide open and David is on the phone when they arrive. He's still wearing his coat and tie. He must have come directly from his office. He, for once, is in a panic.

"Yes, I'm certain that she met with foul play. She promised me she'd keep in touch and I haven't heard from her."

David waves them inside, then holds up his hand, indicating they should wait until he gets off the phone.

"I realize she hasn't been missing long enough to file a formal complaint but I'm certain... "

Before Miki and Ida can exchange significant looks, David slams down the phone.

"Leah's gone missing and I can't get the police to do anything. They moved pretty darned quick when they thought she was a suspect in a murder."

"You have any idea where Charlie is? He might be able to help," Miki interrupts to ask.

David shakes his head as his hand goes to his forehead as if to keep it from shaking.

Miki again feels that cold hand on her shoulder.

"You up for a visit to a houseboat with a God's eye?" Miki asks Ida.

"That's crazy, Miki. We should be warning the 'family,'" Ida answers.

"If they haven't been clued in by now, it's probably too late. And we might dig up a lead for Charlie to follow."

"Maybe that biker cat will have more blow," Gab interjects.

"What are you people talking about?" David asks.

"Would you mind if Gab stays here while we run over to Gate Five and back?" Miki asks David.

"Well, okay. But I'm driving up to the sheriff's office to demand they take action. He'll have to stay here by himself."

Miki sees Gab sneak a peek at David's well-stocked liquor cabinet. He must need something to smooth out the rough edges of his coke high.

"You sure you don't want me to come along?" he asks lamely as David heads out the door and Miki and Ida follow. No one bothers to answer him.

Peggy Crawford

"Where's Jennifer? Where's my baby? Didn't I tell you to watch her?" Crawford screams at Red.

"I took her to the bedroom. When I left, she was playing with her doll like always."

Crawford lets Red have it. She slaps him – hard.

"Fool. Bastard. Pig! You're the lamest of them all."

"Them?" Red responds, taking hold of Crawford's wrists and holding her at arm's length. "Them?"

Crawford's brain almost short circuits it runs so hot, so fast and furious. She says nothing but her mind is awhirl with recollection laced with hostility.

"Yes, them. My father, my stepfather, Edge, dozens of lovers in between. The enemies who creep into your bed and force themselves on you to satisfy their dirty little wet dreams with their pitiful little peckers, then beat you up to prove what a big man they are after they've shot their load, long before you've even gotten warmed up, if that disgusting thought was ever even the whisper of a thought in your mind."

Red pulls her toward him. His face looms large. Then he shakes her like a rag doll. Crawford's eyes jiggle but that does not dull her disgust, her disdain, her intense focus on finding her baby, Jennifer.

Contain the fury. Harness the anger, she tells herself.

Aloud she says, "You haven't got a prayer of pulling this deal off without me."

"Is that so?"

"Suppose I turn you in?" she asks.

"I'll return the favor."

"A judge and jury - who do you think they'd believe?"

His sex-addled brain, scrambled with crystal meth and amphetamines, dulled by alcohol, lurches to an uncertain stop.

Slow wheels of thought flicker in the corners of his eyes.

"All right. But when this is sorted out..."

He turns, heads through the sliding glass door, and disappears into the night in search of Jennifer.

Crawford follows and is greeted by the lights of Sausalito, Belvedere, the sound of traffic coming down Waldo Grade, the background rumble of a major metropolitan area, as seen from Gate Five, a place where residents believe they are enjoying "the last free ride." Here, Beat meets hippie, dropouts collide with intellectual renegades, the underworld mates with flower children. And the junk these people have accumulated, the rickety walkways, all the nooks and crannies, only serves to further infuriate her and frustrate her efforts to find her missing daughter.

"Jennifer... Jennifer," she shouts over the water and down the rickety wooden walkways.

Boats grind in their moorings. The fruity smell of shit and brackish water assails Crawford. She looks in the places where little people would hide. When the wind gusts die down, she sways down the walkways through an uncomfortable heat, sticky just like back home.

"Sweetheart! Mommy's not mad at you. I'm sorry I hurt Leah and wouldn't think of doing it again. Come to Mommy and you'll see. Sweetheart?"

As she searches, she worriedly thinks. Where is my darling Jennifer, so young and so helpless? Doesn't she know that Mommy only wants what's best for her? Doesn't she realize that Mommy is arranging things so that we can live far away, above the fray? Jennifer must never suffer the way I have... never. She's going to have everything that Mommy never had. No hand will ever be raised against her. No one will force himself upon her. No one will bend and twist her spirit trying to break it. She will be free.

She calls, croons, again, "Jennifer. Jennifer!"

Red stumbles against a sculpture made from a rusted boat anchor, shiny Detroit hubcaps, live plants, and driftwood.

"Aww, man," he mumbles in disgust. He's stepped in dog shit.

As he scrapes the mess off his shoe, he realizes that Crawford's Achilles heel has been exposed. It's Jennifer.

He has only a moment to savor this insight when suddenly the wooden pier gives way underneath him.

A loud crash followed by a splash and a profane exclamation pierces the night. Red has ended up in the putrid water of Richardson Bay.

The tide is going out. Quicksand-like mud, filled with who knows what, is being exposed farther and farther from the shoreline. Red will have a devil of a time getting his bulky body free of that muck.

A porch light comes on in front of a nearby houseboat. The door opens. Two scraggly-haired flower children emerge, arm in arm. They are naked.

"Hey, man, what's happening?" the male hippie mutters as he looks left, then right, unable to identify the source of the disturbance.

"Yeah, like, what's happening?" his girlfriend asks, clutching her boyfriend around the waist and running her free hand through her long blond hair.

Red makes loud, abusive but unintelligible sounds as he thrashes around in the shallow water. Crawford is forced to focus on Red.

"Didn't this guy ever learn to swim?" she asks herself. "Guess not. He sounds like he's in a panic. No way he's going to drown. The water's only waist high."

She yells to him, "Stand up, idiot."

Then she realizes Red's bulk will make him sink deeper into the mud if he stands up. He could be pulled underwater and drown. Can't have that. Not now. Call attention to us.

"Is that your boat?" Crawford asks the hippie and his girlfriend.

"Well, like, yeah man."

"Mind if I borrow it for a moment?"

Crawford jumps in without waiting for an answer.

"Far out," Crawford hears one of them say as she lands in the rowboat.

Miki

"Did you hear that? It sounded like someone falling into the water."

"There's always some sort of weirdness going on around the Gates," Ida answers Miki with a dismissive flick of her wrist.

Ida lived on a houseboat for several months with Gab and the kids when they first moved up to the Bay Area from LA. That's when she landed a job at the Trident and it's when Gab got into jewelry making. Some of the Trident waitresses lived on houseboats in the Gates and Gab fell in with some Beatnik jewelry makers. They got by, by the skin of their teeth.

Miki and Ida make their way along a cluttered walkway. The houseboat with the God's eye is easy to find. Miki decides that when they get there they'll ask if there's any coke for sale. Then they'll see what develops.

The sliding glass door leading into the houseboat is open when they approach it. The darkened front room is silent, ominous. The cold hand on Miki's shoulder is impossible to ignore.

"Hello. Anyone home?"

Miki sticks her head inside. Nothing moves, but an angry impression of violence and danger pervades the room. She and Ida enter. They notice that a blanket thrown over the sofa has a bulky bulge in it.

"What's that?" Ida asks, nodding toward the bulge.

They cross the room, anticipating who knows what at any moment. Miki pulls up one edge of the blanket. Underneath is a body with a mop of frizzy, dark hair.

"Leah?" Miki whispers under her breath. "Leah? Are you all right? Can you hear us?"

Ida shakes Leah gently while Miki holds up the blanket. Then Ida leans down close to Leah's face.

"She's breathing but she's completely out of it."

A cat jumps up on a nearby table and cries. The two women jump, almost scream. Miki's a dog person. Cats give her the creeps.

"We've got to get her out of here – now," Miki realizes.

The cold hand on her shoulder informs her. A tsunami of evil intentions is chasing them down.

Miki and Ida bundle Leah back up in the blanket. Between the two older women they stand Leah up and pull her arms over their shoulders.

No problem. Leah's a shrimp compared to them.

Looks like there is a virtue to getting older and putting on a few pounds.

They drag her a few steps. Leah automatically, like a robotic doll, begins moving her feet. Her legs wobble but she adds momentum and support to their forward progress.

"That's right, honey. We're going to take you home. Get you out of this place."

The breeze is freshening outside. Gate Five litter, strewn in all directions, hurtles through the air. Wind chimes ring and clatter incessantly. Rowboats, houseboats, rub enthusiastically against their moorings. Dogs bark disjointedly. The turbulent sounds send Miki, Ida, and Leah scurrying down the wooden walkway leading to the parking lot and the Mercury Cougar. Without warning, Ida lets out a stifled scream and stops short. Miki and Ida almost let go of Leah. A little girl has grabbed Ida's leg. The little girl points with a pudgy finger.

"Leah," she says.

"Do you know Leah?" Miki asks.

The little girl nods gravely.

"Can I go with you?" she implores.

"Where's your mommy?" Ida asks.

"She hurt Leah," the little girl answers. "I don't like her any more."

Without another word, Ida takes the child's hand and squeezes it. Leah stumbles and mumbles something incoherent. Her head flops from one side to the other, her eyes struggle to remain open, as the four of them proceed along the bouncy walkway. When they reach the parking area, they pass a local landmark, an old paddlewheel boat, the Charles Van Damme, rumored to have been a gambling boat back in the Gold Rush days.

Unexpectedly, ominously, the wind dies down. For a moment they live in a vacuum. Then it hits – a gigantic bolt of lightning and an immediate, fierce rumble of thunder that engulfs the parking lot and rattles all of the surrounding area with it. The murky waters of Richardson Bay glow. Phosphorescent ripples, small sparkling crests of waves, surge excitedly away from the boiling water created by the bolt of lightning where it made a connection with the Bay.

Ramshackle Gate Five shudders, shakes, creaks and moans. A white-hot glow immediately turns red, violet, green, and orange in turn, then rushes outward as if from the impact of an atomic bomb.

In the light created by this phenomenon, the women see a bulky, mud-covered human form in the water. Slowly sinking, it shakes and contorts with nightmarish anguish as the lightning fades from the sky. The charged water sluggishly returns to its normal wayward movement. Two body parts of the mud-covered man remain visible: one hand that sticks straight out and one of its fingers, the middle one, stretched to its limit and his face which mimics the face depicted in the "Scream" painting. These also, slowly, majestically, sink beneath the muddy waters of Richardson Bay.

As Miki, Ida, Leah, and Jennifer take in this terrible sight, they see a woman in a dinghy rowing toward the man. As he subsides into the waters, the dinghy changes course and hastily heads back toward the rickety dock.

Tough Guys from Chicago

Standing in the parking lot, looking out over Gate Five as the storm hits, are the tough guys from Chicago.

"What the fuck?"

Eddie's eyes bug out. He's amazed, alight with puzzlement. Weirdos are poking their heads out of their hovels. A crowd is forming fast. Frankie instantly surveys the situation.

"Shit," he says. "Not a good idea to do the dame in the rowboat now. We'd stand out in this crowd - two guys in suits wearing raincoats. The locals are all wearing hippie shit."

Frankie slips his gun and silencer into a specially designed shoulder holster.

"Why didn't you whack the broad first?" Eddie wonders.

"Didn't someone say to pump her before we whack her? I know I heard that," Frankie snaps back. Inwardly he thinks, "Eddie shouldn't have pointed out I fucked up. If it was anybody else I'd..."

"Naw. That was Luigi, Frankie. Remember? He don't count, not in my book he don't."

"You've got a point there, Eddie."

"You got your eye on where that broad is headed?" Frankie asks Eddie.

"I got her," Eddie answers.

"We're just a coupla guys strolling up a shitty walkway toward our GTO, the fastest getaway car in town."

"Never had a hit go down quite that way before," Eddie says as they get into the car. "That lightning bolt hit right when you pulled the damn trigger. You didn't even need the silencer."

"We wait here until the scene clears," Frankie begins. "Then we whack the broad."

Eddie nods, pulls out the binoculars and focuses on Crawford.

"Too bad we got to whack her, Frankie. She's a knockout."

Cop cars, a fire engine, and the rescue squad bump down the unpaved road toward the harbor, red lights flashing, sirens blaring. Frankie and Eddie's car stands out in the assemblage of beat-up old cars and VW camper vans.

"Goddamn Frisco," says Frankie. "Why couldn't we get an assignment in Chicago or even New York? Someplace decent."

Charlie

Cocoon-wrapped Charlie mentally recites to himself a mystical nursery rhyme made up by himself on the spot.

"I cannot run.

"I have no legs.

"I cannot scream.

"I have no mouth.

"I cannot breathe.

"I have no lungs.

"I cannot bleed.

"I have no blood.

"I have no mind, no consciousness.

"Yet I am aware."

Trapped. Imprisoned.

Charlie's body continues to function, causing everlasting and uncontrollable disorientation and dislocation.

Maya...

Charlie rattles the iron bars of his invisible cage with nonexistent hands and screams with nonexistent vocal cords into the airless space in which he is enclosed. Nonexistent noxious vapors clutch and constrict his throat. He suffocates, gasps for air, as he struggles toward the surface.

Which way is up?

Panic. Horror. Isolation. Dissolution.

I'll never make it.

Laughter seems to break out all around him. He feels he's being watched, inspected, analyzed.

Waste seems to rain down upon him. He thinks he sees his tormentors playfully throw knives in his direction. They cut off his penis. His blood mixes with sewage. He's left to rot in the burning midday sun. Yet he has never left the torture chamber.

I'm drenched in sweat.

So thirsty...

I'm bone dry.

Must drink, must drink, must drink.

He believes he is falling from the top of the world's tallest building. The pavement moves rapidly toward him, ready to crush his face, his bones, his body, his being.

I'm being stoned by wild-eyed strangers.

I'm being pulled apart on a rack by evangelical monks in long, brown robes.

No one wants to hear my confession – my contrite, repenting moans.

So thirsty.

So thirsty.

Maya...

If I could just drink, just taste soothing, velvety liquid.

But water, the elixir of life, seems so far away, too far to reach without legs, without a mouth, without blood.

Fear

Primal scream.

Maya

Rage, rave and rant through this terror.

Fight. Fight back.

It's called living.

If I just had some water, something to drink.

A pitcher and a glass... My kingdom for...

Maya...

On that metal table...

Within reach...

If I could just move my hand...

Why can't I?

Has my spinal cord been severed?

Where am I?

The glass...

The pitcher...

I can smell the liquid...

Feel its presence in this antiseptic room.

Remember...

He's looking into a mirror.

His face morphs once, twice, a dozen, a million times. It breaks apart and disappears.

In the mirror of life he sees – nothing, no thing.

Remember...

Orpheus steps through the looking glass and into the other side, passes through Hades, the Underworld, the unknown, looking neither right nor left.

Time never was...

Must navigate the perils of Hades.

The multi-headed deity, the one I'm bringing back.

No hero – not I.

"Remember..."

His heart is a torrent of emotions.

Isobel, Linda, Leah and, yes, Peggy - forgive me.

Humanity looks on with distaste, disgust, undisguised revulsion. He is convinced he's an untouchable, shunned and forced to live in a cave at the edge of civilization. He's an animal, the lowest of the low, an insect, vermin, polluted soil-soul broadcast across the universe. He will be plowed under so the experiment can be begun again.

Water...

Never was...

If I just could reach that pitcher.

If I could just lift up my...

A rumble...

The table rocks and rattles.

The room goes inky black.

Beyond the veil...

I am swallowed by the Void.

Lord?

My hands...

They're free. I can move them.

His leg slides effortlessly across the harsh mattress surface on which he lies.

He sits up.

His head spins.

He's going to be sick.

Not yet.

"Time..."

He extends his leg down into unfathomable depths.

It touches the floor and tingles.

He's alive but not yet reconnected to this body.

"Never was..."

He trips over something – is it a black blob, a demonic body, a bolt of cloth? It's his pants.

"Remember..."

He picks them up.

And stumbles forward.

Water or escape?

Flow on...

Footsteps rush toward him through deep space.

No time, no place, to hide...

His head, his arms, his stomach convulse, contract, dissolve, touch infinity, become a point, expand, magnify, glorify, reveal.

Snap to.

Sentient again.

React.

Fight or flight.

An adrenaline surge of vital juices from the pre-human dimension rumbles through his cranium.

Self-preservation, a force that must be reckoned with, comes to life.

Flickering lights...

The impression of a shape approaching.

He lunges forward, springing like an unleashed beast toward his attacker. This time, instead of being a hallucination, his foe is flesh and blood.

Fury fills his being, the rage he has carried since birth, possibly the pain of birth, possibly in the DNA passed on to him from eons long ago.

In his hands his pants are a weapon with which he strangles this shape, this threat. He is unchained, released. Nothing can stop primal juices, self-preservation.

Nothing.

No more...

"Remember..."

Lost in space but his body functioning, he pulls on his backpack and races out the door into the eternal darkness of the depths of the mansion.

Mr. Big

"What happened?" Mr. Big wants to know.

"A bolt of lightning struck the power line and our back-up generator got fried, sir. Our power grid is wiped out."

"The prisoner?"

"Jorge has gone to check on him. Without power, that sub basement's a black pit. Diablo..."

The underling does not finish his thought. It's not necessary. Mr. Big has spent many years in the wilds of Colombia building this syndicate. He has heard the talk of Diablo, the Devil. And once, just once, he saw... something.

But this is not the time to think or talk about the past. Cool heads must prevail. Another underling rushes into the room.

"The prisoner has escaped. He strangled Jorge and stole a car. Got out by crashing through the electric gate while the electricity was out. What do you want us to do?"

"What?

"Charlie Foxhawk Carter killed Jorge," Mr. Big mutters in disbelief.

Jorge was like a son to me, Mr. Big laments. Inwardly, he recognizes that Jorge's end was inevitable. So be it, he resolves as he cold-heartedly calculates the commands he must issue to salvage this situation.

"What do I want you to do? Nothing. Let's see how Ms. Crawford deals with adversity. And, if she passes this test, she's worth doing business with."

"Bueno, senor..."

Peggy Crawford

Flashing lights, spotlights, headlights, and the warning lights on an ambulance illuminate the packed-dirt parking lot on Gate Five Road. A commandeered rowboat pulls Red's remains shoreward. The rescue squad rolls a gurney along the rickety wooden walkway leading out over the water past makeshift houseboats. Police radios blare. Volunteer firemen stand in small groups, dressed in full regalia, talking and drinking coffee. There's nothing for them to do but they have no intention of leaving.

Clumps of houseboat residents lurk as discreetly as possible on the fringes. They're not eager to be questioned, but they can't help being curious. The carnival of public death is being acted out.

And Jennifer is nowhere to be found.

She's not likely to be hiding in someone else's houseboat. I taught her to distrust strangers, Peggy reflects. And she's too careful to fall into the putrid bay water like Red did, she concludes. Has she met with foul play? Could she have given up and gone back to our houseboat?

Again she calls out, "Jennifer. Jennifer, honey..."

The houseboat is empty. That pain-in-the-neck Leah Travail is gone too.

What just happened here? Crawford is brought up short. She tries to think it through. Did the lightning strike first, before Red let out his dying yelp? Did he jerk backwards just before the lightning struck? Did I imagine hearing the ping of a bullet just before the lightning bolt?

That was when she had ducked down for cover.

Did that save my life? Have Jennifer and Leah been spirited away by the shooter, if shooter there was?

Outside, the cops are formulating theories and rounding up the usual suspects, looking for answers that they'll never find. The cops are very methodical about some things: harassment, paperwork, asking questions, sticking their noses in where they don't belong.

Fuck them. Fuck Leah. Fuck everybody and everything. Everybody but Jennifer. Somehow Jennifer must have hooked up with Leah Travail. Somehow they got out of here. That has to be it. They'll most likely head toward Leah's brother's house. Where else could they go? Crawford asks herself.

Crawford changes her clothes, melts into the crowd and slips away.

Hitching a ride is a snap. In the vehicle, Crawford replays Red's death in her mind. She's convinced Red was shot. She draws a conclusion. It was a hit. No question about it.

That probably means I'm next in line. Jennifer and I have got to make tracks, fast. Who was the shooter? How did they know we would be at Gate Five? If it was a hit, who authorized it?

Keep your eyes on the prize, honey.

First things first – rescue my baby.

Lt. Cooper

"Thought you might be interested... Just picked up a call from Marin on the police scanner. Dead man found floating in Richardson Bay near Gate Five in Sausalito after a gigantic bolt of lightning struck right next to the houseboats. Officer on the scene is calling it homicide. No reason given. Kinda screwy, don't you think?"

A crushing pile of paperwork that threatens to slide off Lt. Cooper's desk confronts him. His old buddy, Dave Jenkins, the desk sergeant, gives Cooper his usual deadpan look.

"You think this has anything to do with... " Cooper begins.

"Your pal Carter has a way of being involved where weird meets murder. Take that screwy Bob White case," Jenkins fires back before Coop has time to finish.

That's not unusual. Jenkins may look like he's asleep but he's right there, all the time. Cooper and Jenkins have worked together since they graduated from the police academy in the same class.

Tired – that's how paperwork makes Cooper feel.

"He's not my pal, Davy. But you're right. Better check it out. I need some fresh air anyway. Want to come along?"

Cooper's chair scraps along the floor as he gets up. It's been a long day and it looks like it's going to get longer. Jenkins shakes his head and puts his beefy hands on his expansive hips.

"I'll leave that to you while I ride my desk. That way I'll make it to retirement," Davy replies.

It's one of their standing jokes. And Jenkins may be right.

Cooper picks his sports jacket up and throws it over his shoulder. He doesn't bother to button his collar or straighten his tie. No surprise inspections likely. He's headed toward alternative lifestyle country, Marin County.

"What's the matter, Davy? Lost your sense of fun?"

"Ha. Some fun. Spare me."

They both laugh. Cooper starts for the door, pauses and asks, "Punch me out, will ya? And if I don't check in in an hour put out an APB on Charlie Foxhawk Carter. He's mixed up in this somehow, I'm thinking."

"He's that kind of guy all right, Lieutenant." Jenkins purposely waits a beat, enough time for Coop to start to turn toward the door, before landing one more one-liner. "And remember – go with the flow."

Charlie

Bending knots of fragmented nonsense...

Flickering shadows of unearthly dimensions...

Looking from the inside and seeing the closed lid of a coffin, buried six feet under.

The tattered remains of Charlie's pants and his backpack are on the seat beside him. Driving naked in San Francisco.

He careens around a corner and through a stop sign, just missing a trolley car and a wandering pedestrian.

The night is interrupted by the finger of God.

A blinding bolt of lightning shatters the laid-back grace of Market Street near the bottom of Twin Peaks.

The trolley line snaps and sparkles in sympathetic recognition of the bolt of lightning.

288

In his backpack, blue powder magic potion, courtesy of a Mt. Tam holy man, unleashes its powers by remote control...

"Hello," Charlie pleasantly salutes.

The sky above is dark and angry.

Great billowing clouds boil and roll through the inky velvet night.

The wind speaks out in protest.

First, it's a whisper originating in alleyways.

Then, it's a clearing of the throat that rattles trashcans.

Finally, it's a blast that rocks rows of apartment buildings and forces people walking on the street to lean into the howl.

KMPX, the home of underground music, playing at the moment a cut from the new Traffic album, develops a serious case of static.

Charlie descends from the haze of a violent mirage, the edge of insanity, to turn the dial.

He's bringing in the station, seeking its signal, as he fumbles with the connection between soul and body.

Navigate life like water overcoming obstacles over, under, around and through.

That's been Charlie's mantra for the last few years.

Right on.

He's muttering to himself, to the world at large, to unseen creatures that crowd his brain cavity and spill over into the electric-blue street.

"What is consciousness?

"What is consciousness...

"What is consciousness!" he chants, just as Timothy Leary chanted to his drug-addled adherents.

The macro and the micro, the alpha and the omega, the finite and the infinite, the positive and negative, generate sparks and collide.

"What does it matter?

"Anti-matter...

"Splatter..."

His galloping steed, his internal combustion engine, fires forward at speeds which always approach but never reach a destination.

"Cosmic metaphysical equation..."

Another explosive bolt of lightning sends surges of galactic power through the San Francisco grid and zaps the awareness of city residents, shocking them out of their complacent soma sleep.

Paradise has been put on red alert. There's a momentous change in the making.

Charlie's Multi-headed Goddess rides a seashell shoreward to broach a sacred subject.

Landing...

Miraculously.

The radio static disappears.

In a surprise move, the music, a narcotic more potent than a thousand shots of the best heroin, dips down and out.

The normally laidback voice of the KMPX announcer intrudes.

"Woo. Get back. I've got a real news flash. Lightning, high winds and RAIN are headed our way. Hold on tight. Looks like it's going to be a bumpy ride."

Charlie's alien companion, the car, spins and slides, slips and rocks.

The clouds above, the heavens, angrily explode, shaking the ground with earthquake vibrations that become rumbling thunder.

The Multi-headed Goddess speaks.

All those who listen (only Charlie?) are knocked witless so that their senses can be restored.

All those who ignore are readied to be ground up and discarded back to the elements from which they came.

It is a dangerous night to be out and about.

Charlie Carter to the rescue – of himself, of his friends, of the "family," of all the laidback outsiders and discards of the world – the woebegone and forgotten...

Front burner time for the dispossessed.

Ride 'em, cowboy.

Tony

Hear thunder rumble. See boiling, angry clouds. Smell the freshening air filled with urgent messages from surrounding trees, bay waters, earth, a prison.

Nowhere...nothing...

Tony is deep within the bowels of a shattered mind, filled with turgid flashes.

"Augh, augh, augh," coughs his sluggish brain.

He cautiously cranes his neck upward to see lightning crackle.

Dark, foreboding clouds ominously alarm his eyes.

Rushing winds push, bunch, scatter those same clouds in the turbulent sky above.

Within Tony's cranium, continuous screaming, a piercing, tormented bellow.

A gigantic bolt of lightning thunders. The sky in all directions becomes a blinding white light.

Tony crouches... in bushes... seeking refuge... primordial man... hunkered... down...

Nowhere... nothing... cellular... molecular...

He is a human animal, a human animal hiding.

Nothing... nothing...

Word images jitter through Tony.

"Love... Leah... Coward... Bloody knife... Edge... body..."

Black...Blank...Void...

"Family... Respect... Lost..."

Black...Blank...Void...

"Aww...Aww...Aww..."

Tony moans and hollers until his throat is raw and ragged.

He is hunkered down within and without...Primordial man...

Nowhere... nothing...

Void... Void... Void...

Lightning... Thunder...

Clouds rushing... Wind bending trees...

Howling... Roaring...

Storm approaching...

Hiding... Crouching...

In bushes...

Nowhere... Nothing.

Crouch... In bushes...

"Wait...

"For signal...

"Coming..."

Sheriff Whelan

"Shot? The man was struck by lightning," Whelan shouts, trying to make himself heard above the noise of the storm.

Multiple lightning flashes glow over Richardson Bay, San Francisco Bay, round the rim of the Bay Area with alarming regularity. Gale-force winds batter the ramshackle houseboats, rattle the unstable walkways, and cause sailboats to smash against docks. Whitecaps develop in this normally turgid, murky tributary.

"Right. Yes, sir. Lightning. That's what it looked like at first, sir. But when we finally got him ashore, we found this here hole in his temple. See?" Whelan's deputy, Nick, shouts in reply.

"What're you talking about, boy?" Whelan hollers before looking where Nick is pointing.

Nick makes himself scarce, leaving Whelan to talk to himself.

"Can't help getting mean sometimes with all the aggravation I've got to put up with. Everybody wants something. Politicians, heavy hitters, big contributors to campaigns. Buzzards."

Whelan thinks about the guy who made a sizable contribution to his campaign fund and then happened to mention the sheriff should look the other way if big changes come to the Marin drug scene.

Hell's bells, he thinks. I don't give a hoot what those no-good drug takers do as long as they don't mess with the well-being of the good solid folks who put me in office or cause the Sheriff's Department's arrest and conviction record to plummet. Sure, I took that their money and ran. Now this... What's going down here ain't part of that deal. No sir. You better believe it.

Fuck this Mr. Big and those federal authorities. They're on their own. Just let 'em try to get back at me or take back their money.

Without warning, the rushing wind changes direction. A lightning bolt strikes close to shore. The residents of Gate Five have crawled back to their tumbledown houseboats, looking for cover.

293

Whelan and his deputy grab hold of slimy wooden pylons for support and protect their hats.

Whelan's stomach convulses, again.

Doc warned me about spicy foods. Should have listened.

Christ. Got to take a crap. Not an attack while I'm in command. Undignified.

Shit.

Feel rotten.

Whelan sees Cooper approaching. Before he can speak, Whelan shouts with false bonhomie, "Lt. Cooper, as I live and breathe. What brings you to our humble neck of the woods? Business or pleasure?"

"Sheriff Whelan."

Three gigantic, jagged fingers of light explode in the sky above. A thunderous eruption immediately follows the blast. The wind rips in one direction and then the other. Whelan and Cooper both stagger, hunch up their shoulders, and tuck in their heads.

"Jesus, Mary and Joseph."

Whelan crosses himself. Cooper bows his head. They were both once altar boys.

"What do you think?" Cooper asks.

"Rain. Plenty of it."

Their eyes scan the active sky above.

Was Cooper raised on a farm too? Whelan wonders. I remember my pappy never allowed any of us to wish for rain. Thought it might spook it away. Hope I haven't jinxed our chances this time.

"What you got here?" Cooper asks, cutting short Whelan's mental rumination.

"You drove all the way over here to find out?"

Getting no reply, Whelan charges on.

"What makes this corpse so all-fired interesting to you? Something I should know about?"

"Word on the street in the City is that a new outfit is moving in and taking over the drug action," Cooper concedes.

"How does a man struck by lightning connect to that?" Whelan responds. He wonders whether Cooper has somehow connected him to this drug takeover story Cooper just mentioned.

The wind dies down suddenly. The horizon rim is still being peppered with lightning strikes. One dazzling and thunderous bolt lights up what's left of Alcatraz. Dark shadows of evil manifest themselves, even in Paradise.

"The police scanner said the man was shot in connection with a lightning death. Circumstances seemed odd to me. Wanted to check it out for myself. Who knows? Might connect to our investigation."

"Well, you may have something there, Lieutenant. You may just have something. And what would I get for my trouble if I help you out?"

"The thrill of helping out one of your own, Sheriff, and being the one doing the arresting when and if we run these bastards to ground."

"That's a start. That's for darn sure a start."

Damnation, Whelan thinks. Why did this hit have to happen on a night like this? But I might get something out of it by putting a tail on Cooper.

The wind picks up. The approaching storm swirls like a waterspout round the Bay, gathering force over water.

Miki

"Murdered Edge." Leah, still looking pretty rocky, spouts, unsolicited.

She and Miki are seated in the breakfast nook of her brother's house.

Miki puts down the cup of tea she was about to hand to Leah and gives her a hug.

"Not now, honey. No need for you to think about that."

Miki feels guilty too. She felt the cold hand on her left shoulder and ignored her queasy feelings about Edge. She let "family" members down. Now Leah and the rest of the "family" are fast descending into troubled waters.

"You're not alone, sweetheart. We're all in this with you," Miki adds, trying to comfort Leah.

Leah is looking into Miki's eyes but she doesn't seem to see Miki. "What is she seeing? How can I help?" Miki wonders.

"Drink your tea. We'll talk later."

"Tastes good..."

Leah holds the cup with both hands. She's fried, burnt, spent.

Miki knows that what Leah needs is peace and quiet. She also knows that there's no way she will get any for the time being. Danger lurks everywhere.

Jennifer watches Leah with close attention. A glass of milk and a chocolate chip cookie remain untouched on the kitchen table in front of her.

What big blue eyes. How still she sits, Miki observes. I'm not the motherly type but isn't it a fact that most children are in constant motion? Why isn't this one?

Leah forces a tired but positive smile onto her face.

"Scared?" she asks Jennifer.

Jennifer moves her head slowly from left to right and back again. Then she puts her finger into her mouth and begins sucking.

Tears stream from the corners of Leah's eyes but she holds her smile.

Now there's someone who'd make a great mom, thinks Miki. Hope she gets a chance.

"Want mommy?" Leah asks.

Jennifer lowers her eyelids, looking inward. Then she opens them and looks back at Leah. Those impenetrable blue eyes, light-attracting orbs without ending, seem to engulf and swallow Leah. This child is the child in all of us. Jennifer nods her head a fraction.

Both Miki and Leah wonder, what does the future hold for this innocent living amid the ruin created by adults?

"Don't be frightened, honey," Ida interjects, breaking the spell with well-meant words of encouragement. "You're safe with us."

Jennifer turns her head to Ida and sees Miki as well. The two are hovering with tea for Leah, milk for Jennifer, bagels for all heating up in the oven.

So, what else is new? Feeding people, making them comfy, the basics. Start from there.

Miki feels the job is tougher in this huge Victorian house filled with expensive furniture and learned books. She doesn't find the house inviting. How could anyone really relax and let it all hang out here?

It feels like I'm in the house of a distant, austere foreign dignitary; the house of a rich, stern relative who lives out on Long Island; the house of a tyrannical elder who delivers tongue lashings and looks down her nose at my family and me. "Don't track up the house. Don't sit down on the furniture. Don't break anything. Don't spill anything. Don't get caught picking your nose or scratching your butt.'

Thump.

Leah uses both hands to put her teacup onto the table. She slides her chair closer to Jennifer, then leans forward and takes Jennifer's hands in her own.

Miki wonders, "What is it that Leah never had time to tell me when she visited our place with Edge? Does it matter now?"

Jennifer looks into Leah's deep, dark eyes.

They share God's secrets – love, hope, reassurance, renewal, thinks Miki.

Can Jennifer see in Leah's eyes that she is in crisis, a being awash with nothing solid to latch onto? The vessel in which they all are sailing is coming apart in the surrounding heavy seas of the tsunami crashing down on laid-back Marin.

"Chocolate chip cookie... Warm milk... Bubble bath... Clean clothes," Leah tells Jennifer with a smile.

The front door flies open at the end of a long hall as a particularly violent bolt of lightning strikes, illuminating the entry way and rattling windowpanes with deep, guttural thunder.

"Who the hell do you think you are, stealing my child away from me?"

Peggy Crawford, with disheveled auburn hair and deranged green eyes, springs into the hallway on the coattails of the blinding flash and the rumble of thunder.

Miki, Ida, Leah, and Jennifer jerk to surprised attention. Leah clasps Jennifer to her breast. Jennifer, outwardly docile, eyes her mother who is suddenly upon them, trying to separate Leah from Jennifer.

"Let go of her, you bitch," Crawford screams.

Leah resists. Crawford, primal juices thundering through her brain, slaps Leah hard. Leah falls back, more in shock from Crawford's explosive energy than from the force of the blow.

Miki and Ida recover from their shock in the same moment. They each grab one of Crawford's arms. Crawford fights like a banshee, kicking, scratching, screaming, wiggling her body in wild, contorted ways, but her struggles are hopeless. Miki and Ida gain the advantage. They press Crawford against the kitchen wall.

"What the hell do we do with her now that we've got her?" Ida pants.

"You bitches'll pay for this - stealing my child," Crawford spits out with real venom.

Miki and Ida look at each other without releasing their grip.

"Better tie her up, I guess, until we can get some reinforcements."

Ida nods.

"Where can we find some rope in this place?"

Leah is clutching Jennifer's hand as hard as she can. It takes her a moment to react.

"Workshop... Garage... I look."

As Leah turns to the back door, a double roll of thunder that sounds like a kettledrum echoes off the steep hillsides surrounding the house. Little Jennifer, who had been silent throughout the evening, screams in terror. The others follow her eyes to the doorway of the breakfast nook, where two men with guns stand.

"Freeze. Don't move a fucking muscle."

One hellion, three bug-eyed women, and one bug-eyed child stare down the barrels of two guns. These men are not locals. They look like something out of a "B" grade gangster movie. They're trenchcoated goons wearing muddied Italian leather shoes, gunsels hired to do somebody's dirty work.

"Find some rope, Eddie, and tie them up," Frankie commands.

He waves his gun at everyone in the room. It has a silencer, making the slender barrel appear outlandishly long.

Ida releases her hold on Crawford. Miki curls her lip but does the same. Leah continues to clutch Jennifer's hand, hard. Jennifer, little Jennifer, seems to have taken a trip into the ozone. She's had too much for one day.

"What the..." Miki mutters, readying herself for what will come.

Crawford's transformation is amazing. She goes from pinned banshee to femme fatale in a flash.

"What brings you big boys calling?" she asks boldly.

Frankie, holding everyone at gunpoint, sneers. He has what one might, in a pinch, call a handsome face.

He gives Crawford the eye.

"Too bad we've got to waste you. You're prime... prime."

Frankie holds his gun steady but he's not ready to squeeze the trigger. He's waiting for Eddie to get back with the rope. Eddie can be heard clumping from room to room, pausing momentarily to search, then moving on. Occasional crashes interrupt his venture. Eddie is not a patient man.

Frankie smirks. That Crawford is worth a second look and a third.

Has their fate been postponed by lust, at least for the time being?

"Bet he thinks he'll be doing her a favor by humping her. Something pleasant for her to think about and be grateful for when he whacks her," Miki speculates.

"Back up against that wall. All of you."

Frankie makes another motion with his gun toward a blank wall without windows. Leah and Jennifer join Miki, Ida, and Crawford.

"We await our end just as our relatives did at Auschwitz," Miki reminds herself. "No gas for us, though. A nice, familiar, American-made bullet will do the trick."

Eddie begins whistling far off in the back of the house.

There's a man who loves his work. He's a real humanitarian.

The noise of the storm masks the entry of two more men, men in suits not near as fancy as Frankie and Eddie's. Coming from the direction of the garage, they step out of the shadows into the kitchen, guns drawn.

"Drop it slow and drop it easy."

Frankie jerks in momentary surprise but professionalism takes control. He fires. His silenced gun emits a string of light popping sounds.

At the same moment, the two officers' guns erupt with a thunderous roar that fills the kitchen and the breakfast nook.

Everyone hits the deck, seeking cover.

Amazingly, no one is hit.

Frankie squeezes off another shot from his new position at the doorjamb. Miki and Ida are trapped in the crossfire.

Eddie rushes toward the gun battle.

"Frankie. Frankie. What's going on, Frankie?" he hollers.

Then he's silent, cautious.

"Federal agents. Give yourselves up, now. Backup is on the way. You'll only get yourselves hurt if you keep this up," one agent states in a monotone that authorities seem to have learned from a secret manual.

The fed is right. Someone is likely to get hurt. Eddie lets loose with a round. It thuds into the wall above the heads of the feds.

Crawford, Jennifer in hand, has already escaped through the door leading to the garage. Leah follows.

Charlie

Mighty thunder rumbles and roars. Cosmic electrical displays flash in all directions. Prodigious thunderheads bark explosively as they march across the sky. The Lord is putting on a show.

On Charlie's shoulder sits a parrot with unnaturally brilliant colors. The parrot alternately eats away at his earlobe and chants magical formulas into his tattered ear.

"What was that again?" Charlie keeps repeating over and over, moving closer to the parrot and then retreating when the parrot takes another bite of his ear.

"To Tony's, to Tony's, to Tony's," repeats the parrot.

The car Charlie's driving, a nondescript gray Chevy, glows brighter than the most garish DayGlo poster on sale during the height of the Summer of Love.

Onlookers, fellow drivers on the lanes of life, wave and make gestures. Charlie responds.

"Mother always said being polite never hurt anyone."

Charlie rides on wheels of gold on a blue, diaphanous cloud that extends outward, toward but never meeting infinity. All around the cloud on which his transformed car rides, whizzing lights shoot by – nighttime, time-exposure photographs that reveal the comet's tail of car lights streaking away and beyond.

Bodiless faces, frozen in space, pop out of this kinetic movement...

"To Tony's, to Tony's, to Tony's," they implore.

Charlie smiles and nods good-naturedly.

Overhead, glorious revelations of the Supreme Being thunder, quake, belch and fart. The Multi-headed Goddess emerges from his belly button.

"What a marvelous night for a drive through the subatomic universe," Charlie bellows.

At the toll plaza leading to the Golden Gate Bridge, Charlie slows.

"Have I entered a race? On which track should I run?

"Everyone else seems to know."

He's holding up the stampede. He's been caught dawdling again. He slams down hard on the gas pedal.

"To Tony's," Charlie shouts, as if he just received the message.

His chariot lunges forward. G-forces press his body into the plastic seat covers. His hair shoots straight back and turns into flowers. His ear becomes a salad that disgusts the parrot and makes it squawk. Several bodiless heads frown and raise their eyebrows in alarm. His DayGlo vehicle threatens to break away from the diaphanous blue cloud approaching infinity but never arriving. His golden tires show signs of turning to lead.

Odd whining and scraping noises surge through the dashboard. An announcement in galactic gibberish performed by the ever-popular Multi-headed Goddess airs. The voice of God is captured.

Is it fully understood and interpreted?'

Nobody knows. The message is a level above comprehension where what is known is unknown and what is unknown becomes us.

"Surely, this is a hoax, a ridiculous joke designed to enchant innocent fools and bamboozle unbelievers.

"Is there a Beyond beyond Opposites?" he blabbers with incredulity.

Charlie pierces the mountain's navel as he enters the Rainbow Tunnel. Fluorescent lights bounce off of damp concrete walls heavy with the weight of the surrounding hillside. On the Waldo Grade beyond, a lightning-and-thunder-charged landscape overshadows the spectacle of emerging into glorious, glamorous southern Marin. A torrential rain of monumental proportions approaches.

Anticipating the future, Charlie turns on his windshield wipers and dials down the radio so that he can hold out his hand to catch lightning, the first raindrops. Leaning his head out of the window, he howls, sliding down the Waldo Grade doing forty-five. No one seems to notice. He's a forgotten man.

From the highway, Charlie sees that there's a disturbance of some sort at Gate Five. What else is new? He stays on course for San Quentin Village.

Humans, lice on the skin of the living earth, scamper about in all directions, convinced that what they do matters.

"Life is but a dream, sh-boom, sh-boom. Hello, hello again."

The parrot squawks, "To Tony's to Tony's to Tony's."

His chariot comes to rest in the turnout for the San Quentin house. Golden wheels overhang the steep hillside in front of his magical vehicle. Charlie and his parrot look off into the endless waters of the

Bay. Then up, up, up the hillside Charlie goes. The front door flies open before him.

"Charlie. Where have you been? We've been so worried about you," someone seems to say.

But when Charlie looks, that someone is nowhere to be found.

"Who? Who?" Charlie shouts, rotating his head from side to side. "Who wants to know?"

No answer.

"Who? Who?" he repeats in wonderment.

"You must be cold. Better put on some clothes," that same someone seems to suggest.

"Sensible advice. Where did I leave them?"

"In the backpack you strapped on after you parked your chariot," that someone answers.

Charlie nods to acknowledge the kind reminder.

"To Tony's, to Tony's, to Tony's," the parrot squawks.

"We've arrived," Charlie responds.

After putting on some clothes, Charlie takes the brooch from his backpack and puts it in his pants pocket.

"A keepsake," he announces to the room at large.

Outside, a crescendo of lightning bolts strike with unabated fury followed by ferocious thunderclaps. For some unaccountable reason, it seems prudent to make his way outside the San Quentin house. The disturbed air inside the house seems much more dangerous than the monumental rainstorm's approach outside.

Leah

"Edge's journal. Where is it? Take me there," Peggy Crawford orders as the car shoots out of David's driveway onto Blithedale.

Crawford is sitting in the passenger seat holding a knife. It's pointed at Leah. Leah is driving the mobsters' car; conveniently, they left the key in the ignition. Leah's having trouble handling it.

"Driving a projectile," she tells Crawford.

Jennifer – poor, innocent Jennifer – sits silent, all but invisible, in the back seat.

Is that the story of Jennifer's life? Do adults ignore her in dangerous situations just when she needs them the most?

My gut cries out for her, to her, Leah responds in silent sympathy.

Lightning bolts and thunder ignite with alarming regularity. The darkened sky flickers with multiple fractious light displays. Drought-dried tree limbs crack and fall. Power lines go down. Sparks from live wires on the ground make firecracker explosions.

The citizens of laidback Marin are tucked away in their cottages. They smoke reefer, snort coke, take opium suppositories as they seek shelter from the approaching storm. "Far out. Too much," they murmur, glued to their windows. Thunderstorms are rare in the Bay Area. This one is memorable.

God is more fun than TV. Puts on a show wilder than the wildest Western, more captivating than a hologram. Outrageous...

Leah? She hangs on, trying to concentrate on driving along the back road toward Larkspur.

"What kind of mother..." Leah starts.

Crawford interrupts instantly.

"Not everyone grows up in a house with a white picket fence. Ain't all it's cracked up to be anyhow."

"Ten years... see what Jennifer says to that... " Leah punches back.

Crawford snickers. Her face is no longer pretty. It's pinched and drawn. She has no intention of taking Leah's jab lying down.

"You're not a mother. If you were, you'd understand all I'm thinking about is Jennifer. That's my mission in life. Jennifer knows that and she'll remember that." She turns to Jennifer. "Isn't that right, honey?"

The car turns onto the San Quentin main road. The wind roars. Some of the gusts must be near hurricane force. Tree branches whip backward and forward with frightening velocity. Without warning, a mammoth treetop crashes into the road behind them. The crash and clatter of the tree's downing penetrates the howling wind. That mess won't be cleared away from this road any time soon, which means no one will be driving into or out of San Quentin Village any time soon either.

Primordial Man, Tony

Tony, Primordial man, advances with caution up the treacherous hillside, keeping to cover.

Bang. Boom. Crash.

Trees tremble. Bushes tumble.

Wind thrashes. Lightning flashes.

Dark, black, starless night has arrived.

He heads for the back door of the San Quentin house.

Inside...Inside...Hurry...

Reawakens, snaps back, brought on by chairs, tables, rugs, totemic objects, bed connected to consciousness once occupied by Primordial man.

Silence...Seeming quiet inside amidst turmoil and increasing chaos outside.

Meditate. Dive deep within.

Go beyond troubling images...

Knife in hand... pool of blood... Edge dead, vacant eyes glaring into him...

Murder...

Dive deep... into the quiet at the center of the storm...

Blank... Black... Void...

He meditates seated squarely on his meditation pillow placed on his prayer rug at the center of the dilapidated San Quentin house, seeking to block out disturbance which threatens inner peace.

Then what...

Remains in meditative lotus...

Overlayed by Primordial man.

Blank... Black... Void...

Charlie

The overpowering smell of desperation and agony rides on the whistling wind. The towers and walls of San Quentin glow under spotlights' glare, a fortress of human suffering in the near background.

"Important. Got to get this act together," Charlie tells his parrot out loud.

It understands.

San Quentin Village, like most of southern Marin, is dark. Major power lines are down. Trees pulled up by their roots are thrown haphazardly in all directions. The heavens above dictate with violent fury...

Death... Death... Death walks the land.

It is calling. No sentient being can escape its frigid hand as...

The cycle of birth-death-rebirth beckons... And the wheel – the ever-lasting rotation of reincarnation – karma – fate – without surcease deludes humanity with the cloak of ignorance, the veil of forgetfulness.

"Give me voice, Multi-headed Goddess," Charlie roars into the howling wind.

The parrot's cocked head inspects him quizzically.

"From the heart, a likely place to worship God," the parrot responds.

"Tony. Tony and Leah are in trouble. Must warn them, must help them to get away, save all that can be saved," Charlie responds urgently.

"Make your way within. Dive deep," the parrot squawks.

"The Kernel, the Core, therein the secret lies that will release us," Charlie insists, for all the woebegone and forgotten of this world, now and forevermore.

A golden moment of speculative clarity with a sharp edge of dark and comic cosmic humor takes hold, then dissolves.

The glorious union of two innocent souls, Leah and Tony, has resulted in rape, humiliation, pain, murder. A high-powered drug deal that is still solidifying but will result in a reshaping of the hip scene in Marin, all of which hinges on possession of a journal written by a mad, wily-coyote chemist, Edge - Is that the nub of it all?

In the deal's wake, who and what will become the flotsam and jetsam of this crushing storm? Will the transformation following this windy night, thunder-and-lightning filled, and approaching torrential rain be over in a week, or even the months and years that follow?

"Bury that past and turn it to dust with the cleansing hand of Nature," answers the divine Multi-headed Goddess.

"For all eternity and the infinite now," Charlie proclaims, faltering and fluttering into prophetic delirium.

He is a sentient being forced out of Paradise and made to wander the uncertain middle ground of Purgatory, seeking the shelter of a cave filled with shadows, the place where shamans live and give voice to our collective consciousness.

"Some supplicants will perish. Some will fall by the way. The chosen few will crash through into the Beyond," the Multi-headed Goddess reminds him.

Charlie nods, enlightened.

"This is the moment, the moment that grabs us and takes us around, behind, beyond and through.

"Water is the way to clarity with the kind help of you, oh wise and treacherous Multi-headed Goddess."

Tough Guys from Chicago

Frankie puts a round into the wall just above the fat feds' heads.

Frankie thinks to himself, They ain't going nowhere. We got 'em penned down from both sides. And there's no more real estate to protect their lard asses in the kitchen.

"You might as well come out and take your medicine," he shouts.

The dry taste of death slides to the back of his mouth and the stillness of the grave draws near. He's transported with a thump to the altar rail of the church he attended as a child. Hogwash, pure hogwash, he thinks. All my sainted mother's doing. May she live to be a hundred.

"Who gets to whack 'em, Frankie?" Eddie asks excitedly.

Frankie and Eddie's friendship began on the playground at elementary school. They attended the same church, played in the same neighborhood hangouts. Frankie took care of Eddie. He doesn't know why. Maybe he felt sorry for him.

Why did I take him on? He sure was the runt of the litter. Boy, did the guys beat up on him. Not after I took him on. We've been buddies ever since. Mom, I did one thing on the up-and-up. I stuck with my pal through thick and thin.

Frankie yells at the two fat fuck feds.

"I told my pal Eddie here, 'We won't have to whack the feds.' You guys are too smart to let that happen, right?"

He gets no response.

Frankie checks. The two dumpy broads are huddled under the kitchen table – one overweight, one medium. Easy targets, but who cares? They're not his primary target. His targets, the looker and her kid, are gone.

Did they make a break for it through the garage door?

He yells to the two fat fuck feds again.

"We got no quarrel with the broads here. You pull out. We disappear. Easy. Clean. Right?"

Still no response.

Fuck it.

Frankie nods to Eddie, signaling the old fast break, squeeze play. Punctuate it with a little lead.

He fires twice. Eddie makes his break. The feds fire off a round.

"Fuck," Eddie hollers. He's been hit. And just when Frankie was getting ready to fan his gun in the feds' direction.

Eddie jerks. Two wild rounds blast into the floor. The gun drops from his hand.

"You okay, Eddie?"

Eddie stumbles back out of sight before he answers, breathing heavily.

"It burns like crazy, Frankie. I'm bleeding bad."

"Fucking feds," Frankie growls to himself. "That's it. Nobody fucks with my buddy Eddie. Nobody. So everybody's got to pay. Never wanted this damn assignment in the first place. Nothing but a bunch of fruitcakes and weirdos out here in California. Who gives a damn about them? The feds will die first, then the broads. The paid hits will follow."

Frankie steps out into the open, blasting away into the kitchen counter that protects the feds. He is rounding the corner of the counter ready for anything when...

The front door slams open again. The howling wind blows a dead tree branch through the doorway. The lights flicker and dim, then snap off. The house is dark, illuminated only when lightning flashes again and fills it with murky shadows. Eddie groans.

Then Frankie hears Eddie pick up his piece. Eddie lets loose with three shots in rapid succession. One of the plainclothesmen hollers from behind the counter.

"Eddie always was a good shot," Frankie thinks.

A cone of light from a flashlight points in Eddie's direction. One carefully aimed shot from a very big gun explodes Eddie's skull. The back of his head breaks apart like a watermelon and a thin trail of blood trickles from his mouth.

"Throw your guns down and surrender," Sheriff Whelan thunders.

He's holding the flashlight and gun as a cloud of smoke from his cannon rushes by his face.

Frankie fires off one quick one in Whelan's direction, then spins behind the counter. He's planning on taking at least one cop with him.

"No sense in all of us getting killed," one of the feds behind the counter comments, a gun pointed right at Frankie's chest.

Mexican standoff.

Frankie chuckles, and tells himself, I guess I've been living in a movie all along.

Going to finish out this script the way it oughta be wrote.

Sorry, mom. I go out blazing."

BOOK FOUR

Confrontation

Explosive lightning bolts, like blasts from heavy gun emplacements or missile launch sites, pepper the night sky. Reports from thunderous rumbles threaten to shatter windowpanes and send shivers down trees. A mighty gust of wind shakes the San Quentin house.

The front door flies open. A lightning bolt, another growling grinding report, gale-force winds, and three guests enter.

"Get lost, fast," Peggy Crawford commands, cool, hard, determinedly glaring at Tony.

Leah accompanies this surly woman, the one who just spoke, and her solemn daughter, Jennifer.

Head rotating from side to side in slow motion, a thought flickers across Tony's consciousness amid on-again, off-again moments of Void blankness. He has seen this surly woman somewhere before.

"I said, beat it. Get lost," Peggy Crawford barks.

Jennifer recedes into the murky shadows of the front room where Edge was murdered. Her finger automatically moves toward her mouth. She clings to Leah's hand.

"Leah?"

Tony ignores Crawford and the knife she threateningly waves, focusing on Leah's angelic face.

The same springy black curls that captured his heart that very first day at Miki and Peter's house highlight her pale skin. The same aura radiates from her. The same celestial being beckons him closer.

"God, she's beautiful. And she's back... back here," his mind bellows.

Tony's eyes plead with Leah to ignore the dangers of the present moment, put aside the violence that has surrounded her for months, and dismiss the unspeakable act that sundered them. He beseeches her to rekindle that spark which once caused her to draw near to him.

That spark was extinguished when Tony's feet of clay were exposed. Tony will just have to get over her in his own time and way.

"Peggy... Peggy Crawford... and daughter, Jennifer," Leah informs Tony. "Want something in house."

Leah's choppily delivered introduction leads Tony to look at Crawford. Remote, far away from this confrontational moment, Leah

312

being the only exception to that rule, he tells Crawford, "Take whatever. Leave," making no move to leave himself.

Crawford snickers.

"This demented fool is a bad hippie joke, a loser. He deserves to get kicked in the balls. Repeatedly," she reflects, flashing back to the first time she saw Tony. That was in Richmond, Virginia, just before Tim Montgomery, a close friend of Tony's at the time, and Crawford headed out for California.

"Go, Tony," Leah urges.

"Staying with you," Tony replies.

"Touching. Where's the journal, Leah?" Crawford demands, holding the knife to Leah's throat as she jerks Leah's arm up and twists it behind her.

"Edge journal," Leah informs Tony, ignoring Crawford and her strongarm tactic.

Tony looks blank, puzzled. In his mind flash oh-too-familiar, fragmented memory images.

Knife in his hand, Edge in a pool of blood... In this house...

Nowhere... Nothing... Void...

Primordial Man...

Crawford decides she is in no hurry. She relaxes her hold on Leah, letting the knife slip away from Leah's throat. As long as she ends up with the journal, so what? No way she's going to meet the delivery date set by Mr. Big without it.

"Stuff in it," Leah continues. "Peggy needs... We loose ends... Get it?"

"Like Leah said, I need that journal," Crawford reinforces after a long pause during which the storm outside rattles and twists the house. Bolts of lightning followed by more booming thunder are seen and heard in the inky darkness framed by the windows that run the length of the front of the house. "You're not planning to cause any trouble, are you, Tony?" she jeers.

Tony does not reply. Crawford patiently adds,

"Just show me where the damn thing's hidden and I'll leave you two love birds to sort things out in peace. Or..."

Crawford jabs the knife meaningfully toward Leah's midsection.

Without warning, Tony lunges between Crawford and Leah, surprising them both. The rattling windowpanes and clattering branches, the repeated reports of thunder and flashes of lightning, cover his move. Crawford jerks her knife in Tony's direction. It rips across Tony's chest, leaving a long, bloody gouge, but it does not stop him. Jennifer jumps backward, forcing Leah backward too.

"Fucking fool," Crawford growls, readying herself to thrust again.

Tony, out of control, crashes into an exposed stud headfirst. Stunned, he falls to the floor. Crawford is back in control of the situation.

"Make it quick, sister. The journal," Crawford demands.

Without a word, Leah stalks out of the front room with Jennifer still clutching her hand. Crawford follows, holding the knife.

"Here... Take... Go...."

Leah reaches into her secret hiding place. Nothing's there. Her brain goes cold and still.

Charlie. Charlie moved it after I told him where it was, she realizes.

"Not here... Can get."

"No more fooling around, sister. The time for games is over."

"Can get," Leah answers. "Let Tony leave... "

"We'll see about that. Move it."

Crawford pushes Leah back toward the front room. Jennifer still clutches Leah's hand. Tony groggily puts his hand to his head and struggles to his feet. And Charlie, entering through the back door, heads toward the front room.

A brilliant lightning flash followed by an immediate and mighty crack fills the house, the yard, the surrounding area. An unearthly glow, the Almighty revealed, seems to vaporize all animate and inanimate objects. A mushroom cloud of expanding gases bulges toward the walls, unnaturally pressurizing the interior of the house. An atomic bomb-like reaction rushes through the charged air, causing colliding particles to expand and explode.

The deafening bellow of thunder is followed by a great, grinding, wrenching noise as the load-bearing walls of the house twist and flex. Violent crackling sounds rip through the flimsy structure. Sparks fly. The house begins to smolder.

Charlie's body fills with light. His brain stem and all synaptic neural connections resonate with the Universe. The front room he enters is transparent, seeming to him like a figment of his imagination that creates a passage from one space-time continuum to the next. His eyes, X-ray vision enhanced, penetrate beyond substance, through shadows, to the white-hot center of it All. He knows what he knows –

is. His is a Voice ready to speak while locked in passionate embrace with the Multi-headed Goddess.

Tony, in and out of his drug-induced delirium, readies himself to attack again.

Leah's been hurt. She needs help, is the only conscious thought he has.

"Knights in shining armor, I presume," Crawford comments conversationally, looking from Charlie to Tony.

She does not bother to look down at the pool of Edge's dark, dried blood that disfigures the shabby carpet.

The walls of the house heat up and pulsate. The wind rushes against the flimsy supports. What was solidly in the real world – the uncared for, deteriorating house – is revealed for what it is – ephemeral effluvium created from a combination of whimsy and hubris. The Void calls out for its elements. The elements hear.

Crawford firmly and resolutely disengages Jennifer's hand from Leah's and shoves Leah aside. Holding Jennifer's tiny yet awesomely powerful hand, Crawford's stance seems to state, "It's a good day to prevail or die trying."

Charlie views the actors, including himself, from high above. He has been instructed and his Voice is lubricated, loosened. It's a good day to mediate with clarity as one of the inspired dead, he tells himself.

Tony's hazy recollection clears momentarily. He remembers Peggy Crawford.

"You! You again!"

He's a poster boy for the banner headline "It's a good day to die over and over."

Crawford smirks, "That's right, lover boy, but we'll save that trip down memory lane for another day."

"Stabbed him! Killed Edge," Tony announces, making an awkward play to reclaim Leah's hand and rejuvenate his self-respect.

"Did you, sweetie? Well, you did do your best," Crawford answers with a throaty laugh.

Leah shouts back, brushing aside the fact that her assertion is based on fragmented images that still form a jumble in her mind.

"I... I murder."

She stands up straight and reaches out for Jennifer's hand. She is determined not to allow Tony to pay the penalty for this, in her mind, righteous murder.

"Keep your hands off my daughter," Crawford growls.

Tony again throws himself at Crawford. Charlie gets there first. He grabs Crawford and smacks away her knife. She snarls as it spins out of her grasp.

"Explain this," Charlie demands, holding up the brooch as if it were a cross and Crawford a vampire.

Crawford crouches, ready to strike. She shields Jennifer from the others and thinks about going for the knife. Then it hits her.

"Where did you find that?"

"Right here in this room," Charlie answers. "Tony, tell us about the last time you saw this woman. It was in this room, wasn't it?"

"This room..." Tony repeats in a monotone.

Tony looks at Leah, his soul mate, the love of his life. He is reminded of his imperfections.

Small fires, licking flames, begin to break out along the baseboard and other exposed wood inside the house.

Tony repeats, "I... I murdered," as his fragmented recollection reminds him, "A knife... blood... hand holding knife... mine... Edge in a pool of blood."

The long drought, the progressive rotting of time, will soon make the house a blazing fire, an out-of-control flaming torch.

"No... I... I murdered... " Leah insists.

The wood will burn clean, eager to reduce itself to ash.

Leah remembers, "In this room, arguing, struggling with Edge. Enraged. Wanted to kill him. Must have."

The wind will whirl convulsively, stirring up the ever-expanding fire.

"No! No, I ... " Tony persists, desperate, pleading.

He takes a step toward Leah. She retreats a step backward toward the oven-hot walls.

The whole structure of the house will soon sag and bow dangerously.

"Tell him. Tell all of us," Charlie shouts to Crawford.

From Charlie's perspective in the heavens above, he sees. He knows. The ready-to-howl blaze might engulf them. But none of them will leave until there is a resolution. He, the one with the magical powers of the Voice given to him by the Creator, Preserver, Destroyer, will see to that.

"You're willing to die to find out who killed a worthless bastard son-of-a-bitch?" Crawford taunts Charlie.

"Are you willing to die because you think you need a journal written by a man you detest?" Charlie tosses back.

Crawford, bitter, dangerous, glares at Charlie.

"All men are animals. Life is hard and bitter. Only the strong survive and succeed."

Jennifer eases away from her mother's protection. She takes Leah's hand and silently eyes her mother.

"Mommy, I'm frightened," she whispers.

A growing flame backlights Jennifer, a white-hot halo.

Charlie, the Voice, proclaims, "I've got hard forensic evidence and witnesses who will corroborate that you were here on that day, Peggy Crawford... And I've got this brooch."

Charlie holds it high. Flames flicker on its surface.

"The journal, hand it over," Crawford replies.

"Your hair is auburn; Red's is fire-engine red, matching hairs found in this room. The forensic comparison will prove they come from the two of you," Charlie responds.

Crawford is not shaken.

"Lover boy's prints are on the knife that is probably in the hands of the cops. Johnny stole his old lady. Crime of passion. Open-and-shut case unless we agree: the journal for the first-hand account. And I get a get-out-of-jail-free card."

"Did it. Me," Tony shouts.

"No. No. Not," Leah answers, horrified.

"Deal?" Crawford repeats, taking Jennifer's hand once again and pushing Leah aside.

"Deal," Charlie states. "And put your first-hand account in writing."

Can either Tony or Leah trust, believe, what Crawford will say? Is their battered memory more accurate? Will Crawford's confession reverse and redirect their torment, bewilderment, anger, bitterness, shattered consciousness?

Crawford begins, "Red and I followed Edge. We parked in the turnout and waited so we could nab Edge when he came out. Suddenly, Tony shows up from above the house. He must have been in the open field on top of the hill. He entered the house by the back entrance. We decided we'd better check things out.

"We went in the back door and looked into the front room. Johnny was slapping Leah around. And he held a needle which he started to inject into her arm. But he jerked around hearing Tony

317

approaching from behind. The needle came out of Leah's shoulder as Tony rushed Johnny. Tony tussled with Johnny, but then Johnny jammed the needle in Tony's neck and injected him with most of the dose he had planned for Leah. Tony landed one punch and crumpled. While all this was happening, Leah struggled toward the front door.

"Out of nowhere, Red rushed into the front room and stabbed Johnny with a kitchen knife.

"Leah split during Red's attack. Tony was out cold. Calm as you please, Red drags Tony over next to Johnny's body, wipes the knife clean and puts it in Tony's hand."

Finished, Crawford holds out her hand, "The journal, if you please."

"And you will put down what you have told us in writing, a statement that will remove suspicion from Tony and Leah in exchange for the journal?" asks Charlie.

Crawford shrugs.

"Done. Red did it."

"What you want is on the shelf above the stove, among all the cookbooks," Charlie reveals.

Crawford retrieves the journal and returns to the front room, smirking.

"You can keep the brooch. Who cares? That little girl is no longer alive. And neither is her father."

Without warning, another massive lightning bolt makes a direct hit on the house. Full propane tanks under the house ignite. A rush of outside air attempts to penetrate inside the house but fails.

Crawford lets out a mighty laugh. She jerks Jennifer toward the front door and rushes downhill, shouting.

"All men are fools. Star-crossed lovers are jokes. And passionate women are their own worst deceivers."

One hand clutches Jennifer's and the other Edge's precious journal.

A collapsing, flaming wall strikes Tony, issuing forth a belch of heat. The weight of evaporating wood, the frying bodies of termites and wood beetles, enshroud him.

"Tony," Leah screams.

Charlie lunges toward Tony just as a falling beam glances off the side of Leah's head and shoulder, knocking her to the floor.

Tony's clothes are on fire. Charlie throws him to the floor and rolls him in a throw rug, trying to damp out the flames. Then he pushes the beam away from Leah. Semi-conscious, she holds her hand to her head.

A great roar, a guttural blast, erupts from the floor of the house. Every wall, every beam, every surface in the house comes alive with fiery flames, an inferno.

Charlie, determined to escape the bonds of the fast-becoming-imaginary walls of the house, throws Tony over his shoulder and drags Leah with his free hand. He makes it out of the back door just in time. A massive fireball, an explosion, catapults them away from the house. The house and its dreams, much brighter now than the glow from the prison, are fast becoming history. Leah coughs, then struggles to sit up.

Leah and Tony's collaborative work of art, the canvas for which Tony provided still photos and Leah provided a painted map of Marin inside a globe seeming to indicate that the county was the whole world, left tacked to a wall in her former studio, incinerates, as does the interior wall. The paint on the canvas and the photos of people and places burst into flame, eager to become part of the invisible world.

The heavens burst open, releasing large, pelting raindrops in massive sheets. The back of the drought is broken by a deluge that will disgorge eight inches of rain in four hours.

Dust that has clung to trees for months is torn from them and hurled toward the ground by the driving rain. The hillside instantly becomes a raging river of mud. Leah, Tony, and Charlie are covered by rivulets of watery dirt. Their skin, their hair becomes gluey and heavy.

Countywide, thunderclaps and lightning mix with rain and sleet. Without warning, baseball-sized hail pounds rooftops, smashes skylights and windows. On top of Mt. Tam, an inch of snow accumulates before turning into sleet and dangerous ice. Chaos reigns in Paradise.

Inky darkness filled with pounding raindrops, sorrow and pain – the stuff of existence – surrounds Leah, Tony and Charlie. They are karma's children, bathed in material-world ignorance, possessed of the feverish longing to be freed from the wheel. They have become an illustration of the *I Ching's* Hexagram 3, Difficulty at the Beginning, wherein a blade of grass struggles to push its way free of the earth encrusted with rocks, roots, and other obstructions as torrential rain, lightning and thunder fill the nighttime sky.

EPILOGUE

(Very late Winter 1971 - 1972)

Charlie

After the storm, uniformly gray skies laden with rain overtook Marin and the whole Bay Area. The reservoirs were recharged. The grasses on the barren, rocky hillsides turned green. The rainy season restored the balance of Nature in Northern California.

Taking in the moody glory of it all, I, fog coming out of my mouth with every panting breath, dressed in sweats and wearing a beanie, jog on a trail that is taking me to downtown Mill Valley.

Expunging the clutter in my mind with cleansing air that refreshes my lungs, my entire body, that's what I'm doing, I tell myself.

Piffle.

My fragmented thoughts continue to whirl round and round.

Coke and a new laundry list of designer drugs have flooded Marin from, what many say is, an LA source. Peggy Crawford, it appears, managed to pull off her big deal, no doubt with the help of Edge's journal.

She's feeding those greedy to indulge in forgetfulness, those who want to see life through an altered state of consciousness that makes indulgence seem like moral fiber, and insight the result of balancing ingested chemicals.

Let him who is without guilt cast the first stone.

My thoughts and prayers go out to little Jennifer. Where is she this evening?

Reaching downtown Mill Valley, I sit down on a bench outside the Depot as Herman rides up on his bike. He smiles pleasantly, takes a seat beside me in the rapidly disappearing light, and gets out a pouch of tobacco and rolling papers. Before undoing the makings, he offers the pouch and papers to me. I decline with a wave of my hand.

It's cool and damp – bracing. Few people are out and about. A large bird, impossible to identify in the uneven light of sunset, flickers across the sky. It's carrying away the day on its wingspan.

"You sure got Tony and Leah out of some hot water," Herman comments as he snaps a match across his fingernail and the match explodes into flame.

I nod ambivalently without commenting.

"You heard Al shut down the Western Front?" Herman asks after taking a drag of his homemade cigarette and pulling a piece off tobacco off his lip. I rouse myself.

"I guess he lost interest about the time Luigi got diagnosed with pancreatic cancer," I respond.

A dog wanders up and sticks his nose in Herman's lap. Herman pets him.

"Seems Edge's murder was pretty much the end of an era around these parts," Herman speculates.

"I reckon so."

"Miki and Peter had their cottage sold out from under them."

"Yeah?"

"Peter's studio job dried up. They've moved up to Sonoma. He's repairing home audio equipment for a living."

"No kidding."

"And Miki's got a job bookkeeping."

"Ida and Gab?"

"They moved to Montana with the kids. I hear they're splitting up. Reminds me of a line in one of Big Phil's songs, 'Going to Montana soon. Going to be a dental floss tycoon.'"

Herman puts out his cigarette carefully. His beat-up red bicycle leans against the bench.

"What about you, Herman?"

"Me? What can they do to hurt you after you've lived in Beatnik pads in the Village, North Beach, and Sausalito, not to mention slipping out of Poland and escaping from Hitler and the Nazis with your Jewish parents just before war broke out?"

To most people, Herman's a joke. After all, he lives in what used to be a mechanics' shop during World War II, when Gates Three and Five were part of a thriving naval shipyard. He scavenges for food from the garbage bin behind the Big G Supermarket. He rides his rattletrap bicycle on car-choked roads in Sausalito and Mill Valley while he keeps a mint-condition, red 1958 MG convertible on blocks in the asphalt-paved front yard of his Quonset hut home. His favorite hexagram in the I Ching is Number 62 – Preponderance of the Small – not exactly a happening thought in hustle-bustle America.

321

He rides away on the bike path that runs along Miller Avenue and leads to Sausalito. I make tracks. We've got guests coming over tonight. My running shoes pound rhythmically along the path I take as I approach the gathering night.

Tony sets up a borrowed 16mm projector and connects a tiny speaker to it after opening up the screen and placing it at the far end of our cramped front room in the shack Tony and I just moved into. We live behind the main house, down a very steep hillside with no driveway leading to our abode. The rent is cheap; our furnishings are meager. It's powered by pirated electricity.

We, that is Molly and David (they got a babysitter) and Harry (my "family" members, of course including Tony), have just finished eating Chinese takeout, celebrating our new digs and the completion of Tony's first film, "Cat Woman, Moon Water," wherein Tony sings the blues about losing his soulmate, Leah Travail.

Surprisingly, the opening shot of Tony's directorial debut shows the trunk of Tony's Plymouth Duster opening. Inside, wrapped in a well-worn horse blanket, are Tony's Nikon still camera, his 16mm Beaulieu motion picture camera and a bag in which are Tony's slide collection and his rolls of exposed 16mm.

I am transported back to the day I discovered Tony's cameras in the trunk of his car and the bag containing Tony's treasure trove. The San Quentin road had just been cleared of storm debris. Tony was recovering at Marin General and I was picking up some things for him. His lungs were seared. Two ribs were crushed. He had a severe concussion. And then, of course, there was the massive injection of an unknown substance or substances into his system. Full recovery could take years, a lifetime.

Tony was wearing the two cameras when he raced to the rescue of Leah as she was struggling with Edge on that fateful day. Somehow the film camera started recording and one still photograph was taken. The mostly useless still photo and eleven minutes of silent film that jiggled around and captured odd angles became the frustrating but illuminating documentation of Edge and Tony's fracas, the murder and its aftermath. After extensive review of the footage along with Crawford's notarized statement and my forensic evidence, Tony and Leah were cleared of suspicion in the murder of Edge. It was determined that Leah had fled the scene with Bianca in hand before Edge was stabbed, and that Tony was out cold during the murder.

No frame of the film footage captured Edge being stabbed. A wall and part of the ceiling were all that could be seen at that moment. Both Red and Crawford were identifiable in frames before and after the fatal blow. The film ran out before the two left the San Quentin house but not before Red was seen wiping the knife clean, dragging Tony over to the knife and imprinting Tony's fingerprints on the knife. Whelan's office declared Red was the culprit. I let it ride even though I had doubts about that conclusion. Crawford was also on the scene and her motive was much stronger than Red's, in my opinion.

During my rumination, the film cuts from Tony's car to the burned-down wreck of the San Quentin house. The ruins are intercut with still photographs Tony took of the house as well as candid photography both still and motion picture of activities that took place while Tony and Leah lived there –

Leah doing a Salutation to the Sun in the front yard of the San Quentin house,

Bianca lounging on various pieces of furniture and hunting prey in the yard,

People visiting them,

Leah cleaning house in front of the shared mural,

Leah meditating,

Leah asleep,

And the Richmond San Rafael Bridge and the upper reaches of the San Francisco Bay at all times of day, night and in all types of weather.

The next to last shot in this intercut montage returns to Tony sorting through the charred remains and finding fragments of the mural that Leah and Tony were constructing. The last shot zooms in on a twisted, fire-damaged photograph of Leah.

The film then transitions to its central theme – Leah, her life journey during the time she and Tony were together. A barrage of motion picture and still photographs capture a vibrant, exuberant, animated Leah during happier times:

Dancing down the streets of Mill Valley, hands in her pockets, curly hair bouncing gaily, white tennis shoes tapping out a lively tune to the beat of freedom,

Miki and Peter's pad, where Leah and Tony met and "family" members congregated

(Leah and Miki hugging and engaged in conversation,
Peter, beatific, playing a sitar,

Harry focused on his fingering while playing a guitar,
Big Phil with his impish smile,
Herman playing dominoes,
Peter and Miki looking at each other lovingly),

Leah and Tony promenading past guests attending the christening of their enchanted cottage and exchanging a kiss applauded by all,

The interior of Gab and Ida's teepee at night with a fire burning in the center,

Leah and Tony on excursions around Marin

(Hanging out in the open field above the San Quentin house,

Watching the sunset from a Mt. Tam overlook where the boiling sun disappears into the Pacific Ocean,
Going to various beach locations,
Attending a fair at the Marin Civic Center,
Leah fishing in front of the San Quentin house).

While this cascade of images visually overwhelms us with celebratory joyful moments, Tony reads selections from his thoughts, poems and stories, all of which evoke Tony's angst, despair, self-loathing, and sorrow for the collapse of their relationship and for the tragic circumstances that overtook their lives. The striking contrast between the images and Tony's commentary is given added emotional depth by the insertion of blues songs and snippets of other recording artists. What results is a heartfelt, heartbreaking assemblage of chaotic impressions that make no sense intellectually but are a shot to the gut viscerally.

I find myself thinking back to the last time I saw Leah.

"Got a plan?" I asked as I put out a hash-laced cigarette that Leah had declined to share.

David, Leah's brother, had given me a very generous check. Leah had seen to that.

"Leaving tomorrow," Leah answered, reflective and remote. "Leaving the Bay Area."

"Can't get away from yourself, you know."

We were standing in the doorway of the guest cottage David had been letting me use rent-free. A hillside blocked out the setting sun but the air and the sky above were illuminated with a golden light that gave to our conversation a surreal, otherworldly quality.

"Are you blaming yourself for the big changes going down in Marin?" I queried.

"Put that way, it sounds outlandish," she replied.

"Listen. What if Miki hadn't been dealing drugs? Edge wouldn't have been attracted to the 'family.' You would never have met him. What if no hippies showed up for the Summer of Love? What if Ken Kesey never thought up the idea of acid tests? What if Timothy Leary stuck to his psychology and never dropped acid? What if Kerouac never took to the road? What if Moses never led the Jewish people out of Egypt and received the sacred tablets on Mt. Sinai?"

Leah held up her hands and shook her head fending off my hypothetical bullshitting.

"If you want to talk... about anything... any time," I offered, contrite, apologetic.

She gave me a brief smile of acknowledgement before going into the house. Her cat, Bianca, followed her, just as she followed Leah from Memphis, followed Leah while she lived with Tony, waited for Leah while she lived with Edge, and fled with Leah from the murder scene.

The film comes to its end. Silence.

Our guests soon leave. What can they or anyone say?

Tony retreats to his room and closes the door. I ignore the puzzle sitting on a card table and don't bother to throw the I Ching.

Lying in bed, a mattress on the floor, I hear a fox call, an owl hoot. I stare into the damp chilly night.

Let go...
It's over...

THE END

"O Mother Tara, this world is Your madhouse!
What shall I say of Your virtues?
Giving up Your elephant, you ride on a bull like one depraved.
Willfully you cast aside Your jewels and pearls and put on a garland of skulls.
Unmindful of others, You roam the cremation grounds.
Says Ramprasad, You must lead me beyond my wanderings in the maze of the world."
Sri Sri Ramakrishna Kathamrita – IV Section XVIII, page 262

ACKNOWLEDGMENTS

First and foremost, I want to thank my wife, Margaret, for editing and helping promote and market this novel and for being by my side to offer encouragement and critical input throughout. And I want to thank Eudora Arthur, our publisher, for her invaluable advice and guidance.

I would also like to thank those people, through the years, who have been good and loyal friends through thick and thin. Particular mention must be made of my brother, Sid, and his wife, Gail; and my cousin, Judy Spencer Merrill.

And I want to give particular thanks to those people who were a part of my life during the early 1970s, most notably Beverly and David Tresan, David and Edie Brown, the David and Sharon Litwin family, Lhary Meyer, and the ever vibrant and evocative Marin County, California and its inhabitants. You are in my thoughts and dreams always.

ABOUT THE AUTHOR

Frank Cervarich was born in Richmond, Virginia but left his heart in the San Francisco/Bay Area. He has written, edited and produced numerous programs for television, film, and video during a forty plus year career in the business. He lives with his wife, Margaret, in Maryland.

Made in United States
North Haven, CT
30 July 2023

39723453R00184